W9-AZX-870

Praise for the Novels of Beverly Connor

"Calls to mind the forensic mysteries of Aaron Elkins and Patricia Cornwell. However, Connor's sleuth infuses the mix with her own brand of spice as a pert and brainy scholar in the forensic analysis of bones. . . . Chases, murder attempts and harrowing rescues add to this fast-paced adventure." —*Chicago Sun-Times*

"Connor combines smart people, fun people, and dangerous people in a novel hard to put down."
—*The Dallas Morning News*

"Connor grabs the reader with her first sentence and never lets up until the book's end. . . . The story satisfies both as a mystery and as an entrée into the fascinating world of bones. . . . Add Connor's dark humor, and you have a multidimensional mystery that deserves comparison with the best of Patricia Cornwell."
—*Booklist* (starred review)

"In Connor's latest multifaceted tale, the plot is serpentine, the solution ingenious, the academic politics vicious . . . chock-full of engrossing anthropological and archaeological detail." —*Publishers Weekly*

continued . . .

PAPER M CONNOR
Connor, Beverly,
Scattered graves : a Diane
Fallon forensic
investigation / Beverly
Connor JUL 9 '09

Peabody Public Library
Columbia City, IN

"Connor's books are a smart blend of Patricia Cornwell, Aaron Elkins, and Elizabeth Peters, with some good, deep-South atmosphere to make it authentic."
—*Oklahoma Family Magazine*

"Crisp dialogue, interesting characters, fascinating tidbits of bone lore, and a murderer that eluded me. When I started reading, I couldn't stop. What more could you ask for? Enjoy."
—Virginia Lanier, author of the Bloodhound series

"Beverly Connor has taken the dry bones of scientific inquiry and resurrected them into living, breathing characters. I couldn't put [it] down until I was finished, even though I wanted to savor the story. I predict that Beverly Connor will become a major player in the field of mystery writing."
—David Hunter, author of *The Dancing Savior*

"Fans of . . . Patricia Cornwell will definitely want to read Beverly Connor . . . an author on the verge of superstardom." —*Midwest Book Review*

"Connor's breathtaking ability to dish out fascinating forensic details while maintaining a taut aura of suspense is a real gift." —*Romantic Times* (top pick)

SCATTERED GRAVES

A DIANE FALLON FORENSIC INVESTIGATION

BEVERLY CONNOR

DISCARD
Peabody Public Library
Columbia City, IN

AN OBSIDIAN MYSTERY

OBSIDIAN
Published by New American Library, a division of
Penguin Group (USA) Inc., 375 Hudson Street,
New York, New York 10014, USA
Penguin Group (Canada), 90 Eglinton Avenue East, Suite 700, Toronto,
Ontario M4P 2Y3, Canada (a division of Pearson Penguin Canada Inc.)
Penguin Books Ltd., 80 Strand, London WC2R 0RL, England
Penguin Ireland, 25 St. Stephen's Green, Dublin 2,
Ireland (a division of Penguin Books Ltd.)
Penguin Group (Australia), 250 Camberwell Road, Camberwell, Victoria 3124,
Australia (a division of Pearson Australia Group Pty. Ltd.)
Penguin Books India Pvt. Ltd., 11 Community Centre, Panchsheel Park,
New Delhi - 10 017, India
Penguin Group (NZ), 67 Apollo Drive, Rosedale, North Shore 0632,
New Zealand (a division of Pearson New Zealand Ltd.)
Penguin Books (South Africa) (Pty.) Ltd., 24 Sturdee Avenue,
Rosebank, Johannesburg 2196, South Africa

Penguin Books Ltd., Registered Offices:
80 Strand, London WC2R 0RL, England

First published by Obsidian, an imprint of New American Library,
a division of Penguin Group (USA) Inc.

First Printing, February 2009
10 9 8 7 6 5 4 3 2 1

Copyright © Beverly Connor, 2009
All rights reserved

OBSIDIAN and logo are trademarks of Penguin Group (USA) Inc.

Printed in the United States of America

Without limiting the rights under copyright reserved above, no part of this
publication may be reproduced, stored in or introduced into a retrieval system, or transmitted, in any form, or by any means (electronic, mechanical,
photocopying, recording, or otherwise), without the prior written permission
of both the copyright owner and the above publisher of this book.

PUBLISHER'S NOTE
This is a work of fiction. Names, characters, places, and incidents either are
the product of the author's imagination or are used fictitiously, and any resem-
blance to actual persons, living or dead, business establishments, events, or
locales is entirely coincidental.
   The publisher does not have any control over and does not assume any
responsibility for author or third-party Web sites or their content.

If you purchased this book without a cover you should be aware that this
book is stolen property. It was reported as "unsold and destroyed" to the
publisher and neither the author nor the publisher has received any payment
for this "stripped book."

The scanning, uploading, and distribution of this book via the Internet or via
any other means without the permission of the publisher is illegal and punish-
able by law. Please purchase only authorized electronic editions, and do not
participate in or encourage electronic piracy of copyrighted materials. Your
support of the author's rights is appreciated.

ALSO BY BEVERLY CONNOR

DEAD HUNT
DEAD PAST
DEAD SECRET
DEAD GUILTY
ONE GRAVE TOO MANY

To Hubert Connor

ACKNOWLEDGMENTS

A special thanks to Anne Bohner, Kristen Weber, and Robbie.

Chapter 1

Diane Fallon studied the Neanderthal child staring at her from his perch. His chubby face didn't look all that different from his modern *Homo sapiens* cousins. He was smiling shyly at her from atop a boulder outside the rock shelter, his plump little fingers grasping the surface of the rock.

"Will you lookee here . . ."

For a fraction of a second Diane was startled, as if the resin figure of the Neanderthal had suddenly come to life. She smiled to herself and turned to see a lanky kid, she guessed about thirteen years old, looking wide-eyed at the Neanderthal exhibit. Behind him stood Sheriff Bruce Canfield of Rose County and an older man she did not know.

The sheriff was holding a cardboard file box, the kind with a lid and handholds on the sides. His wide-brimmed sheriff's hat sat on top of the box. Canfield was a large man in his late fifties with a full head of dyed brown hair. He was wearing his khaki sheriff's uniform and Diane thought he looked a little sheepish.

She hadn't heard them come in, with all the noise created by the staff working on the dioramas for the new human-evolution exhibits.

"Hello, Diane," said the sheriff. "Sorry to barge in here like this." He set the box on a nearby table. "This here's Arlen Wilson and his grandson Henry. Arlen has a farm out in the county." The sheriff's

Peabody Public Library
Columbia City, IN

booming voice echoed across the room, and several exhibit preparers glanced their way, then back at their work.

Arlen Wilson, the grandfather, was a man who looked to be in his sixties. He was taller than the sheriff by an inch or two. He had a ruddy complexion, white thinning hair, and the beginnings of a beer belly hanging over his belt. He and his grandson both were dressed in worn jeans, short-sleeved plaid shirts, and baseball caps.

"Nice meeting you," Arlen said. He took off his cap and grinned broadly as he shook her hand.

The teen, Henry, was not as tall as his grandfather. He was close to Diane's five nine and about as lean as she was. From the broad grin on his boyish face, Diane surmised he was happy to be here in the museum.

"I heard you was doing something to the primate room." Henry turned to his grandfather. "Lookit how real they are."

Diane was afraid Henry was going to reach out and touch them, as she was often tempted to. He looked at each small scene in turn—the child on the boulder, a man making stone tools, a Neanderthal burial. On another pass, his gaze finally saw the little girl in the back of the cave hiding behind a rock, peering out at the other child. Henry grinned.

"She playing hide-and-seek?" he asked.

"Maybe," said Diane. "That's for you to decide. We're trying to make each exhibit tell small stories, but you have to supply some of the plot from what you see."

"Wouldja look at the way he's staring right at us," the kid said, pointing to the child on the boulder.

"Each scene has one figure making eye contact with the visitor," said Diane.

"I like that," said Henry. "It makes them look so alive, like they're watching you."

"The artists have just finished a Cro-Magnon," said

Diane, "one of the oldest modern humans. He looks at you out of the corner of his eye as he stands sideways to you. It's an odd sensation, but fun." Diane smiled at Henry before she turned back to the sheriff, glad to see that the new exhibit was getting a good review.

"What can I do for you?" She eyed the box sitting on the table.

Henry, who was leaning rather far into the diorama, spoke up before the sheriff had a chance to answer.

"Tell me, what do you think happened to them? Did we kill them off, or did they marry with us and disappear, or did the weather get them?"

"I didn't know you're interested in Neanderthals, Henry." The sheriff chuckled.

"We watch a lot of those shows," said his grandfather. "The ones on PBS and the Discovery Channel."

"I don't know what caused their extinction," said Diane. "Right now it looks like they did not interbreed with us. So far, scientists haven't found any Neanderthal DNA in our gene pool."

"Those scientists need to come to my jailhouse on a Saturday night," said the sheriff.

They laughed, and Diane made a move to address the box.

She reached out to touch the lid.

"What's in the box?" she asked the sheriff.

"It's probably nothing, just pieces of animal bone . . . but you never know. Henry may have a point," said the sheriff.

Diane raised her eyebrows, looked at Henry, and started to open her mouth. Arlen Wilson spoke first.

"The land next to mine is owned by a man from Detroit. He sometimes asks me to tend it for him. He got the idea he wanted to plant ryegrass and put some cattle on it this winter. I guess he was gonna ask me to tend to them too. I'll have to tell him to hire somebody else. I'm not a cattleman." Arlen shook his head.

"Anyways, I was plowing it before planting the rye-grass, and my grandson Henry likes to look over fresh-plowed ground."

"I find the neatest stuff," said Henry. "I've got a whole collection of arrowheads. I once found an Indian-head penny."

"This time he found some bones—pieces of bones. I thought it was nothing, just the bones of some animal. But Henry thought we should call the sheriff."

"I figured it like this," said Henry. "The pieces are all about the same size. Mostly. And they look chopped up. Well, you don't get rid of animals that way. If an animal dies, you either bury it or haul it out into the woods for the buzzards and coyotes—you don't chop it up in small pieces."

"He thought they might have gone through a wood chipper," said Arlen. He and the sheriff chuckled.

"We just thought it was worth a look," said the sheriff, still appearing a little embarrassed. "You know, just in case."

"Then, let's have a look. We'll use the lab through here," said Diane.

She led them through double doors into a room with cabinets and counter space, sinks, and work islands—all metal and shiny. One end was stacked with materials that had overflowed from the exhibit preparations.

Diane donned a pair of gloves she pulled from a box on the wall, tore a sheet of brown paper from a roll mounted on the wall, and spread it out on one of the shiny tables. She set the box down and opened it to find wadded-up newspaper. She gently removed the paper. The box was filled with pieces of bone with moist dirt clinging to their surface.

"We didn't want to wash them up," said Henry. "I don't think you're supposed to do that, are you?"

"You did right," said Diane.

She picked out several pieces of bone, put them on the table, teased the dirt away from them with her fingers, and set them aside. The pieces were all of similar size, but not so small that she couldn't recognize them.

"I'm afraid that Henry is right," said Diane. "They are human, they're fairly fresh, and they show definite tool markings as a result of being chopped up, probably in a wood chipper."

"I knew it," said Henry. "I knew it."

Chapter 2

"Well, damn. Well, damn. Are you sure? Of course you're sure. Well, damn." The sheriff slapped his hat against his thigh and looked up at the ceiling. "All I need is a maniac running loose in the county. You're sure, aren't you?" he asked again. "Could it be a pig? I understand pigs are like humans."

Both Arlen and Henry looked at Sheriff Canfield with identical bewildered expressions.

Diane grinned at him. "The tissue is similar. That's why pig valves can be used in heart surgery and why pigs are sometimes used in forensic research. But the shapes of the bones are very different." She picked up several pieces of the broken bone. "This is the distal end of a phalange, this is a piece sliced off a greater trochanter, this is the petrous portion of the temporal bone, this is a piece of occipital—all of it is human."

"Okay, I was just hoping that you were having an off day," he said. "I don't suppose you can ID the victim?"

Diane cocked an eyebrow at him. "Right now I can't even tell you if it's one individual or more than one. If we get lucky—"

"You mean there may be more than one body? Well, hell," said the sheriff.

"I don't know," said Diane. She looked from Henry to Arlen. "Are these all the bones you found?"

Henry nodded. "We just looked in that one spot

where they turned up in the plowed ground," said Henry. "We didn't go digging around."

"How big a field are we talking about?" asked the sheriff.

"Well," said Arlen. "The part we was plowing's a three-acre bit that's circled by trees. It's connected to a bigger, fifteen-acre field by a path just about wide enough for me to get the tractor through. A creek runs along the far edge in the woods. That's why the owner wanted it seeded. It's where the cows would go to get water. Not that he's really going to put cows there. He'll change his mind."

"So we have eighteen acres to search?" interrupted the sheriff. "That's just great."

"Well, I don't know if if you'd need to look at the fifteen," said Arlen. "See, the owner had me plow the three-acre field a couple of years ago. So it's easier digging if you're of a mind to bury something. The fifteen-acre parcel's rock hard. Two years ago the owner got it into his head he wanted to plant sunflowers on the small piece and grow peanuts on the larger field. He changed his mind—he's always doing that, doesn't really know anything about farming—and ended up not doing anything with either field. So, I'm thinking that maybe whoever did it used the small field only, being as it's kind of off by itself and the dirt was already roughed up from the earlier plowing."

"Did you hear anything like a wood chipper?" asked the sheriff.

"No. And might not have. Our house is about five miles away," said Arlen. "Sometimes you can hear things through the woods—depends on the weather."

"How long do you think they've been in the ground?" the sheriff asked Diane.

She picked up one of the fragments and examined it, felt it. She put it to her nose and sniffed it. She did the same thing to another one.

"I'd say not more than a few months—could be a few weeks," she said. "This is fairly new bone. Chopped up like this, the flesh would decompose very quickly."

The sheriff sighed. "I suppose I can get those archaeology students at the university, like we did before, to grid and sift," said the sheriff, more to himself than to Diane and the other two.

Diane looked at the box of bone fragments. She had successfully reconstructed bones from an explosion and from plane crashes. She should be able to do something with these.

"If you can find the right pieces . . . ," she began and picked up the petrosal. "This is the auditory canal." She pointed to an opening in the bone. "I can make a mold of the canal, measure the angle, and estimate the sex of the person who owns this piece, with a little over eighty percent accuracy."

"Well, that'll be a good start," said the sheriff. "What about DNA? Can Jin give us a profile?"

Diane smiled to herself. No matter what fascinating thing she could do with bones, DNA was always going to be king.

"If any DNA survived," she said. "And that's a big *if*."

"Why?" asked Henry. He hovered over the box like it was his stuff inside. His grandfather gently pulled him back.

"DNA is very fragile," said Diane. "It degrades quickly."

"Then how can they find DNA in Neanderthals—they're something like thirty thousand years old—and not these bones?" asked Henry.

"That's a good question," said the sheriff. "Those Neanderthals have tougher DNA?"

The three of them looked at Diane as if demanding an explanation for what looked to them to be a contradiction.

"No," said Diane. She put down the bone fragment and stepped back from the table so she could look at the three of them.

"For DNA to be preserved, it has to be protected from the elements. The Neanderthal skeletons that have survived to modern times were buried deep in the ground or inside caves. That gave them enough protection. Even then, scientists had to look for DNA in inner protected places like the roots of teeth and deep in the long bones."

Diane gestured toward the box of bones. "I doubt these remains were covered with more than a thin layer of soil. Chopping them up caused them to decompose quickly and destroyed most of the places that DNA could be preserved."

It was written on their faces that they weren't convinced—after all, she could just see them thinking, thirty thousand years verses a few weeks. Diane took a deep breath. "Okay. Until fairly recently the problem was that even when there was DNA present, there was simply not enough to do anything with. We now have better methods of copying the DNA, duplicating it to make more of it."

Diane stepped to the table and began putting the bones back in the box. She kept the petrosal out, got a smaller box from a cabinet, and dropped the bone inside.

"Well, just how does that work, exactly?" asked the sheriff. "I hear all the time about copying DNA, PCR tests, and this and that, but I don't understand how you can copy something like DNA. They always talk about it as if they were making a Xerox copy."

"I don't understand it either," said Henry.

Jin would be better at this, thought Diane.

"Every living thing has a mechanism to copy its DNA—if we didn't, we couldn't grow or make new cells. And there is not a lot of variation across the animal and plant kingdoms in the way the copying is done. One of the big breakthroughs came when people working with DNA figured out how to make that copying process happen in a test tube."

For a fraction of a moment Diane thought she could stop there with her explanation, but no. The three of them were looking at her again, demanding an explanation of how one goes about copying DNA. Jin wanted to do a computer teaching program for the museum. It was a good idea. Diane wished she had one now. She smiled at the three of them, actually glad they were curious. Curiosity was good for museum business.

"It's an enzyme—polymerase—that makes the copies of DNA when a cell divides. We can use polymerase from certain organisms, such as the bacteria *Thermus aquaticus*, in a test tube to mimic the natural procedure. Polymerase and some other chemicals unzip the DNA helix, use both sides of the helix as templates, copy them, and zip them back up, re-forming the helix." Diane whorled her finger around for emphasis. "Millions of copies can be made."

She knew they were going to ask how, and she regretted that she wasn't a better teacher. Occasionally she taught classes in physical anthropology at the museum for Bartram University, but they were mainly hands-on courses about the very basics of bones and the human skeleton.

But Henry didn't ask for details. He wanted to know about mistakes.

"I remember somebody saying you get errors when you make a lot of copies from a little bit of DNA. Is that true?" he asked.

"That was a problem with some of the earlier processes," said Diane. "But the *Thermus aquaticus* polymerase compares each duplicate with the original and corrects errors as it copies."

Henry grinned. "Now, see, that's just plain amazing. That's just like science fiction."

"It is that," said the sheriff. "Kind of hard to wrap your brain around." He paused a moment as if studying what she had told them. "Is there any possibility you can get some DNA from these bones?" he asked again.

"Yes," Diane reluctantly agreed, "there is a small possibility that there may be something we can use, particularly if we are lucky enough to find some intact teeth or bone marrow."

The sheriff grinned broadly. That was what he wanted

to hear. Diane sighed inwardly; she might have been able to avoid the whole explanation if she had just said yes in the first place. She put the smaller box containing the petrosal in with the other bones and put the lid back on the box.

"If you and your grandfather like, you can tour the museum before you leave. I'll call for a docent if you want a guided tour," said Diane.

"Thank you. We might just look around some," said Arlen Wilson. "But Henry here knows this place pretty good."

Diane picked up the box and escorted the three of them out of the lab, through the unfinished human-evolution exhibit, and out into the main hallway. Diane and the sheriff stood off to the side, away from the flow of people visiting the museum. The sheriff watched Arlen and his grandson as they disappeared past the museum store toward the dinosaur exhibit.

"Arlen and his wife, Mary, are good people," he said. "They raised Henry and his brother, Caleb Miller, since they were just little fellas." He looked back at Diane. "Arlen's daughter and son-in-law were kind of wild. Not in a real bad way. They didn't do drugs or anything. Just liked having fun. Got in a boating accident on the lake—going too fast, as usual. Killed the daughter, Arlene, and left Caleb Senior in a coma for a couple of years before he died too. Real sad. Arlen and his wife did a good job raising the boys, though. Caleb will be finishing up at Bartram this year. And you see how Henry is. Bright kid. Both of them are."

He shook his head. "Henry was excited about finding the bones. He doesn't quite see the tragedy behind it. It's adventure to him. But I'm afraid folks are going to be pretty upset finding out somebody's been put through a wood chipper."

Diane remembered when she had thought of forensics as an adventure. One mass grave ended the romance for her. She paused and waved at one of the visitors who was waving at her, trying to remember his name. She turned back to the sheriff.

"As the archaeology students are sifting for the bone, they need to look for bug parts too—carapaces and the like. David . . . ," began Diane.

The sheriff was shaking his head before she could finish. "I've got nothing against David, and I know he's good with bugs. But the crime lab is different than when you were running it."

"Get an entomologist at the university then," said Diane.

The sheriff nodded and leaned his shoulder against the wall, rolling the brim of his hat as he spoke.

"I wasn't real fond of the last police chief in Rosewood; you know that; but we worked things out. But this new mayor and the people he put in, they're arrogant and pushy. Why did you guys vote them in?"

I didn't, thought Diane, but she didn't say it. She shrugged. "There was a lot of petty crime, and Jefferies promised that as mayor he would do something about it. I think a lot of voters responded to that. The last administration concentrated on drugs and violent crimes and less on burglaries, but more people are actually affected by break-ins. Plus, Jefferies is fairly young. Rosewood tends to see itself as Atlanta and wants young blood."

"Don't I know it. Rosewood's always been too big for its britches. We didn't need a crime lab in the first place. No offense intended, but the GBI lab was just fine." He sighed. "You know, it's awfully hard sometimes to get burglars. Even if you know who it is—proving it's another matter. Have these new guys done any better than the old bunch?"

"I don't know," said Diane. "I don't keep up with local politics or the police blotter." Diane shifted the box to rest on a hip.

The sheriff shook his head and rolled the brim of his hat again. Diane wondered why it didn't have a permanent roll in it.

"The new head of the crime lab, now, Bryce . . . he's a piece of work," said the sheriff. "You know what he did?"

Diane shook her head.

"Early on, when we had that killing at the tavern near the county line, Bryce showed up to work the crime scene. I hadn't called him and didn't intend to. We had the GBI coming. I told him I wasn't using the Rosewood crime scene unit. He got all huffy. I thought me and my deputies were going to have to escort him back to the city limits. Felt sorry for Neva. I like her, and I know she must have been embarrassed."

He shook his head. "And now Mayor Jefferies is talking about incorporating Rosewood and Rose County. Hell, if we wanted to have Rosewood politics, we'd move into the city. He's not going to get anyone in the county to vote for that, I can tell you."

The sheriff stopped, finally, it seemed, running out of wind. He stood up straight.

"Well, I guess I need to let us both get back to work," he said. "I'll go directly to the Bartram Archaeology Department and ask about some students to do the sifting. We'll bring any more bones we find straight to you, if that's all right."

Diane nodded. "That's fine. Take care, Sheriff. Good to see you again."

"You too," he said and took his leave, weaving his way through a crowd of schoolkids getting on the elevators to the second-floor exhibits.

Diane's cell rang. It was Jin calling from the DNA lab in the basement of the museum.

"Boss, you got to help me. I've had to lock down my lab," said Jin.

Chapter 3

"Locked down?" said Diane. "What do you mean?"

"I mean that Lloyd Bryce sent this guy, Curtis Crabgrass, from the crime lab to apply for a job—"

"His name is Crabgrass?" said Diane.

"Maybe it's Crabtree," Jin conceded. "Curtis Crabtree. Anyway, I told him the DNA lab is not hiring right now. But the guy won't take no for an answer. He tried to bully me into giving him a job. I finally got him out the door, but he tried to come back. I had to lock him out."

"Is he violent?" asked Diane.

"Not exactly violent, yet, but he did some shoving. Now he's hanging out at the door talking on his phone."

"You say Bryce sent him?"

"Yeah, like it was an order to me from Bryce that I should give Crabtree a job in the DNA lab."

"I'll be right down."

Diane shoved her phone in her pocket, picked up the box of bones, and headed for the DNA lab.

"What on earth does Bryce think he's up to?" she muttered.

Visitors were gathered in front of the bank of elevators, waiting to go up to the second-floor exhibits. She worked her way past them and balanced the box of bones on her knee as she unlocked the private elevator, the one that went all the way from the subbasement to the attic. It was quiet inside the elevator, and she tried to clear her thoughts as she rode down to the recently renovated basement that housed the brand-new DNA lab.

The elevator door opened and Diane saw Curtis Crabtree in front of the glass doors to the DNA lab. She had glimpsed him in the parking lot but had not known his name. She remembered David telling her that Bryce had hired two new people—a young woman whom David and Neva called Lollipop because she always had one in her mouth, and a man who David was sure was some kind of thug. This must be him, she thought.

Curtis Crabtree had dark curly hair and a fair complexion that made his day-old beard look dark on his thin face. He was wearing corduroy bell-bottoms, a white shirt open at the neck, and a gold chain hanging among wisps of black chest hairs.

Jin saw her through the glass door and came out, locking the door behind him. His jet-black hair was cut short. He had on jeans and a white lab coat and wore a decidedly irritated expression on his face.

Deven Jin was formerly one of Diane's crime scene crew. He was now head of the new DNA lab run under the auspices of the museum. DNA labs all over the country were backed up with work, and Jin was getting just about more samples to analyze than he could handle himself. The lab was proving to be a lucrative addition to the museum. He had not advertised yet, but he was planning to hire another technician. But Jin was picky. He had to be. Diane could imagine that Curtis Crabtree in no way met Jin's criteria.

"This is Curtis Crab . . . tree," said Jin, waving a hand in the direction of Mr. Bell-bottoms and Gold Chain.

Crabtree stood with his arms folded, frowning at Jin.

"Look," Crabtree said, "Lloyd Bryce appointed me

as the link between the Rosewood Crime Lab and the
DNA lab. He wants me to run all the samples that
come from our unit. What's the problem?"

Diane set her box down on a nearby coffee table.
"Lloyd Bryce has no authority to appoint anyone to
the DNA lab," said Diane. "All DNA personnel decisions are made by Jin and reviewed by me. We have
strict protocols for access to our laboratory services.
Those protocols do not allow for an agency submitting
DNA samples to use our equipment to analyze it
themselves."

Crabtree had a staccato laugh that she imagined
would become annoying very quickly.

"Funny," he said. "This is different. We aren't just
any agency. If you want the business of the Rosewood
crime scene unit, this is how it's going to be done.
This is our policy." He stood with his chin jutting out,
his body rigid as his eyes shifted from Diane to Jin.

Jin rolled his eyes.

"Then we will have to forgo doing your DNA test-
ing," said Diane. "The Georgia Bureau of Investigation has an excellent DNA lab. You can take your
proposal to them—or to any of the other labs across
the country."

Crabtree hesitated a moment, as if he had expected
her to give in and now didn't know quite how to proceed. He didn't laugh.

"You better rethink this. You don't know what you
are getting into," he said.

"Mr. Crabtree," said Diane, "I think you had better
go. Even if we were hiring right now, you've disquali-
fied yourself by your aggressive behavior."

"What? You're kidding. I was just defending myself.
He started it." Crabtree pointed to Jin.

"Jin started it," Diane repeated. "Are you in the
third grade?" She pointed to the stairs. "Please leave.
This area is off-limits to you."

Crabtree narrowed his eyes to slits. "You're a foolish woman," he said. "A very foolish woman."

He stood there in front of them for several moments

as if deciding whether or not to dig his heels in. Suddenly he turned and headed for the stairs. Diane and Jin watched him leave.

"Cheeky bastards," said Jin.

"Aren't they," said Diane. She took her cell from her jacket pocket and called the crime lab and asked for Lloyd Bryce.

"I think there has been a misunderstanding," said Bryce when Diane had briefed him on the encounter. "Curtis is enthusiastic in everything he does. He was probably just being an assertive applicant. Your guy is just overly sensitive."

Diane sat down on one of the leather chairs in the small sitting area near the entrance to the lab. She put her feet up on the oak coffee table and rubbed the middle of her forehead with the tips of her fingers. Jin sat in a chair opposite her and leaned forward, his elbows on his knees.

"Enthusiasm aside, Mr. Crabtree's behavior was inappropriate," said Diane. "I explained that we cannot accommodate your DNA requirements. Our protocols don't allow it."

"I believe we can come to some compromise on this," Bryce said.

"What kind of compromise?" said Diane. "Certification standards require that we use only highly trained technicians who function under our direct supervision and authority."

"I have another employee whom I can recommend," he began.

"Neva would be acceptable, if you wish to transfer her to us. But she would need extensive training and, as I said, she would function one hundred percent under our authority."

Jin grinned. He would like to have Neva. They were a team when he worked in the crime scene unit. Neva was a former police officer given to Diane by the Rosewood Police Department when Diane started the crime scene unit. Now that Diane was no longer head of the unit, Neva worked for Bryce.

"I'd rather keep Neva working crime scenes," said Bryce. "I was thinking of Rikki Gillinick. She's very bright."

"Rikki Gillinick?" repeated Diane.

Jin jumped out of the chair and came at Diane shaking his head. Diane waved him back.

David had told Diane about Rikki, also known as Lollipop, and her inability to understand the difference between what she knew and what she believed, and how she carried her preconceptions with her to crime scenes.

David was another of Diane's former crime scene crew. He was a friend she had worked with doing human rights investigations. David took the news that Diane was being replaced hard and more than once had said he was going to quit. He and Neva frequently joked about the unit over their weekly dinners with Diane, their way of debriefing, Diane supposed. Their biggest complaints were Bryce's assigning David to do only lab work, taking him out of the field, and putting the inexperienced Rikki on the larger cases—like the murder of Judge Karen McNevin. Neva was sent to process a downtown break-in while Bryce and Rikki worked the judge's scene. David analyzed the evidence collected by Bryce and Rikki, and the police arrested the brother of a man the judge had put away. It was a slam dunk according to Bryce, but Diane had sensed that David was not satisfied with the way it was handled.

Rikki as a DNA tech was out of the question.

"We are committed to the protocols that regulate us and ensure the quality of our work," said Diane. "I'll tell you what I told Mr. Crabtree. The GBI has a fine DNA lab. Perhaps you can work out something with them."

"Look, Diane, I know you are ticked at being replaced as the crime lab director, but don't let your emotions cause you to overlook the merits of working with us."

That did pique Diane's ire. She straightened up and put her feet on the floor.

"Lloyd," she said, "the DNA lab tests and analyzes samples. There is no 'working with' anyone in the way that you are suggesting. And Crabtree is off-limits here. That's the end of the discussion."

"You're being foolish," he said.

That word again. "I don't think there is much point in continuing this conversation." Diane flipped her cell shut.

Diane called security and made arrangements with Chanell Napier, her head of security, to post a guard in the museum basement at Jin's lab until further notice.

"That's a hell of a note, isn't it?" said Jin. "We have to post a guard to keep out the crime scene people."

"It's a peculiar turn of events," agreed Diane, standing up. "Call me if there are any more problems."

Diane took her box of bones and rode the elevator up to her osteology lab—adjacent to the Rosewood Crime Lab. She entered, locking the door behind her. Like the DNA lab, the osteology lab was part of the museum—and her domain. She liked being in the quiet room. Its shiny tables, white cabinets, and sterile atmosphere were calming to her.

She set the box down on one of the metal tables and donned her lab coat and a pair of gloves. Then she tore a piece of white paper from a roll, spread it on the table, and began taking the broken bones from the box. She examined each piece as she laid them out, looking for anything of note that might be clinging to them, examining them for tool marks. All of them had deep cuts. Diane tried to keep the image out of her mind of someone feeding body parts into a wood chipper.

She picked up a fragment cut from the left zygomatic arch—the cheekbone. Muscles anchored to the head for chewing pass through the zygomatic arch and attach to the lower mandible. She noted that the piece she held in her hand was small compared to the early hominid replicas she had been working with for the Neanderthal exhibit. Small zygomatic arches meant smaller jaw muscles and were thought to be indicators of the introduction of tool use in early hominids. Before tools were developed for slicing and dicing food, the jaw was the power tool, and a big muscle gave a significant advantage for survival. After tools came into use, just any old size of zygomatic arch had survivability. At least that was one hypothesis.

She had a brief unbidden mental image of a head going through a chipper. She pushed it from her mind.

Diane took the bones to one of the sinks, put them on a screen, and gently sprayed the dirt and detritus off them, passing the runoff over a finer-meshed screen to filter out smaller items, and from there catching the wash water in a plastic tub. She placed the cleaned bones on a drying screen and the screen onto a rack. Returning to the finer-meshed screen, she collected the fragments that had dropped through the holes of the first screen.

A small object caught her eye, and she picked it up. She recognized it as a piece sliced from the greater horn of the hyoid bone—the small bone in the throat critical to speech that anchors the tongue and is connected to the muscles of the jaw and larynx.

Higher apes don't have hyoid bones, but Neanderthals did—ones very much like human hyoids—which led to the hypothesis that Neanderthals had the same higher-order speech capability that humans have.

The hyoid bone, the zygomatic arch—tiny clues to human evolution. The pelvis, bones of the hand, shape of the skull, cranial capacity, shape of the spine and the long bones—bigger clues. And then there was context— stone tools, hearths, graves, and grave goods—more big clues. All the tiny clues and big clues together provided an idea of what early ancestors of man were like. These were the things she was incorporating into the exhibit. Diane hoped that the bone fragments she had of this unknown skeleton held as many clues to who the individual was and why he or she was now in bits and pieces.

Something metallic, partly covered by the detritus in the dirt on the small screen, reflected a glint of light. She picked it up and swished it in the water. It was a piece of thick wire, iridescent blue-green in color. She turned it over in her palm and examined it before she took it to the dissecting microscope—one that allowed her to view three-dimensional objects. The microscope confirmed that the mashed piece of metal had been round or oval. Was it from a piece of jewelry? Earring? From a body piercing? She labeled it and bagged it. A tiny clue.

Diane looked at the bones on the drying rack again. They were a mixture of fragments from the skull, pieces of rib, sections of long bone. When they dried she would start laying them out in anatomical position on the table. Who knew, maybe she could put Humpty Dumpty back together again—after a fashion—provided it was one individual. So far she hadn't seen any indication that there was more than one.

She picked up the petrosal and examined it. It should produce a good cast of the ear canal. Determining the sex would be another good clue.

As she put the petrosal back on the drying screen, she noticed something on one of the occipital bones. On the corner of the piece was some beveling. The fragment was not big, and the beveling could be an artifact of the chipper—probably was—but it was something worth looking at, especially if she could find the adjacent bones. There was a possibility it was a gunshot or projectile wound. That would be a big clue.

A half-inch piece of metal, a petrosal, a possible bullet hole—not even a handful of clues, but she had just begun, and who knew what else the sifters would find in the field.

Diane doffed her lab coat and gloves, washed her hands, and was ready to lock up her lab. As she was hanging her coat on its hook, she heard voices.

The wall she stood next to separated her office from the crime lab. She knew that on the crime lab side of the wall was a large walk-in supply closet. The voices seemed to be coming from there. The wall wasn't thick. There had been no reason to make it sound-proof when they constructed the closet as part of the crime lab. Odd. The closet was not a place one usually held conversations.

Though slightly muffled, the voices were loud enough for her to hear some of the words. She stopped and listened when she heard Bryce's high-pitched speech pattern and another voice that sounded like Curtis Crabtree's.

". . . apply for . . . job, not beat him up."

"I didn't . . . wasn't taking applications . . ."

". . . you've screwed . . . up now . . ."

"Easy to fix . . ."

There was the sound of a door opening.

"What the hell do you want?" Bryce's voice was no longer in hushed tones.

"Oh, sorry." The new baritone voice was David's. "I need some evidence envelopes. The four-by-nine-inch size. And a resupply of phenolphthalein for my blood test kit—here we go."

She heard some rattling of supplies.

"We have more supplies in the cabinets if you can't find what you're looking for," David said.

"If you have what you need, go," said Bryce.

"Sure thing," she heard David say, and the door closed again.

Diane smiled. She didn't have any doubt that David interrupted them on purpose just to make Bryce uncomfortable. She immediately frowned. She hoped David wasn't getting reckless in his dealings with Bryce. It wasn't like David to be reckless, but lately he'd been so moody. She let the thought slide.

Diane stood there, reluctant to move, not wanting to be heard near the wall. For several moments they said nothing. Then Curtis spoke.

"I have to go . . . later."

She heard the door open and close—presumably leaving Bryce in the closet by himself. The oddity of it brought another half smile to her lips. Strange. After a moment she heard the door open and close again. After another moment, she stepped back from the wall quietly.

Chapter 4

Diane was disturbed by Bryce and his employees, but it was nothing she could put her finger on. There was just something not right about the way Bryce was trying to encroach on the DNA lab. David said Bryce was a control freak. It was probably nothing, just his aggressive, slimy personality.

If she was honest, she thought to herself, there was a tiny speck of truth to Bryce's accusation. She had been angry when the new chief of police, Edgar Peeks, showed up with no warning and introduced Bryce as her replacement as director of the crime lab. But that was three months ago and had nothing to do with Curtis Crabtree coming down to the DNA lab insisting on a job. Diane shook the nagging feelings as she left for home.

Home. That was another change in Diane's life of late. Her neighbors had asked her to move out of her apartment because, through no fault of her own, too many unsettling and sometimes horrific things had happened there. The neighbors had been awakened by the arrival of the police just one too many times, and they were frightened. Diane understood that. Everyone needs peace in their lives.

She was staying with Frank Duncan temporarily until she found herself a new place. Frank was a detective in the Metro-Atlanta Fraud and Computer Forensics Unit. Atlanta wasn't far from Rosewood, and

Frank drove into the city daily to work. He wanted her to move in with him permanently. She was thinking about it, but she was also thinking that she wanted her own house. Despite Frank's terrific hospitality, she still felt like a guest. Somehow, coming into someone's house and using it as her own didn't seem right to her.

However, for the moment, the arrangement was working out better than she had expected. She had gained a measure of peace in her own life by moving in with Frank. And if the truth be known, no longer being director of the crime lab gave her time—a priceless commodity. She had time to design the new primate exhibit, she had more time to spend with Frank, she was learning to play the piano, and she'd been caving three times this month alone. And she was even considering getting a dog, maybe an Irish wolfhound or a Lab. Life was good. She was thinking about her good life as she turned into the driveway.

Frank's house was a Queen Anne set back from the road. It was a house much like Frank—traditional, reliable, solid. It had polished hardwood floors, sand-colored walls, and oak and walnut furniture as substantial as the house itself. It always smelled like furniture polish and always shined.

Frank wasn't there when Diane arrived. He'd left a message on his answering machine saying he wouldn't be back until the following day. It wasn't uncommon—Frank traveled a lot in his job—but it was a shame; it was nice when they both got home early. Diane spent the evening watching the Sci Fi channel—that was also nice. Frank wasn't the science fiction fan she was, and Diane would not subject him to a Star Trek marathon if he was home.

Frank called just before Diane got into bed.

"How was your day?" she asked as she snuggled into the softness of the down mattress.

"Good. Love putting the white-collar guys away. They never expect it. I've been chasing a spate of identity theft complaints. Those are always fun to track down. And I got an Atlanta mortgage embezzler who's been on the run with a few million of his company's money. They picked him up in Hawaii."

"Wonder why he didn't go outside of U.S. jurisdiction if he went that far," said Diane.

Frank started laughing. "He thought he had."

"You're kidding?" Diane grinned as much at Frank's mirth as at the humor of the failed escape. She could just see his eyes crinkle and sparkle as he laughed.

"I kid you not. It made my day. Another good answer for all those kids who ask, 'Why do I have to learn this? I'll never use it.' So, tell me about your day."

Diane told him about the progress on the exhibits, but not about the bones found in the farmer's field. Sliced-up bones weren't a conversation topic she wanted to have before she went to sleep. They talked for almost an hour. A good end to the day.

The morning brought sunshine and sparkling frost on the ground. It was a great day to be outside and a great day to take the scenic route to work. It was a little longer, but it was her favorite route, especially in the morning when there was little traffic. The narrow road went through a short patch of woods that were beautiful even in winter when most of the trees were bare of leaves. The trees had shades of bark that ranged from dark brown to tan to almost white, interspersed with the greenery of spruce, cedar, and magnolia trees. And you never knew when a doe and her fawn might be grazing along the roadway or dashing for the woods.

As she drove, Diane listened to classical music on the radio. On the hour, the news came on, and she started to change stations but stopped when she heard that the first item of local news was about the bones. She frowned as the anchor described it as the wood-chipper murder and told of the crushed bones of an unknown victim found by Rose County farmer Arlen Wilson and his grandson. Sheriff Canfield explained to a persistent reporter that the bones were only recently found and he didn't yet know whom they belonged to but that a forensic anthropologist had the bones and it was hoped she would be able to shed light on the identity of the victim. Diane noticed that he was careful not to say *victims*. Rumors of more than one wood-chipper murder would become a nightmare. The reporter asked if the forensic anthropologist was Diane Fallon of the RiverTrail Museum of Natural History. Canfield said yes. Diane frowned again. The last thing she wanted was the reporter calling her.

The interviewer asked the sheriff about possible DNA, and he went into a lengthy explanation of DNA and why they might not be able to find any in the bones. Diane had to smile, listening to the lecture she had given him just yesterday. He must be having fun.

She was about halfway to the museum and in the deepest part of the wooded area when she saw blue flashes of light behind her and the intermittent siren that meant to pull over. She found a wide place on the side of the road, pulled her SUV onto the shoulder, and waited with her hands on the steering wheel. She looked in her rearview mirror at the approaching officer. She knew him. Not good. It was Harve Delamore, and he was grinning like he'd just caught his biggest fish ever.

Last year Douglas Garnett, the chief of detectives for the city of Rosewood and Diane's former boss when she was head of the crime scene unit, had put a reprimand in Delamore's file for overly aggressive behavior with a suspect. Diane had given a sworn statement as a witness to the incident. Diane was not Delamore's favorite person.

He looked different than last time she'd seen him—a little leaner, and he'd shaved his head the way a lot of men do these days when they are going bald. Delamore was in a patrolman's uniform. It was a summer uniform even though the temperature had been near freezing overnight. The term *hot-blooded* fit him, she thought as he approached. The uniform meant he had been demoted from his rank of detective for some reason. Probably some additional offense. Harve didn't strike her as a man who learned very quickly.

Damn, he's probably going to be in a mood, she thought. *Probably write me up for everything he can think of. Well, damn.*

Diane rolled down her window as he approached. She decided not to say anything until he spoke, asking for her driver's license, probably her insurance papers, probably the deed to the museum. She really didn't have time for this. She knew her brake lights were in working order; she hadn't been speeding; there had been no stop signs or red lights to run. He just wanted to jerk her around.

She turned her head toward Officer Delamore as he bent down to the open window. Before she realized what was happening, he'd reached through the window and grabbed her arm with one hand and opened the door with the other. He held her tight through the window as the door swung open. Diane reached behind her, feeling for her cell phone in the center console. She got her fingers on it, but he jerked her hard toward the open door and she dropped it.

"Well, if it's not the bitch who messed up my life." His voice was a snarl and his face was twisted in some kind of weird satisfied rage.

She was pissed herself. "What the hell are you doing?" Diane screamed at him. "Have you gone nuts?" That reprimand was a year ago. What had set him off now? she wondered.

"Shut up, bitch."

Harve reached inside the open door and dragged her out of the vehicle. Her cell phone clattered to the pavement. He looked down at it, smirked, and ground his foot onto the top of it.

"Uh-oh, no signal," he said.

Diane loved this road because she was usually the only one on it. Now she prayed for someone to drive by. But no one did. She was alone.

"Harve, think about what you're doing. This will ruin you," said Diane.

"I told you to shut up, you damn stupid bitch. You're going to get what's coming to you."

He had her by her left arm, which meant she had one arm and two legs free. She put them to good use. She kicked his shin hard, kneed him in the groin, and rammed the palm of her right hand into his nose with all the strength she could summon. He didn't see it coming. He was stunned and let go, and she jerked away. She had been lucky. She'd caught him off guard. It wouldn't happen again. She had to get away from him.

He was blocking access back into her SUV, so she had to run. She sprinted for the woods, thinking maybe it was a mistake even as she did it. On the one hand, someone might drive by and see her if she ran down the road. On the other hand, he would just run her down with his car.

Harve Delamore was a big guy, but he was all show muscle and not much real working muscle. That would be helpful if she were male. But show muscle or not, testosterone in the male gives muscles a spectacular advantage. Harve was stronger by far than she was. But she had stamina, and she could run. Which she did—as fast as she could. Diane could run long distances, and she had another advantage. She knew these woods.

There was one big problem in all that optimism. Harve had a gun. She thought he would be reluctant to shoot her, though; he wanted to hit her. She saw it in his eyes when he held her. He wanted to pound his meaty fist into her face. So maybe he wouldn't use his gun.

She was in the air, jumping over a fallen tree, when the gunshot roared in her ears. In the same instant, pieces of bark flew off a tree to her right. He was trying to scare her. Or else he was a really bad shot. Right now, either one would do, as long as she could keep running.

It was hard to shoot a moving target in these woods—lots of trees to get in the way. But she had a serious problem. Males run fast for short distances, and she didn't have enough of a head start. Diane ran faster. She heard the sound of him gaining on her: heavy footfalls, limbs breaking, grunts and curses. She pushed herself to the limit.

He was close behind her. His breathing was heavy. He was getting out of breath. Good. She tried a sharp turn to throw him off balance, slow him down. It didn't work. He knocked her to the ground, then pulled her up by her arm, breathing hard. He had his gun in his hand. He laid the barrel against her temple.

"I've got you now, bitch, and there's no help. This is a dead end for you."

Diane kicked and hit at him as he dragged her through the woods. He turned abruptly and hit the side of her head with the barrel of his gun. Diane literally saw stars. Disoriented, she felt herself dragged deeper into the woods, away from the highway. She tried to keep her bearings. She heard rock crunching under foot and felt her pants snagging. She tried to right herself, but he jerked on her arm and she fell again. He was enjoying dragging her over the rough terrain.

She tried to calm her fear, clear her head, think of a plan. She didn't fight. If he knocked her out, she was done for. If he jerked her arm out of the socket, she was done for. She thought she knew where she was, and that could be either good or bad. Harve came to an abrupt stop. Chances were, he knew where he was too, and apparently he thought it was good for his purposes.

They were at Chulagee Gorge. It was a gouged-out drop of more than five hundred feet formed by a river that had dried up eons ago. Mike, Diane's geology curator and caving partner, used the cliff face to teach rock climbing to members of the caving club. He said that a half billion years ago, the quartzite rock here was a sandy beach on the coast of Laurentia in the

Iapetus Ocean, which sounded to Diane like a place of fantasy or science fiction. She'd liked it.

Mike insisted that if you climb a rock face or explore a cave you should know what it's made of and where it came from. Sometimes the caving club members' eyes glazed over as they listened to the petrogenesis of the rocks they were waiting to climb. But one thing Diane remembered from his lectures was that quartzite is very hard.

She had climbed parts of the cliff face many times—but always with safety ropes because of the great height. It wasn't a particularly difficult climb. There were plenty of handholds and footholds in the quartzite and schist formations. But it was nearly impossible if you had never climbed before.

Harve Delamore didn't strike Diane as a rock climber. Rock climbing, like caving and scuba diving, is a way of life. You have to do it a lot if you do it at all. It's dangerous to let yourself get out of shape or out of practice. Diane was also betting that, like many bullies, Harve was a coward. She was betting her life on it.

There was the gun to contend with. He had been holding it in his free hand while he dragged her. She watched for an opportunity and tried to think of a way to take it. Getting in a wrestling match with him for it was a last recourse, but it might come to that. She would lose most likely, but with no other options, she would still try if it came to that.

Her arm and shoulder ached from being gripped and dragged, and her head hurt. She pushed the pain to the back of her mind. She'd had a lot of practice doing that—pushing pain back until it was just an annoyance. Not even to mention the times she had been beat up, stabbed, and shot, she'd done some difficult caves and wrenched her muscles more than once. But you have to keep going. You can't stop.

Diane had practice putting fear in the back of her mind too. Every caver has moments of panic while caught in too tight a squeeze, or becoming lost—

discovering new passages, they call it—or trapped on unstable ground. You learned to control the panic, make the surge of adrenaline work for you.

But the fear a maniac generates in you is something different. Diane found humans far more terrifying than anything nature had in store. It was a struggle to keep the dread in this moment from overwhelming her.

Delamore pulled her to the very edge of the precipice. Her fear redoubled as she realized his intent. He was going to throw her into the gorge—perhaps after beating her or shooting her, or God knew what he had in mind.

She struggled. He slapped her across the cheek. She stood with her back to the drop-off, her heels at the edge. She could hear the wind whistling up from the depths below. This wasn't the plan she had in mind.

With a devilishly evil look in his eyes, he gave her a sudden push backward. She was off balance; she couldn't stop herself. She was going to fall. This was it.

He grabbed her wrist and pulled her back to him. It was so quick, it made her reel. She grabbed at him with both hands. He laughed.

"Oops, almost fell. Be careful," he said. His voice dripped with mock concern.

He pushed again. And again pulled her back.

"Uh-oh, you're going to fall."

Again his shove pitched Diane out over the chasm with only her feet on the edge and his hand around her wrist, her other hand grabbing on to his arm. He pulled her back.

"It's a long drop down. Sure you're up to it?" He laughed.

It was clear he intended to torture her with fear. But one of these times he was going to let go or miscalculate, and she would be gone.

Diane had an idea, but she had to put it in motion before he tired of his game. If he pushed hard enough and she couldn't grab on to him or on to something, she would die. No chance of catching hold of something on the way down. What would make him continue the game?

Ross Kingsley, her FBI profiler friend, said positive reinforcement—a reward—will continue a behavior. But the catch is, what does the perp consider positive reinforcement? She knew immediately what Delamore wanted, and she loathed the thought of giving it to him. Harve Delamore wanted to hear fear, to hear her begging. That would be his reinforcer.

"Look, please stop this," she said. "Please."

It rather shocked Diane that she was having a hard time pleading, even for her life. What on earth did that say about her priorities? She inched to her left and pleaded again.

"Not such a big deal now, are you?" he said.

He pushed her again and pulled her back. This time Diane dropped to her knees.

"Better watch out," he said. "It's a long, long way down." He laughed.

"Please stop this. Please, you're scaring me," she said.

Diane had seen a possible weapon on the ground, and now it was under her hand while she was on her knees begging for her life. A hard piece of quartzite. Jagged edges. He pulled her to her feet.

"Please, please, please," he mocked her. "Come on, beg me, you damn bitch. I want to hear you beg some more."

Diane struck his gun hand as hard as she could with the jagged rock. She struck and struck again and slashed in quick succession—three times before the gun slipped out of his hand, bounced off his foot, and disappeared over the edge and into the gorge.

DISCARD
Columbia City, IN

Chapter 5

The gun was gone, but Harve Delamore still held her arm tight in his grip. He was stunned and in pain, and he was furious. Diane was quick. Before he could hit her with his free hand, she slammed the rock down on the wrist of the hand that held her arm. He yelled and let go of her, but pushed her backward in anger. She had expected that, though; she fell to her knees immediately to keep herself upright as she slid over the edge of the cliff.

She dropped in a free fall through the air, preparing herself for what she knew was below. Eight feet or more down the side of the cliff, she landed solidly on a sloped ledge where the rock protruded from the sheer face of the cliff. The momentum caused by Harve's push sent her scrambling to find purchase. She shifted her weight forward and fell to her hands, not hard, but enough to let her grab the rock and stop her descent as she slid toward the edge.

"I guess you're in trouble now, bitch. That'll teach you to mess with me," Harve yelled down at her. "What's going to happen to you now, huh? There's nobody gonna come to your rescue."

Diane ignored him. She pulled herself back on the ledge and took the time to scuff the soles of her shoes on the rock to dislodge any detritus and loose pebbles that had accumulated from her trek through the woods. Thank God she didn't have on heels or leather-bottom shoes. She rubbed her hands on the surface of the rock and then on her clothes, trying to remove the sweat. More episodes like this and she would need to start carrying a chalk bag in her pocket, she thought wryly. She took off her jacket to give herself more range of motion. It dropped into the ravine.

She started climbing down, looking first for places to plant both feet before she moved. She'd climbed this very spot many times before. She knew where the footholds and handholds were, and that helped her to go more quickly.

But Mike told them never to get cocky with rock. "It can change from weathering, microschisms. You still have to test your holds. Don't expect them to be stable because they were the last time you climbed."

She wasn't being cocky with the rock, but it was critical that she hurry. Delamore would do something. She found her footing and descended inch by inch as fast as her level of confidence let her. Rock climbing was slow work—at least for her—and she could hurry only so much. Her first goal was to get space between the top of the cliff and herself in case Harve decided to climb down after her. *But surely he won't*, she thought. With her luck, though, he would probably turn out to be a closet climber.

"Where do you think you're going?" yelled Harve.

The slope of the rock changed at the bottom of the ledge. She braced her feet against the rock face, located her handholds, and gently swung down under the ledge, catching the vertical surface with the balls of her feet, bracing herself, then moving each hand. Rock climbing has a rhythm to it. To Diane it was not so different from music. Each change in slope of rock, each fissure, horn, corner, handhold, foothold, and overhang had its own cycle of movement. A twist in the hips could make the difference in a successful grip. When all the pieces were taken together, it was almost a dance.

"Hey, you talk to me, you damn bitch. Where do you think you're going?" he yelled again. He sounded genuinely puzzled, as if she had taken flight or something equally unexpected and impossible. "You come back here," he demanded.

Yeah, right, thought Diane.

She rarely climbed solo, certainly not on a rock face this high. It was dangerous without the safety of rope. Diane was good with rope. She liked it; she knew how to manipulate it, tie it. Rope was good. Hanging with her bare hands on the side of a cliff, she wasn't so sure about. But she had judged Harve Delamore to be more dangerous than the rocks. She kept the level of the risk from her thoughts, reminding herself that she had climbed this face many times—albeit on rope—and she had never fallen. She was lucky he'd dragged her to this section of the gorge. There were other places on the cliff face that she could not climb.

Diane continued inching her way down, always being careful. You feel the full weight of the laws of physics on the side of a rock face. Concepts like *gravity* and *equal and opposite reaction* suddenly become very real.

A rock the size of a melon bounced off the slope beside her. Harve was throwing boulders at her. *Well, shit.* She glanced up. She could see him grinning even from a distance.

She climbed to her right, where the slope of the rock would give her a measure of shelter. It was a harder climb, but she couldn't survive a hit from a rock. Another one the size of her head bounced near her, breaking on impact. At least he wasn't a good shot. Diane braced her feet and found her handholds. She slowly moved to a safer place as the rocks rained around her from above. He was throwing anything he could find, as if he suddenly did believe there was a possibility she might get away from him.

Diane found a place under a ledge where she could stop and rest. She heard him yelling but couldn't understand what he was saying, though she did hear the word *bitch* a couple of times. She looked for footholds. They were harder to find in this route, and her shoes weren't the best for climbing, but they did hold trac-

tion better than she had expected. Her muscles felt
good at the moment—the stretching and exertion always felt good. She'd been afraid Harve had sprained
her arm, jerking her around the way he had, but other
than being sore, it seemed fine. This would work after
all. She started moving again, putting one hand in a
crack and another on a protrusion of rock. She pushed
on the rock with one foot, finding a toehold with the
other.

As she moved along, she began hearing scraping
sounds overhead. *What now?* she thought. She turned
her head and looked up, but her view was obstructed
by an overhang. She stopped and listened. He was
climbing down. The crazy bastard was climbing down
the rocks.

She started descending again. After several feet,
Harve came into sight. He was making his way down
a large crevice between the ledge she had climbed
down from and the adjacent rock. It looked to the
untrained eye like an easier route, but it was decep-
tive. It was difficult to prevent your feet from becoming wedged in the crevice.

"Are you nuts?" Diane yelled at him. "You can't
climb down here."

"Scared, little girl?" he shouted.

"*You* should be scared. You're not a rock climber,"
she yelled back.

"How do you know? I do this every weekend," he
sneered.

"No, you don't," Diane said under her breath. "I
know all the climbers and cavers."

She wondered whether he had a backup gun. No,
he would have used that instead of throwing rocks.

"If you can do this, I can," he shouted.

So that was it, she thought. He wasn't going to let
a girl best him. Well, he was wrong. Diane was in her
element. She felt calmer than she had since he'd
dragged her out of her vehicle.

She moved horizontally on the rock face, heading
toward an easier path. A few feet from her was a slab of

rock that looked vaguely like a sheep's head plastered sideways against the cliff. Climbers called it Ram Rock. It had several creases and protrusions that were like features—eyes, a nose, an ear, and a horn. All made easy hand- and footholds. She had it in her mind now to climb back up to the top and run for her car, since Harve was down here.

"I played football," he yelled. "I could've gone pro."

He sounded closer. She looked over at him. He was perhaps twenty feet to her left and above her position. He was working his way down the crevice and having a difficult time, going too fast.

"Did you play ball on a vertical field?" said Diane.

He didn't respond. She watched as his foot slipped and slid down the crack. He grabbed at the rock. He stopped with a jerk when the crack widened to a tiny ledge. He looked startled, then scared. After a few moments he apparently thought he was safe, because he grinned at Diane. He pulled a knife out of his belt and pointed it at Diane, making small circles with the blade.

"You don't have time for that," said Diane, calmly. "You need both your hands."

"I'll teach you to fuck with me," he said.

Then he looked down. He shouldn't have. Below them at the bottom of the gorge was an old car someone had long ago pushed off the edge of the cliff into the canyon. At this height it looked like a child's toy. The tops of tall pine trees swayed in the wind four hundred feet below them.

Diane saw his face change. He grew pale, his eyes widened, and she knew his pupils were dilating. It happened so fast. He was panicking.

Harve hugged the rock, not moving. Diane thought she heard him moan.

"Stay calm," she shouted. "Don't let go of the rock. Hold on with both hands." *Why am I helping him?* she thought. *Let the bastard fall.*

He whimpered.

"Breathe slowly and evenly," said Diane.

"Help me," he said in a quiet voice. "Help me."

Diane had seen people panic on the rocks, but they were tied to ropes. If his panic got out of control, he would free-fall to the bottom.

"Harve, listen to me. You're standing on a small ledge. You can stand there for a long time until I get help. Try to stay calm."

"I can't," he whimpered.

What a change, she thought.

"Concentrate on holding on. Don't look down," said Diane. "Look up. Look how close you are to the top."

Harve brought his gaze around and looked up. They were no more than fifty feet down. He whimpered again. *It must look impossible to him*. She was sure the tension in his muscles that panic brought was making them ache.

"Listen to me, Harve. Breathe more slowly. Relax just a little bit. You're in a good place. You have a place to stand. Just stand there and I'll get help."

"I can't," he whimpered.

"Yes, you can. Concentrate on something else. Why did you come after me?"

Harve was silent for a long moment, and Diane repeated the question.

Silence again. He wasn't talking.

"Harve, can you talk?" she asked.

Harve squeezed his eyes shut. "Oh, God, oh, God, oh, God," he whispered.

"Breathe," she said. "In and out. You are in a good place. You could stay there all day if you had to."

He was paying attention. His breathing didn't sound so ragged.

"You sound good. Just keep calm. Panic is your enemy, not me. When you panic, you're in trouble," said Diane. "When you feel better, I'm going to go to call for help. Rescue will come and get you out of here, but you have to hang on."

"You'd like that, wouldn't you?" he said. "Have me waiting here while you go get help. Pretending to be my friend."

"I'm not pretending to be your friend. Obviously we aren't friends. But I don't want you to die out here either," said Diane.

He looked up, apparently reassessing his situation, deciding maybe he could climb back up after all.

"I'm not going to die. You are." He took aim with his knife, preparing to throw.

"Don't do that," shouted Diane.

He grinned, reared back, and threw the knife hard at Diane.

Chapter 6

Diane flattened herself against the rock face and watched in horror as the knife whizzed in a spinning blur toward her. She had no way to dodge it, nowhere to go. She threw one arm up in a defensive move just as the deadly blade struck the rock next to her abdomen and glanced off her waist.

The sudden move, the twisting of his body from throwing the knife, had shifted Harve's center of gravity, spoiled his aim, and left him struggling to hold himself upright. The laws of physics are hell when you're balanced precariously. His grip slipped on the rock. His arms flailed wildly, and his foot became caught in the crack. Diane heard the ankle break as his body fell backward, headfirst, his foot trapped in the fissure. He screamed, hung there for a moment; then his foot slipped from the crack and he fell five hundred feet to the bottom of the gorge. Diane didn't look. There was no way he could survive; there was nothing on the way down that would break his fall, nothing to grab on to, no help, no hope. Diane winced when she heard the thump of his body impacting on the rocks at the bottom. She felt sorry for him, living his last moments in terror.

She didn't move for several long moments. She felt drained, her energy gone with Harve. Her heart beat faster and she felt sick. She couldn't throw up. Not here. After a couple of minutes, her nausea subsided, her head cleared, and she moved again. She climbed over to Ram Rock and up to the top. It was an easy climb for her.

She walked to her car to call for help. Her cell lay on the pavement, smashed beyond use. She walked back to Harve's vehicle and called dispatch on his police radio.

"Who is this?" the female voice interrupted.

"Diane Fallon," she said.

"You're a civilian. You aren't allowed to use this channel," the voice said.

Diane started to tell her, *Okay, I'll go to the museum up the road and call 911.* "I'm trying to report—"

"Ma'am, you have to get off this channel. Where are you calling from?"

"A police car. I don't know the number," said Diane. "It belongs to Harve Delamore."

"Where is the officer?" said the dispatcher.

"He's dead. He fell into Chulagee Gorge," said Diane.

"Where are you?" the dispatcher asked.

Diane gave her location. She got out of the police car and walked to her own vehicle, climbed in, and locked the doors. She was shivering, so she started the engine and turned on the heater. She looked in the rearview mirror at herself. Her face was a puffy, blood-smeared mess. Her blackened eye was swollen half shut. Her hair was in tangles, blotched with dried blood. She suddenly felt the way she looked. She put her forearms on the steering wheel, rested her head gently on them, and waited.

It wasn't long before she heard the sirens, faint at first, then growing louder and louder—coming in high volume to the rescue of a downed officer.

Diane didn't move until she heard a knock on her window. She jumped. It reminded her of how all this had started. She didn't have the strength to do it again. This time she wouldn't roll down the window.

She lifted her head. It was Izzy Wallace. She smiled

wanly and rolled her window down, glad to see a friendly face. Izzy looked at her.

"What the hell happened?" he asked. "Wait a minute. I'll come around."

He picked up the smashed cell phone and looked at it, worry on his face. He walked around and got in the passenger side of Diane's red SUV.

Diane explained all the events of the morning—from being pulled over by Harve Delamore to the fall.

"So he's at the bottom of the ravine?" said Izzy.

"Yes. His gun is down there somewhere. I knocked it out of his hand. His knife is down there too. So is my jacket. My billfold with my driver's license is in it," she said.

"We need to go to the police station, and you will have to give a statement again. We need to take a picture of you too. You look like hell," he said.

Diane looked at her face again in the rearview mirror. Her left eye was black and swollen, and she had a huge bruise from her eye to her jawline. And there was the blackening dried blood. She looked at her mouth and her teeth. Thank God, her teeth weren't damaged.

"I didn't think he would come out on the rocks," Diane said. "If you've never climbed before, it's scary. I thought I could get away from him that way."

"Harve never had the best judgment," said Izzy. "You know there's going to be some who will blame you."

"I know. Does he have a family? A wife and kids?" asked Diane. "Are his parents still living?"

"He has an ex-wife. They didn't have any kids. I think his parents are dead. He has a brother somewhere. I don't think they got along."

"That's sad," said Diane.

Izzy escorted Diane into the police station, took a picture of her and her face, and walked her to one of the interview rooms.

"This won't take long," he said.

Janice Warrick walked in and frowned at her. "You look awful. Have you been to a doctor?"

Before Diane could answer, Curtis Crabtree came in with a patrolman and told Janice to leave.

"I caught this case," said Janice. She looked at each of them. The large frown line between her eyes deepened.

"The chief is taking it," Curtis said.

The patrolman had thin light brown hair that looked slightly windblown. His name tag said he was Officer Pendleton. Of the two, he looked the most angry— and grief stricken. Izzy had said Delamore's friends would blame her.

Neither said anything. They just stood against the wall across from her, staring. Diane was surprised that Curtis was there. Perhaps like Neva, he was a police officer or a detective before he was recruited to work in the crime scene unit. Like any new broom, the new mayor had done a lot of sweeping. Diane was one of the people he'd swept out. In the wake, new people were hired. There were many in the police department now that she didn't know.

Diane didn't say anything either. She sat and waited, hoping it wouldn't be too long. She ached all over, and her head throbbed where Delamore had hit her. She closed her eyes and rested her head in her hands. She hoped that frustrated them—her not being able to see them stare at her.

The door suddenly opened, and Edgar Peeks, Mayor Jefferies' new chief of police, burst into the room. He had dark hair, hazel eyes, and almost a baby face, were it not for the day-old beard he seemed to always wear—perhaps because he had such a baby face.

He pulled up a chair and sat opposite Diane, glaring at her for several moments.

"You are in a lot of trouble," he said.

Diane said nothing; she simply gazed back at him thinking that, no, she wasn't in trouble; the police department was—one of their officers just went berserk and tried to kill her.

"Have you nothing to say?" he asked.

"You haven't asked a question," said Diane. She was wondering why she was being treated as a perp instead of a victim. "I told the policeman on the scene what happened."

"We're not going to forget that you're responsible for Harve's death," Pendleton said. He had his fists curled, like he wanted to fight.

Diane wondered how "not forgetting" was going to manifest itself. Were Delamore's friends going to stalk her? Pull her over every time they saw her? What?

"How do you think I am responsible?" she asked him.

"He's dead because of you," said Pendleton.

"How?" repeated Diane. "I tried to get away from him. He shot at me, beat my face in, tried to push me off the cliff, and tried to kill me with rocks and a knife. All the while, I was trying to get away. If you blame me because I wouldn't die, then you need to seriously rethink your values. I'm sorry you lost a friend. Truly I am. But I did not push him or in any way entice him to follow me out onto the cliff. He did that all by himself in an effort to harm me. Now, I'm really too tired for this."

She started to rise.

"You aren't going anywhere," said Peeks, "until we get some answers."

"Then ask me questions," she said. Diane put a hand on her throbbing head and closed her eyes for a second.

Peeks looked surprised, as if he hadn't expected co-operation, as if he would have preferred to hammer some kind of confession out of her instead.

"You said he was on the cliff when he fell. Why was he there?" asked Peeks.

"He was there because I was. He was chasing me." *I thought we covered this*, she thought.

"On the side of the cliff? Are you saying you were running from him on the side of the cliff in Chulagee Gorge? See, that doesn't make sense." Peeks looked back at Curtis and Pendleton, who were standing behind him near the wall. "Does that make sense to you guys?"

"It doesn't make sense to me," said Pendleton.

Diane was wondering if they thought she lured him out to the cliffs and threw him over the edge. Did they not remember how big he was compared to her?

Curtis said nothing, just stood smiling, as if he was enjoying himself. Actually, of the three of them, he looked the most friendly.

"Why would you go there? Do you know how steep that cliff is?" said Peeks.

"It's a five point seven," said Diane.

The three of them looked blank, startled, and clearly puzzled.

"What?" Peeks said.

"You asked me if I know how steep it is. I assume you were asking me about the degree of climbing difficulty. So, yes, I know."

Diane realized why they didn't believe her story. They didn't think that she, in her nice azure pantsuit and Hush Puppies, would climb out onto the side of a steep cliff—or anybody would for that matter. They had a point.

"I've climbed that cliff many times," said Diane. "I'm a caver and I do a lot of rock climbing. I thought if I went out on the cliff, he wouldn't follow. I was wrong. He thought that if I could do it, he could too, especially since he was an ex–football player. That's what he was doing out there. He didn't fall from the top. He wasn't pushed. He was about fifty feet down on the face of the cliff, coming after me. He panicked and fell. I was twenty feet away from him at the time."

"You said he panicked," Pendleton said after a moment. "He just suddenly panicked? Why?"

"He looked down," said Diane. "Rock climbing isn't a sport he had experience in. We were almost five hundred feet up on the side of a cliff. He didn't realize how frightening it would be when he looked down. It happens. I tried to talk him out of the panic."

"You told Officer Wallace that he attacked you. Now,

why would Officer Delamore do a thing like that?" asked Peeks.

"I have no idea. He didn't say. He just kept calling me a bitch," said Diane.

Peeks leaned forward, glaring at Diane. "You know, I'm having a hard time buying your story," he said. "There's a lot of holes in it. A lot of holes. And you're going to stay here until you fill them." He was almost shouting.

"I don't think so," said Diane. She rose, and Peeks started to reach for her when the door to the interview room opened.

"I don't think so either."

Chapter 7

Colin Prehoda, the museum's lawyer, came in and took a serious, considered look at Diane.

"Have you seen a doctor?" he asked.

"No. I've not been allowed to leave," she said.

Curtis and Pendleton stepped forward. Peeks jumped up. For a moment Diane thought the three of them were going to attack her lawyer.

Prehoda was taller than all of them in the room, and heavier. He wasn't overweight, or even slightly chubby; he was just a big man. Diane thought he was probably very imposing in court.

"You're leaving now," he said.

"I've got a dead officer," said Peeks.

"Who attacked my client," said Prehoda. "Do you know why he did that?"

"She hasn't told us," said Peeks, staring at Diane with puzzling hatred.

"I told them I don't know why he attacked me," said Diane.

"There you have it. She's given you all the information she has. Now she is going to the hospital. If you have any more questions, you can contact me."

Prehoda helped Diane out of the chair and guided her toward the door. Peeks didn't try to stop them, but his face was dark with anger.

"This isn't over," he said to Diane. "Don't think

you are free of this, and don't think any of us are going to let this go until we get to the bottom of it."

"Good," said Prehoda. "We expect to be fully informed of your findings as to why an officer of this police department conducted unprovoked assaults with the use of deadly force upon my client, whom, I remind you, is an officer of the court in good standing. And I must warn you against harassing her. I won't tolerate it, and I'm sure you have more pressing concerns than appearing in court. Don't think that I'm bluffing. I think you know me better than that."

Prehoda led Diane out of the room and out of the police building. Diane could feel the stares as she passed through the station. She also noticed that not all of them were hostile. Outside, Prehoda walked her to his car.

"I'd prefer to go to the museum," said Diane.

"I'm sure you would, but we need to take you to the ER. Not just for your safety, but for legal issues," he said.

Diane got in and saw that her jacket was in the front seat along with her purse.

"Who called you?" she asked.

"Garnett," he said.

Douglas Garnett was the chief of detectives. Diane knew he was having a difficult time with the new administration. She hoped this didn't put him further on their bad side. She assumed that either Janice or Izzy had alerted him.

Colin took Diane to the hospital. She didn't have to wait long to be seen. After a lot of examining, blood taking, prodding, and a head X-ray, the doctors pronounced her fine. She thought she was. She was sore but didn't feel seriously injured.

Diane didn't know Chief of Police Peeks, and his hostility toward her was puzzling.

"What's going on?" she asked Colin as he drove her to the museum.

"I don't know," he said. "The mayor and the people

he's picked are giving a lot of people trouble, particularly in the police department. Garnett has asked me to handle appeals of several firings. He suspects that he himself is going to be replaced soon."

"Mayor Jefferies does seem to be blitzkrieging his way through the government, doesn't he?" said Diane.

"That's the word for it. Neither he nor Peeks gives notice. They just show up and fire," he said.

Diane told Colin about Curtis Crabtree appearing unannounced at the DNA lab and demanding a job.

"I've noticed that Jefferies has an inordinate need for control," said Colin. He grinned suddenly. "Did you know that he and Peeks both wear pinky rings embossed with the profile of Alexander the Great?"

Diane smiled and it hurt. "No, I didn't know that." She shook her head at the thought. "How sophomoric."

Colin had arranged for her car to be brought to the museum. It sat in her parking space as they drove up. Diane looked at the people flowing in and out of the museum and asked Colin to take her around back.

"I don't want to scare away the visitors," she said.

"Do you have a change of clothes in your office?" he asked.

"Yes, and a shower. I'll be fine. Thanks for the rescue," she said.

He drove around to the rear of the museum and Diane started to get out.

"Can we get the crime lab out of the museum?" she asked. "I'd really like to reclaim the real estate."

"I'll look at the contract. Right now, I'd have to say no, not until the contract expires. But maybe I can get creative."

Diane thanked him again and got out at the loading dock. From there it was a short distance to the private entrance to her office.

Diane showered, washed her hair, dressed in clean clothes, and was about as refreshed as she was going to get. She took a couple of aspirin to dull the pain and walked to her assistant Andie's office and waited for the reaction.

"Oh, God. What happened?" Andie's eyes were so wide, Diane could see the whites all around her irises. "Your face . . . What happened? Are you all right? You better sit down."

Mike, the museum's geology curator and Diane's caving partner, was there. He and Andie stared open-mouthed at her. She had tried makeup but washed it off. Maybe theatrical makeup, she thought.

"I was passing the path to the gorge and I thought, what the heck, I'll do a little solo climbing before I go to the museum," she said.

Mike took her hands and looked at the scraped fingers.

"You did?" His voice was filled with such incredulity that Diane almost laughed.

He looked at her, amazed, obviously unable to make sense of why Diane would go climbing in her street clothes, alone—not sure if she was joking, and wondering how she'd gotten so beat up.

"What did happen?" asked Andie.

Diane explained the episode with Delamore, trying to keep it objective, but she suddenly felt more shaken than she'd realized. She sat down on the sofa and hoped they didn't notice how suddenly weak on her feet she was.

"I've been at the police station, then the hospital ever since," she said.

"Oh, my God," said Andie. "I was a little worried when I couldn't get you on your cell."

"Delamore stomped it into the pavement," said Diane.

"He tried to kill you?" said Mike. "He hit you?" Mike sat down on the stuffed chair next to the sofa. He reached over and touched her face with his fingertips, then let his hand drop.

"I'm fine. I've looked worse after we've been caving," she said.

"No, you haven't," said Mike.

Thanks, she thought.

"Can I do anything to help?" he asked.

"You've helped immeasurably already. Thanks for insisting that I learn more about rock climbing. It saved my life," she said.

His lips turned up into half a smile. "Every caver needs to learn rock climbing," he said. "I guess so does every museum director–crime detector."

As Diane started to stand, Mike reached out and helped her up.

"You think you need to rest up a bit?" he said. "Seriously. I've seen you look better."

"I've got a lot to do," she said. "I need to keep busy." *I just saw a man die,* she thought. He may have been trying to kill her, but it was still disturbing to see someone die. Her heart ached with the thought of it. *Focus,* she thought. "Andie, would you mind going downtown and buying me another cell phone?"

"Sure," said Andie. "Any particular kind?"

"Something useful," she said.

"Sure. I'll do it right now." Andie jumped up and grabbed her purse and coat from the closet. "You've had several reporters call about the wood-chipper murder. Was someone really murdered by being put in a wood chipper? That's awful."

Diane was afraid of this.

"No," she said simply, not wanting to discuss a case, but wanting to dispel any rumors. "I imagine you'll be getting more calls when the news outlets find out about Delamore. I'm not in for any reporters." Diane wondered whether Harve Delamore had anything to do with the bones found in the field. She knew he didn't like her, but why did he attack her now? Maybe he'd heard the news report.

Andie was about to leave when the door to her office opened and Jonas Briggs, the museum's archae-ologist, came in along with Henry Miller, the young boy who'd discovered the bones, and another young man.

"Found these young men looking for you . . ." Jonas stopped. "What happened to you? You look like you lost a wrestling match with a grizzly." His white tooth-brush mustache bobbed up and down as he spoke. Jonas had snow-white hair and equally white bushy eyebrows over bright blue eyes. He looked like a kindly grandfather—or a wizard.

"You're half right. Just a little mishap on the way to work. Henry, how are you?" she said before Jonas could question her further.

"I'm fine, Miss . . . I mean, Dr. Fallon," he said. "This is my brother, Caleb."

"I remember the sheriff mentioning Caleb." She held out her hand and he shook it.

Henry and Caleb didn't favor each other. Henry was going to be much bigger than his older brother.

Caleb nudged his brother and smiled warmly at him. "Go ahead," he said.

Diane could see how fond Caleb was of his younger sibling. The thought of it made her smile.

"So, what brings you here?" she asked.

Henry looked at his brother, who nodded at him.

"When I was here yesterday," he said, looking back at Diane, "I . . . well, I really like it here, and I was wondering if there are ever any jobs for someone my age. I'm in eighth grade."

"So, that makes you, what, thirteen, fourteen?" asked Diane.

"Yes, ma'am," he said. "I'm fourteen—almost—in a week."

"Well, we have a student after-school intern pro-gram you can apply to," she said.

"See," said Caleb, gently poking his brother on the arm. "I told you it wouldn't hurt to ask." He turned to Diane. "He was real shy about asking, figured you'd say no, but I told him it never hurts to ask and that he should always let the other person be the one to say no—don't do it for them." Caleb looked very self-satisfied.

"Good advice," said Diane. "Andie, can you get him

the papers to fill out and some information to take back to his grandparents?"

"Sure thing." Andie went to a filing cabinet.

Mike and Jonas left, waving good-bye. Jonas looked back at Diane one last time and shook his head.

"You go to Bartram, I understand," Diane said to Caleb as Andie looked for the forms. "What do you take?"

"History and computer science," Caleb said. "I'd like to go to graduate school in advanced computational methods."

"So, you have one foot in the past and the other in the future," said Diane. "That must be interesting."

Caleb grinned. "Yeah, a little cognitive tug-of-war sometimes, but I like them both."

Andie handed Diane the application form and several brochures.

"Show the brochures to your grandparents and fill out the form and bring it back. You'll be called in for an interview, but that will be mainly to make sure you are really interested. I'll put in a good word with our education director," Diane added.

Henry grinned. "I like the dinosaurs. Do you think I could work with them?"

"It will probably be with a variety of things— everything from dinosaurs to rocks to conservation. You still interested?"

"Oh, yes, ma'am," he said.

Diane liked Henry and his brother Caleb. They were polite and smart. She would like to clone them.

"Can I take your picture with Henry?" asked Caleb, pulling out a digital camera.

Diane unconsciously touched her face. Andie looked distressed. For a moment, Diane thought she was going to forbid it.

"I'll Photoshop the bruises out, I promise," said Caleb.

What the heck. "Sure," she said and let him take a picture of her with Henry.

Diane saw them to the door and told Andie she was

going upstairs to her osteology lab. On the third-floor overlook, she glanced down and saw Henry and Caleb looking at the dinosaur bones. She smiled, walked down the hall to her lab, and went in.

The first thing she noticed was a treacly smell of perfume, and she wondered whether Neva, who had wanted to work with Diane's imaging computers in the lab vault, had changed perfumes. But Neva didn't usually wear it as heavy or as sweet as the aroma she smelled. Diane walked into her office just off the lab and stopped abruptly. There was a young woman sitting at her desk. Her first thought was that it was Goldilocks sitting in her chair.

Chapter 8

"Can I help you?" said Goldilocks. "Are you lost?"

Diane stared at her, wondering whether perhaps the woman had escaped from an asylum.

"Oh, by the way," Goldilocks continued. "I'm Dr. Jennifer Jeffcote-Smith. I've just arrived from California."

And you got lost somewhere over Utah, thought Diane.

"Nice to meet you, Dr. Jeffcote-Smith, I'm Dr. Diane Fallon and I'm wondering what you are doing in my office."

Jennifer Jeffcote-Smith, attired in a powder blue silk suit that matched her eyes and went great with her shoulder-length wavy blond hair, stared blankly at Diane for a moment.

"Oh," she said finally. "Well, this is awkward."

The expression on her face looked to Diane as if Dr. Jeffcote-Smith thought it was awkward only for Diane. There appeared to be a tiny gleam in her eye and an almost imperceptible twist at the corners of her evenly lipsticked mouth that could easily turn into a smirk.

"No, not awkward," said Diane. "I'm sure it must be some kind of strange misunderstanding." *Like I just walked into a parallel universe.*

"Lloyd said you—well, aren't working here," she said.

"That would be Lloyd Bryce?" said Diane.

"Yes; let me go get him. This had better come from him, don't you think?"

Dr. Jeffcote-Smith rose and started out the door.

"Oh, I need to get in the vault to familiarize myself with the equipment. I understand it's state-of-the-art. If you would write the key code down for the door, I'd appreciate it." She walked out of the office, across the lab, and out the door that led to the crime lab.

Diane was still speechless at the effrontery. What was Bryce thinking? Obviously Bryce had asked either Neva or David to let the woman in the lab. No one else had the code to Diane's door.

It was several minutes before Jennifer Jeffcote-Smith returned with Lloyd Bryce. He came bustling in with a deep frown on his face, his dark eyes ablaze with annoyance. He wore jeans, a brown sport coat, and a yellow-gold shirt. Diane could tell it was an expensive shirt, but oddly, it made him look cheap. He wasn't a tall man. He was trim, had dark short hair, and wore too much aftershave. She tried not to breathe deeply.

Diane hadn't liked him from the beginning and wasn't sure why. Now she was beginning to think her initial reaction had been a premonition.

He hesitated a moment, studying her face, but he didn't ask the obvious question. "Diane, you are just making a fool of yourself." Bryce sounded a bit like a machine gun with words for bullets.

Dr. Jeffcote-Smith's mouth was definitely starting to look like a smirk. She was enjoying this, and Diane wasn't sure why. She'd never met the woman.

"I think not, Lloyd," said Diane. "Look at that brass plaque on the wall. What does it say?"

"Aidan Kavanagh Forensic Anthropology Lab. I've read it. I don't know who Aidan Kavanagh is, but he has nothing to do with this. You don't work here anymore. I've hired Jennifer to be the new forensic anthropologist, and that's that. Any effort to hang on will only prove humiliating to you. Now, go run your little museum."

"Aidan Kavanagh has everything to do with this," said Diane evenly. "His father is the major funding source for this lab. The other major funding source is the museum. This is a private lab, privately funded, under the control of the RiverTrail Museum of Natural History and its director. That would be me. This lab predates the crime lab, and there are no public monies involved. It is not an agency of the city of Rosewood. You have no authority here whatsoever."

Bryce stared at her like she was speaking a language he didn't understand. Perhaps she was. Perhaps *you can't do this* was completely foreign to him. Jennifer's smirk had lost some of it's momentum. In her eyes Diane saw what looked like fear. That was odd too.

"You would say anything," he said at last. "I've seen contracts."

"This is not a matter of what I would or would not say to keep my lab. It's a matter of legal record. What you saw may have been the contract the forensic lab has with Rosewood, but apparently you didn't read it. There is not so much as a paper clip that passes between these units that is not recorded and checked by accountants. When Rosewood had their idea of putting the crime lab in museum space, the contracts were carefully worked out between the city attorneys and ours. At no time did this forensic anthropology lab relinquish any of its connection to the museum. It belongs to and is administered by the museum."

She hoped like hell that Colin and the museum accountants could find a way to break the contract with the crime lab and get rid of this damn nuisance. Bryce had suddenly become a major pain in her backside.

One problem with breaking the contract was the taxes the museum would have to pay each year. That was the little blackmail scheme the last administration had thought up. They upped the taxes because of valuable assets the museum owned, then offered to forgive them if Diane would house and run the crime lab.

She thought they could work around the taxes. They hadn't fought it at the time because she and the board liked the idea of the crime lab. And it had worked out well. She had not, however, accounted for such a change in the thinking of new administrations—she should have.

"You are a disturbed woman who can't let go, and you've concocted this tale," said Bryce. "I'll have the city attorney look at the contract right now." He grabbed his cell, punched in a number, and spoke to someone in low tones.

Jennifer had retreated from the two of them and was leaning against one of the metal tables. She had her arms wrapped around herself as she gazed around the room. She looked both angry and scared. Diane wasn't sure who she was angry with, her or Bryce.

"Now do we have everything under control?" said Diane when Bryce was off the phone.

"This thing about the forensic anthropology lab is not finished by a long shot," he said.

"No, you're wrong. It's over," said Diane.

"We'll see. In the meantime, Jennifer will be working here," he said.

"Have you heard nothing I said? This is my lab, and I don't need an assistant," said Diane.

Out of the corner of her eye she saw Jennifer flinch at the word *assistant*. Diane needed to ratchet the tension down, but she wasn't sure how, other than give away her lab. And she wasn't going to do that, even temporarily.

"Jennifer is the official Rosewood forensic anthropologist. She is the person all skeletal remains will be given to for analysis. What will you need a big lab for then?"

David had told her Bryce was clueless. She'd thought David was just overly critical, but apparently he was right. The man really didn't know anything.

"Bryce, Rosewood gets how many skeletons a year? Almost none. Virtually all of the bones we analyze come to me from neighboring counties, other states, and other countries. I'm all for Rosewood having its own forensic anthropologist, but the city will have to

supply her with a lab and equipment. You can't ask
the museum to do it. Now, I have work to do."

"I'll see you later today—with the police if necessary," said Bryce. He stomped out of the lab.

Diane looked over at Jennifer.

"I need to get my purse," she said.

Diane followed her into the office. "You moved
here from California?" said Diane.

"Yes, with my family. My husband quit a job he
loved in order to support my career," she said, retriev-
ing her purse from the bottom drawer of the desk.

Diane hardly knew what to say. She should have
been kinder to her. This had to be a blow. Bryce may
not have believed her, but Jennifer knew something
was not right.

"I'm sure they'll find you very good lab space,"
began Diane.

Jennifer looked sharply at Diane. "I don't need
your pity."

Diane was surprised at her vehemence. "I wasn't
offering you pity," she said, "just friendliness."

Jennifer put her purse under her arm and walked
out of the office, the heels of her Dolce & Gabbana
pumps clicking on the floor like ricocheting bullets. *At
least she's rich,* thought Diane.

Diane stood for a moment staring at the closed
door. "This has got to be the strangest day," she said
under her breath.

She saw that the watercolor of the lone wolf hunting
that she kept on the wall, the only decoration in her
osteology office, had been taken down and was leaning
against the wall. She walked over and picked it up.

"Now, why didn't Goldilocks like you?" she said to
the picture. "Maybe she's friends with Little Red Riding Hood." Diane hung the painting back on the wall.

She then changed the key code on the doors to the
lab. Safely locked in, she went to the drying racks to
look at the wood-chipper bones.

She put on her lab coat and gloves, stopping momentarily to see whether she could hear any more

closet conversations. All was quiet. She checked the bones. They were mostly dry, and she began laying them out on the table in basically anatomical position. They looked like a fossil find—like Lucy laid out with her tiny ribs and scant bones. Diane had only seventy-two pieces of bone to work with.

She picked up the petrous part of the temporal bone, the bone she hoped would reveal the sex, made measurements of the fragment, and recorded them. She mixed up casting compound and began making a cast of the acoustic canal. She set the poured cast aside and examined the rest of the fragments one by one, looking for any anomalies, any cut marks that might not have been made by the wood chipper, anything that might have identification value. She reached for a piece of the hip bone that included the pubic symphysis—the place where the two sides of the hip bones join. The surface was rugged with well-defined grooves, which meant the person was young—late teens, early twenties.

Diane turned to get the camera to photograph the piece when she was suddenly jarred out of her thoughts by very loud yelling coming from the crime lab next door.

Chapter 9

Diane stood for a moment, uncertain what to do. The voices were coming from deeper within the lab and not the closet. She reached for a phone to call the crime lab when she heard her name.

Okay, she thought, *it's somehow about me. I am the landlord, so to speak, and this sounds serious. Landlords check into serious noises.*

She walked to the adjoining door, unlocked it, and entered the crime lab. It hadn't changed much, still all glass and metal cubicles and fancy equipment. The voices were clearer now. One was Sheriff Canfield's; he was red faced and very angry. He was standing in front of Bryce, yelling at him. Bryce was backed against a desk, staring wide-eyed at the taller sheriff.

A woman with long blond hair in a ponytail, wearing khaki slacks and a pink polo shirt, sat in one of the cubicles with her door open. Her eyebrows were raised and her lips turned into almost a smile. *Must be Rikki.* Diane thought the look on Rikki's face was far too excited. She was obviously enjoying the confrontation. Diane glanced around the room but didn't see Neva.

"Did you really think you could get away with this? What goes on in the heads of you people? We didn't elect you . . ."

Bryce caught sight of Diane. He straightened up and pointed a finger at her.

"What are you doing here?" he said.

"I heard the yelling," she began.

Sheriff Canfield turned and saw Diane's face. "You've been hurt," he said. "What in the world happened to you?" His concern was obvious and sincere.

"Police brutality," she said.

Bryce shook his finger in her direction. "Get out. This is none of your business."

Bryce's callousness angered Canfield just that much more. "It is most certainly her business," said Canfield. "Now, get the bones and give them to her right now. Do you hear? Now!"

"Sheriff, we've hired a forensic anthropologist to analyze our bones, if you will give her a chance," said Bryce. His voice and manner were remarkably calm, considering the situation.

"I don't give a shit if you hired Britney Spears to buy your underwear. You don't get to decide who the bones go to; I do."

"What's going on?" asked Diane.

"This son of a bitch waylaid my deputy on the way to bring you the rest of the bones we've found so far—and it was a lot of them, with some hair and fingernails mixed in. My deputy was on his way to your lab with them when this dirtbag stopped him and took them away from him. He and a security guard damn near wrestled them out of my deputy's hands. My deputy told me Bryce said he would deliver them to you, but I knew better."

"We didn't wrestle them from him," said Bryce.

"How did you know they were on the way?" Diane asked him.

"Huh?" Bryce looked at her, silent for a moment. "We didn't. The security guard and I just happened to be out there when the deputy drove up."

"The bones," repeated the sheriff. "Get the damn bones and give them to Diane. And if you ever do anything like this again, I'll put your ass in a sling."

Their attention was diverted at the sudden sound of

the elevator. After a moment the doors opened and
Jennifer Jeffcote-Smith stepped out, carrying a tray with
three cups of coffee.

"Jennifer," said Bryce, "give the sheriff back his
bones."

She gave one of the coffees to Rikki and brought
another to Bryce. The third she held in her hand.

"I haven't finished with them," she said. "I just got
them an hour ago."

"I don't care," said Sheriff Canfield. "You shouldn't
have had them in the first place."

Jennifer looked at Bryce, then the sheriff, and
finally Diane. Her eyes narrowed when her gaze got
to Diane. It lingered a moment; then she suddenly
switched her attention to the sheriff and laid a dazzling
smile on him.

"I'm perfectly capable of analyzing those bones,"
she said.

"I'm sure you are, ma'am, and I'm not questioning
your credentials or your abilities. We've got a jurisdiction issue here. Please pack up the bones and give
them to Diane," said Canfield.

Jennifer looked at Bryce and he nodded. She audi-
bly sighed and walked over to the room that was David's photography studio.

Diane stood with the sheriff, wishing she hadn't
come into the crime lab, thinking that maybe it wasn't
a good thing for landlords to check out suspicious
noises after all. As she waited, she studied Bryce, who
stood looking at nothing in particular, the corners of
his mouth turned slightly down. Trying to usurp Canfield's jurisdiction was a stupid thing to do, even if he
thought it was a way to poke Diane in the eye. Why
had he done it?

Jennifer wasn't gone long—and she came back
empty-handed. They all looked at her. Diane thought
she looked alarmed, but she quickly regained her com-
posure. She walked to Rikki's cubicle.

"Did you move the bones?" she asked Rikki.

"Why would I?" said Rikki. "I don't do bones." She

put the end of a pencil in her mouth, and Diane wanted to tell her not to pick up things in a crime lab and put them in her mouth.

"Okay." Jennifer cleared her throat. "The, ah, bones aren't where I left them. Has someone been in my lab?" Her voice had a slightly higher pitch and a strained calm quality to it.

"What?" said the sheriff, looking at Bryce. "You've lost them?"

"*I* haven't lost them," said Bryce. He turned to Jennifer. "What do you mean they're not where you left them? Where did you leave them?"

"In my lab," she said. "They were in tubs on the table, and now they are gone."

"Could you have put them somewhere else?" asked Bryce.

"No. They aren't where I left them. Someone must have come in and moved them while I was getting the coffee," she said.

"Well, don't this just take the cake," said the sheriff. He glared at Bryce. "I suggest you find my evidence. It didn't just walk off by itself. I'm sure you keep a log of everything that comes in and goes out of this lab, don't you? I know that Diane did."

"I assure you, Sheriff, we will make every effort to find it," said Bryce.

"I don't want to hear about your efforts. I want my evidence," said the sheriff.

"Maybe we'd better ask Diane," said Bryce. "You will notice that she can waltz in here anytime she wants."

"Now, why would she steal the bones?" said Canfield. "She's the one who is supposed to have them. Quit pointing fingers and get me my evidence. I can't believe this. You're the one who hijacked it. Don't go blaming other people for your foul-up."

Diane decided that this would be a good time to leave Bryce to his hunt.

"Let me know when they've been found, Sheriff," she said as she turned to go back to her lab.

She felt oddly ill at ease turning her back on Bryce and his crew, as if when she got back to her lab there would be a knife sticking between her shoulder blades.

Diane wrote a preliminary report for Sheriff Canfield on the results of the analysis of the few bones she had. She had learned very little from them, and it didn't look like she would learn much more. She would take a sample down to Jin to see if he could extract some DNA.

She read over her summary again. She hadn't found any fragments to suggest there was more than one individual. The lateral angle measurement of the auditory canal made it probable the individual was male. The pattern on the pubic symphysis suggested he was in his early twenties. The piece of metal could mean that he had some type of body piercing. That was it: not much, mainly suggestions. She packaged and labeled samples to take to Jin and locked them along with the bones in her vault and changed the key code.

Diane locked up her lab and left via the museum side exit. As she passed the break room, she saw Jennifer Jeffcote-Smith sitting at one of the tables drinking her coffee. From the steam rising out of the cup, it looked hot. She didn't look happy. Diane hesitated a moment, then went in.

"Come to gloat?" asked Jennifer when she saw Diane.

"No," said Diane pulling up a chair.

"Then what are you looking at?" said Jennifer.

"I think I'm looking at a scapegoat," said Diane.

Jennifer looked up sharply. "What's that supposed to mean?"

"You know, Lloyd Bryce has a temper, and he loses it easily," said Diane.

"You will have to be more clear," she said. "Or just leave—that would be good too." She continued to sip her coffee, breaking eye contact with Diane.

"He didn't lose his temper with the sheriff, and Canfield was laying into him pretty hard."

"So?" said Jennifer.

"You need to ask yourself why," said Diane.

"This is your story. You ask yourself why," she said.

"Because he *wasn't* angry," said Diane.

"Look. Will you get to the point or leave? In case you haven't noticed, today hasn't been a good day for me." Jennifer set her coffee down. She twisted her wedding rings.

It hasn't been a good day for you? Diane thought to herself. *Look at my face, lady.*

"How long were you out of your lab?" asked Diane.

"What do you mean?" Jennifer asked.

"How long were you gone getting coffee? It was about noon when you came up. That's a busy time for the restaurant," said Diane. "It could have taken a while."

"I didn't keep track of the time," she said.

"Doesn't matter. It wouldn't take long for somebody to get the bones," said Diane.

Jennifer folded her arms and gave Diane her full attention. "Why do you say I'm a scapegoat?" she asked.

"They hire you to come to Rosewood from California with the promise of a lab and equipment. Then they discover they don't have a lab and equipment, so either they will have to stock one for you or let you go. You said you moved your family here and your husband quit his job. That sounds like grounds for a suit to me if they let you go. However, they could sandbag you, then fire you and maybe save a lot of money. After today they can let you go and say it was because you were incompetent."

"I'm not incompetent." Jennifer raised her chin and glared at Diane.

"I'm not saying you are. I'm just talking about a scenario—one you need to keep in mind," said Diane.

Jennifer was quiet for a long moment. "Why are you telling me this? You may have been the one who stole the bones."

"I didn't, and blaming me isn't going to help you. I'm just giving you a heads-up," said Diane.

Jennifer's blue eyes glistened as if she were about to tear up. "It wasn't supposed to work out this way," she said.

"No, I don't imagine it was," said Diane. "What color was the hair?"

Jennifer looked at her, puzzled. "What are you talking about?"

"The sheriff said they found hair. What color was it?"

"Dark—very black. I was thinking it might be Asian or Indian. Why?"

"Because, if most of the bones are gone, we need all the information we can get. What about the fingernails?" said Diane. "What did they look like?"

"I really didn't look at them. I just looked at the bones. And before you ask, there wasn't much to look at. They were all in pieces. There wasn't much to be done," she said.

"What about the skull bones? Did you notice anything on the occipital that might look like a bullet hole?"

"I hadn't gotten around to identifying the parts yet. I had just begun separating them into categories. I put them in separate tubs so they wouldn't get lost. I didn't want to put them on the table. My lab isn't really a lab." She took another sip of her hot coffee. "Why would you ask about a bullet hole in the occipital anyway?" Jennifer looked at Diane suspiciously.

"I have the first bones that were found," said Diane. "I saw something that might be beveling on a piece of occipital. I had intended to try to piece the skull together—see if perhaps it was a bullet hole."

"They were in too many distorted pieces. It wouldn't be possible," said Jennifer.

"Maybe and maybe not. Did you notice anything that suggested there was more than one individual?" asked Diane.

"I hadn't gotten that far. Frankly, Bryce had me running errands most of the morning—getting stuff for my lab. We were going to convert the darkroom into a lab."

Diane stood up. "I'm sorry this is happening," she said. "I really am." She turned to go, then turned back. "Out of curiosity, whose idea was it that you go get coffee? Was it your idea or someone else's?"

"Bryce . . . ," Jennifer began and suddenly stopped. The look in Jennifer's eyes told Diane everything she needed to know.

She left Jennifer there, figuratively and literally crying over her coffee. Diane felt very tired. She decided to go home. Maybe Frank would be there.

Chapter 10

Frank wasn't home, but he hadn't left a message saying he wasn't coming. Diane sat down at the piano to practice as soon as she had put her things down. Frank had a baby grand piano, and he was teaching her how to play. When she had first seen his piano, she remarked, the way people do when they see a beautiful piano, "Oh, I wish I could play." He said he would teach her, but she resisted the idea at first. She thought she should learn on some lesser piano. Somehow, the quality of her playing and the quality of the sound of such a fine piano didn't seem like a good match. But there was something heavenly about sitting down and listening to the sound of the hammers striking the strings, even if all you could play was "Off We Go to Music Land." Today she played to keep her mind focused more than anything else.

Fortunately she had progressed since those beginning lessons and was now learning a nocturne by Chopin. It was from a book of easy classic pieces for the piano; most of the notes were taken out, leaving the basic melody and some harmonic chords. But it was pretty and she could play it—a little.

She hadn't been playing long when she heard the door open. She stopped.

"Don't stop on my account," said Frank. "It's sounding good."

"It's still not right, and I'm not sure . . ."

She heard him put his car keys in the small ceramic

tray he used for that purpose, then his watch, and the change in his pockets. After a moment she smelled the scent of him—a mixture of Frank and aftershave. He came up behind her, put his face next to hers, and kissed her jawline.

"You're treating the measures as if there were a slight rest at the end of each one. Measures are just that—a unit of measure. Play right through it." He put his hands around her, under her arms, and began playing the piece. After a moment he switched to the full Chopin, adding the notes that had been left out for beginners like her. He included the grace notes, the trills, the full range of keys along the keyboard. He stopped abruptly.

"See?" he said.

Diane laughed, stood up, turned, and kissed him. "Yeah, I get it. I need more practice."

Frank's jaw dropped when he got a look at her face. "Diane, my God, what happened?"

"Did you hear anything on the news?" said Diane.

"No," he said. He came around the piano bench and touched her face and put his arms around her. "What happened?" he said again.

They sat down on the sofa and Diane leaned against him and told him about Delamore, the cliff, the death.

"You almost died," he said. "Diane . . . why didn't you call me?"

"I didn't want to upset you, and I was all right. As it turned out, he was in more danger than I was."

"Diane . . . ," he said again, as if saying her name over and over would ensure she was really there. "Really, now I'm serious. I've had some experience with trauma and death—"

"As I well know."

"Well, yes," he said. "You have to believe me, for your own emotional well-being, please have someone get me whenever you are involved in any way in a severe trauma. Death and near-death experiences affect you in ways you cannot handle alone."

"Are you saying I need your strong shoulder to lean against?"

"Yes, that's what I'm saying. It's no weakness on your part . . . or mine. It's a human need."

"So, when you get shot up, you need my shoulder as well?" she said.

"You know very well that I do," Frank said.

"That's very sweet," Diane said.

"Call me if anything even remotely like this ever happens to you again."

"Okay, I will."

"You promise?" he said.

"I promise."

"Okay. Tell me the rest of it," Frank said.

"Edgar Peeks thinks I killed him," she said. "I believe he would have arrested me had not Colin Prehoda arrived to spring me."

"Peeks strikes me as incompetent. Spence Jefferies wants to hire people who are loyal to him regardless of their qualifications. I doubt if Peeks can make a case even when he has one."

"Maybe not, but he can leak it to the papers that I'm a suspect. That wouldn't be good for me or the museum."

"Don't worry about it now." Frank kissed the top of her head. "Other than hanging on the side of the cliff, how was the rest of your day?"

She told Frank about Bryce hiring Goldilocks the forensic anthropologist from California and putting her in the museum forensic anthropology office. She told him about Jin having to strong-arm Curtis Crabtree, who was apparently also a detective. Then she told him about the closet.

Frank laughed during the whole narrative.

"They were in the closet having a conversation?" he said, with a characteristic twinkle in his eye. "How big is the closet?"

"Pretty big," said Diane. "Small room size. I suppose that was the most private place they could find."

"How could he not know the forensic anthropology lab belongs to the museum?" asked Frank.

"I don't know. It's true that I haven't done any work for the crime lab since Bryce took over. Nothing has come up. That's not particularly unusual. Maybe that's why he thought I was no longer working as the forensic anthropologist. But I would have thought the new administration would have known." She shrugged. "It's straightened out now. I feel sorry for the forensic anthropologist he hired. She was totally broadsided today. I don't know why David or Neva didn't tell him the lab belongs to the museum."

"Why didn't David tell you about the forensic anthropologist?" asked Frank.

Diane hesitated a second and sat up. That was a good question.

"Perhaps he didn't know about it," she said.

"He didn't know?" said Frank with a raised eyebrow. "Is that likely?" He pulled her back to him.

"No. David always knows everything going on in the lab. He didn't tell me because he wanted me to be surprised and more inclined to rip Bryce a new one." She stared at the fireplace and wished there was a fire in it. "I'm worried about David. He is really very levelheaded, despite his playing at being paranoid. But lately he seems truly paranoid. Losing the lab was a blow to all of us, including me. And now is not a good time for either of us."

The two of them had worked together as human rights investigators. They probed and recorded the worst behavior of humankind in hopes of achieving even the smallest amount of justice. In South America they were uncovering mass graves filled by a particularly vicious dictator. He struck back at them hard. In the massacre he led, Diane had lost her adopted daughter, and both she and David had lost many good friends.

Diane had spent months in despair and on benzodiazepine. When she finally stepped back into life again, she couldn't go back to doing the work she had done before. The offer to be director of RiverTrail Museum of Natural History was a salvation. She was several months into her position when David Goldstein showed up and asked for a job. Like her, he had been aimless since the massacre, walking a fine line this side of sanity. He wanted to work in Diane's newly established crime lab. There he felt he could actually bring bad guys to justice.

And now it was coming up on the anniversary of the massacre. Every year it was hard. Every year they managed. This year David had had his comfortable rug pulled out from under him when the new mayor of Rosewood decided to rearrange the spoils of his election victory.

Frank reached out a hand and grasped hers. "I know," he whispered.

Diane had been able to adjust to being replaced as director of the crime lab mainly because of Frank. Living with Frank held nice surprises. He was the most levelheaded, reasonable person she had ever known. She hadn't realized how calming it would be just being with him on a daily basis.

The last things Frank did before going to bed were to play the piano—some beautiful piece—then, before turning out the light, he wrote in a journal. After their first several days living together, Diane mentioned that she hadn't known he kept a journal.

"It started when Kevin was younger. Cindy and I were in the middle of our divorce, and Kevin was having trouble dealing with it and with some problems at school," Frank had told her. "I could see he was suffering. I started reading psychology books and searching the Internet. I was looking for some way to help us both through a rough time. There's a mountain of junk psychology out there. You'd be surprised how little of it has any factual basis. But you know how we detectives are . . ."

"Handsome and sexy?" Diane had said.

"Thorough. We leave nothing undone. I uncovered a couple of articles on new research into how people can make themselves happier."

"I have some ideas on how I could make you happier," Diane had said, smiling at him.

"I'll take you up on that." He had kissed her.

"Tell me about your journal first," she had said.

"Had I known you were such a tease," he'd said. "The research involved a simple technique which I thought at first was too good to be true. But it turns out it works. Every night before I go to sleep, I think of three good things that happened that day and I write them in my journal. Then I spend a moment thinking about why they occurred. That's all there is to it."

"And this works?" Diane remembered being incredulous.

"It does. It worked for Kevin, and it works for me. It helped Kevin realize that not everything was going wrong in his life. It's very subtle, but it works. It immediately improved my dreams, and I noticed that I had a happier outlook on life. It has a long-term calming effect on me. Hadn't you noticed?"

"You've always been a calm, happy guy," Diane had told him. "According to your brothers, you were born that way."

"This still helps," he'd said.

"You write down things that go well in your job?" Diane had asked.

"Sure. If I solve a case, or if I see something nice like a dog riding down the road with his head hanging out the window and a smile on his face, or you. I write a lot about you. Just a sentence or two, like the times you returned from a caving trip with no bruises or near-death experiences. Then I go to sleep having thought only about the good things during the day and not about the meanness I saw or the guy that got away."

Diane adopted that habit. She didn't write it down.

She just went to sleep listing in her mind the good things that went well during the day. Frank was right. It was subtle, but it worked.

Diane was wondering what three good things she could possibly think of from this stupid day. Being with Frank was definitely one of them. She started to kiss him when the telephone interrupted the moment and Frank went to answer it.

"It's for you," he said, coming back with the phone in his hand. "There's something going on at the museum that needs your attention."

Chapter 11

"What happened?"

Diane was in the sitting room off of her office with a docent, Andie, the night security supervisor, two parents, and a seven-year-old boy with tears in his eyes. The father was pacing up and down, uncertain whom to be angry with. The furniture in Diane's office suite was very comfortable—plush sofa, stuffed chairs—but everyone in the room looked as if they might be sitting on nails. It didn't help that Diane's face looked like the loser's in a heavyweight boxing bout. The child kept glancing at her as if she were an ogre who might grab him and eat him at any moment.

"Emily, what happened?" Diane asked the docent again.

Emily was a tall athletic girl whom Diane understood was quite successful in track at Bartram University. She said her athletic training served her well running after kids. Emily opened her mouth to speak, but the father beat her to it.

"You were supposed to be watching him," he said to his wife.

Emily looked away as if wanting to give them privacy, or not wanting to be witness to anything unpleasant or embarrassing. Andie slumped down in her chair. Diane said nothing, preferring to let them get out their frustrations for the moment.

The wife glared at him. "You were supposed to babysit. You knew I had a class tonight. You just had to go out with your buddies when they called."

They were both young, not yet out of their twenties, Diane guessed. The wife looked tired around the eyes; her dishwater blond hair was limp. The father kept running his fingers through his red-brown hair in what appeared to be a nervous habit. Both looked as if they were fighting feelings of guilt.

"Well, you shouldn't have brought him here," said the father.

"This is supposed to be a safe place," she said. "The guards aren't supposed to pull guns on you."

Diane's jaw dropped. She looked at the security supervisor, Blake Cassey. He was shaking his head even before she spoke. He held out his hands, palms facing Diane as if that would ward off the accusation.

"One of the guards drew a gun?" Diane said.

"We're going to sue," said the father.

"Museum security wasn't involved in this," Blake said quickly. "It was the dar . . . It was the west wing guard at the crime lab, and he didn't actually pull a gun."

Blake had almost said *It was the dark side*. That's what the museum staff called the crime lab in the west wing.

Diane turned to Emily, who, as nearly as she could figure at this point, had the most information. "Perhaps you had better start from the beginning."

Emily tucked a loose tendril of her dark hair back in its clasp and took a breath.

"Mrs. McConnel was in the gemology class," she began. "Ethan was coloring at a desk and decided to walk about. When they discovered he was missing, Andie—she was in the class too—called upstairs to us. Two of us docents were still in the office. We always have someone there when classes are being taught, for times like this." She smiled, showing a row of perfect white teeth.

"There are typical places kids like to go, and we know where they are. The dinosaurs are the most popular. I started with the third-floor overlook. Kids see it when they are on the first floor and want to go up there to look down. Sure enough, I saw him walking past the snack room onto the overlook. And I ran after him."

"In the meantime," said Andie. Her auburn curly hair was like a cloud around her face. Andie looked like Little Orphan Annie a lot of the time, a persona she often played up. "Mrs. McConnel called her husband and I called museum security—and you."

Diane noticed that both the docent and Andie were using what Andie called their happy-talk voices, obviously trying to play down the frightening aspect of the event, making like it was really a grand adventure that Ethan McConnel would remember fondly when he grew up. It seemed to Diane that the most likely thing Ethan would remember was her bruised and swollen face.

"I had his hand," continued Emily, "and we were looking at the pterodactyl when this guy, the night guard for the crime lab, came out of the hallway, the one leading to the . . . to the crime lab. He started telling us that we were trespassing and to get out. He patted his gun and told us if he caught us there again we'd be in serious trouble with him, and with Mr. Smith and Wesson. I would have argued with him about just who was trespassing, but Ethan was getting upset and I wanted to get him out of there."

"You did right." Diane turned to the McConnels. "I'm sorry this happened. Someone in the crime lab overstepped their authority and used bad judgment. I will make sure nothing like this happens again."

"Isn't the crime lab part of the museum?" said Mr. McConnel.

"No," said Diane. "They rent space. The crime lab belongs to the city of Rosewood."

"But don't you run it?" he persisted.

"No," said Diane.

"It's that change in administration you and your buddies voted in," said Mrs. McConnel.

The husband let out an exasperated breath. Diane was glad she wasn't riding home in their car tonight.

"Say what you want, but the burglary rate is way down under the new get-tough policy," he retorted.

"Now, how would you know? Are any of your buddies on the police force?" she said.

Ethan put his hands over his ears. Diane guessed he did that a lot.

The husband nodded his head up and down. "Barrel knows a cop or two," he said.

The wife turned to Diane. "Would you trust anyone whose mother named him Barrel?"

The father stood up. "Let's go, Barb. I'm sure these folks don't want to listen to us bicker." He turned to Diane. "I expect you to do something about that guy. He can't go around threatening little kids with guns. Come on, little buddy," he said to Ethan. "Let's go get some ice cream."

"I'll take care of it tonight," Diane assured him. She turned to the security guard. "Take the McConnels by the museum shop on the way out. I believe it's open late tonight. They got in some new kaleidoscopes. Ask the clerk to give Ethan one."

Ethan's face brightened at the mention of both ice cream and a gift, though Diane suspected he didn't know what a kaleidoscope was. What was important was that his parents smiled too.

When the McConnels were out of the office, Diane stood up. "Emily, let's go see the guard."

"Sure thing." Emily stood, looking ready for a fight.

Diane's museum office was on the first floor in the east wing. The crime lab was on the third floor in the west wing. They walked to the elevators located in the lobby and rode up to the third floor.

"The gemology class seems popular," said Diane, making conversation.

"Any class that Mike teaches is popular," Emily said.

Mike Seeger was curator of the geology collection. Diane could imagine he was popular with the women, with his winning, slightly crooked smile and lean good looks.

"Lots of women sign up, then," commented Diane.

"Men too," said Emily. "They love to hear about his adventures."

Diane smiled. "I'll bet they do."

Mike was also employed by a pharmaceutical research company to look for extremophiles—organisms that can live in the most severe environmental conditions. The company paid Mike a good salary to go to some of the more dangerous places in the world to find them. It was like a paid adventure to him.

"I don't see how Neva stands it," said Emily. "If my boyfriend had such a dangerous job, I'm not sure I could. I don't even like to think about it. He just got back from exploring an ice cave. Isn't that dangerous enough?"

"Very," said Diane. She didn't like to think about Mike's other job either.

They got out at the Pleistocene Room overlook and walked through Exhibit Preparations, where several people were working, then down the hall, past the break room, and onto the dinosaur overlook. The guard was coming out of the break room and spotted them.

"That's off-limits," he said, coming after them with a soda in one hand. "Nobody is allowed beyond this point." He pointed to the entrance to the overlook.

Diane didn't stop until she was standing with her back to the security camera so that the guard had to face it.

"Do you know who I am?" she said calmly.

"It doesn't matter. Nobody goes beyond the break room," he said.

Diane noticed he was caressing his holstered gun. She honestly couldn't tell if it was a nervous habit or a threat.

"You're wrong. The only thing that should matter to you is who I am," she said. "I'm the director of this museum, and this overlook is museum property. For that matter, the crime lab is on museum property."

He grinned. "But you aren't in charge of the crime lab anymore."

"I am in charge of the museum, and I'm telling you, you cannot keep any of my staff or museum visitors out of this area. Are we clear about that?"

"I have my orders," he said, putting his hands on his hips in such a way that it looked like he could grab his gun at a moment's notice.

First Curtis, and now this one, thought Diane. *Where does Bryce get them: Thugs Are Us?*

"I don't care what Bryce has told you," said Diane. "You are not to be here threatening my staff or my visitors. Do you understand?"

"I understand the man who signs my check," he said. "Now, I think it's you ladies who should leave."

He stepped toward them. Diane held her ground.

"You were warned," said Diane when they were almost nose to nose. "Come on, Emily."

Diane walked over to the elevator that was on the back side of the overlook and punched the button. The doors opened almost immediately, and the two of them stepped in. Diane could see the smirk on the guard's face in the elevator mirror.

Just before the door closed, he said, "I heard about your close call today. You never get enough, do you?"

Diane held her tongue, but her blood was boiling.

"That didn't go real well," said Emily as the door closed.

"On the contrary," said Diane. "It couldn't have gone better."

Emily looked puzzled.

They got out at the first floor and walked across the museum, back to Diane's office. Mike was there talking with Andie and Blake, the security supervisor.

"I want the videos to the overlook," Diane said to Blake.

"I have the one that shows Emily and the little kid," he said handing it to her.

"Get the one that was taped just now with the two of us," said Diane.

"Is everything okay?" asked Mike. "I just let my class out."

"Everything's great," said Diane.

"Did you rip him up?" said Andie.

"He wouldn't budge," said Emily. "I can't believe the nerve."

Diane smiled, walked behind her desk, and reached for the phone. She called Lloyd Bryce's home.

"Yes." His voice sounded irritated. *Probably saw the museum name on caller ID*, thought Diane.

"You have another out-of-control employee, the night guard at the museum entrance to the crime lab. He's at the dinosaur overlook and is threatening my visitors and employees. You rein him in now," said Diane in her most undiplomatic tone of voice.

"Go to hell," he said loud enough for everyone in the room to hear. "You never knew how to keep the crime lab safe. That's why you had so many people breaking into it. Well, I do." He slammed down the phone.

"Wow," said Mike. "The guy has anger issues."

Emily and Andie were wide-eyed.

Blake shook his head. "You want me to take some security up there?" he said.

Diane smiled. "I don't want to risk a shoot-out at the dino overlook. What I want is for you to call and tell me what the monitors show he is doing."

Blake called security and talked to the person watching the monitors. "He is? Thanks, Leeanne."

"He put a chair on the overlook and sat down facing the museum approach. What's the guy think he's doing?" Blake asked.

"He's doing what he was told to do. Thumbing his nose at me," said Diane, smiling.

"You seem awfully happy about this," said Mike.

"I am," said Diane. She picked up the phone and made another call.

Chapter 12

"Colin, this is Diane Fallon. I'm sorry to call you at home so late."

Colin was a workaholic. Diane wasn't completely sure he ever slept. He was well-known for staying all night in his office. Diane imagined his office furniture to be as comfortable as hers. She had been known to stay all night at the museum a time or two herself.

"That's all right, Diane. What can I do for you? Peeks isn't bothering you, is he?" He sounded like he was eating, but that didn't mean he wasn't also working.

"No, not yet. I just had an unfortunate situation at the museum."

Diane explained about the incident with seven-year-old Ethan McConnel, the docent, and the crime lab's night security guard.

"I explained things to him, and he was equally threatening to me. I called his supervisor, Lloyd Bryce, who not only refused to rectify the dangerous situation but, I fear, encouraged the confrontation. The guard is now sitting in a chair on the overlook. I have tapes of each incident. The father of the seven-year-old is threatening to sue. Is this something we can use?"

"Yes, it is. It absolutely breaks the terms of the contract, makes it null and void. You know Rosewood is short a judge for the moment, so this will take a little longer, but it won't be too long. In the meantime, what are you going to do about the guard?"

"Tonight I'm going to evacuate the third floor. Tomorrow I'll tell Bryce the guard cannot return. If I can't get any satisfaction from him, I'll call the chief of police—Peeks will be piqued by that. Oh, and a couple of other things happened lately too."

She related the stories about Jin's job applicant at the DNA lab and the incident with Goldilocks, the new forensic anthropologist. She left out the conversation in the closet and the lost bones.

"This guy Bryce is out of control. Lucky for us. I'll start on the paperwork."

He said that the same way Diane would say she was going caving. He loved his work. Diane smiled.

"Thanks. Again, I'm sorry to disturb you," she said.

"Not a problem."

"Wow," said Andie when Diane had hung up. "Are you really going to kick them out? What's wrong with Bryce?"

"I don't know," said Diane. "But right now I have to go upstairs and ask the people working on the third floor to go home."

"I think the archivist is working late too," said Emily.

The third floor was mainly offices and work space. The docents' offices were there, so were Exhibit Preparations, the Library and Archives, and Education.

"I'll make sure everyone is out," said Diane.

Emily's hazel eyes clouded. "Do you really think he is dangerous?" she asked.

Diane smiled. "Can't take a chance, can we?" she said.

Emily still looked worried, and Diane felt guilty. Part of her did feel that Bryce and some of his people were out of control, but she didn't really think the guard would shoot anyone. She was just taking advantage of the opportunity to use Bryce's bad judgment against him.

"Most of this is just posturing by Bryce," she said. "But I need to stop it, and I want to make sure no one from the museum has to cross his path until I get it cleared up. No one should be afraid they will face a man with a bad attitude and a gun during the course of their day at the museum."

Emily nodded and gave Diane a faint smile, and Diane patted her on the shoulder.

"This guy is the definition of *hostile workplace*," said Emily. "It's just so weird."

"I'll say," said Andie. "But weird is what we do here." She grinned at Diane.

"Good night, Andie," said Diane. "I'll see you in the morning."

Andie nodded, said good-bye, and started to leave. She lingered at the door momentarily, as if there might yet be fireworks to see. Diane shooed her away.

"Mike, you mind coming with me? There's something I'd like you to help me with," said Diane.

"Sure thing, Doc." Mike grinned. "I love working here. Always something going on."

"I'll go too. I need to get my purse," said Emily. "It's in the docents' office."

The three walked out to the elevator and rode up to the third floor. The guard was still there. Diane saw him at the far side of the building as she was about to enter Exhibit Preparations. He was sitting in the chair looking like a troll guarding the bridge, popping something—candy or popcorn—into his mouth and staring down the hallway.

Mike looked down the long hallway at him. "So tell me," he said. "Which Billy Goat Gruff am I?"

"Well, I know I'm the littlest one," said Emily, "so I'm out of here." She waved at them and went to the docents' office.

Diane went to each department on the third floor and told her employees to go home. That done, she told Mike what she was planning and the two of them walked down toward the west wing overlook. The guard stood up as she approached, expecting, no doubt, another confrontation. He was grinning, ready for it.

Shipman. That was the name on his uniform. G. Shipman. He was a large, broad-shouldered fellow with short dark hair and a broad face with a nose that looked like it had been broken at least once. Diane wondered whether he was a bully when he was in school.

"You're going to have to bring someone bigger than that skinny runt," he said, pointing at Mike. "He's not much better than the broad you brought last time."

They ignored him, and before Shipman realized what Diane was about, she'd pulled the metal accordion gate from its slot in the wall. He ran at her, lunging at the expanding door, trying to wrestle it from her, grinning and staring her in the eyes the whole time. Mike stepped in and slammed it in the latch. Diane locked it.

Shipman's muscles, Diane guessed, were like Harve Delamore's—all show. Mike's were not. It was nice to have the testosterone advantage on her side this time.

"Hey, you can't lock me in," he said. He shook his hands as if they hurt. Probably stung after Mike grabbed the gate from him.

"I'm not," said Diane. "I'm securing the museum. There's a stairwell and an elevator to the left and right of the overlook. They lead down to the first floor. There will be guards at the desk and they can let you out. Or you can go through the crime lab to their private elevator," said Diane. She closed the fire doors and locked them too.

As Diane and Mike walked to the middle bank of elevators, she called security on her cell and told them to turn on the night lighting.

After a few moments they were plunged into darkness except for the foot lighting. They heard a muffled yell but couldn't hear what Shipman was saying. She pushed the button for the elevator and the doors opened immediately. They got in and the doors closed, drowning out all sound.

"I thought something was up the way you talked to Bryce—a little harsher than your usual tone."

"Bryce had already lost two battles with me. I knew he wouldn't want to lose a third, and I didn't want to tempt him into being reasonable by making nice with him."

"Doc, I didn't know you could be so manipulative," he said.

"Of course you did," retorted Diane.

Mike folded his arms over his chest and leaned against the wall of the elevator. "Exactly where did this get you?" he asked.

Mike was wearing tan slacks and a dark gray sweater, dressier than his usual Dockers and polo shirts. She was glad he was back. She hadn't liked the idea of his ice caving any more than Neva had.

"The terms of the contract between the museum and the City of Rosewood specify that neither the crime lab operation nor any of its employees shall put the museum, its staff, or any visitors in danger," said Diane. "When the lab left my control, Vanessa and the board wanted the crime lab gone. I confess, I had already been thinking about it even before Vanessa suggested it. It would be nice to have the space back."

"So Bryce really stepped in it this time," said Mike. "When Neva gets off work her muscles are knotted up worse than mine after a hard rock climb. She really doesn't like the guy. And neither does David from what I hear. Neva's worried about him."

Diane didn't say anything for a long moment. Finally she spoke. "We're coming up on the anniversary of the massacre," she said at last. She didn't elaborate. People who knew her well knew what she was talking about. "It's always hard on both of us. This year, more so on David."

"Oh, Diane, I'm sorry . . . I hadn't realized. I don't think Neva did either."

The elevator doors opened.

"It's not something we bring up without cause," said Diane as they stepped off the elevator into a stream of people leaving the museum restaurant.

Diane unlocked a door and ducked into the primate section to avoid being noticed by anyone she knew. The room had an eerie feel in the dark with only the foot lighting. The Neanderthal figures looked even more real in the dark shadows.

"Are you going to be all right?" Mike asked.

"Fine. David will be fine too. How about you? Is that a new scrape on the side of your face?" she asked, deflecting any talk about the massacre.

"Frostbite. I got it in the ice caves. I have to tell you, ice caves are among the most beautiful places on earth, but I really hate them."

"Don't they have more experienced people with ice caves . . . ? I mean, that isn't your thing," said Diane.

"We had ice cave experts doing the climb too. I didn't really have to do that much. I wanted the experience. But now that I've had it, I much prefer the regular old caves we explore," he said. "Though I have to say, the volcano expedition several months ago was interesting."

They crossed over to the east wing lobby. Two of her security guards were on duty. Diane greeted them as she walked past.

"You got a phone call from Lloyd Bryce," said one of the guards. He grinned. "He said you locked his guard in the west wing?"

Diane stopped. "I did no such thing. Mr. Shipman has several egresses to choose from if he wants to leave. If Mr. Bryce calls again, I'm not here."

"Sure thing, Dr. Fallon."

Diane left Mike in the lobby on his way to pick up Neva to take her to a late dinner. Diane went to her office and called Frank to tell him she would be home soon and that she would tell him all about her latest adventure.

Home, she thought as she hung up. She still hadn't made up her mind whether to settle in with Frank or to get her own place. She wished she could do both. She sat in her chair listening to the water fountain on her desk. The bubbling, flowing sound was soothing.

Diane didn't feel like she had just won a major battle. She thought she would feel more jubilant now that the museum had a way to reclaim all that space in the west wing and rid itself of a growing problem. She sat there feeling a little sad, not unlike the way she had felt when the chief of police and the mayor had replaced her. It had hurt more than she let on, more than she had told anyone, even Frank. In truth, she loved the crime lab and she had enjoyed it being in the museum. She knew Vanessa had too.

Vanessa Van Ross was the real power behind the museum. She was old Rosewood going back several generations. She had money and she had power—but not enough power to change the new mayor's mind. Vanessa wasn't aware that Diane knew she had gone down to the mayor's office after he fired her to talk him out of it. It must have been an odd feeling for Vanessa—being turned down. It didn't happen often.

Diane got up, put on her jacket, and turned out the lights. She walked through Andie's office and opened the door to leave. Neva and Mike were standing there ready to knock. Neva was dressed in jeans and a short, lambskin-lined suede jacket and gloves. *It must be getting colder outside*, thought Diane.

"Well, hi," Diane said. "Did you forget something?"

Mike shook his head. "Neva wanted to talk to you," he said.

"It's David," said Neva. "Did you know he resigned today?"

Chapter 13

"Resigned?" said Diane. "When?"

Neva shrugged. "I just know he left a letter on Bryce's desk. I'm really worried about him. He hasn't been himself lately," she said. Her dark brown eyes looked moist. She ran her fingers through her honey brown hair, but her bangs fell back in her eyes.

"Come in," said Diane.

Neva frowned at the sight of Diane's face, but she didn't say anything. Probably knew that Diane was tired of people noticing.

Diane turned on the light in Andie's office. Mike and Neva sat on the sofa; Diane sat on a chair in the small sitting area in the corner of the office. The cottage-style stuffed furniture with its floral design and matching rag rug of pink, blue, and green were pretty and tranquil. It made Diane feel like she should be entertaining Peter Rabbit's mother. She guessed that was what Andie had in mind.

"He hasn't been the same since you left the crime lab. You know David hated politics to start with. Now . . ." Neva shrugged again. "I know he never talked much about himself, but he talked to us about other stuff. Now the only time I have a conversation with him is when all of us have dinner. At work, it's strictly business. He keeps to himself."

"Do you know where he is?" asked Diane.

Neva shook her head. "I tried calling his cell but didn't get an answer. I went by his house while Mike was teaching his class tonight. He either wasn't home or didn't answer the door."

"What about his rooms in the basement here?" asked Diane.

"I went down there before I left. Unless he locked himself in and is not answering the door, he's not there." She hesitated a moment, looked over at Mike, then back at Diane. "I know this is a hard time . . ." She let the sentence trail off.

"Sometimes David likes to be by himself, especially now," said Diane. "And you know he won't suffer fools—gladly or otherwise."

"I know that," said Neva. "Mike's been telling me what Bryce's been doing. Bryce has this thing about control. That's what makes him so hard to work with. I can't tell you how many crime scenes we've arrived at way late because he takes forever to assign one of us to go. By the time we get there, the scene has already been compromised. Often he'll just send Lollipop by herself." Neva rolled her eyes.

"You had no clue that David was going to resign?" said Diane.

"Not really. Neither of us have been happy up there. Jin is counting his blessings that he's in the DNA lab. Frankly, I was thinking about applying for a job there when he gets around to hiring. It worries me that David would quit with no job lined up."

"Don't be too worried. I'll look for David and speak with him," said Diane.

Neva looked relieved. "Maybe you could talk him into coming caving with us sometime," said Neva.

"Not a chance in hell," said Diane. "He'd rather work a crime scene with Bryce."

Neva laughed. "You think he is all right, then?" she said.

"I believe so," said Diane. "I'm not really worried." This wasn't exactly the truth. She had been mildly concerned about him too. But she didn't want to worry Neva.

"I'll let you get home, then," said Neva. "You must feel awful, everything you've been through today."

"Not as bad as I look," said Diane. But it really was. She and Mike stood up. Diane rose with them.

"Good to see you, Neva. I'm glad you came by," said Diane.

She missed working with them every day. The four of them had worked well together.

"I have to tell you, Bryce is very angry with you," said Neva. "He is always quick to temper, but I've never seen him this angry."

"How did he not know that the forensic anthropology lab belongs to the museum?" asked Diane.

"He wouldn't listen to any advice or information that David or I tried to give him, so we quit trying. But I would have thought he knew about your lab." Neva shrugged. "I'm sorry about letting them in there. I hadn't meant to. They caught me coming out of the lab."

"It's all right," said Diane. "I changed the code on the locks to make sure they don't get back in—it wasn't aimed at you."

"I thought you would," said Neva. "I'd prefer not to know how to get in the lab until Bryce understands where his limits are."

After Neva and Mike left, Diane called Frank and told him she might be delayed. Then she retrieved her cell phone from her pocket and called David's cell number. She didn't expect him to answer, but he did and she was surprised at the amount of relief she felt.

"David, are you all right?" asked Diane.

"Sure," he said. "Why wouldn't I be?"

"Neva said you resigned." Diane sat back down in Andie's plush chair.

"It seemed like the logical thing to do," he said. "I just couldn't in good conscience work for the guy anymore."

"Where are you?" asked Diane.

"I'm driving home."

"Neva has been trying to get in touch with you," said Diane.

"I know. I just didn't want to talk to her yet. I'm feeling guilty about bailing out on her without warning. I'll call her later."

"What are you going to do?" asked Diane.

"I thought I'd apply for a job at the museum. I have lots of skills."

"That sounds like a plan," said Diane. "Why don't you come to my office tomorrow?"

"I'd like to take a little break first. You know, get this month over with."

"I understand. So you're going to take a vacation?"

"Yeah. I think so," he said.

"Keep in touch."

"Sure," he said. "Don't worry."

When they hung up, Diane sat in the chair for several minutes thinking about David. It was one of the more strained, noncommittal conversations she'd ever had with him. She put her face in her hands and rubbed her fingertips across her forehead as if she could smooth out her thoughts. Instead she only made her face hurt. David seemed off to her, even for David in troubled mode. She couldn't put her finger on what it was, but it didn't feel right to her. She went home to Frank with an uneasiness in the pit of her stomach.

Diane liked rounding the drive and seeing the museum early in the morning. Until it came into view, she never knew exactly what she would see. The stone structure could be bathed in the glow of sunrise, or it could be shrouded in fog, glistening wet after a rain, or dark and gothic during a downpour.

This morning the building had a golden glow as the sun just rising above the tree line reflected off the granite. A fog from the pond rose from behind the building, giving the scene an ethereal, misty halo. The dark, leafless trees looked like long dark fingers caressing the building.

The granite structure was a beautiful gothic-style

building with large rooms decorated with Romanesque moldings, polished granite floors, and mahogany-paneled walls. It began life in the 1800s as a museum on the first floor, with the upper floors rented out as office space. In the early twentieth century, the building was converted into a private medical clinic that closed down in the 1950s under mysterious circumstances—a history the employees loved to speculate about. The building then stood empty until Milo Lorenzo and Vanessa Van Ross decided to make it into a museum again.

There were stories told by the docents of bodies buried in the subbasement—the hidden results of medical mistakes or fiendish experiments from the building's dark past as a medical clinic. Good ghost stories are always fun.

As she drove up to her parking lot, she saw two figures rising from their seats on the steps, obviously waiting for her. It was Henry and his brother, Caleb.

"I'm sorry for coming so early," he said. "Caleb has to go to work and I have to go to school."

"That's all right. There are a lot of early birds around here," said Diane.

The blast of warm air felt good as they entered the building. Chanell Napier, Diane's head of security, was at the desk speaking with one of the guards about to go off duty. She was a slender African-American woman with a cheerful round face and a levelheaded disposition.

"Blake told me about last night," she said. "I can get a few guards and retake the third-floor overlook if you like."

Beside her, Diane saw Henry and Caleb exchange glances. *That had to sound strange*, she thought. Of course the whole thing *was* strange.

"I'll handle it with Bryce," said Diane. She turned to Henry and Caleb. "You here to return the application form?" she asked.

Henry nodded, handing it to her.

"I've been trying to interest him in archaeology."

Jonas came strolling over with a wink. "I could use a good assistant."

Henry grinned proudly at his brother. "This is Caleb's last day on his job," he said. "He's going to work at the university."

"I'm going to be working in the Advanced Computational Methods Department." Caleb grinned. "It's what I've been wanting to do."

"Beats working that boring job at the bank," said Henry.

"That's the truth," said Caleb. "I'm real excited. Almost as excited as Henry."

"Do you think they'll accept me?" asked Henry, suddenly looking a little worried.

"I'm sure they will," said Diane.

"That's a shoo-in right there," Jonas stage-whispered in Henry's ear. "Everyone around here does what Dr. Fallon says."

Diane laughed. "I wish."

"Sheriff Canfield had people out scouring the field again," said Caleb. "He said somebody stole the bones?" Caleb looked incredulous.

"Grampa said the sheriff's fit to be tied," said Henry.

"Have they found anything else?" asked Diane.

Caleb shrugged.

"I heard Grampa say they found a bullet," said Henry.

"People are always shooting around there," said Caleb. "I'm surprised they didn't find lots of bullets."

"The hunters are crazy," said Henry. "Sometimes they don't pay any attention where they shoot."

"Sounds like here," said Jonas. "Is the third floor safe?" he asked Diane. "I heard we had a troll on the overlook."

Henry and Caleb looked curiously at each other.

The third floor overlook is getting a reputation, thought Diane.

"It's safe," said Diane. Jonas was kidding, but she was a little annoyed with him. She didn't want any rumors flying around.

*   *   *

When Diane got to her lab, she retrieved the box of bones she had selected for Jin to try to get a DNA sample from. She thought she would run into Shipman again when she opened the overlook, but he was gone. Perhaps Bryce had gotten rid of him. She took an elevator down to Jin's DNA lab. She caught him coming out the door.

"Hey, boss, how are things?"

"A surprise a minute," she said.

"So I hear." Jin shook his head. "You don't look so bad. I got a girlfriend in theater. You want to try some theater makeup?"

"I think it gives me character," said Diane.

"Neva told me David resigned," said Jin. "You know, I'm worried about him. He hasn't been saying much lately. He just goes into his room and shuts the door."

"I think he'll be fine," said Diane. "I have some bones for you to try to get some DNA out of. Please find some," she said, handing him the samples.

"The wood-chipper murder, right? Sure thing, boss." He took the package. "If there is any DNA here, I'll find it."

"Thanks, Jin."

"You tell me if you hear from David," he said.

"Actually, I did hear from him. He's thinking about leaving town for a few days."

Jin was quiet a moment. "You think he'll come back?"

"He asked about a job at the museum," said Diane.

Jin grinned. "That's good. Maybe he's just chilling out."

Diane's phone rang. She took it out of her pocket and looked at the display. It was Andie.

"Andie," said Diane.

"Dr. Fallon, the mayor and a whole bunch of other people are here. They are sitting in my office."

Chapter 14

"The week just gets better," muttered Diane. "Andie, put them in my office, not the sitting room. Move more chairs in if you need them. Call Colin Prehoda and tell him what's up. Don't let them hear you. Offer them coffee. I'll be right up."

"Sounds serious, boss," said Jin.

"Serious, but possibly good." Diane smiled. "Find me some DNA," she said and took the stairs to the first floor.

She stopped in Andie's office and gave her the report she had written for Sheriff Canfield. She scribbled a note on it saying that Jin was going to try for some DNA.

"Andie, fax this to Sheriff Canfield's office," she said and walked past Andie's desk into her own office.

Spence Jefferies, the mayor of Rosewood, was sitting in one of the comfortable chairs. Edgar Peeks, the new chief of police, sat in the other stuffed chair. Douglas Garnett, the chief of detectives, a man whom Diane had worked with successfully on many cases, sat in a straight-backed chair. Diane was surprised to see him there. One corner of his mouth tweaked when he saw her, and he briefly made eye contact. He looked thin to Diane, but it had been a while since she had seen him.

They all stood when she entered but sat back down quickly after they shook hands. She noticed that none had coffee. Diane took a seat behind her desk and surveyed the group.

Mayor Jefferies and Chief Peeks were both sharp dressers, sharper than Garnett, who was somewhat of a clothes horse. Diane noticed the pinky rings that Prehoda had mentioned.

The two men were very different in appearance. The mayor had light brown hair, dark eyes, and a lean face. His prominent nasal folds and rugged complexion made him look older than his actual age. Peeks had dark hair, hazel eyes and that baby face. What they had in common, besides a good tailor, was mean-looking eyes—shark eyes, Neva would have called them—devoid of kindness. *How did you get elected with eyes like that?* thought Diane as she looked at Jefferies.

"What can I do for you?" she said.

"You can explain this," said Peeks.

The chief of police tossed a packet of folded papers onto her desk. It looked like a legal document. So the only niceties they were going to exchange with her were standing when she entered the room and shaking her hand. Diane picked up the papers and looked at them. Sure enough, Colin had been busy. Just as she was about to speak, she heard noises from Andie's office.

The door opened and Colin came in carrying his own chair. He was a snappy dresser too. Diane was beginning to feel underdressed for the occasion in her plain navy pantsuit. Colin wore his boyish smile, one that had fooled many an opposing counsel. He turned his chair around and straddled it with his arms resting on the back.

"This is Colin Prehoda," said Diane. "He drew up the document you just handed me."

"We're acquainted with Mr. Prehoda," said the mayor.

Diane was about to speak again when there was more commotion. This time it was Lloyd Bryce. He was also carrying his own chair. *Andie must be out of chairs by now*, she thought. She noticed that he wore an identical pinky ring. So—an Alexander the Great club?

"I hope this is everyone, or we'll have to go to the auditorium," said Diane.

"Now, why exactly have you come?" she asked again.

"What's this business about shutting down the crime lab?" said Peeks.

"I wouldn't know anything about that," said Diane. "These papers simply direct that the crime lab be removed from museum property."

"We have a contract with the museum," said the mayor.

"Mr. Jefferies," said Diane. "The contract was voided when the crime lab guard threatened a seven-year-old visitor and one of my docents with a gun. The overlook where the incident happened is provided by the museum as a place were visitors may go for a top view of the dinosaurs. It is a heavily used feature of the museum. It does not fall under the jurisdiction of the crime lab."

Peeks started to speak. "It is my understanding the guard never actually pulled his gun."

Diane cut him off. "He showed it to them, referred to it, and emphasized its presence. He ordered them off the overlook and told them if they were to come back again they would be in serious trouble with him and his gun. That is a threat. He was out of control and beyond his authority."

"She exaggerates," said Bryce in a tone that suggested this was an end to the matter.

"I have the videos," said Diane. "Not only of the incident with the child, but of another when he confronted me and the docent, and a third video that shows him attempting to attack me and to wrestle the gate away from me while I was securing the museum. And Bryce, before you say I was locking him in, I would remind you that he had points of egress from the overlook by means of a stairwell and an elevator—in addition to the elevator in the crime lab."

Diane paused, but when none of them said anything she continued.

"The contract has very clear prohibitions against the crime lab putting the museum, its visitors, or its staff in danger. The guard would not listen to reason, choosing instead to bully and to use physical force and threats. When I asked Bryce to intervene, to rein the guard in, he refused—with some rather foul language. It was clear that Bryce was in support of the guard's actions. I had no choice but to execute the provisions of the contract to protect the museum," said Diane.

"You could have given us a heads-up on this," said the mayor.

"I could not delay. The crime lab was out of control and I didn't know how much worse it was going to get. I had already been forced to evacuate the entire third floor of the museum to remove my staff from the danger presented by the belligerent guard."

Bryce made an explosive noise that Diane took to mean she was exaggerating again.

"The incident with the security guard was just the latest and the worst in a long list of contract violations. Bryce sent Curtis Crabtree with instructions that he was to work in the DNA lab that is owned and operated by the museum. There are no open positions in the DNA lab and he was so informed by the DNA lab manager. But Mr. Crabtree wouldn't take no for an answer. He refused to leave and got physical when he was told that the lab was not hiring. And in a separate incident, in clear violation of his authority, Bryce tried to dismiss me as head of the museum's osteology lab and install someone he had flown in from California and promised the job to."

Bryce squirmed in his chair and looked angry, impatient, and dismissive.

"Frankly," said Diane before he could speak, "I'm at a loss to understand what is going on. But it is clear that the actions of the director of the crime lab and members of his staff are interfering with and disrupting the operations of the museum, putting its staff and visitors in danger, and soiling its reputation. It has to stop here and now. The museum is responding by removing the crime lab from its premises."

"There is a matter of the taxes we have forgiven," said the mayor.

Ah, yes, the over-the-top taxes, thought Diane.

"That is being addressed as well," said Colin.

They all turned and looked at him, as if they had forgotten he was there.

"I'm not a potted plant either," he said, giving them one of his charming grins.

"Is there no room for negotiation?" asked the mayor. "Perhaps the museum security unit could take over all security."

Diane shook her head. "That would not be acceptable. As I have indicated, the actions of the security officer are only one complaint among a long list."

"I see," said Mayor Jefferies. "Of course the city attorney will have to look over all this. We only have your word."

"The contract provisions are clear," said Colin. "And let's not forget the videos and many independent witnesses."

"Look," began Diane.

"There is some question as to the ownership of the bone lab," interrupted the mayor.

Diane raised her eyebrows. "No," she said, "there is not."

"I think the bone lab was turned over to the city when the crime lab was installed," Jefferies continued.

Diane shook her head, as did Colin.

"That dog isn't going to hunt," Colin said.

"No," insisted Jefferies, "I believe Garnett told us that when the crime lab was established, the bone lab went in with the arrangement. Isn't that right, Garnett?"

Jefferies turned to Garnett, who looked at him, at

Diane, and back at Jefferies. Bryce had a bit of a smirk on his face. Colin sat up straight, watching Garnett.

"I don't know where you got that idea," said Garnett. "The forensic anthropology lab has always been part of the museum. The city has never had any stake in it. I have tried to brief Chief Peeks many times about this, but so far he hasn't had the time, so I'm not surprised that things are a little confused."

The silence that followed was uncomfortable. The mayor stared at Garnett for a long, hard moment. Diane couldn't see his face straight on, but the view she did have didn't look good. Garnett held his gaze and they were locked that way until Diane spoke.

Gregory Lincoln had been Diane's boss at World Accord International, where she was a human rights investigator. He was a career diplomat and a good friend. He would often give her little tidbits of his diplomatic wisdom—mainly because Diane had no skills herself in that direction. One of the things he told her was that sometimes it is useful to leave the opposition with something to save face.

"You could move the lab to where ballistics is done. It's next to the police station and the chief could keep an eye on it," she said.

Not much to save face with, but it was a bone. A bone that they ignored.

"There is another item," said Peeks. "This document says you own several pieces of equipment in the crime lab."

"Yes," said Diane. "That is true. The museum does."

The previous city administration often would not want to foot the bill for a piece of expensive equipment, holding out for the museum to buy it. And Diane did buy several items and leased them to the crime lab, with the proviso that the museum had access to them as needed. The largest piece of such equipment was the mass spectrometer—an item she was sure the current administration was going to hate to lose.

The mayor turned to Diane and looked at her with

Peabody Public Library
Columbia City, IN

his cold, dark eyes. It must have been the way he looked at Garnett a moment ago. Definitely shark eyes.

"Are you sure you want to do this?" he said in such a way that Diane was sure it was a warning. "You realize that you may be arrested at any moment for the murder of Officer Delamore and we can deal with your replacement."

Colin sat up straight again. He was starting to look as dangerous as the mayor. *Good*, thought Diane.

"That has nothing to do with the danger to the museum the crime lab represents," said Diane. "I'm sorry it has come to this, but there is no choice. I can't have a tenant who deliberately and repeatedly violates the sanctity of the museum. And I certainly can't have out-of-control people with guns on museum property."

"This is out of the blue," Peeks said. "Why didn't you try to resolve it instead of broadsiding us?"

You're a good one to talk about broadsiding people, she thought.

"I did try to resolve it. Bryce told me to go to hell loud enough that everyone in the room heard him."

Jefferies and Peeks turned their gazes on Bryce. He visibly cringed.

"We aren't going to take this lying down," said Peeks.

Diane kept her voice calm and reasonable. "I didn't think you would. But I hope you see that I have to protect the museum. We can't have our visitors or employees endangered and we can't leave ourselves open for lawsuits when some gun-toting cowboy decides he's going to threaten a child."

"You know I'll make calls and inform people that you aren't the person we are using as forensic anthropologist," said Mayor Jefferies. "You won't have anything to do in that big lab of yours."

Diane laughed. Jefferies first looked surprised, then angry. Diane could see he didn't like being laughed at.

"You think I'm joking?" he said, leaning forward.

Colin started to stand, but Diane spoke before he got to his feet.

"I think you have a big job ahead of you," she said. "You will have to call every county and city in every state in the United States. Then you will have to start calling cities and countries around the world. I don't think you know how this business is done."

The mayor's face flushed. He said nothing. But Diane could see he wanted to. He had forayed into an area he knew nothing about and he had made a mistake and an empty threat. He wasn't going to do it again. Diane had no doubt he would look for behind-the-scenes ways to sabotage her career.

"I think," said Colin, "we would consider that to be defamation and would act accordingly."

Diane stood up. "I think we have said all there is to say."

Jefferies, Peeks, and Bryce all looked as though they would like to climb over her desk and strangle her. Instead, they simply rose from their seats. They didn't shake hands. Diane was glad. They would probably crush her fingers.

Peeks stared hard at her. "As soon as the investigation into Delamore's death is complete, expect to be arrested. Start getting your affairs in order."

He turned and they all filed out of the room. Garnett glanced at her briefly, then turned and left with the others. The look in his eyes made her feel doubly uneasy.

"What was that about my osteology lab and Garnett?" she asked Colin after the delegation had gone.

"I don't know. That was strange and unexpected. They couldn't hope to get away with claiming the forensic anthropology lab." Colin shook his head. Some of his black hair fell in his face and he brushed it away with his hand. "The only thing I can figure is they were trying to tell you they are going to make it hard for you to get them out of here."

"Do you think they will make a lot of trouble?" asked Diane. "The mayor was very angry."

"They will make trouble, but I don't know how much. If they take us to court, we'll have to present proof and defend our position against their claims, warranted or not." Colin stood up and stretched. "The idea of moving the crime lab next to the police station is a good one. Maybe they'll take the suggestion and this will be over soon. I expect they won't drag it out. We'll see. I wouldn't worry too much about Jefferies attacking you personally. That would put him in a world of trouble. And as for Peeks' threat, I wouldn't worry. He's just trying to scare you."

"Not if they own the crime lab," said Diane. "Which they do. I have to tell you, I'm worried. What I don't know is why they just didn't go ahead and arrest me. I know they will."

Colin didn't say anything for a moment. "They want you to reconsider moving the crime lab. It's blackmail."

"I can't give in," she said.

"I know. It if comes to you being arrested, you have a lot of pull too. Vanessa and her family will have a fit. And you know Vanessa when she is pissed," he said.

Diane thought he was just trying to cheer her up, but she thought he was right about the blackmail part. Perhaps they saw that as leverage.

Colin left and Diane sat in her office for a long while thinking. She hadn't voted for Jefferies. She hadn't liked the way he came out throwing mud from the beginning, and she was surprised he appealed to so many people. He had a shoot-first-and-ask-questions-later attitude about suspects that reminded her of third-world dictators. So far, the only official action he had taken that she agreed with was to approve new bulletproof vests for the police officers.

She wondered how much of her relish in going after Bryce, Peeks, and Jefferies came from her desire for payback. She realized she was not above wanting it for the way the whole crime lab directorship was handled. The thought made her ashamed. She suddenly felt not so different from them.

She went home early. It felt like a storm was coming.

* * *

Diane spent the time until Frank got home playing the piano. It was calming, and she needed calm. The mayor and his friends had disturbed her core more than she realized at the time. She had gone head-to-head with the last mayor and it was no big deal. As a rule, authority didn't scare her. These guys did. They seemed mean and she knew they were willing to lie. Lies are wicked weapons.

After Frank got home they went to a movie and had a late dinner, and an even later evening. Diane awoke late the next morning. Frank was already dressed and drinking coffee when she got up and walked into the kitchen.

"Ah, I knew the smell would get you in here." He handed her a cup.

"I'm going to be late to the museum," said Diane. "Why didn't you wake me?"

"You were sleeping so soundly, I thought you needed it. Besides, I haven't been up that long myself. I'm late too. I'm going to have to run by McDonald's for breakfast."

He kissed her cheek. "I'll see you tonight."

The telephone rang and Frank grabbed it. Diane rarely answered the phone when he was home.

She could hear from the conversation that the call was from Ben Florian, Frank's partner. She watched Frank's face change from a grin to a look of utter surprise and shock.

"Thanks for calling, Ben."

He hung up the phone and looked at Diane for a moment.

"That was Ben. He was on his way to work and heard the news."

"What news?" asked Diane.

"Mayor Spence Jefferies was murdered last night."

Chapter 15

Diane and Frank stood staring at each other for several long moments, astonishment and disbelief reflected on both their faces.

"Murdered?" Diane said finally. "The mayor? I just saw him yesterday."

She always thought it strange that people would say that, as if having just seen someone should have afforded them protection against death. But there she was, saying it with the same surprise in her voice. She wanted to say *Are you sure?* but that was just as silly.

Murdered—a dreadful word, even applied to someone she didn't like.

"Who?" she asked. "How?"

"He was apparently killed at home, shot in the back of the head. They don't have a suspect yet."

"When did it happen?" asked Diane.

"Late last night," said Frank. "Ben didn't have a lot of information. He just heard it on the news."

"Well," said Diane, "this is certainly unexpected."

There was a time when she would have been one of the first on the scene. She would have known last night that there had been a murder and by now would have collected a truckload of evidence. But now she was like everyone else in Rosewood—one of the last to find out. That was good, she told herself. Nothing like getting called out late at night to look at someone with the back of his head shot out. Now she could go to work and, like most everyone else, simply speculate about what had happened.

"The detective in charge will probably want to talk to you," said Frank. "Just because you talked with him yesterday."

Diane nodded. "Probably so. The chief of police was there too." Diane smiled halfheartedly. "He'll probably say I did it then and there and moved the body." She kissed Frank again. "You're going to be late."

"Have a good day," he said. "I may be late tonight. These identity thefts are becoming a real bear."

"I'll be here playing the piano," she said.

"I laid out a finger exercise book for you." Frank gestured toward the room with the piano.

"I saw it. The cover said *The Virtuoso Pianist*. The words *virtuoso* and *Diane Fallon* will never be heard in the same sentence."

"Forget the word. Do the exercises. They'll strengthen your fourth and fifth fingers."

"My fingers are very strong," protested Diane, looking at her hands.

Frank took a hand and kissed the tips of her fingers. "Strong enough for rock climbing, but not for the piano. Trust me. You'll find those seventh cords you have trouble with a little easier. See you sometime tonight." Frank kissed her again and left, carrying his cup of coffee.

Diane stood at the door, sipped her coffee, and watched him get into his car. She smiled and waved as he pulled out of the driveway. It felt so domestic. She closed the door. *I don't have to think about murder anymore*, she thought as she got ready for work. *I have to think about Neanderthals—and maybe getting arrested.*

"Have you heard?" said Andie when Diane walked into her office. She had a newspaper spread out on her desk.

"About the mayor? Yes," said Diane. "That's a shocker."

"And he was just here. Do you think someone will come talk to us about him?" said Andie, excitement dancing in her eyes. Diane thought Andie would have had her fill of murder when Diane was director of the crime lab.

"Probably," said Diane.

"Strange, isn't it? So far the police don't know anything," said Andie. "Or at least they aren't telling the news what they know. You don't think you'll be a suspect, do you? I mean, you were suing him."

Diane noticed Andie didn't seem at all disturbed by the prospect of her boss being a murder suspect. Maybe Diane's being a suspect was starting to be old hat to her.

"I doubt it," said Diane.

Diane went to her office and sat down at her desk. It was unsettling having the mayor gunned down. It was too much like third-world-style politics, a breakdown of the rule of law. The thought gave her an urge to want to stop it. She got on her computer and looked up the story on the Web. The online media didn't have much more than Andie had told her.

Mayor Spence Jefferies was found in his kitchen, shot in the back of his head. He was found early this morning by an aide who came around to the house when he couldn't get in touch with the mayor about a meeting scheduled for this morning. Diane reached for the phone, then stopped. Who did she think she was going to call? Why was she calling anyone about this anyway? She didn't do murder anymore. She stood up and left her office.

"I'm going to work on the Neanderthal exhibit," she told Andie.

"Sure thing, Dr. F," said Andie, not looking up from the newspaper.

"I wish we could use a fountain," said one of the exhibit planners, standing back, looking at the diorama of the Neanderthals. "Real water falling from the rocks would be so cool."

"And the mold and mildew would look so real," said another.

"True," said the first.

Diane started to say something about the placement of vegetation when her phone rang. It was Kendel, her assistant director. Diane answered it with a tinge of expectation of good news.

"I did it," said Kendel.

Diane could hear the excitement in her voice even over the static of the weak signal between the cell phones.

"You were able to get it?" said Diane. "Kendel, that's great."

The staff working on the exhibit all stopped at the sound of Kendel's name. They all knew she was negotiating for a set of Neanderthal bones—a real coup for a small museum like RiverTrail. The museum had casts of various skeletons on display, but none of the real thing.

"It's the most expensive thing we've purchased," said Kendel. "But, I have to tell you, they are a nice set of bones. You're going to like them."

"Good job, Kendel," said Diane. "Really good job. We're all looking forward to seeing them—hopefully the public will too."

Kendel had just recently gotten her mojo back after being accused of stealing artifacts—an accusation that nearly cost her her career. Having her back to her old self meant good things for the museum. Kendel was skillful at acquiring quality collections.

"She got the Neanderthal skeleton?" the staff said simultaneously when Diane got off the phone.

"Yes, she did," said Diane. She started to elaborate when her phone rang again. This time it was Andie.

"Dr. F, you have a policeman here to see you," said Andie.

"I'm sure it's about yesterday's meeting. I'll be right there." Diane eyed the diorama again and made a suggestion about where to place more vegetation before she left to see the policeman. She wondered if Peeks had sent him to arrest her. She sighed.

The policeman was Izzy Wallace, a friend of Frank's and a man who had not liked Diane very much in the beginning of their relationship, believing she was all wrong for his good buddy Frank. Later, Diane had identified Izzy's only child as one of many students who died in an off-campus explosion. Rather than hating the messenger, he had changed. The experience had formed a kind of bond between them. They both had lost an only child to violence.

Izzy had lost a lot of weight. He used to be a big, barrel-chested guy, but he was thin now. Not lean and trim, but almost wasted looking. Diane guessed it was grief. She ushered him into her sitting room.

"How are you and your wife doing?" she asked.

He shrugged. "One day at a time. People at church have been real helpful." He sat down on the edge of the sofa. "You know, you always want somebody to make sense of it." He shook his head in a mournful way. "But there just isn't any sense to it."

"No," said Diane, "there's not."

He turned down an offer of a drink.

"Not unless you have something stronger than soda," he said with a weak laugh.

Diane wasn't sure if he was completely kidding. She sympathized. She had gone through all the stages of mourning too. She sat down in the chair next to the sofa.

"I keep meaning to hide some good Kentucky bourbon here for difficult times. But we have so many demanding days, I'd be drinking all the time," she said, smiling.

"I hear you there," he said. "Difficult times. They keep coming, don't they?"

"Sometimes it seems that way," said Diane. "What can I do for you?"

"It's about the murder," he said.

"Jefferies was here just yesterday," said Diane, "about the crime lab."

She was surprised they'd sent Izzy and not a detective to interview her. Not that Izzy couldn't do a good job, but she thought he worked the desk now. She supposed they figured she had little to add to what they already knew. After all, Garnett was also in the meeting. He could tell them everything she could.

"I know," said Izzy. "I didn't come to talk to you about that—that is, not exactly. We—me and several police buddies—would like you to investigate."

Diane hadn't expected that. "What? Me? Why? I can't intrude on an ongoing investigation. Certainly not one of this significance. And I have no standing to investigate."

"We got it figured out," said Izzy.

"I don't understand. Why would you want me to investigate?" she asked.

"Because Edgar Peeks will be in charge of the investigation," Izzy said. "We don't trust him."

Diane was still not understanding. She'd heard there was no love lost between the rank-and-file policemen and the new chief of police, but she didn't know why. So why would they want her to investigate?

"I don't—" began Diane.

"It's not out yet, but they're arresting Douglas Garnett for the murder," said Izzy. "Peeks is just going to hang it on him with no investigation. And that'll be it."

Chapter 16

"They're going to arrest Garnett? That's ridiculous," said Diane.

"It is, but lunacy has never stopped the likes of Edgar Peeks before," said Izzy.

"Tell me what happened. Why does he think Garnett is the murderer?" Despite herself, Diane leaned forward, anxious to hear the story.

"After they left here yesterday, Garnett and the mayor got into a big argument down at the police station. I tell you, you really pissed Jefferies and Peeks off when you told them to take the crime lab out of the museum. They considered it the jewel in their crown. It was really important to them." Izzy grinned broadly. "I've never seen Chief Peeks so mad."

"I wasn't taking away the lab. I just told them to move it," said Diane. "What was the problem?"

"They wanted the whole enchilada—the crime lab, the bone lab, and the DNA lab. They especially wanted the DNA lab, and as long as the crime lab was in the museum, they had a chance of getting control of all of them—they thought. You come along and throw a wrench in their plans. Then they find out the city doesn't even own some of the expensive equipment in the crime lab; you do. Like I said, they were really pissed. Warrick—you remember her?"

Diane nodded. Janice Warrick was a detective she had butted heads with when she first moved back to

Rosewood but who later became a trusted colleague if not a friend.

"Well, Warrick overheard the mayor talking to Peeks about replacing you as director of the museum," he said.

Diane laughed. "What? The mayor has no authority over the museum or me."

Izzy nodded and gestured with his hands. "I know, but you see, that's the way they look at everything. You'd think Jefferies was elected emperor of the universe and not mayor of Rosewood. They're crazy. And let me tell you, you were making them crazier."

"Who knew I had so much power," Diane commented drily. "Did they say how they proposed to replace me?" said Diane.

"No, but I wouldn't have put anything past them," said Izzy.

Diane hadn't liked the mayor, or the people he associated with, and had serious doubts about which direction their moral compass pointed, but still she was surprised at the picture Izzy was painting of them.

She said, "I know they wanted Garnett to lie about who the forensic anthropology lab belonged to, but how could they possibly think they would get away with that? I keep more records than the IRS."

"I don't know. They just like to throw everything at an enemy at once, hoping to overwhelm them, I suppose. Make them more willing to negotiate. That's why they threatened to arrest you, you know. They don't have much of a prayer to do that."

"Why?" asked Diane.

"Because the bottom of the gorge is just across the county line. The GBI handled the scene. Didn't you know that?"

Of course, the county line; she had forgotten. Diane felt an overwhelming sense of relief. She realized that she was truly afraid that she was going to be arrested and framed.

"You been worried about that?" he said.

Diane nodded.

"Can't say as I blame you. Who knows how those people think? They might have tried to come up with something. I know they would have pulled some other dirty trick out of their hat to back up what they were saying about your bone lab. They would have given you a run for your money. Kept you real busy dealing with them anyway."

"Tell me more about Garnett and the mayor," said Diane.

Izzy sat back on the couch.

Diane could see this was going to be a long conversation. "Would you like me to have the restaurant send us up lunch?" she asked.

"That would be nice," said Izzy. He grinned. "You sort of have a little kingdom here, don't you?"

"A lot of people think so," said Diane.

"Sort of queen of your domain," he said.

"No, just the queen's knight. Vanessa's the queen," said Diane.

"I hear you there. Lunch would be nice. I tend to skip meals since Evie's been working with this anti-drug group. She's trying to make some meaning out of Donald's death. I guess I should learn how to cook, but I don't have much of an appetite anymore."

Diane ordered a couple of steaks, baked potatoes, a salad, and chocolate cake, and asked that it be brought to her office.

"I won't turn down a good steak," said Izzy. He looked like he might have found his appetite.

Diane took a pile of books and papers off the table and readied it for lunch. She and Izzy made small talk until it arrived. He seemed to appreciate the break. Diane knew what a struggle it was for him and his wife—looking for meaning where there was none, looking for closure that didn't exist.

"They tell me you moved from your apartment," he said.

"They asked me to leave," said Diane. "Too many things happening in and around my apartment for them."

"I hadn't heard that. Who asked you to leave?" said Izzy.

"My neighbors. They met with my landlady and took a vote."

"You know that's not legal," said Izzy. "You could have fought it."

"I know, but I understood their position. Sometimes you just need some peace," said Diane.

Izzy nodded. "You're right about that. Sometimes you just need peace."

He stared off in the distance for a moment, then looked back at her and gave half a laugh as if embarrassed for getting lost in thought.

"How's Frank treating you?" he said. "He hasn't played that accordion of his for you, has he?"

Diane laughed. "No, but he is teaching me the piano," she said.

"Piano. That's nice. Evie plays a little bit."

It didn't take long for the order to arrive. Izzy looked at the food like he'd never seen food before, or like it reminded him of a life he used to have. Diane remembered what it was like to not have an appetite, having grief eat at the pit of your stomach so you thought it would never hold anything again. She also remembered that when she began eating again, her body started coping better.

"This is really good," said Izzy after taking a couple of bites of his steak. "I can't remember the last time I had a really good meal. I need to bring Evie to the restaurant here soon. We haven't been out together since, well, since before . . ." He let the sentence trail off.

"I do like the food here," said Diane.

Izzy ate a few more bites, took a long drink of tea, set the glass down, and paused as if not really wanting to talk about what he had come for. Diane understood. This must be a tiny respite for him.

"You ever wonder why Garnett didn't just find a new job, maybe in Atlanta, the way they were treating him? It would have been the smart thing to do rather than waiting for them to replace him like we all knew they would." Izzy didn't wait for an answer. "He did it for the rest of us. Peeks began showing himself early on, and Garnett saw what political animals Peeks and Jefferies were. Not that Garnett's a stranger to politics himself, but he's always been good to the people under him."

"And Peeks wasn't?" said Diane. "Didn't he and Jefferies purchase new state-of-the-art bulletproof vests for the police?"

Izzy made a derisive noise. "State-of-the-art my . . . Those vests were so old they wouldn't stop rubber bullets. Everything they did was just for show. They made sure the newspapers made a big deal of it, but like I said, it was just show. We figured they ordered out-of-date vests and pocketed the rest of the money, but we can't prove it."

"That's disappointing," said Diane. "Did anyone inform the newspapers?"

"We tried to leak it, but they sent a couple of vests—good ones—over to the newspaper office to show them. They're slick. Garnett thinks Jefferies was planning a run for governor and maybe from there to senator, and we were just a stepping-stone."

"What do you think?" asked Diane.

"I agree. We were just a stepping-stone."

"You said Garnett stayed to help. With what exactly?" asked Diane.

"Peeks likes to replace people. You know that; you were one of them he replaced. But you at least had another job. He was getting rid of people who didn't have a fallback position. People with families, people with a pension coming. Garnett fought for them. He got Colin Prehoda involved. Put a stop to a lot of it. Prehoda drove them crazy too. They hated not getting their way. They started in on Garnett, trying to remove him. Had him investigated by Internal Affairs, accused him of malfeasance when he was chief of detectives. It blew up big when he refused to say you turned over the bone lab to the city. Garnett was heard threatening the mayor. He said somebody like him didn't deserve to be around decent people, didn't deserve to be around at all. Something like that."

Wow, thought Diane. She had no idea she had become such a part of local politics. "Is there any other evidence against Garnett?" asked Diane.

"He was seen leaving the mayor's house at the right time," said Izzy. "Really, I'm not sure what they have. Peeks isn't saying much."

"What does Garnett say?" asked Diane.

"Nothing much at the moment. Colin Prehoda's his attorney, and you know how they are. They tell you to shut up," said Izzy. "That's probably a good thing."

"Who is working the crime scene?" asked Diane, hoping that it was the Georgia Bureau of Investigation and not Bryce."

"I don't know that anybody is right now," said Izzy. "But I imagine it will be Bryce. At least Neva and David will do a good job."

"David resigned," said Diane.

"Oh. I'm sorry to hear that." He paused for several moments. "You know, I just can't see Edgar Peeks inviting the GBI in."

"He may not have a choice. Having a mayor gunned down might attract the people in Homeland Security," she said.

"I don't know if that would be good or bad," said Izzy. "I don't trust Bryce. He doesn't seem too bright to me. On the other hand, I don't want the state or the feds to get the idea that Garnett might be involved. Sometimes it's better to deal with the devil you know."

"What do you want me to do?" asked Diane.

"Find out who killed the mayor," said Izzy.

"You don't want much. I don't have any standing in this. I wouldn't be allowed to investigate," she said.

"Like I said, we got that worked out. There's a private investigator in Atlanta who's going to let you work under his license. Prehoda's setting it up. You just have to let him hire you, temporary like," said Izzy. "It was my idea," he added, grinning.

Shit, thought Diane. She liked the idea.

Chapter 17

The house that Spence Jefferies lived and died in was one of the larger homes in Rosewood. It had a bright gray stone exterior, arched windows, several chimneys, and dark gray multiple roof peaks embellished with small tapering towers. It had a circular drive with a locked gate at the entrance, which was why Diane was standing on the street in the cold waiting for Colin Prehoda to come let her in.

Douglas Garnett had hired Colin as his attorney. Colin had set it up so that technically Diane and the detective agency she was temporarily attached to worked for him. That way, most of her discoveries would be the work product for his client. This gave her access to the evidence and got her past those who did not want her involved.

Most of the police she had dealt with on this case were forthcoming, anxious to help. They supported Garnett. But there were those who were against him. Very few people were undecided. A few were hostile to the point that when they met her in the hallways they brushed close to her, hitting her shoulder with theirs as they passed. Diane supposed that was meant to intimidate, but she didn't find it particularly intimidating. For her it delineated whose side they were on. It was like wearing a uniform, showing your colors, flying a flag. It had been an interesting couple of days.

As she waited outside the gate she studied a floor

plan of the house. It was a little over five thousand square feet. The trouble with large houses is there are too many doors leading to the outside. She doubted that all the doors were even listed on the floor plan she had. It was a drawing given to her by Colin, and not the registered blueprints for the house. The drawing didn't show the basement. She was willing to bet there were several more outside doors to the basement.

Then there were the windows—big houses have lots of windows. Of course, big houses have alarm systems. The mayor's hadn't gone off the night he was killed—leading everyone to believe that he knew who killed him, had let the murderer in.

Colin said there was an approach from the rear of the estate, a sort of service entrance that featured a gate, which was usually locked. Colin said the mayor preferred coming in that way because it was hidden from the front and no one could tell when he came and went. *Another way for a killer to come and go unnoticed*, she thought. The mayor didn't have cameras at that service entrance.

Diane had seen the autopsy reports. Colin had convinced the judge that it was in everyone's best interest to move things along quickly. But getting information about the crime was like pulling teeth. Shane Eastling, the new medical examiner, was slow to comply with the judge's order to give all the information to Colin. Eastling had delayed, saying the reports weren't ready, that his copier was broken, that he had to be out of his lab for a while, that his secretary was out sick. Diane camped outside his office with a portable copier and he finally complied. It didn't surprise her that his unfriendliness bordered on hostility, but it was unusual—Diane normally got along well with medical examiners.

It did come to her attention that Shane Eastling was a friend of Jennifer Jeffcote-Smith and had recommended her to Bryce. Perhaps Eastling thought Diane should have given up her lab and her position as forensic anthropologist to Jennifer. A rather unreasonable view to take, she thought.

The autopsies showed part of what Diane already knew—the mayor had died from a gunshot to the back of the head. According to the reports, the mayor had a contact wound and no defensive marks.

Bryce's report was interesting in what it left out—blood evidence. They had collected no samples. They did find fingerprints belonging to Garnett in the kitchen and on a table in the foyer. Investigating detectives had located a witness who saw Garnett's car leave the mayor's house. They had a security-camera tape showing Garnett enter and leave through the gate. Neither Diane nor Colin had seen the tape. It was another piece of evidence Peeks was delaying giving to them, and it made Colin suspicious. If it showed Garnett, that was powerful evidence in the prosecutor's favor. So what was the problem? Diane suspected Lloyd Bryce and Edgar Peeks were just generally trying to give them a hard time.

Diane hadn't spoken with Garnett yet. She wanted to get the feel of the crime scene before she met with him face-to-face. Colin told her Garnett had indeed met with the mayor at his home very briefly. Garnett told Colin he was trying to reason with the mayor about the crime lab. He said he was trying to convince the mayor that Diane's idea of putting it near the police station was a good one and that the city would have more control over it there than in the museum. Garnett also said the mayor was threatening to fire Neva.

"So, that's what Garnett was doing there," said Diane. "He was still trying to protect his police officers." At least Neva had a fallback position at the museum, she thought. Garnett probably didn't know that.

Colin drove up in his charcoal Escalade and parked it behind Diane's red Explorer. He got out and greeted Diane as he crossed the street. He walked up to the gate and looked at it as if expecting it to open.

"I'm going to have to keep pushing on everything," he said matter-of-factly. "The crime scene crew said they were finished, but when I asked to do a walk-through, Peeks tried to stop me, saying they are still finishing up. The guy's throwing up road blocks at every turn. However"—he patted his coat pocket—"I have our ticket in—a court order. And this." He stuck his hand in his pocket and pulled out a key that he dangled before him with a smile.

The black wrought-iron gate was equipped with a simple lock, not one that would keep a serious gate crasher out, but it was apparently causing Colin some problems.

"That's the problem with skeleton keys; you have to fiddle with them. There," he said as the gate opened.

"They didn't give you a key?" said Diane.

"No. Peeks said he would meet us. But I'm dubious of any good intentions on his part, so I brought my own. I doubt he is here. I don't see his car. These gates are pretty straightforward."

"What about the house?" asked Diane. "How are we going to get in?"

Colin grinned. "This house used to belong to a client of mine. He gave me a key to one of the side doors that Spence probably didn't get around to changing the locks on."

"Which door is it?" Diane looked at her floor plan.

"To the basement, around back. It's not on the drawings I gave you," he said.

Diane stopped in the middle of the circular drive to get a good look at the house. All the curtains were drawn. Bryce said they had left things as they were, but she didn't know if they really had. Like Colin, she was dubious. There was no shrubbery near the windows, no place an intruder might hide. The windows were all closed. She wouldn't be able to tell until she got into the house whether they were locked. She looked at the second-story windows. They were closed as well.

"You'd need a ladder to get to the second floor,"

said Colin. He stood beside Diane with his hands in his pockets, looking at the house.

Diane glanced over the rough stone exterior. "A rock climber could do it," she said.

"Really?" said Colin. "A rock climber could climb up that wall—with no trees or ledges to grab on to?"

"Sure. My geology curator could climb the face of the museum," she said.

"The museum? Really? People can actually do things like that?" he asked.

Diane nodded. "Mike is among an elite group who can do very difficult climbs. But this house wouldn't be that hard. I could do it."

"You could? Amazing. I had no idea. That's so Spider-Man."

"I can't spin a web," said Diane.

"Glad to hear it. I was starting to feel inferior," he said. "So, if one of the upper windows was unlocked, a skilled rock climber wouldn't find it too difficult to climb up and get in the window?"

"That's true," said Diane. "Or a second-story man. You know, don't you, there is a class of burglars who specialize in that MO."

Colin looked around. "I don't see any sign of Peeks," he said. "He probably thinks he's letting us cool our heels waiting for him. So, shall we go find our basement door?"

"We could try knocking on the front door first," Diane said. She started toward the door. "I think it's open." There was a small crack where the door stood open about an inch. "I think we've maligned Mr. Peeks unnecessarily and he's probably been listening, snickering at our paranoia."

Colin laughed. "I hope so."

Diane opened the door and walked into the foyer. The first thing she saw was Garnett kneeling on the marble floor next to the body of Chief of Police Edgar Peeks.

Chapter 18

The second thing Diane noticed was the pool of bright red blood staining the white marble floor. A small trickle of blood had flowed toward the wall. For such an expensive house it was surprising that the floor wasn't completely level.

They stood there for a moment staring at one another before anyone said anything.

"I guess Peeks showed up after all," said Colin.

Garnett slowly stood up. "I called the police," he said.

Diane just then heard the distant sirens.

"I know this doesn't look good," said Garnett.

"What happened?" she said.

"We can discuss that later," said Colin.

Always the lawyer, thought Diane. *Colin doesn't want me to hear anything just yet.*

"I found him like this," said Garnett. He wanted to profess his innocence. Natural reaction—guilty or not.

Diane's gaze darted around the foyer. They were standing at the base of a winding staircase that led to the second floor. To the left, the room that was labeled PARLOR on her drawings looked to be a study—all dark wood and leather. The desk was covered with papers, and the wood filing cabinet was open. Several books were piled on chairs.

From where Diane stood, she could see into the living room. The drapes covered the windows and

French doors. She saw no bloody footprints on the white marble. Too bad. Nothing's ever easy.

"Did you see anyone else?" asked Diane. "When did you get here?"

"Just a few minutes ago. And no, I didn't see anyone else," said Garnett.

"Why are you here?" asked Diane.

"Colin told me to come," he said.

Colin looked startled. "No, I didn't."

"Your secretary sent me a text message to meet you here," Garnett said. "On my cell phone."

"My secretary doesn't text. She's against it," said Colin. "Inexorably."

Diane frowned at Garnett. "Shouldn't you be too experienced to fall for this?" she said. "Obviously someone set you up. Why didn't you call Colin or me before you came?"

"I'm ashamed to say, it didn't occur to me. I knew you were coming. I thought you wanted me to walk you through my visit here the other night," said Garnett.

"How did you get here?" said Diane. "Where's your car? Where's Peeks' car?"

There were so many questions running through her mind, and she wanted to get answers to most of them before the police arrived. But the sirens were getting louder.

"The back way. That's what the text said. It said, 'Front locked, use back.' My car's parked behind Peeks'. His is in the small garage. Mine's right behind it."

"No other cars?" asked Diane. She noticed Colin wasn't stopping her. Probably decided the questions might be useful.

"None," he said.

"This isn't good," said Diane. "How did you get in the house?"

"Through the garage into the kitchen. I called out. When no one answered, I came to open the front door for you to get in when you arrived. This is what I found."

"The door was cracked a bit; did you do that?"
she asked.

Garnett shook his head. "No. I stopped here when
I found him."

Diane took a quick look at the body. He lay face-
down with one arm out to the side and the other one
under his torso.

"I'm going to see if he's dead," she said.

Diane knew he was dead, but she wanted to touch
the body to see how long, and she wanted all of them
to be able to state a reason when the police asked if
they touched the body.

It was warm. Peeks hadn't been dead long.

He wore a suit, good quality, and as far as she could
tell with him sprawled out on the floor, it fit. She gently
lifted his coat to see if his gun was there. It was. She
saw the holster for his cell phone. It was empty. She
wondered if he had it in his hand under his body.

Diane gently replaced the edge of his suit coat in
its former position. She stood up and glanced at the
corner of a fruitwood hall chest on which there sat a
bust of Alexander the Great. Didn't need Freud to
figure that one out. The chest had fingerprint dust on
one corner near the bust.

She wanted to go through the house, particularly
the kitchen, but the house was a crime scene—again—
and she knew better than to contaminate it. But she
was tempted. Colin and Garnett stood quietly looking
at her. She imagined they could read her mind, and she
wasn't sure they would stop her if she decided to go
through the house. But she didn't. It *was* a crime scene.

"Did you hear anything at all?" said Diane.

"Nothing at all," he said.

Diane heard sirens draw close, then abruptly stop.
They were here. She turned to Colin. "When it's released again, I want to go through the house."

He nodded. They waited as the police came through
the door. The first person in was Curtis Crabtree.
Diane guessed he was playing detective today. Behind
him was Janice Warrick. *Partly good*, thought Diane.

Janice was a friend of Garnett's. Shane Eastling, the medical examiner, walked in behind them, then Lloyd Bryce and Rikki Gillinick.

"What happened?" Janice was the first to speak.

"I need all of you to get out of my crime scene," said Bryce.

"Just a minute," said Janice. "Right now it's *our* crime scene. And I want to know what happened."

Colin spoke up first. "We came here to walk through the crime scene, and this is what we found."

Diane noticed that Colin didn't elaborate. Neither she nor Garnett said anything. But they couldn't go with this story for long. Garnett and Janice made eye contact. She knew there was more. Diane looked at Bryce standing holding his case, doing a slow fume, then at Curtis. He had a smirk on his face as he looked from Garnett to Diane.

"Eastling," Curtis said to the medical examiner, "look at the body and tell me what you can. Bryce, you have the scene after that." The sound of his voice indicated he was in charge and no one had better argue with him about it.

"I'll talk to the witnesses outside," Curtis added.

He said it as if he were going to beat them up. *This isn't going to be fun*, thought Diane. All in all, she'd rather be having her teeth pulled.

Two policemen were outside. Diane didn't recognize one. The other was Pendleton. He also gave Diane the evil eye. Janice came out after a moment.

"Gunshot to the back of the head," she said. "Like Jefferies."

Curtis nodded. "What the hell happened?"

Garnett began speaking. Colin shot him a look, but Garnett went ahead. He always had such contempt when suspects hid behind lawyers, as he often put it. Diane guessed he was unwilling to do the same—even if there was good reason.

"I got a text message for me to come to the house," he said.

Colin opened his mouth to speak, but Garnett waved him off.

"I thought it was from my lawyer. It was not. I got here and found the body. I called the police immediately. Diane and Colin arrived a few minutes later. That is all I know."

"Well, it looks like you are in a bit of hot water," said Curtis. "You were arrested for killing the mayor. And through some miracle or jurist malpractice you get out on bail, and the first thing you do is go kill the chief of police."

"I didn't kill him," said Garnett.

Curtis called over to the two policemen and told them to take Garnett into custody. Colin didn't try to stop them. Diane assumed he was going to make his case to the judge, deciding that Curtis wasn't a person to be reasoned with. Diane agreed.

"Don't say anything until I get there," said Colin.

"He's already said enough," said Curtis.

Colin ignored him and started for his car.

"Just a damn minute," said Curtis. "I'm not finished with you. The chief of police has been murdered and I find you on the scene. You've got to answer some questions."

"I have a court order saying I have a right to be here," said Colin. "We entered and found the body."

"Garnett was already there when you entered?" said Curtis.

"He had just gotten there, yes," said Colin.

"But you hadn't asked him to come," said Curtis.

"What I say to a client is privileged," said Colin.

"Garnett just said—" began Curtis.

"Nevertheless, what we say to each other is confidential and protected," interrupted Colin.

Curtis turned to Diane.

"She works for me in my representation of Garnett," said Colin. "Anything that passed between us is protected as well."

"I could put her in jail until she talks," Curtis said,

looking at Diane. "She may still be arrested for killing Delamore."

"Is that what the GBI said I did?" asked Diane.

Curtis ignored her. "Did any of you touch the body?" he asked.

"I did," said Diane. "I checked to see if he was dead."

"He was shot in the back of the head," said Curtis.

"I didn't know what his wound was," said Diane. "I only saw blood. He could have needed help. I had a duty to see if there was anything we could do for him."

Curtis studied her for a moment. Then he turned to Colin.

"How did you get in the gate?" asked Curtis. "It was locked."

"Really? When you got here it was locked?" said Colin.

"No, smart guy, the gate has been kept locked since the mayor's death," he said. "How did you get in?"

"I have a court order, and Peeks was meeting me to walk through the house. He said he was going to leave the gate open for me. Presumably that's what he did."

Colin didn't seem to mind lying to the detective. Diane felt uncomfortable with it, but she understood. She kept her mouth shut and her face noncommittal.

"He said . . . ," began Curtis, and stopped.

"Who said what?" asked Colin.

"Nothing," said Curtis.

So, Diane thought, Peeks told at least Curtis he was going to keep them waiting at the gate. That wasn't a surprise.

"We have told you all we know. Now I'm going to my client." Colin turned and walked off.

"Let him go," said Janice. "He's right."

"The hell he is," said Curtis, but he didn't try to follow. Instead he turned his attention to Diane.

She assumed that Colin figured that anyone who could scale a wall could take care of herself.

"Do you have anything to add?" he said.

"We came here to look at the house. I don't suppose you'd let me do that," said Diane.

"Hell no," he said. "That court order isn't any good now. There's been another murder."

"I figured as much," said Diane.

Diane could see that Curtis was in a personal quandary. He really wanted to do something to her. But at the moment all he could manage was harsh words, and not many of those. He looked as if he would like to smack her right there.

The ambulance arrived at that moment. It came up the drive and halted a few feet from them. Diane was relieved. That gave Curtis something else to think about.

"You know where to find me," she said and turned and walked off as Colin had.

She half expected him to run after her, tackle her to the ground, and handcuff her, but she heard no footfalls. She walked down the drive and out the gate. It was with some relief that she climbed into her SUV and drove off.

She didn't drive far. At the first opportunity she pulled off the road and took out her cell phone. She sent a text message to Detective Janice Warrick and asked her to take pictures of the house and surfaces. She didn't know if Janice had a camera with her, but if she did, perhaps she would at least get some views of the interior of the house. Diane didn't know now how long she would have to wait to get inside the house.

She drove back to the museum and parked in her spot. As she got out and started toward the door, a small Asian woman, about fifty years old, dressed in a pantsuit, with a camera around her neck, approached her.

"Are you Dr. Diane Fallon?" she asked, smiling.

"Yes," said Diane, smiling back.

The woman handed Diane a sheaf of folded papers. "You've been served. Have a good day."

Chapter 19

Well, this is just great, thought Diane, standing on the steps looking at the papers she had been handed. *I'm being sued. And didn't the sweet little lady just look so touristy with her camera around her neck.*

Diane opened the paper. *Jennifer Jeffcote-Smith vs. the City of Rosewood. Well,* thought Diane. *I'm not being sued. Rosewood is.* She skimmed the document. *And for a lot of money.*

She hurried up the steps and went to her office before any other strange person caught sight of her.

"You've gotten a lot of calls," said Andie as she handed Diane her mail. "Reporters are calling every five minutes. They want to know about the wood-chipper murderer."

"Refer them to Sheriff Canfield," said Diane.

"I do, but they want to talk with you," said Andie.

"Too bad," said Diane.

"They also want to ask about Delamore," said Andie.

"Tell them no comment," said Diane.

"Vanessa phoned. She's back. I told her about the Neanderthal bones that Kendel bought. I hope you don't mind. I couldn't help it. It's just so cool."

Diane smiled as she went through the mail. "That's fine. Was she excited?"

"Oh, yes. She's already planning the opening party for the exhibit."

"It's going to be a while. We have a long way to go," said Diane. "Anything else?"

"You got several calls from someone who wouldn't leave a name, some woman."

"Probably the process server who just gave me this." Diane waved the papers.

"Process server? Are we getting sued?" Andie's eyes went round and worried.

"No. Rosewood is. Ms. Jeffcote-Smith, the newly hired forensic anthropologist, was fired. Her lawyer wants me as a witness," said Diane.

"Oh, well, as long as it's not us," said Andie. To her, anything associated with the museum was "us." Diane appreciated her loyalty.

Andie handed Diane several pink pieces of paper. "Here are the other messages. Nothing urgent. Someone wants to donate his collection of fossil coprolites. I took his name."

"That's redundant," said Diane.

"What?"

"Fossil coprolites. Coprolites are fossils," said Diane, opening a letter from the president of the local Rotary Club. They wanted her to speak next month at their meeting.

"What kind of fossils are they?" said Andie.

"Fossilized excrement," said Diane.

"Oooew," said Andie. "It must have been a prank, like the guy last month who wanted to sell us the carved baculum coffee stirrers."

"Quite possibly." She smiled at Andie. "I'll be in my office. You can field all the scatological inquiries," she said.

Diane sat down behind her desk and went through the messages. Andie was right. Nothing urgent. Most were from various vendors. Diane sorted through her messages and put most of them aside. She picked up the phone and called Vanessa, who had just returned from a family reunion in Ohio.

"How was your trip?" said Diane.

"Lovely, interesting, and a bit tiring. Never seen so many really old people in one place," she said, laughing. "You know it's going to be either terribly interesting or terribly boring when your doctors want to come along to your family reunion.''

Vanessa's family was long-lived and the object of study for the Center for Research on Aging. Her grandmother had recently died at 114 years old. Her mother was approaching a hundred, and several other members of her family were centenarians. Diane imagined the whole family together was too much of a temptation for the researchers to resist.

''I imagine they reveled in the data,'' said Diane.

''Oh, yes. Mother has a cousin who just turned a hundred and three, and of course my father's side has several over a hundred.''

''Your father's side? I don't think I realized that side was long-lived too. Coincidence or arranged?'' Diane asked, smiling into the phone.

''That is one of your science fiction allusions, isn't it? Heinlein,'' said Vanessa.

''I didn't know you were so well versed in science fiction,'' said Diane.

''I'm not. I think it's dreadful, but I have a cousin who kept going on about *Methuselah's Children*.''

''One of my favorite books,'' said Diane. ''I can see how it appealed to your cousin.'' Diane paused a moment, absently fingering the summons on her desk. ''Andie said she told you about the Neanderthal.''

''Indeed she did, and I am elated. Have you seen the bones yet?'' she asked. ''Are they nice ones?''

''Kendel says they are,'' said Diane. ''She's delivering them herself.''

''Let me know the minute they arrive,'' said Vanessa.

''And I've filed notice for the crime lab to move out of the museum,'' said Diane.

''You've been busy. I'm glad we are reclaiming the space. I liked the crime lab; it was fascinating, but it's just not the same without you in charge,'' Vanessa said.

Diane took a breath. "I suppose you've heard the news in Rosewood," said Diane.

"I heard that the mayor and chief of police have been murdered. I must say, I'm shocked. I didn't like Jefferies, but to be murdered in your own home, that's a frightening thought. And this just a month after Judge McNevin. What is happening to my town?" said Vanessa.

"I don't know." Diane filled her in on the meeting with the mayor before the murders, including the fact that he wanted to have her replaced as director of the museum.

"What? How on earth did he plan to manage that?" asked Vanessa.

"I don't have any idea. I think they were just talking through their hats," said Diane.

She told Vanessa about the debacle with the new forensic anthropologist and about the subpoena. As she spoke she heard a commotion in Andie's office. It sounded like someone was pushing their way in.

"I need to go. There's apparently someone insistent on seeing me. Let's have lunch at the museum this week and talk about the primate exhibit." Diane finished the call with Vanessa and went into Andie's office.

A middle-aged woman wearing a flowered dress stood in front of Andie's desk. She had dyed blond hair with gray roots and carried about fifty extra pounds evenly distributed over her body. She had a large black purse hanging on one arm and two-inch black heels that looked to be too small for her feet.

"I need to see her. I've been calling all day. Now, let me see her. I'm not leaving 'til I do."

"Is there a problem, Andie?" asked Diane.

The woman turned toward Diane. "You're Dr. Fallon. I recognize you. I need to talk to you. I've been everywhere else. Please just give me a minute."

"This is Mrs. Donovan," said Andie. "Her son has been arrested for killing Judge McNevin."

"Why do you need to see me?" asked Diane. "I'm the museum director."

"Everybody knows you're more than that," she said.

Mrs. Donovan's face was haggard and worn, wrinkled before her time, but she had beautiful blue eyes that now beseeched Diane.

"Come in. I'll give you a few minutes," said Diane. She stood aside and gestured to her office.

"Thank you," she said and walked past Andie's desk and into the office.

Diane followed, leaving the door open a crack, and sat down at her desk.

"I'll get to the point. I'm Clarice Donovan," she said, sitting down in the chair in front of Diane's desk, scooting it closer at the same time. "My son is Evan Donovan. He's been accused of killing the judge that put Bobby away for life. Bobby's my other son. I know my family's troubled. It would be what they call *dysfunctional* on the *Dr. Phil* show. I know Bobby's done some bad things, and now he's in jail paying for it. But Evan's a good boy—I mean, he might do some little things, but he wouldn't kill nobody, and he didn't do this. I can't find anybody to look into it for me. The lawyer they assigned to him won't do nothing but try to get Evan to plead guilty. Well, he's not guilty. Isn't that lying in court if you say you done something and you didn't?"

"What is it you think I can do?" asked Diane. *The woman must be truly drawing at straws if she ended up here*, she thought.

"You can look into it. I know they say they got the evidence, but they can't have. They've made some mistake."

"Why did you come to see me?" repeated Diane.

"The crime lab here did the evidence," she said.

"I'm no longer director of the crime lab," said Diane.

"But you could talk to the person who is," she said.

If you only knew. "I assure you, the current director won't listen to me," she said.

"But you could look into it. Somebody has to. You can't just lock somebody up and have no one look into their case," she said.

"People have looked into it. That's why he's been arrested. His lawyer will have to—"

"Haven't you been listening? His lawyer won't do anything. The prosecutor and the detectives won't even talk to me—and now they're dropping like flies themselves. I don't know what the world is coming to. It's just gone crazy."

She stopped and took a breath and moved her chair a bit closer to Diane's desk.

"That's one good thing about my boys being locked up. They can't be blamed for what's going on now. All I'm asking is that you look at the evidence. Surely you can do that. Something is wrong."

Diane sat there wondering why in the world she agreed to talk with the woman. There was absolutely nothing she could do for her, and she wasn't sure how to politely get her out of her office—short of agreeing to do something.

"I can't promise anything, but I'll see what I can do. Don't expect anything. As I said, I'm not in the loop anymore," said Diane.

The woman relaxed back in the chair. "That's all I ask."

"Why are you so sure he didn't do it?" said Diane.

She leaned forward. "Because he was at home with me. But who's going to believe a mother?"

"Okay. Just remember, I can't promise anything."

The woman nodded, apparently satisfied that she got a positive response from someone. Diane saw her out the door.

"I'm sorry, Dr. Fallon. I couldn't get her out," said Andie after Mrs. Donovan had gone.

"She's a determined mother," said Diane. "I'm going to do some paperwork." *Hopefully in peace.*

Diane hated paperwork, but after a day like today, paperwork sounded like fun. She went back into her office and shut the door.

She had made her way through all her budget reports when she heard someone in Andie's office. *Maybe I should think about soundproofing my walls— or moving my office and not telling anyone.*

Andie knocked on the door and opened it. "Detective Warrick would like to see you."

"Okay, thanks, Andie. Send her in."

Janice Warrick walked in carrying a folder. Her short brown hair was ruffled and she smoothed it over.

"Why don't we sit at the table," Diane said, pulling out a chair.

Janice sat down and laid the folder on the table. A stack of photographs spilled out.

"I got the photographs you asked for," she said. "I had to take them with my camera phone. It's a good one, but it's still a camera phone. I printed them out for you." She gathered them back into a neat stack.

Diane was surprised a phone could hold that many pictures. She took the first one off the stack and looked at it. It was of the kitchen where Jefferies had been found.

"What is this on the floor?" Diane said. "They outlined the body?"

"Yeah, I didn't think you guys did that anymore," said Janice.

"We don't. It introduces an unnecessary contamination to the crime scene." Diane frowned. It wouldn't do to criticize Bryce's methods; it would only make her look bad.

Diane went through the pictures. "Where were Garnett's prints found?" she said.

"In the hallway—the foyer, I guess you call it—on that chest of drawers next to that statue—you know, the head of some guy."

"Alexander the Great," said Diane absently. "Where else?"

"On the kitchen counter," said Janice.

"Nowhere else? Not on any door facings, tables, chairs?"

"No, just those two places. The kitchen print was a full handprint, and the one in the foyer was four fingers on the right hand," said Janice.

"I need to speak with Garnett. Can you get me in?" said Diane.

"Sure. That shouldn't be a problem. You've found something?"

Chapter 20

Garnett sat across from Diane at a table in the small room. He didn't look good. He had dark circles under his eyes and his face looked pale and haggard. Diane imagined a sharp dresser like him hated the neon prison jumpsuit.

The room they were in was specifically for conferences like the one she was having with him. It was also used for interrogations on occasion. The walls were painted a strange shade of pink. Rumor had it that someone thought the color sapped prisoners' strength when they looked at it. Diane wondered why they had orange prison suits, since that color was supposed to energize and excite. She thought they must have just gotten the paint cheap. At least the room wasn't dull gray.

"A witness says you were at the mayor's house the night he was murdered. Tell me about it," said Diane.

He smiled slightly. "Strange being on the other end. I never realized you sounded so harsh." He folded his arms on the table and sighed. "I wasn't there long. I didn't get past the entryway at the front door. The mayor said he didn't have anything else to say and that he was busy. I left. That was it. Apparently someone saw me drive away. It was dark, but I suppose they recognized the car. No, wait. After I went out the gate I pulled over and turned on the light to make a call. A car went by. They could have seen me.

Doesn't matter. As I understand it I was also on the security camera, and I admit I was there."

"How did your prints get in the house?" asked Diane.

Garnett's shoulders went up an inch and fell. "I was also there the evening before. But I wasn't there long then either."

"Tell me about it," said Diane.

"That morning Peeks told me he wanted to replace Neva and Izzy. He said Izzy wasn't pulling his weight. It wasn't true. I could have told him Izzy was still grieving and to cut him some slack, but I didn't. The man had no compassion." He shook his head. "I don't know what he had against Neva. She's very competent." He smiled. "Much more than I thought she would ever be. She really blossomed at the crime lab."

"So you went to talk to the mayor about it that same night?" prompted Diane.

"I got there around eight o'clock that evening. It was dark, of course."

"Was anyone else there besides the mayor?" asked Diane.

"Peeks was there; that's all. He arrived the same time as I did."

"What did you touch?" asked Diane.

Garnett wrinkled his brow. "What?"

"The fingerprints. What did you touch?" she asked.

Garnett sat back and thought a moment.

"I knocked on the door. Didn't use the knocker. Just my knuckles on the wood. The mayor opened it. Peeks came up just as I got inside and brushed past me, almost knocking me over. He likes doing that. I touched that table by the wall—chest or whatever it is—to steady myself. Peeks patted me on the back and said something like 'Sorry, fella.' We all went into the kitchen, where Spence was making nachos in the microwave. I told the mayor I didn't think letting Izzy or Neva go was a good idea."

Garnett shook his head, put his hands flat on the table, and looked at them. His wedding ring was gone, and his watch, taken and put in a labeled envelope until he got out of jail. Diane wondered if sitting in a cell was giving him a new perspective on things.

"What happened?" asked Diane.

"He started off by telling me how Izzy wasn't pulling his weight. Same words Peeks used. I told him Izzy worked the desk and was good at it. Peeks said I had low standards, that Izzy was lazy. I told them Neva was a fine officer. They said she spent too much time working at the museum for you, but they might hold off on both of them if I would consider searching my memory about the disposition of the bone lab. That I should remember that you turned over the lab to the city."

"Surely they didn't think that would work," said Diane.

"Apparently my testimony was part of some plan they were concocting. I don't know. I told them the whole thing was ridiculous; they didn't have a hope in hell of getting your lab. Evidently they thought it was theirs to begin with. I never briefed them on who owned the bone lab. They knew you had just put in the DNA lab, and I think they wanted to put one of their own people in it to eventually replace Jin. But they thought the bone lab was part of the crime lab. It was a blow to find out it wasn't, and they just didn't want to let go. To tell you the truth, I don't know what they had in mind to do about it. Except maybe force you to change your mind by threatening to arrest you for Delamore's murder."

"What else did you touch?" asked Diane.

Garnett thought a moment.

"I remember leaning on the kitchen counter, you know, that island in the middle of the kitchen. I put my hand on it and leaned over to talk to the mayor. I told him what they were doing was unfair and if he hoped to get elected again, he should tone it down. He got really pissed. Then suddenly he calmed down and asked me about you."

"About me?" said Diane.

"He wanted to know how to unseat you as director of the museum."

"That is so strange," said Diane.

"Isn't it? I told him better men have tried and failed. He really didn't know much about the museum. He mentioned something about going to the board of directors. I didn't say anything. I thought I'd just let him see how that worked out for him." Garnett laughed.

Diane couldn't imagine what the mayor was thinking. Of course, the mayor who preceded Jefferies had tried to do the same thing, but for different reasons. He had wanted the land the museum was on—or thought he did.

"So there are just two things you remember touching— the kitchen counter and the hall chest," said Diane.

"That's it, I'm pretty sure. I left soon after. It wasn't like he was going to invite me to share his nachos." He looked at her quizzically for a moment. "I know that look on your face. What are you thinking?"

"It appears that the hall chest and kitchen counter were the only two places they dusted for prints," said Diane.

It took a moment for a look of surprise to cross Garnett's face.

"They were only looking for my prints—Peeks must have told them where to look," he said. "Who worked the crime scene? Not Neva?" His eyes clouded over.

"No, it was Rikki and Bryce," said Diane. "And probably Curtis Crabtree."

Diane stood up. "Don't worry. I think we'll get to the bottom of this soon." *Now that all your enemies are dead.* The thought came unbidden into her head. She shook it off. "I need to speak to Colin. You don't happen to know what other evidence they have against you?" asked Diane.

"No, I don't. . . . Not really," he added.

Diane sat down again. "Tell me what you know," she said.

"The gun used in the killings was one that was used several years ago in a robbery. It should have been in the evidence room. Not many people have access to that room. Only the police."

She didn't like where this was going. It wasn't a good thing when all the suspects were policemen.

"Did they find the gun itself?" she asked.

"No," said Garnett.

"Was it the same gun that killed Edgar Peeks?" she asked.

"I don't know."

"Anything else you need to tell me?" she asked.

"I can't think of anything . . . except that I usually need more evidence than what they have on me to lock someone up. You think Prehoda can get me out of here?"

"I don't know. If he can overcome the drama of you being found standing over Peeks' body," she said.

"I don't know how many times I've heard perps say they've been set up. I've never believed them; not once," Garnett said.

"It does happen," said Diane.

She knocked on the door and the guard came to take Garnett back to his cell.

Diane walked up to the squad room to speak with Janice. She needed to get Janice to take point on Garnett's case. They somehow had to give Curtis Crabtree something else to do, and she wasn't sure how to accomplish that.

Chapter 21

When Diane got to the squad room, Buford Monroe, the chief of police under the previous administration, was standing with Edward Van Ross, who was the president of the city council of Rosewood—and Vanessa's son. That's why the city council hadn't done anything yet, thought Diane. Edward was out of town and they were waiting for his return.

Behind Van Ross stood the former police commissioner, who had also lost his job with the change in administrations. Jefferies said it was redundant to have a police chief and a police commissioner in a city the size of Rosewood and getting rid of the commissioner would save a huge salary. Diane had agreed with him about that. She still did. The commissioner had run for city council and won a seat. Standing there in front of the squad room with Edward Van Ross, he and Monroe both looked vindicated—like they wanted to say, *I told you so*.

"The council met today," Edward Van Ross was saying when Diane arrived, "and appointed me acting mayor until we have a special election. As one of my first acts I have reinstated Buford Monroe as chief of police."

Diane looked around the room at the faces. Most were smiling, but there were a few who looked sullen—hired by Peeks, no doubt, they had pooled their fortunes with his; and now it looked like they had picked the wrong side. She wondered if Harve

Delamore had been a Jefferies supporter. As she looked over the gathering, she noticed that Pendleton was smiling. Interesting. Maybe he would be willing to talk with her about how Bryce and company handled the crime scenes.

"I'm sure all of you will welcome Chief Monroe back and do all you can to help during this crisis," continued Van Ross.

Diane hoped he wouldn't talk long. She wanted to have a word with Monroe. She spotted Colin Prehoda standing with his back to the wall. He nodded when she made eye contact and pointed to a bulky envelope he had in his hand. She worked her way over to him.

"I finally got the security tape," he whispered to her. "It was found in Peeks' apartment, of all places. Janice discovered it, thankfully."

"Have you looked at it yet?" Diane whispered.

"No, I thought we'd go to your office or mine and have a look," he said.

"I came with Janice and I need a ride back, so let's go to mine," she said.

Van Ross was ending his speech. He made mercifully short ones. He joked that that was why he was elected president of the city council. Diane, followed by Colin, walked up to the front. Edward Van Ross gave her a hug and mentioned how much his mother was looking forward to the Neanderthal bones. He also offered his sympathies for her injuries.

She shook Buford Monroe's hand and said softly that she was glad to have him back and that she needed to speak with him. Having just been hugged by Edward Van Ross gave her some political credits, she imagined. They stepped away from the crowd.

"I think it would be a good idea to replace Curtis Crabtree as the primary on the murders. Janice Warrick would be a good replacement," she said, coming right out with what she wanted, hoping frankness was the best way.

"Why?" he asked.

"Crabtree isn't objective, and he seems divided between the crime lab and being a detective. I think Janice would be better.

"I can't be seen to favor Garnett. Even though I believe he is innocent," he added. "I don't want to load the deck in his favor by eliminating any detective who isn't on his side."

Diane let the bad metaphor go, even though she hated bad metaphors. "I understand, and you are correct in that position. Janice was reprimanded by Garnett—actually demoted by him—but she has worked her way back up to detective and clearly sees this objectively, the way a good detective should. Putting her in charge wouldn't be seen as making a judgment in his favor; it would be seen as making sure everything is evenhanded and not based on grudges." It wasn't a good argument. But she didn't think it had to be. Buford Monroe didn't like any of Peeks' cronies, and he knew that Curtis was one of them.

Monroe was nodding the whole time. That was a good sign.

"There's merit to what you've said," he mused.

"I want all this put behind us and not have it reflect on those who were part of the past administration. I want it done well."

Monroe seemed to be considering, but Diane knew he had already made up his mind. He was a political animal, and the idea of clearing the names of those under the last mayor—namely, him—appealed to him. Diane waited patiently.

"Okay, I see your point and I agree. I'll make the change right away." He looked around at the people still in the squad room. "I'm afraid there is a lot of housecleaning I'm going to be doing before this is over." He looked like he relished the idea.

"I don't envy your task," said Diane, still sucking up to him.

He shook his head. "I don't either."

"Thanks for speaking with me," she said.

He nodded. "Glad to be working with you again," he said.

Colin was talking with Edward Van Ross, so she sought out Pendleton. He was still hostile, but he agreed to speak with her when she said she was working to clear Garnett.

"Can you tell me anything that you thought was out of the ordinary going on at either crime scene?" she asked. "You've been to crime scenes before and know how they are done."

He shrugged. "They are all different. I wasn't at the Jefferies crime scene, but at Peeks'. Bryce and that Rikki chick were looking for something. Some kind of list, I heard them mention."

"Do you know what kind of list? Names? Numbers?" asked Diane.

"No. They didn't say," he said.

"Anything else?" she asked. "Did they check for fingerprints?"

He had been slouching but stood up straight. "Now that you mention it, they didn't dust for prints at all. Now, that's strange. Another thing. That Rikki chick pocketed something she found on the floor near the body. I thought it was a silver pen, but I don't really know what it was. Something shiny. I thought it was something she dropped maybe. That's all I know."

"Thank you for talking to me," said Diane.

"The GBI said that Harve wasn't pushed. Something about the math and something about his foot injuries being consistent with your description. But I don't know why he would have gone after you. I know he didn't like you, but . . . this is just strange." He shrugged and left before Diane could comment.

When she and Colin left, Diane was glad to get out of the police station. She never found it to be a comfortable place even before the Jefferies administration. On the way to the museum she told Colin that Monroe would be putting Janice Warrick in as lead detective.

"How did you pull that off?" said Colin, looking over at her, then back at the road.

"By trying to be both logical and political. Not easy," she said.

"That will make our job easier. Maybe the worm is finally turning," he said.

"I had Janice take pictures inside the mayor's house," said Diane. "I noticed when we were there earlier that there was fingerprint powder only on one corner of the hall chest—no place else. When I saw the pictures of the kitchen, I saw the same thing. There was fingerprint dust only where Garnett had touched the countertop." Diane related her discussion with Garnett to Colin.

"So, Bryce or what's her name—Rikki—didn't try to find any other prints, just Garnett's." Colin whistled. "Wow."

"I assume they acted on orders from Peeks, but I don't know," said Diane.

"That's both good and bad. Good in that it looks like they were trying to frame Garnett. But the prosecutor could see it as a motivation for Garnett to kill Peeks."

"Janice will interview Bryce," said Diane. "I'll be interested to see his explanation. Her pictures also showed that the house appeared to have been searched after the mayor's body was discovered and the police had turned the crime scene over to Bryce. Janice said the original crime scene photos taken by the police didn't show the disarray that her photographs did. I can't be sure, but it looks like Bryce may have been looking for something—or he has a very messy style of working a crime scene. Officer Pendleton said that Bryce and Rikki were looking for some kind of list and that Rikki may have taken something from the crime scene."

"What do you think it could be?" asked Colin. He pulled into the museum parking lot and into Kendel's space.

"I have no idea. Janice also said the mayor's com-

puter was heavily encrypted and no one has been able
to see what is on his hard drive," said Diane.

"That's interesting. I think. But even I have a pass-
word on my computer," said Colin.

"I got the idea that this is a little more heavy-duty
encryption. I'll ask Frank about it," said Diane.

"Frank Duncan?" said Colin. "He's Atlanta, isn't
he?"

"Yes. The Metro-Atlanta Fraud and Computer Forensics Unit," she said.

"We've met. Not a guy a defense attorney likes to
have on the stand," said Colin. "Nice guy, I've heard."

"I've heard that before," said Diane. "Yes, he is a
very nice guy."

"You dating him?" asked Colin.

"Yes. I'm staying at his home while I'm house hunting. My neighbors kicked me out of my apartment."

"What? Neighbors can't do that. Why?" said Colin.

Diane explained about the various times she had to
have the police come to her apartment when someone
went after her—the attacks, the blood. "They got
scared."

"You want to fight it?" he said.

"No. My neighbors across the hall attend funerals
for fun and once broke into my apartment looking for
a cat they thought I was keeping against building policy. I had a downstairs neighbor whose ancestors were
members of the Donner party. I was sort of ready
to move."

Colin laughed out loud.

They put the security tape from the mayor's house
into Diane's machine. The images were dark and
fuzzy. She thought the mayor would have had better
equipment. The video surveillance cameras were motion activated. Something had caused the tape to start
recording. They watched for more than a minute before they saw anything. It was a deer going into the
woods.

The next sequence showed Garnett's car pull up and park. He got out and walked up to the door and was let in. They watched the view of the car for another few minutes. Finally Garnett came out. He wasn't in the house long, but it would have been long enough to shoot the mayor. Garnett got in his car and drove off. After another several minutes of nothing happening, the tape ended.

"That wasn't helpful," Colin said. "Why do you think they didn't want us to see it?"

"I have no idea. Maybe because Garnett wasn't in the house long. Let's watch it again," she said.

Diane rewound the tape and they started it again. Colin got closer to the monitor. The second time was equally unhelpful.

"I think you're right," said Colin. "It was the timing they were worried about."

As he spoke, Diane rewound the tape and watched it again. This time she put the machine on slow motion.

"This has to be one of the more boring jobs," said Colin.

There it was, three minutes after Garnett left. Right where the deer had gone into the woods earlier—a figure. It had been just a blink at regular playback speed. The figure came from behind a large tree at the edge of the woods. Was he, or she, there the whole time? The figure moved quickly into the cover of the trees.

"I'll be damned," said Colin. "That's what they didn't want us to see. Someone else was there that night."

Diane's VCR fed the image through a computer. She used it for the very thing they were employing it for now, watching and analyzing museum surveillance tapes. She rewound the tape and started the playback again. She stopped the motion on the figure.

"You can't make anything out," Colin said. "Can this be enhanced?"

"Probably some," said Diane staring at the image.

The running figure wore a hoodie with his or her hands in its pockets.

"We need a way to find out who this is," said Colin.

Diane sat staring at the picture, feeling sick. She knew who it was.

Chapter 22

Diane sat in the living room of Frank's house in the dark, watching the fire she'd built and wishing he was home. But how could she talk to him about this? There was no one she could talk to. She thought briefly of Mike, her caving partner. He was the only one who wouldn't be duty bound to report what she told him, but she didn't want to drag him into this either. She knew what Frank would say. Knowing the right thing to do is not hard. Dealing with the consequences of doing the right thing is the hard part. So is living with the consequences of not doing the right thing. *Damn.*

She picked up her phone again and called. No answer. She left another message. She wanted to scream the message, but she calmly told the voice mail that it was urgent and to call back, please. She got up and went to the piano, opening up the finger exercise book that Frank had said she should try. It was both hands and all sixteen notes. It was what she needed, something that looked impossible. She gave it a try.

She was still working on the exercise when Frank came home. She didn't hear him until he spoke.

"I'm glad you've really gotten into those exercises," he said.

Diane jumped.

"Sorry, I didn't mean to startle you." He sat down beside her. "Your fingers aching yet?"

"Not yet. Well, maybe a little," she admitted.

"Are you all right?" he asked.

"No," she said simply.

"You want to tell me about it?" he said.

Diane turned to him. "I'd like to. But you're sworn to uphold the law." She smiled in spite of herself.

Frank laughed. "Sounds like you've had another interesting day. There is some discretionary room in my code of conduct. Want to give me a try?" He stood, pulling her up with him and kissing her forehead. He led her into the living room.

The fire had died to glowing embers, illuminating very little. Frank turned on the light and Diane shaded her eyes, feeling like a vampire. She realized she had been playing the piano in the dim light of dusk. Frank stoked the fire until it blazed again. The warmth felt good.

"What's this about?" he asked.

"First, how was your day?" asked Diane. "We always talk about my day, which inevitably ends up dominating the conversation."

"That's because your life is more interesting than mine," said Frank, grinning. "This is starting to sound like it's going to be a really interesting story this time." He paused and Diane said nothing. "Okay. My day was a bit frustrating. We've had a big upsurge in identity thefts all over Atlanta—individuals and businesses—and I'm finding them hard to track down. I suspect we have an organized theft ring in operation. What's mainly happening is the perpetrator is taking out loans in victims' names, then disappearing with the money. The trail is almost entirely electronic. Many of the victims are large businesses in Atlanta. Now, see, mine's rather boring. Tell me about your day—after I get us some coffee."

They ended up ordering a pizza—large, thin crust with mushrooms, pepperoni, and sausage. They ate it and talked about music.

"You're right," Diane said. "The seventh chords are easier even after only a couple of times of doing the exercise. I'll be able to hang on to a rock face with my pinkies after this. Who knew?"

"All pianists," he said, taking his last bite of pizza. "Now, tell me about your day."

They took their coffee into the living room and Diane described it, beginning with finding the body of Edgar Peeks and ending with looking at the videotape. She didn't say anything about the figure she and Colin saw in the tape.

"I heard about Chief Peeks," said Frank. "Ben says I should move to Atlanta, where there's less crime."

"I tell you, this has rattled the community. The city council has finally done something now that Edward Van Ross is back in town."

"They hardly do anything without his approval," said Frank. Diane knew he liked Van Ross, but she also knew he disapproved of his power. "Now, what's your dilemma?" said Frank.

"I recognize the figure on the tape," she said.

She picked up the file from the coffee table and took out a still photo she had made of the figure caught by the late mayor's security camera.

"You recognize this? How? It's so fuzzy it could be a bear for all I can tell."

"It's the tilt of the shoulders, the gait, the angle of the head. You can recognize people just looking at the body—if you know them," she said.

"Yes. I've done that. And I've been wrong. Can be quite embarrassing. Who do you think it is?" he said.

Diane started to say, but was saved by the sound of the door chimes. Frank went to answer it, and Diane sipped her coffee by the fire, wrapping her hands around the cup to warm her cold fingers.

"Look who's here," said Frank as he entered the room with David.

"I got your messages," said David.

Diane stared at him for a moment. "I thought you were going on vacation," she said.

"It's a working vacation," he said. He sat down on the couch opposite Diane and Frank.

"David," began Diane. She hesitated. "I've been really worried."

"Don't be. I haven't gone off the deep end," said David.

Frank sat back and looked at Diane a moment. He had guessed who she suspected was in the photograph, she realized—probably even before David came. There weren't many people besides Frank himself that Diane would worry about so much.

"I hope not," said Diane. She noticed that David had come in carrying a briefcase.

"As I said, I haven't gone off the deep end, but I have been delving into conspiracy theories," he said.

"Okay, I can see we're going to need more coffee," said Frank. "Please wait; I don't want to miss anything."

"David," said Diane when Frank walked out of the room. "Were you at the mayor's house the night he was killed?" She showed him the picture from the surveillance tape. "I'm probably one of the few people who would recognize you."

David stared at Diane for a long time. He frowned. "I've been in a quandary about this," he said. "You don't think I killed him, do you?"

"Of course not, but Garnett's in jail, and everything seems to be going to hell. I just need to know what's going on in my corner of the world. What were you doing there?"

"I was casing the place. I wanted to find out when I could break in and plant a bug."

"What? David? What? Have you gone completely nuts?" Diane hardly knew what to say.

David smoothed out the back fringe of his hair. "I know it kind of looks that way. But I had my reasons."

Frank came in with three mugs of coffee. "I think I remembered how you like your coffee, David," he said. "One sugar and one tablespoon of cocoa powder."

"That's it," he said. He took the mug. "This feels good. It's chilly outside. Gets into your bones."

Frank took Diane's old coffee and put it on the mantel and gave her a fresh cup. He sat down beside her with his own mug of coffee and took a drink.

"I hope I didn't miss anything," he said.

"Not much," Diane muttered.

"Okay, David, what's your conspiracy theory?" said Frank.

"I started noticing strange things in the lab," David said.

Frank laughed. "This is sounding like a horror movie," he said.

David smiled. "It is. There was something hinky about the crime scenes Bryce sent me and Neva to. There were some he did not want us to go on."

"Who did he send?" asked Diane.

"He would go, or he would assign Rikki after she came," he said. "Or no one went. He called it prioritizing."

"Did you ask him about any of it?" asked Diane.

"Sure. Many times. He told me he was in charge of the crime lab now and how he made decisions was none of my business. Soon after, he assigned me to the lab full-time and stopped me from working crime scenes. When the judge was murdered, Bryce assigned Neva to work a convenience store burglary, and he and Rikki did the judge's crime scene."

"You don't think he just wanted to do the high-profile crimes himself?" asked Frank.

"No," said David. "I think he had an agenda and I think it involved the mayor. And I don't think it was legal."

Both Frank and Diane stared at him in silence. Diane was beginning to wonder if he hadn't gone over the edge. But this was David. She knew him. She trusted him.

"You're going to have to give us some more explanation," she said.

David opened his briefcase. The snap of the latches sounded loud in the quiet room. He took out a folder, placed it on the coffee table, and opened it. Diane saw a chart of numbers with notes scribbled at the bottom. Frank reached for it, examining the page.

"You remember the rash of burglaries we had last

year? Remember how Jefferies made a big deal over
the charge that the old mayor and his administration
couldn't do anything about crime, especially crimes
against the average homeowner? He hammered over
and over on the point that the old police chief
wouldn't even deal with home burglaries. How the
police told victims they probably wouldn't be able to
get their property back."

"Yes," said Diane. "I remember. Unfortunately,
that's what the police usually did say when a house
was burgled."

"And remember how the burglaries went down after
Jefferies had been mayor for a while?" said David.

"Yes," said Diane.

Frank studied David's notes. "Where did you get
these figures?" he asked, not looking up.

"The police department, court records." David gestured toward the paper Frank was holding. "I checked
into the numbers. Total burglaries went down, but the
arrest rate for burglaries stayed the same as it was
under the old mayor. So did the conviction rate,"
said David.

"What are you saying?" said Diane.

"He's saying the whole thing was staged to win the
election," said Frank. "That the mayor or his supporters had to be behind the surge in burglaries. Okay, you
have my attention. What else do you have, David?"

Chapter 23

"Is that what you are saying?" said Diane. "Jefferies was behind the rash of burglaries?"

She sat openmouthed, staring at David. With what she was finding out about Jefferies from Garnett and others, she didn't know why she should be so surprised. But she was. What David was suggesting was beyond political control of jobs or lying to try and claim her lab. If it was true, this was serious criminal activity he was engaged in to get elected.

"Yes, I think he was behind the burglaries," said David.

She took the sheet from Frank and looked at the numbers. "So, he got someone to burgle the homes, then had them stop a month after he came into office? That seems incredible."

"It does," said David, "but how else do you read the numbers? How would the burglaries decrease but the arrest rate stay the same? Maybe it could have been a burglary ring that just happened to move on a month after the election. Nice and convenient for Jefferies. I prefer my conspiracy theory."

"What about the crime scenes?" began Diane. She paused a moment. "Were those the ones you and Neva were excluded from?"

"You got it," said David. "The newspapers reported that the stolen items were recovered in several instances. Good stories. Jefferies wanted to make sure the voters knew they did the right thing by electing him. But why weren't the perps arrested?"

"You have more?" asked Frank. "This investigation you've embarked upon—is that why you resigned?"

"Yes. I didn't tell Neva about my suspicions. I wanted to collect more data and I didn't want to involve anyone else, just in case it turned out I was completely bonkers after all. That's why I didn't say anything to you," he said to Diane.

"What else do you have?" Frank asked.

"This next stuff is what I find really disturbing," he said, pulling some photographs from his file.

Diane saw photographs of fingerprints, of crime scenes, trace evidence, more notes. David had been busy.

"Bryce should have just fired me," said David. "I don't know why the stupid son of a bitch thought restricting me to the lab would keep all his dirty little secrets hidden from me. The lab is where most of the work is done."

David picked up a photograph of several fingerprints. "These are from the investigation of the murder of Judge Karen McNevin. Bryce worked this scene. Rikki hadn't been hired then. He brought all the evidence back for me to process. The first thing I noticed on the lifting tape—besides the fingerprints—was a lot of trace."

He pulled out another photograph taken through a microscope. It showed small particles with a cubic crystal habit. Diane recognized sodium chloride. There were other particles she didn't recognize.

"Salt," said Diane.

"This salt was on all the trace lifts—some on the fingerprint lifts, and in fact, on all the trace from the crime scene," said David.

He picked up another photograph. This one showed a close-up of some trace fibers supposedly lifted from the crime scene. There was something else stuck to the cellophane, some kind of red-brown flakes. Diane didn't recognize them.

"The flakes are peanut skins; the other tan particles are pieces of peanuts," said David. "They are also pervasive in the trace from the judge's crime scene, including the dog hair that was lifted from her body. It was consistent with the accused's dog. Bryce lifted the hair with the fingerprint tape, and it has the salt and peanut parts all over it."

David stopped and looked up from the pictures. "Let me tell you something about the murder," he said.

He took out the crime scene photographs and laid them on the table. Frank's coffee table was now covered in photographic evidence.

"Judge McNevin was shot at home," said David. "It was on a Saturday. Saturdays her husband took their two kids to a movie, or someplace equally entertaining. Saturday was Karen's day to stay home and catch up on her law journals. People who knew her knew she would be alone in the house on a Saturday afternoon. Her husband said she liked to soak in the tub while she read. She had a tub tray she used to keep her journals on and a glass of wine. She'd gotten out of the tub, put on a robe, and was in the bedroom when she was confronted by her killer and strangled to death."

Diane and Frank listened as David spoke, not interrupting. Diane wasn't sure where this was going, but she was developing a hard knot in the pit of her stomach. Frank's living room was lit only by task lighting, and in the growing darkness the recesses were fading into shadows. Diane got up abruptly and turned on the overhead chandelier, and suddenly everything in the room was made visible again.

"I'm sorry," she said, looking at Frank and David staring at her. "I just needed light."

David hadn't taken a drink of his coffee for a while, and it was probably growing cold. One reason he said he liked putting chocolate in it was that it tasted better when it got cold. Diane thought she should warm it for him. But then she wondered if she was just trying to delay hearing what he had to say, delay the dreaded thing to come, whatever it was. She mentally shook herself. *This is just stupid,* she thought. *It's the time of year. It always does this to me, keeps me off balance. As it does David.*

"Go on," she said.

David pulled out the autopsy photos.

"Where did you get the autopsy photographs?" asked Diane. "I had to camp out in Shane's lab practically to get him to give me anything."

"I hacked into his computer," said David.

Diane and Frank both raised their eyebrows.

David raised his palms and shrugged. "What do you do when it's the people in authority you suspect of being criminals? I collected most of this stuff before I resigned, so technically I was authorized to see it."

"Go on," said Frank. From the deep crease in his forehead and the frown on his face, Diane could see he was worried too. She wasn't sure whether he was concerned about David or about what David was saying.

"Lloyd Bryce worked the crime scene. He wouldn't allow either me or Neva to come with him. Got rather sharp about it, as I recall. He came back with the evidence for me to process. I found all this trace.

"Now, I happened to know Judge Karen McNevin and her husband. They were friends. Karen was deathly allergic to peanuts. She had a very fast reaction when she came in contact with them and always carried an EpiPen. She couldn't even touch them. At parties she stood far away from anyplace where there were mixed nuts. She wouldn't have any in her home.

"On the other hand," continued David, "Evan Donovan, the man accused of strangling her to death, is an avid peanut eater. I spoke with his friends. He even does that thing where he puts them in his Coke. His house is littered with salted peanut parts. I know, because I broke in and looked. The trace evidence came from his house and not the crime scene."

David sat back and waited.

"Couldn't it be transfer?" said Frank.

"On the lifts, the salt residue covers the entire square from corner to corner. If it was transfer, it wouldn't have covered the tape that thoroughly and evenly. Bryce lifted the fingerprint and trace from Donovan's house and was rather sloppy about it. Also look at the autopsy report. There is no evidence in the pictures or mention by the ME of an allergic reaction. She would have had a serious skin reaction if Donovan had touched her throat with peanut residue all over his hands." David let out a breath. "This evidence is why I quit."

"You're saying Donovan was framed," said Frank. He said it more like a statement than a question.

"Evan Donovan was made to be a fall guy. He was raised in an abusive home. Both he and his brother Bobby have low-normal IQs. Evan has a temper. He threatened Judge McNevin when his brother Bobby was sentenced."

"Why was she killed?" asked Frank.

"If you wanted to take over a town, what would you do?" said David. He didn't wait for an answer. "Get elected as mayor, start appointing friends to powerful positions, get yourself a crime lab, a bone lab, a DNA lab, and get your own judge appointed. But there was a little hitch. There was no vacancy on the bench. So one of the current judges had to go."

"This is some conspiracy theory. If the mayor had been successful in all this, what was the point? What was he going to do with it?" said Frank.

"I don't know," said David. "But if he was into criminal activities, like drugs, for instance, it's good to have the crime lab on your side. If you want to control who goes to jail and who goes free, it would be a nice thing to have a DNA lab. And what a good place to have all three of those—a small town where all three labs are housed in a museum. These kinds of labs are usually in big cities, which are harder to get control of. Rosewood probably looked like easy pickings, especially since Jefferies once had family here." David stopped and steepled his hands. "If we want to find out who killed the mayor and the chief of police, we need to do a little victimology. I think we need to find out exactly who Spence Jefferies and Edgar Peeks really are and what they were into."

Chapter 24

Diane and Frank studied and tried to digest David's collection of information, discussing the permutations and possibilities that would explain the evidence. Diane was finding it mentally exhausting. She spotted another folder in David's briefcase and pulled it out.

"What's this?" she asked.

"Oh, that's my sociological research," he said. He took the folder from Diane and opened it. "This is interesting."

The first page was a map. On closer examination, Diane recognized it as a map of the voting districts in Rosewood.

"The red dots are burglaries," said David. "Notice that they cluster in areas where voting is traditionally the heaviest."

"The mayor was that organized?" Diane was incredulous.

"It's better than that," said David. "I analyzed the homes that were burgled. It was always a prominent member of some group—church, Lions Club, Rotary—and usually at least two members of the organization were victims. These are people with lots of connections and social networks who would talk about it at their club meetings and with their friends and acquaintances, thereby making the problem look even bigger. Having at least two members as victims just increased the perception that crime was rising at an alarming rate. Our late mayor was a clever devil."

Frank noticed that his neighborhood was one of those David had marked.

"I do recall some folks down the street had a problem," said Frank.

"I think one reason you weren't hit," said David, "is that you work in Atlanta. You'd talk to fewer people in Rosewood about being a victim. And you are a detective, so you might just take it upon yourself to go after the perps."

"I would have," said Frank.

"How would he get this much information?" said Diane.

"Easy. One good graduate student could gather it for him. Besides, these days almost everything is online. And there's the good old-fashioned way: join the local chamber of commerce and they'll give you a truckload of information on their members, on businesses, demographic profiles, neighborhood maps—you name it, they've got it. Jefferies had to live in Rosewood for at least a year before he ran for mayor. I think he used that time to gather information. Remember, he had Rosewood connections too. His grandparents lived here."

"I didn't know that. What else do you know about him?" asked Diane. "I know he moved here from Atlanta, but I don't know much more than that."

David pulled several pages from his folder. "More sociology," he said, smiling.

Diane recognized the pattern of information. It was a social network diagram. When she worked for World Accord International, her team would do a social network analysis of the villages they were going into. That let them know who the community leaders were and what their range of influence was.

"The diagram starts with Spence Jefferies and lists the people he went to college with—Edgar Peeks and Lloyd Bryce."

"Didn't Jefferies go to the University of Pennsylvania? You aren't telling me that Lloyd Bryce graduated from Penn?" said Diane.

"Diane," said David, "you know very well that a

person can be both smart and stupid at the same time."

"I'm just amazed that he had scores good enough to get in," she said.

"He did," said David. "They all went to the Wharton School of Business."

"Really? I hardly know what to say. That's a hard place to get into. But what qualified Bryce to run a crime scene unit?" asked Diane.

"Nothing," said David. "Was that not obvious?"

"He really got into Wharton on his own?" said Diane. She was having a hard time wrapping her brain around Bryce having any intelligence whatsoever.

David laughed. "Bryce's scores were the highest of any of them."

Diane shook her head. "Who knew?"

"Exactly how do you know?" asked Frank. "How were you able to get such personal information?"

"Part of the information I got from Bryce himself. He likes to brag," said David.

"And the other parts?" asked Frank.

"Through investigation," said David.

He and Frank held eye contact for several moments.

"You're a good investigator," said Frank.

"Yes, I am," said David.

Diane could see Frank wanted to ask more questions. And he probably realized he would get no satisfactory answers. David was very secretive about how he did things.

She looked at the diagram. It showed circles with the names of Lloyd Bryce, Edgar Peeks, and Spence Jefferies, with lines connecting all of them to one another. Edgar Peeks was also connected to several policemen he had hired. Lloyd Bryce was connected to the guard at the overlook, to the DNA tech/detective he wanted Jin to hire, to Rikki Gillinick, and to Jennifer Jeffcote-Smith. Jennifer was also connected to Shane Eastling, the new medical examiner.

"Do you think Shane Eastling was a member of Jefferies' little cabal?" asked Diane.

"I don't know," said David. "It could be that he simply knew Jennifer and recommended her. But he would have had to know Bryce was looking for a forensic anthropologist—ergo he would have to know Bryce in some capacity. However, it could have occurred in passing—at a crime scene Bryce mentioned he was looking and Shane knew somebody. I haven't done full research on Shane yet. Nor do I know where Bryce found Rikki or Curtis, or where Peeks found the policemen he hired. There's a lot I don't know."

"It's hard to fathom," commented Frank. "Where did Shane Eastling go to school, do you know?"

"Cal State and the University of Chicago," said David. "He grew up outside of Los Angeles, as did Jennifer."

"You know," said Frank, "you should just turn this over to Janice Warrick and let the police take over from here. Now that the principals at the center of this are dead, they're no longer a problem. That is, except to discover what they were up to and who killed them. But it's not your problem to solve. With the things Diane discovered about how Bryce mishandled the crime scene, Garnett should be in the clear." He paused and smiled. "The detectives are probably now looking for the shadowy figure," he added.

David winced. "Look, I suppose I need to talk about that," he said.

Diane didn't say anything. Neither did Frank. The three of them sat in the light of the chandelier staring at one another.

"I pulled the LUDs on all their phones," said David. "There was nothing that wasn't expected. That surprised me. Then I happened to remember seeing Bryce talking on a cell that was different from the one he normally uses. And I realized—they used prepaid cells for their activities."

"What exactly were their activities?" asked Frank. "You've made a convincing case that they were up to something, but do you have any idea exactly what that was?"

"No. I haven't a clue. That's why . . . That's why . . . Well, damn. Look, like I told Diane earlier, I was casing the mayor's place looking at who came and went. I was also looking for an opening to put a bug in his house. I thought it was important to find out what he was up to, since I was convinced that he killed a judge and he staged a rash of burglaries for his own political advancement."

"Bug the mayor's house?" said Frank. "You were really going to do that?"

"I couldn't think of anything else. And yes, that means I was there the night he was killed. But the only person I saw that night was Garnett. I believed he was innocent, but I didn't know it for a fact. I didn't hear anything. There were no gunshots."

He stopped and took a breath. He looked miserable.

"I've been agonizing about coming forward. I didn't want to muddy the waters. From my point of view, I knew I wasn't the one who killed them. Until Garnett was arrested, I had no idea anyone would blame him."

"What are you going to do now?" said Frank.

"I don't know. Come forward but leave out the part about wanting to bug Jefferies, I guess. But I don't have a good story as to why I was skulking around in a hoodie. I thought I might say I wanted to report Bryce but was undecided, so I just stood outside his house trying to figure out what I should do. Lame, I know. But the truth—well, more or less."

"For now, Garnett is in the clear, I think. I'll find out," said Diane. "You can tell the truth. Say you had all this evidence that Jefferies may have been involved in a murder, but you couldn't go to the police because you thought the chief of police was in on it. So you decided to investigate Jefferies yourself. That's all true. You don't have to say you were going to plant an illegal bug. But first, let's see what's up." She turned to Frank. "What do you think?"

"That sounds like a plan," he said. He looked at David. "One way or another, you're going to have to clear up your presence on the video."

David nodded. "I should have thought of the simple explanation. That's the trouble when you embark on a life of crime. Your thinking gets muddled."

Diane went to the phone and called Colin Prehoda. He would know if Garnett had been released. She dialed his cell and he answered on the first ring.

"Diane, I'm glad you called. There are some things I need to tell you."

After listening to Colin, Diane hung up the phone and sat back down on the couch beside Frank.

"Well, the good news is they've dropped the charges against Garnett on the murder of Jefferies because the evidence was muddied by Bryce. The bad news is it was a bullet from Garnett's gun that killed Edgar Peeks—and Garnett had his gun on him when Colin and I found him over the body."

Chapter 25

"What are you saying?" said Frank. "Garnett shot Edgar Peeks?" He looked as disbelieving as Diane felt.

"That's what the police are saying," she said. "That's what ballistics shows, and it sounds very much like what Colin believes."

"Who did the ballistics?" said David.

"I'm sure they did it at Rosewood's ballistic lab," said Diane. "Unless they sent it to the GBI, but I doubt they did that. I didn't ask."

Diane was still reeling from the news. She grabbed Frank's hand. It was warm.

"I don't believe it," she said. "I can't believe Garnett's a murderer. Something is wrong."

"What does Prehoda want you to do?" asked Frank.

"He wants me to continue to investigate, but he's up against the wall on this one. He says if we can discover what the mayor and his friends were up to, then we can show that Garnett had reason to fear them, that he had reason to fear for Rosewood. I didn't have a chance to tell him about Judge McNevin. He was in a hurry. But it will certainly reinforce his thinking."

David stood up. "I have to go downtown right now. They need to know I was there."

He looked at all the papers and photographs lying on the coffee table as if it was going to be impossible to pick them all up and get them back in order.

"Wait on that," said Frank as David bent down to

pick up his briefcase. "It won't change the ballistics
evidence, and right now you're under the radar. That
gives you an investigative advantage."

Diane looked at Frank in surprise. She thought he
would be the one to insist that David go to the police
immediately and identify himself as the person in the
video. David was surprised too. He looked blankly at
Frank for a moment, still stooped over his briefcase,
then slowly sat back down. He let out a deep breath.
Diane understood his relief. The revelation could
ruin David.

"A few minutes ago," said Frank, straightening
the papers on his coffee table, putting them into or-
derly stacks again, "I said this is now the police's
business and they should be the ones to deal with it.
But I've since rethought that position. I've been
looking at your network diagram and it's got me
wondering."

Frank put a stack of photographs down and leaned
forward, resting his forearms on his knees.

"In the beginning, it looked to you like the mayor
was in charge of this conspiracy, cabal, or whatever
you want to call it because he was the mayor, he was
in the highest leadership position. But was he the
leader? Maybe, maybe not."

Frank put the tips of his fingers on the page with
the diagram. "You were able to network only the people who were actually seen together. Any one of us
could have made this diagram from what we knew
about the official relationships among these people.
Consider the possibility that this is all that's meant to
be seen. Are there others involved we are unaware
of? How many people in the police department are in
on whatever it is? For that matter, what about other
areas of the government, or businesses in Rosewood?
What about the people the mayor and his buddies put
in the police department? What are they doing now?
Taking up the banner? I hate to say it, but I think
you have to continue doing what you are doing until
you can answer those questions."

David didn't say anything for a moment. He just rubbed his hand over his bald head. "Right now I'm at a loss for where to look," he said. "That's why I wanted to listen to what went on in the mayor's house. I was hoping for a new lead. I mean, what the hell was his goal? It had to be more than what we see."

"He lived in Atlanta before he moved to Rosewood," said Diane. "Perhaps the answer lies there. Does he have any relatives still here?"

"No relatives. His grandparents are dead," said David. "He had an advertising business in Atlanta, the same one he still owned when he was murdered. They do local Atlanta commercials. From what I could find out, they are squeaky clean."

"Have you looked at companies in any of the other principals' names?" said Frank.

"Peeks worked in a recruitment firm in Atlanta. Bryce was in banking—he was a vice president of a bank in Connecticut," said David. "I haven't been able to find anything suspicious so far. None of the companies are under any kind of investigation. I'm still looking. The only really suspicious thing is they all made a lot more money in their former jobs than they do here. Except the mayor. He's the only one who still had ties to his former business—as far as I know now. As I said, I'm still looking."

"That should tell us something right there," said Diane. "My impression of them is that they don't seem to be the type of people who would take a substantial downgrade in pay."

"None of them had any shadow companies that I can find," continued David. He shook his head. He seemed at a loss.

"How about the next tier down in your chart?" said Frank. "Rikki, what's her name."

David gave Frank a blank stare for a moment. "Damn. I didn't think of Lollipop. That would have required a paradigm shift. I'll do that."

"There's one place you can go that may already

have quite a bit of information on Jefferies," Frank said.

"Where?" asked David.

"Walter Sutton, the ex-mayor," said Diane. "Of course. He would have investigated Jefferies during the campaign—hell, he would have had him followed."

David spent the night at Frank's. They worked out a plan to interview the ex-mayor, Walter Sutton. It would be a little tricky. Diane didn't really want the mayor to know exactly what was going on. He tended to be a sieve when it came to information. They decided to tell him they were helping Garnett. The mayor liked Garnett. Or at least he did the last time they checked. Sutton was not above abandoning people he thought might be a political drag on him. They decided to give him one juicy bit of information to chew on. Diane hoped it would make him more eager to give her information. She had been afraid that Walter Sutton might not want her to know the length he himself would go to to find information on an opponent.

Diane decided to do the interview herself and to go alone. She liked the idea of keeping David off the radar. Sutton would have it all over town that David was investigating. It didn't matter if people knew Diane was looking into the murders. Everyone already knew she worked for Garnett's lawyer.

Diane asked David where he had been holed up. He told her at the museum, in his rooms down in the basement. He'd been eating from the break room and the restaurant. It wasn't that he was avoiding his home, but his computer in his museum basement office was more powerful and was linked to the crime lab—unknown to Bryce.

"There's another thing we have to find out about," said Diane. "What Bryce was looking for in Jefferies' house. I know he was searching for something in particular, not just working the crime scene. Pendleton said they talked about some kind of list. If you had Jefferies' computer, could you find out what's on it? Janice said it's encrypted pretty heavily."

"Maybe," said David. "I could give it a try."

"Another thing," said Diane. "We need to tell Edward Van Ross what's going on—at least about Karen McNevin. He's the acting mayor and he needs to know that Jefferies may have had a judge murdered. Not to mention that his police department may be holding an innocent person for the crime."

"That's a full day you have planned tomorrow," said Frank.

"I know, and I'd better get to bed." She stood up and stretched.

Diane showed David the guest room and wished him good night.

"Get some sleep," she said.

"Actually, I feel better. It's good to get it off my chest. It's been worrying me, especially now—the anniversary. My dreams haven't been good lately."

"You trust David?" said Frank when they were in bed.

Diane was lying with her back up against his chest—*spoons*, she'd heard her grandmother call it. It felt comfortable and safe.

"Where did that come from?" said Diane. "Of course I do."

"Sometimes he's a little strange, and I wonder if he could have gone vigilante on us. I don't think he did, but it has crossed my mind."

"He wouldn't," said Diane. "No more than I would. He'll skirt the law—like breaking into a suspect's home and planting a bug if the circumstances are dire enough. But murder? No. Absolutely not."

"How good is he with computers?" asked Frank.

"You know how good Mike is at rock climbing?" said Diane. "David is that good with computers."

"That good?" Frank said.

"Yes. As good as you are a lover," she said, turning over to face him.

"Wow, he's that good, is he?" said Frank.

*　　*　　*

Diane let David sleep in. For breakfast Frank fixed her one of his good stick-to-your-ribs recipes, oatmeal mixed with fried apples. She left David a note, and she and Frank parted at the door; Frank drove off to Atlanta, and Diane drove to the mayor's office to speak with Edward Van Ross. She had called ahead and found that Buford Monroe, the old-new chief of police, was there. She supposed that Edward wanted Monroe to hear what she had to say.

"Are you all right?" said Edward. His blue-gray eyes were clouded with concern. "I didn't have time to ask you about your misadventure at the meeting."

"It's mainly bruises," said Diane, though her face hurt like hell where Delamore had hit her.

"Would you mind telling us about it?" said Monroe. "I'm getting calls, you know, concerned citizens who want to know why a policeman was killed, what we are doing about it. You know how people are. They don't want to believe there's a bad cop."

Just a bad museum director. Diane had thought it was behind her. She thought since the GBI had done the math for them, she wouldn't have to deal with it. But apparently they wanted to hear what happened from her lips, maybe to look at her face when she told it, just to make sure. So she told them the story again.

The chief of police pulled on his lower lip as Diane spoke. Edward had no nervous gestures. He sat listening, one arm on the table, the other resting on the arm of the chair, his frown deepening as the story progressed.

"Why on earth did you go out on the cliff?" said Chief Monroe when Diane finished the story. "That's what I don't understand."

"Diane is a caver," said Edward. "She climbs rocks. I imagine that was a familiar place for her and one that didn't represent danger—as staying with Delamore obviously did."

The chief looked unconvinced. Not, Diane realized, that he doubted her story, just that he couldn't imagine feeling safe and cozy hanging on the side of a cliff.

"Edward is right," said Diane. "I've climbed that cliff many times. I was familiar with it."

"Ah," said Monroe. He smiled. He seemed to understand now.

"There's something I need to tell you," said Diane. "It's about the evidence David analyzed from Judge McNevin's crime scene. He was very concerned about it and was hesitant to go to Bryce, for reasons which will become obvious."

Diane laid out the evidence to them that David had presented to her. They were astounded by what she had to say. Both of them were silent for a long while.

"This is bad," said Edward. "This is the worst thing that could happen to Rosewood. The credibility of law enforcement and criminal justice and public confidence in our government are at stake. This will not do. How sure are you?"

"The evidence is very compelling, and it convinced me. If you are asking me if it is conclusive—not completely. But it's so compelling that it renders the original theory of the crime improbable," she said. "If the evidence was falsified, as it appears it was, it may mean that the wrong man is being held for the judge's murder."

"We have to untangle this," said Edward. "We can't have anything like this in Rosewood." He turned to the chief. "What does Bryce have to say for himself about irregularities in procedures at the mayor's crime scene?" he said.

"I asked him about dusting only for Garnett's prints," said the chief, "and about several troubling questions that other detectives have brought to my attention. And you know we are being sued for ten million dollars because of that forensic anthropologist fiasco."

Diane wanted to tell him not to get off the subject, but she kept her mouth shut.

"I know," said Edward. "We have our lawyers working on that. What did Bryce say?"

"He denied that he only looked for Garnett's

prints," said the chief. "He denied just about everything we asked him. He kept saying he handled all the crime scenes to the best of his ability. He blamed this Jeffcote-Smith woman for the loss of Sheriff Canfield's bones. I tell you, Canfield is having a fit. To tell you the truth, Lloyd Bryce can plead incompetence and there isn't much we can do, except fire him. That's all we have on him—incompetence."

"Which brings me to another topic," said the mayor, turning to Diane. "We have relieved Bryce of his position. We want you to take back the crime lab."

Diane was silent for a full minute. "The museum," she began, and the mayor raised his hand to ward off what she was going to say.

"Mother and Colin Prehoda drew up new contracts. Nothing like this will happen again. If it should, the crime lab will be moved from museum property at your discretion. No appeal, no higher authority than you," he said.

"Very well," said Diane and wondered why she was agreeing. But deep down she knew. It was the same reason Buford Monroe agreed to take his old job back as chief of police. It was a vindication. No matter the reasons for what had happened, getting fired stung. And vindication soothed the sting.

Another reason she said yes was that in her heart Diane enjoyed the crime lab. She liked to catch bad guys. It was true she had been happy with all her free time, but she was happy with the lab too. Perhaps there was a compromise—making David assistant director, for instance.

"What about Rikki?" said Diane. "I believe she's in the thick of things with the mayor and his buddies."

"You can fire her," said Edward. "Or you can keep her for a while and try to get information out of her. You know how to do these things."

"When do you want me to start?" asked Diane.

"Just as soon as you are able. I have the papers here," he said.

Edward motioned to a clerk and he brought over several papers for her to sign.

Diane read them. So, Vanessa Van Ross and Colin Prehoda drew them up. Everyone was back on board. Diane smiled and signed the contract.

Chapter 26

Diane walked to her SUV in the city hall parking lot. She stopped several feet away and looked at it for a moment. A ray of sunlight peeked through the blanket of winter clouds and reflected off the bright red finish. It looked pretty. She liked her vehicle. *At least it didn't get trashed this time.* She thought about the number of times her attackers had taken their anger out not only on her but also on her car.

As she was about to get in, she saw Janice Warrick and Izzy coming toward her.

"You need to put a steak or something on that face," said Izzy, squinting as if it hurt to look at her. "It still looks pretty bad."

"I know. I tried makeup, but I end up looking like a corpse," said Diane. She stood and waited. From their expressions, she could tell they wanted to talk, probably about Garnett. Izzy shifted his weight from one foot to the other. Janice studied the ground, moving a pebble with the toe of her shoe. They both believed Garnett killed Peeks, and they felt guilty about believing it, thought Diane. They wanted her to tell them they were wrong.

"It doesn't look good for Garnett," said Izzy.

"What about Shane Eastling?" said Diane. "He's been acting kind of . . . kind of like he's on the other side. Could he have substituted the bullet?"

Janice shook her head. "I was at the autopsy. So

was Izzy. We wanted to get the bullet to ballistics as soon as possible."

"We saw Eastling dig it out of Peeks' brain," said Izzy, wrinkling his face.

Diane wondered whether that was the first autopsy he had ever attended. She couldn't imagine it. He'd been a policeman for a long time.

"Chief Monroe is getting less inclined to look for another killer," said Janice. "He wants everything wrapped up real quick. I'm afraid they are going to cut Garnett loose," she said.

"We still want you to look into it," said Izzy.

"I will," said Diane. "I have a hard time believing he killed Peeks. There has to be an answer."

Izzy and Janice both seemed to relax.

"Even if, by some . . . Even if he did kill Peeks," said Izzy, "there must have been a reason that he doesn't want to talk about—like protecting somebody, something like that. And the evidence against him for doing Jefferies is nothing, in my book." He shrugged. "I'm afraid they'll want to lump all the murders together just to get this over with."

"I don't intend to let it go," said Diane. "You know I'm back in charge of the crime lab."

"We heard," said Izzy. "That's great. Bryce is in this up to his eyeballs in some way."

"He's slippery," said Janice. "I interviewed him about how he worked the Jefferies crime scene. He denied framing Garnett. Gave some razzle-dazzle about first finding prints with black lights before lifting them. I told him he'd still have to use special powders." Janice smiled proudly. "He tried to tell me I didn't know what I was talking about. Then he said both of the surfaces where he got the prints were shiny and he could see that only one set of prints was there. And I said, 'Even on the kitchen counter?' He stuck to his story. The chief thought he was just trying to look incompetent rather than guilty. I don't know. Like I said, Bryce is slippery."

"Bryce and Rikki were looking for a list at the crime scene," said Diane. "Did Bryce say anything about a list?"

Janice raised her eyebrows and shrugged. "They were looking for something, I'd wager, but I don't know what. Want me to get Bryce back in?" she asked.

Diane shook her head. "Let's keep it to ourselves right now. Van Ross suggested I might want to keep Rikki on for a while to see if she reveals anything."

"I never realized he could be so sneaky," said Janice, smiling. "He seems so nice."

The cold was getting to Diane and she started to shiver. "I'm going to the museum. There are a few leads I'm working on. I don't know how I'm going to prove who killed Jefferies and Peeks, but I will." She stopped and looked sharply at Janice. "Who took Garnett's gun at the crime scene?"

Janice Warrick frowned. "I did."

Diane's face fell. She thought she was on to something.

"I'll figure it out," she said and got in her car. *I don't know how, but I'll figure it out.*

Diane drove to the museum and parked in her space. She sat there watching people come and go, thinking she should have driven around back and entered by a rear door. She was looking so bad, worse than when Delamore first attacked her. *No kind of makeup is going to hide this,* she thought. And she'd planned on trying to see the former mayor today. *Well, hell.* She got out and walked into the museum and to her office. She got a few stares, but no one said anything. Good. Maybe it looked bad only in the sunlight.

David was in Andie's office waiting for her. Apparently he hadn't slept too late. He looked better. Obviously getting his fears and suspicions off his chest had been good for him.

"David, I'm rescinding your resignation," said Diane.

"What?" he said. He stared at her for a moment, then smiled. "You have the crime lab back."

"Yes, with a very tightly written contract—by Vanessa and Colin Prehoda. I want to go over everything and see what we have to do to get everything back on track. And I want to revisit the crime scene at the mayor's house before I see former mayor Sutton."

The relief he felt was obvious. Diane could almost see all the tension drain out of him as he collapsed onto one of the stuffed chairs. He looked like a man whose world was righted again.

"Nice to have things back to normal," said David. He rubbed his hands together. "What are you going to do with Lollipop?" he said.

"Keep her on and see if she leads us anywhere," said Diane.

Diane went to her office and called Colin.

"Since I'm back as director of the crime lab, I can't be working for you."

"Already severed," he said. "When Edward said he wanted to put you back in the crime lab, I took steps to change our relationship. But I hope you are still going to investigate the deaths."

"Yes. We all need to untangle this mess to get Rosewood right again," she said. "Can you tell me what Garnett says about the gun?"

"This is certainly difficult. I can tell you that he still maintains his innocence."

"I intend to go over the mayor's house again and see if I can find anything new. I'm sure the prosecutor will share with you any discoveries I make."

"You're sure of that, are you? I'll have to stand on him to make certain he does. You've dealt with Riddmann," said Colin.

Diane frowned. "Let's just see what happens."

She turned to David when she hung up. "Now, do you want to go see what condition my crime lab is in?"

Diane decided to enter the crime lab through her osteology lab. David was with her. So was Izzy. She had called Izzy in case Bryce decided to dig his heels in, and she didn't want to involve museum security.

"It's like *The Return of the King*," said David. "I'm Legolas. Though he had more hair and great ears, but I can handle it. Izzy's Gimli. And of course, you're Aragorn. You guys have your swords ready?"

Izzy chuckled. "I forgot my axe, but I have a gun. Will that do?"

Diane shook her head. David was far too giddy. He was acting like Jin.

She punched the key code that unlocked the door between the crime lab and her lab. She'd expected it to be like entering a tomb—dark, long, and vacant. It wasn't, of course. All the lights were on and Rikki was there, sitting in her cubicle working on her computer. Neva was getting a drink from the water fountain near the conference table. David had given her a heads-up; Diane could tell by the look on her face. She came over and hugged Diane.

"Welcome back," she said. "I am so glad to see you. Really glad."

However, Diane didn't think David had alerted Rikki. She looked surprised to see them. But her face quickly reverted back to a sullen expression. It was quite different from the isn't-this-fun attitude she showed when Canfield was blowing his top at Bryce. Bryce had probably told Rikki he wasn't in charge anymore.

What do you know about all this? thought Diane as she looked at Rikki.

Diane shifted her gaze to the rest of the room—a series of tiny labs in glass-walled work spaces containing equipment to examine and analyze almost anything, whether it was a gas, liquid, or solid. The crime lab could identify alloys, crystalline structures, and solutions. The techs could separate compounds into their components, separate large molecules from mixtures, or analyze their concentrations in a solution. They could separate and identify sounds, detect their frequency and intensity. They could analyze impressions, tool marks, and documents. The lab had an impressive array of national and international databases at its disposal—CODIS for DNA, AFIS for fingerprint. They had databases for bullet casings, tire treads, cigarette butts, fibers, shoe prints, animal tracks, hair, fur, textiles, buttons, paint, bugs, plants, and more; and they had software that could match, categorize, correlate, and render a map of all those things. It was a good lab. Diane was proud of it. Now she had to see what Bryce had done to it.

She inspected each room. It didn't look too bad, but in some of the rooms she was dismayed to see a thin layer of dust.

"Something's happened to the air filtration," said Diane.

"We tried to keep the equipment clean," said Neva. "But . . ." She didn't finish her sentence.

Diane knew by *we* Neva meant herself and David. Rikki's cubicle was the worst. There were food crumbs, coffee rings, and clutter all over her work space. And a jar filled with suckers—lollipops.

"You can drink coffee at the conference table, but nowhere else. No food is allowed in the lab at all," Diane said to her.

Rikki's frown deepened. "Bryce let me eat in my own space," she said.

"That's irrelevant," said Diane. "These are the rules now."

Rikki didn't say anything. Diane could see she wanted to glare at her but had the good sense not to. Diane wondered if she would quit. And if she didn't, why? She had been thinking about Edward's suggestion—let Rikki work here and see if she led her to any information about what the heck was going on. She may be just an innocent person who wasn't trained right, or she may be involved in whatever Bryce was. Diane wanted to find out.

"David is going to be assistant director of the crime lab," Diane continued. "In my absence, he's the boss. Miss Gillinick, since you're new here, you will be going on calls with either Neva or David until you get used to the way we do things."

"I've gone on lots of crime scenes by myself," said Rikki. "I do good work."

"That may be true, but I do things a little differently. Just consider this a refresher course," said Diane. "Now, David, call TechClean and have them go over the lab. This would be a good time to get a maintenance check on the equipment and have instruments recalibrated. Find out what is wrong with the air filtration. Do whatever it takes."

"Sure thing, boss," said David. Diane thought he gave the word *boss* a little too heavy an emphasis.

"Neva, I want you to catch me up on all the pending cases. We're also going back to Jefferies' house to go over the crime scenes again." Out of the corner of her eye she saw Rikki come alert. Diane couldn't tell whether she liked or disliked the idea. Maybe this would be a good learning experience for all of them.

Diane motioned to the conference table. "Rikki, I would like you to sit down and tell me everything you know about Sheriff Canfield's bones."

Rikki looked startled. "What? I don't know anything about them," she said.

"I just want you to tell me what you remember about them. Please, sit down," said Diane.

Rikki reluctantly walked over to the table and sat down, interlacing her fingers in front of her. The others sat around the table, including Izzy. Diane was surprised he didn't take his leave.

"What do you remember about the bones?" said Diane. "We need to try to find them. It's important."

"It has nothing to do with me. That was Jennifer's thing," said Rikki.

"But you're a member of the team; we need you to help. What do you remember?"

Rikki looked very uncomfortable with all their eyes on her.

"Bryce brought them up here. He said the sheriff's deputy gave them to him in the parking lot, and I believe him." Rikki lifted her chin as if daring them to disagree. "He gave them to Jennifer and she took them to the darkroom that Bryce told her to make into a lab." Rikki smirked. "Jennifer was really pissed about having to go from that big lab to a dinky darkroom. She hated it."

"What did she do with the bones?" said Diane.

"She got some plastic tubs and started sorting them. I watched her for a while. It's boring work. I don't know how she was sorting them. They all looked about the same to me. Just chunks of bone. I quit watching after a while. She worked for a long time."

"Who asked her to get coffee?" asked Diane.

Rikki shrugged. "I don't remember. She came out for a break and we just talked about getting coffee. We had to take the elevator and go down and around to the restaurant—it's better coffee than the break room. I think she volunteered. I don't remember."

"Did anyone else come up while she was gone?" asked Diane. "Any visitors to the lab?"

"No. I wasn't there the whole time. I went to the bathroom and had a smoke, since the overlook was closed off," she said.

Diane saw both Neva and David wince. She could swear they were about to duck.

"What?" said Diane. "You smoked on the overlook? Did you notice the signs that say this is a smoke-free building? The collections here are sensitive to contaminants like smoke—not to mention the equipment and the evidence. You don't smoke in here, in the bathroom, or anyplace inside the building."

Rikki didn't say anything, just hunched her shoulders. Diane looked at David and Neva.

"Did you know she was smoking?"

"I mentioned to her she wasn't supposed to," said Neva. "So did David. Bryce told her it was all right."

"And you didn't mention it to me?" said Diane.

"What is the big deal?" said Rikki. "A couple of cigarettes a day. This is a big building. We are on the top floor."

"It is a very big deal. And it is not to happen again. However, let's get back to the bones. What happened when you came back from the bathroom? Did you see anyone approach Jennifer's lab?" said Diane.

"No. There was just me and Bryce. Curtis was here for a while. He goes back and forth from here to the police station. I can't remember when he came or left," she said.

"How did you meet Bryce?" asked Diane.

"This sounds like more of an interrogation," said Rikki. "I haven't done anything."

"I'm just trying to verify your bona fides," said Diane. "I don't know anything about you."

"Well my résumé is on file," she said.

"Do you want to work here? I haven't asked you that. Perhaps you don't," said Diane.

"He was at the job fair on campus. I graduated from Emory. He and the chief of police had a booth and were taking applications. They called me a month or so ago."

"What about Curtis?" asked Diane. "Do you know how he knows Bryce?"

Rikki shrugged. "I have no idea."

"Where is the evidence from Jefferies' house?" asked Diane.

"Evidence?" said Rikki.

"The evidence you and Bryce collected from the mayor's house from both crime scenes," said Diane.

"Locked up in the vault, I guess," she said.

"What do you think happened to the bones?" asked Diane.

"Jennifer's bones?" Rikki shrugged. "I think she couldn't do anything with them so she got rid of them and claimed they were stolen. Bryce thinks you took them," said Rikki.

"Okay, thank you for answering my questions, Rikki. First, I think we'll take a look at the evidence from the mayor's house," said Diane.

Rikki's face brightened.

Chapter 27

Diane was puzzled by Rikki's reaction. She found it interesting—but puzzling. Rikki certainly bore watching.

"Is the computer in the vault?" asked Diane.

"It was taken to the police station," said Rikki.

"I think Janice delivered it here," said Izzy. "We didn't have anybody there to deal with the encryption. Bryce said he would find someone."

The room containing the vault was one of the rooms that needed some serious dusting. Diane, Neva, and David cleaned the examination tables before opening the vault.

The vault was the size of a small walk-in closet. Shelves filled with boxes of evidence lined the walls. Diane didn't think it looked quite as neat as when she last saw it, but perhaps she was being hypercritical.

The computer was there sitting on the shelf, its keyboard shoved in on its end beside it.

"Let's go through the evidence boxes first; then you take the computer, David, and see what you can do with it," said Diane.

There were two cardboard boxes with evidence from the mayor's house. Diane took the boxes from the Peeks and Jefferies murders to separate tables and opened them.

She took out the fingerprint cards first. There were four of them. One had Jefferies' prints, one had Peeks' prints, and two had Garnett's prints—one from the hall chest and one from the kitchen counter. That was all.

"Why aren't there more prints?" asked Diane.

"I don't know," said Rikki. "Bryce took the prints. I searched the house."

Diane took out evidence envelopes with blood samples from the Peeks and Jefferies scenes. Again, not enough samples. She took out the crime scene photographs. They were pretty good.

"I took those," said Rikki proudly.

"These are good," said Diane.

Rikki grinned broadly.

Diane studied the stills. The mayor was slumped on the floor, half on his back, beside a bar stool at the island in the kitchen. Blood was pooled under his head. There was a plate of what looked like nachos on the counter. Apparently a favorite of the mayor. A splatter of blood covered the counter in fine droplets.

Diane, David, and Neva laid out the victims' clothes, using a different table for each of the victims. Peeks' silk shirt and cashmere sweater were spattered with blood on the back. It was high-velocity spatter.

"Did you take any blood samples from the clothes?" asked Diane.

Rikki shrugged. "Bryce handled all the blood. He took some samples from the scene. He said that when what has occurred is self-evident, you can sample the evidence. Anything more is a waste of time and money. That was the big criticism they had of you— you wasted money," said Rikki.

"Did he take a representative sample?" said Diane.

"What?" asked Rikki.

"Under his philosophy, he would have to take a representative sampling. Did he?" she asked again.

"I don't know," Rikki said.

"One of the things we need to do is make sure all the blood belongs to Jefferies. We may have the perp's blood somewhere. That way we can reconstruct the crime scene."

"Someone came in and shot the mayor," said Rikki.

"Where did he come from?" said David. "Was he in the house waiting for him? Did Jefferies let him in? Did he know him? Was it a stranger? There's a lot of questions."

"What do you think happened?" asked Rikki. "It looks to me like he had to let him in. I mean, the mayor's house would have been hard to break in to."

"Possibly," said Diane. "But the only way you can get an accurate picture is to collect the evidence. If we are really lucky, the perp will have gotten a nosebleed." She smiled at Rikki.

Diane looked at the clothes again. Both victims had expensive tastes—Ermenegildo Zegna, Just Cavalli, Armani, Ferragamo. She poured out the effects found in their pockets and on their bodies. The two had identical signet rings embossed with an image of Alexander the Great. She rolled her eyes and shook her head.

"Look at this," said David. He handed Diane a watch that belonged to Mayor Jefferies.

Diane cocked an eyebrow.

"Expensive?" asked Izzy.

"About fifteen thousand dollars expensive," said Diane. "It's a BRM Chrono-Automatic watch. Very limited number made."

"Wow, can I hold it?" asked Izzy.

Diane handed it to him.

"What does it do? Is it some kind of computer?"

"It's a hand-crafted watch made with expensive materials," said Diane.

Izzy looked at his watch, then at the mayor's, and shook his head. "I could get me a good boat for fifteen thousand dollars," he said.

Diane noticed how uncomfortable Rikki was getting. She knew why.

"That's a nice watch you're wearing," Diane said.

Rikki gave a small self-conscious laugh. "My boyfriend gave it to me. It's a knockoff," she said.

"You'll have to tell your boyfriend he made a good buy. It's not a knockoff, it's a real Cartier Tank Française. Very nice," said Diane. She wondered whether that was the shiny object Officer Pendleton saw Rikki pocket at the crime scene.

"Really?" Rikki laughed nervously again. "He'll be pleased. How much is it worth, do you think?" she asked.

"It's also about fifteen thousand," said Diane.

"Wow," said Rikki. "He's not going to believe it."

Rikki sounded unconvincing to Diane, but maybe she was just prejudiced. Diane glanced at David and saw that he didn't believe her either. What Diane was wondering now was what it would take for Rikki to quit, to be so afraid of being found out, she would take off. Diane suspected there was a very specific reason she was sticking around.

"Well, it wasn't a robbery," said Izzy, "that's for sure."

"No," said Diane. "It doesn't seem to be a robbery."

She was wondering whether they all were that wealthy, or were they making a lot of money. The mayor alone was decked out in more than twenty thousand dollars' worth of clothes and accessories. The mayor's job didn't pay that much, but perhaps his Atlanta business was doing really well. She had a lot of questions for Janice to look into. She wondered whether Janice had searched Peeks' and Jefferies' homes.

"When are the funerals?" Diane asked. They all shrugged. "It looks like the mayor and his friends had a lot to leave their heirs. It would be interesting to discover who they are."

The door buzzer startled all of them. David went to answer it. After a few moments, he brought Jin back with him.

"IIi, guys," Jin said, raking his fingers through his black hair. "Good to see you back, boss," he said.

"Good to be back," she said. "Is this a social call?"

"Nope, I just found something interesting. You know that guy who wanted me to hire him? Curtis something."

"Curtis Crabtree," said Diane.

"Well, in the scuffle he left some epithelials behind and I decided to run them," said Jin.

"What did you find?" asked Neva.

"He had alleles in common with Edgar Peeks," said Jin.

"Brothers?" asked Diane.

"Cousins maybe; maybe uncle and nephew," said Jin.

"Did you know they were related?" Diane asked Rikki.

She shook her head. "No. It's news to me."

Chapter 28

"No," said Jin, taking a big bite of pizza. "I'm Legolas. I'm always Legolas. You're Gandalf, David. You're the one who disappeared for a while, then came back."

"All I know is," said Neva, helping herself to a slice, "that I'm Arwen, the most beautiful creature in Middle-earth."

Diane listened to them happily discussing their *Lord of the Rings* character preferences. She had tried to get Frank on the phone to tell him they were having pizza in her office, but he didn't answer. Mike had come to join them briefly but had to leave early to get ready for his class in gemology. Izzy had stayed. That was somewhat of a puzzlement to Diane. She didn't know if he was asked to guard her or what.

Rikki had gone home. That was a relief to everyone. They didn't know which side she was on, and Diane thought that, like her, they felt uneasy being constantly just a little dishonest with her.

"Okay," said Jin. "Who's Rikki?"

"Gollum," both Neva and David said together, and they all laughed.

Diane was about to sit down and eat a piece of pizza when she heard a noise in Andie's office. She opened the connecting door just as Andie was entering. She was all bundled up in slacks, a wool poncho, and gloves. She had a cap pulled over her frizzy auburn hair.

"Oh, I'm glad you're here," said Andie. "I have your cell phone. Wait till you see this."

"Would you like some pizza?" said Diane. "We have plenty."

"Pizza? Thanks, but I just ate." Andie took out a box and opened it. "This is great." She slipped the phone from the box, flipped it open, and turned it on. "It's a camera phone like the old one and has all the bells and whistles on it. But it also has this."

She punched a couple of keys and the phone started talking.

"Take a left on Rose Street," it said. "Go point two miles."

Diane looked at the map on the digital screen.

"It has GPS mapping," said Andie. "You just punch in the city and where you want to go and it will tell you how to get there. Cool, huh?"

"Yes, it is," said Diane. "This is nice. It really is. How much more a month is this going to cost me?"

"Just ten dollars," said Andie. "I put all your numbers in it. At least, the ones I know."

"Thanks, Andie, I appreciate it. It's a great phone. You off to your gemology class?"

"Yes, and I hope it's uneventful this time," she said. "Last time, we were just starting on opals. You know that's my birth stone. Mike was saying they have water in them. I don't understand that. He was about to explain when little Ethan turned up missing. And you know the rest." Andie looked at her watch. "Well, gotta go. See you tomorrow."

Just as Andie was leaving, Frank walked through the door. "I thought I'd catch you still at work," he said.

"Hey, Frank," said Andie. "See you." She was out the door.

"Was it something I said?" said Frank, watching Andie leave.

"She's off to learn about gemstones." Diane paused. "I'm director of the crime lab again."

"You always have such eventful days," he said. "So, was the crime lab a reward for almost getting killed?"

"No, it was a reward for not being Bryce," she said. "Because of him the evidence is now suspect from a whole string of crime scenes processed by the lab, and the city's dealing with a multimillion-dollar lawsuit from Jennifer Jeffcote-Smith, the forensic anthropologist he hired. Did I tell you I got served on that?"

"No. For what?"

"Witness for the complainant. You want some pizza? We have plenty. Izzy's here." She lowered her voice. "He's been here all day. I called him to go with me to the lab in case Bryce decided he wasn't going to leave. Fortunately, Bryce wasn't there. Anyway, Izzy just stayed. I'm wondering if Edward or the chief of police sent him as a bodyguard."

"That would be good if they did," said Frank. He followed her into her office.

David and the others were discussing the evidence when Diane entered. They stopped when they saw Frank.

"Hey, Frank buddy. How's it going?" said Izzy. "Come get a piece before it's gone. These guys inhale pizza."

They greeted one another and Frank sat down with a slice and a cold soda from Diane's fridge. Diane caught him up on everything they had discovered so far.

"I called Janice and told her Curtis Crabtree is related to Edgar Peeks," said Diane. "I don't know if that will mean anything. I also told her about the conversation in the supply closet."

"Conversation in the supply closet?" said Neva. She laughed. "Who was Crabtree talking to in the supply closet? And why?"

"He and Bryce were talking. It's the conversation you interrupted, David," she said.

"How the hell did you know about that?" he asked, laughing. "I saw them go in and I wondered what they were up to."

"The supply closet is next to my lab, and the wall is thin. There wasn't much to the conversation, not much more than what I learned from Jin and Izzy. Apparently it was Crabtree's job to get employment in the DNA lab. Now it appears that it was part of some master plan to get the crime lab, the DNA lab, and the osteology lab," said Diane.

"What balls," said Neva. "I can't believe it. Did they really think they could do that?"

"They seemed to. What I don't know is what their master plan was supposed to lead to exactly. David pointed out that the crime lab would be a great thing to control if you were in the crime business—you could frame or free anyone."

"I'll say," said Neva.

"I also asked Janice if they had searched Peeks' residence. She had, and found nothing that would suggest why they had been killed, nor anything to suggest they had been involved in illegal enterprises. Peeks did appear to be living way beyond his means. With Jefferies it's more difficult to tell because of his business in Atlanta. It's successful and might account for his income."

"Could Jefferies have been paying Peeks?" said Jin.

"What for?" said Diane. "That's the thing. What was the business really? Were they just a new criminal organization we haven't heard of? Did they deal in drugs? What? It's scary to think about. They get rid of a judge and have a new one appointed and—"

"Wait? Get rid of a judge?" said Neva. "What are you saying?"

Diane realized she hadn't told them about the tainted evidence from the murder scene of Judge McNevin and about David's suspicions. She nodded to him and he laid out all the evidence for them.

"That's why I quit," he said.

Jin, Neva, and Izzy sat with their mouths open. When David finished, no one spoke for several moments.

"But the mayor doesn't appoint judges," said Neva.

"He could influence the choice," said Izzy. "He's

been making cozy with the governor. If the newspapers can be believed, they shook hands a lot. There was a photo op of them every other day. Evie was in one of them for her work on drugs. She said the governor liked the young can-do attitude of Jefferies. Evie was put off by him. Couldn't put her finger on what she didn't like," Izzy said, proudly showing off his wife's good judgment.

"I told Edward Van Ross about our suspicions today," said Diane. "He's very disturbed about the whole thing, as you can imagine. That's why I think it's important to find out what they are—were—up to and how far it extends. Not only for the sake of Douglas Garnett, but for Rosewood. And we can't forget that somebody killed them. Our most important job is to find out who and why."

"Have you talked to the former mayor yet?" asked Frank.

"I'm going to try to see him tomorrow," said Diane. "I would like Neva and David to search the crime scene at the mayor's house. Jin, go with them and analyze the blood evidence. And David, we need to find out what's on Jefferies' computer."

"Okay," said David. "It isn't going to be easy. Maybe Frank can help."

"Sure," said Frank. "You know how I like codes."

"Good," said Diane. "There's something else I want to discuss. Bryce and Rikki are looking for something. I put pressure on her today, especially with the watch business, and virtually told her she was going to have to relearn the job, and she didn't flinch. I'm not sure why she's sticking around, except that she must still be looking for something and we are her best bet for finding it."

"What do you think it is?" said Neva.

"It has to be something about money. It's always about money, isn't it? She and Bryce must know we are looking at them for some kind of criminal activity, yet they are not leaving. Bryce is suing the city for his job back, according to Janice," said Diane. "Maybe he's innocent, or maybe he's just keeping everyone in the government occupied while they also have Jennifer's lawsuit to deal with."

"If there's something in the mayor's house to find, we'll find it, boss," said Jin.

"Neva, try making nice to Rikki. I want to know what she pocketed at the crime scene."

"You think she'll tell me?" said Neva. "She'll know what I'm up to."

"Maybe, but she might let something slip," said Diane. "Who knows."

"Okay, I'll be as nice as pie to her." Neva wrinkled her nose.

"Tell me this," said Izzy. "If those watches are as valuable as you say and they don't make very many of them, wouldn't the company keep a record of who they sold them to? Wouldn't there be some kind of serial number, like a VIN for a car? Maybe Neva can find out the number to little Gollum's watch. Or maybe there's some kind of receipt in the mayor's house—if she stole it from him. If she's stealing, that'll give you something to bargain with. Maybe we can get her to talk."

Diane looked over at Izzy and raised her eyebrows. "You're absolutely right on all counts," she said. "We'll look into that tomorrow."

"I could do that," said Izzy. "I've worked burglary."

"Okay," said Diane, nodding.

"So, where are we now?" said David. "What do we think happened at the house?"

"Well, I think Bryce and Rikki were right about how it went down," said Diane. "Someone came up behind the mayor and shot him in the back of the head."

"He probably knew his attacker and didn't expect anything," said Neva. "And the shooter didn't steal anything. It was a hit."

"Yes," said Diane. "It was a hit. Both murders look basically the same to me. Same MO. Doesn't have to be an outsider. The shooter could be someone that Jefferies and company were in business with . . . and we don't even know about them yet."

"What about ballistics?" said Frank. "How do you explain the fact that the bullet that killed Peeks came from Garnett's gun?"

"That's one we have to work on," said Diane. "And we need to know if the gun that fired the bullet that killed Peeks is the same gun that killed Jefferies."

"I can't believe that Garnett did it," said Izzy.

"Nor I," said Neva.

"Me either," said Diane. "But we have to put our personal beliefs aside and find the best evidence we can to lead us to the killer or killers."

"How about the other security tapes?" said Neva. "We need to look at all of them to see who's been visiting the mayor over the last month. God, that will be boring. You can do that, Jin." She laughed and punched him on the shoulder. "Or should I say Legolas? You can use some of your elfin magic and get it done quickly."

"We have a lot to do tomorrow, so I'm going home to get some rest," said Diane.

Her face was aching and her arm was sore. In fact, she was tired and aching all over. Sleep would fix everything, and tomorrow maybe they would find a solution. Diane told David to lock up. Izzy stayed with the others. He seemed to be having a good time. She imagined he hadn't had one in quite a while.

She followed Frank home in her SUV. A time or two she thought she was being followed. But when she slowed down to see if she could get a look, whoever it was turned off. *Just being paranoid,* she thought. She pushed on the accelerator and caught up with Frank's Camaro.

Chapter 29

In the previous Rosewood City administration, mayor Walter Sutton and Police Chief Buford Monroe had arranged for the crime lab to be housed in the museum and for Diane to run it. Mayor Sutton and Diane had gotten off to a very shaky start when the mayor tried to talk her into selling the museum property—a deal that could have brought him and his friends a lot of money. The mayor's tactics in trying to persuade her had bordered on threats.

Vanessa had told Diane that Sutton was devastated at losing the mayoral election to Spence Jefferies. It had crossed Diane's mind several times that Sutton was among those who had a motive for killing Jefferies. But in all honesty, she couldn't imagine Sutton doing it or even hiring someone to do it. Then again, if he had learned what Jefferies did to win the election, he would have at least thought about it. Of course, her feelings were colored by the fact that she really didn't like Sutton and hadn't voted for him—or for Jefferies either. She had filled in the write-in spot on the ballot with the name of someone who wasn't even running—ironically, Edward Van Ross. *Odd how things turn out sometimes*, she thought as she drove up to Sutton's house.

Now she would have to act like nothing had ever happened between them. Not hard. She had been doing that very thing ever since the crime lab opened its doors.

Sutton lived with his family in a house that was a white-columned Greek revival on the outside but a more modern floor plan inside. It had a great room, a sunken living room, and a deck on the back. Not as large as Jefferies' house, it was still a mansion. She had been there for a party a time or two with Vanessa and had thought it an unusual combination of styles and not a particularly good layout for people who like to give parties.

Diane parked her SUV in the drive, picked up the folder off the seat, walked up to the house, and knocked. The door was answered almost immediately by a young woman in her mid-twenties.

"Hi. I'm Loraine Sutton. I believe we've met at one of my parents' parties. So nice seeing you again," she said, smiling.

It must have been a rote thing she said to people, for she didn't really notice Diane's face until she got to the end of her greeting. Then she showed the jaw-dropping, startled look that Diane was getting used to.

Diane had tried to make herself look less bruised, but she hadn't gotten any better at applying makeup this morning than she was the previous days. She had given up and left it off, deciding she would just have to forgo trying to look like nothing had happened.

Loraine Sutton was Walter Sutton's daughter. Diane knew she graduated from the University of Georgia. Other than that, she didn't know very much about her except that she and her brother were always very active in their father's campaign. Diane didn't know if Loraine had a job other than that of cheerleader for her father. She had dark brown hair and dark eyes like her mother, and sharp facial features like her father. Her best feature was her skin. It was creamy and blemish free. Her eyes were a little too close together and her nose a little too pointed for her to be called beautiful, but she had an interesting face and a nice smile. She wore a rust-colored pullover sweater and matching wool slacks.

"I'm very happy to see you again," said Diane.

"The family's in the living room. We're all anxious to hear what you've come about. It sounded rather cryptic."

"I know," said Diane. "It's one of those things that is hard to explain briefly over the phone. It's very kind of all of you to see me."

Loraine led her to the sunken living room, just to the right of the entryway. It was a cozy room with lots of fabric—layered oriental rugs, drapes, wall tapestries, upholstered chairs and sofas of jacquard, leather, and various floral designs, all in hues of dark red, brown, green, and gold. There was either a parlor palm or a schefflera at each window. The coffee table was dark walnut with a black marble top adorned with fresh flowers. The marble fireplace had a painting of a horse over the mantel.

The mayor and his son, Albert, rose to greet Diane as she entered the room. The son was like a young clone of his dad—tall, lean, sharp featured. The former mayor had steel gray hair, whereas the son's hair was blond. Diane thought its color probably came from a bottle and it was a little too stylish to look natural. Walter Sutton's wife, Eleanor, came in from another door carrying a tray of coffee and cookies. She was also a slim woman. She was dressed in a peach pantsuit and wore her dark hair up in a French twist. It was a family who could make a good portrait together. Just what a politician needed. Eleanor Sutton stopped for just a moment when she saw Diane's face. They all did. She slowly lowered the tray onto the coffee table. Diane was glad she didn't drop it.

"We're sorry to stare," said the elder Sutton, recovering first. "We were just startled. Were you in an accident?"

"Did you hear in the news about Harve Delamore?"

They had. Diane tried to give as short an explanation as she could of what had happened. But like everyone else, they had questions. She answered them all.

"That is just terrible," said Eleanor. "What possessed the man? Being demoted in rank is hardly the end of the world."

"He evidently had problems," said Diane.

"That's an understatement," said Loraine. She helped her mother serve the coffee.

Whenever Diane visited, she always drank her coffee black because it was just so much easier. She felt uncomfortable visiting and eating at the same time unless it was at a dinner party and she had a table in front of her. She took a cookie offered her, put it on the saucer, and sipped her coffee. Not bad, but not as good as the coffee she made. Mrs. Sutton sat down on the arm of her husband's chair, sans coffee or cookies.

Diane started to turn the conversation to why she had come.

"There are a couple of things I wanted to talk with you about," she said. "I'm sure you're keeping up with what's been going on in Rosewood—the murders."

"Terrible, terrible thing," said Walter Sutton. "I had no love for the man, but this is just terrible. Peeks too." He shook his head as if it were just too much to contemplate.

"There are some things you need to know about the election," began Diane.

She was hoping that in giving them information, she would encourage them to be more willing to give her information in return. Sutton would not readily admit if he had tried to dig up dirt on Jefferies.

"What kind of things?" asked Walter Sutton.

Diane opened the folder.

"You know that during the election a lot was made of the rash of burglaries that occurred during the latter part of your administration," she said.

"Don't I though. It was really bad luck for me. I don't believe for a minute that anything Jefferies did brought the rate down," he said.

Diane leaned forward. "You'd be wrong."

Sutton looked startled for a moment but said nothing.

"A man in my crime scene unit has an eye for data," continued Diane. "The crime rate, particularly burglaries, bothered him. So he started collecting data from police and court records. One of the things he discovered is that, though the number of burglaries went down after Jefferies came into office, the number of arrests for burglaries did not go up."

Walter Sutton frowned. The others looked puzzled for a moment.

"What are you saying?" whispered Loraine.

"I'm saying that it is quite possible the mayor and his close supporters were behind the surge in burglaries. That he conceived and directed them as part of a strategy to make you look bad and get him elected," Diane said. "These are maps—"

"That son of a bitch. That son of a bitch." Walter Sutton's face was flushed with anger. He lunged to his feet, paced a couple of steps, and turned on his heel. "I knew something was not right. Didn't I?" He looked at his family. "I told you something just wasn't right about Jefferies."

Albert reached for the maps. "What are these?" he asked.

"David, my assistant director, mapped out the areas in the city where the surge in burglaries occurred. Notice the neighborhoods," said Diane.

Loraine leaned over to look. After a moment she said, "The heaviest voters."

"And if you look at the individual homes," said Diane, "you will find that the victims are all leaders in their communities. They go to church and belong to organizations."

"To make a big problem seem bigger," said Albert. He shook his head. "It's hard to believe someone could be so . . . so conniving."

It's worse than that, thought Diane. When she discussed her plan with Frank and David, it was agreed she should tell Sutton only about the burglaries, not of their suspicions regarding the murder of Judge

McNevin. Politicians are not known for their ability to keep a secret if knowledge of it makes them look good.

"After the election," Diane said, "instances of burglaries in these areas dropped back to normal. Many stolen items were recovered. But no perpetrators were arrested and tried. This is just raw data, but it's very suggestive."

"I'll say," said Albert.

"I thought you ought to know about it," said Diane.

Walter Sutton sat down again. "I'm sorry the SOB is dead and I can't get my hands on him," he said. His wife put her hand on his arm.

"Spence Jefferies put a black cloud over many of us who served in your administration," said Diane. "You, the commissioner, the chief of police, me—and Garnett."

"It is just terrible about Garnett," said Sutton.

Diane noticed that he was noncommittal about his support for his former chief of detectives.

"Garnett stayed on the force to help out the department," said Diane. "Peeks was shifting duties and people around and making a lot of decisions that were not in the best interests of the rank-and-file police officers. And you know about the bulletproof vests."

"The state-of-the-art body armor," said Sutton sarcastically. "I saw the picture in the newspaper of Jefferies holding them up."

"Those were the only two state-of-the-art vests he purchased. The ones he gave the police officers were long out of date and wouldn't stop rubber bullets, according to the testimony of officers on the force," said Diane.

"That wicked man," said Eleanor.

Diane could see they were all wondering why she really had come. They were politically savvy people and knew there was something now they would be asked to give in return for this information. Diane took another deep breath.

Chapter 30

"I don't know if you are aware, but Edward Van Ross placed me back in charge of the crime lab."

Diane didn't want to go into details about Bryce. It would sound too triumphant, and she didn't want that—even though she did feel it, just a little. She mentally chastised herself. Nor did she want to give away too much information that had to remain confidential.

"I had heard," said Sutton, "and was glad to hear Edward is putting things right. You know I worked hard to get just the right people in positions. People who are qualified. I know the victor gets to make the changes that suit him, but the men he hired had no background in police work."

Diane nodded in agreement. *Be agreeable,* she told herself. "The detectives are trying to find out who killed Jefferies and Peeks," she said. "They are also trying to learn what Jefferies and his friends were involved in. And we all want to clear Garnett. I don't believe that he suddenly became a mass murderer."

"No, of course not," said Sutton.

"My people are going over the crime scenes again. And frankly, we are all playing catch-up. I'm hoping your staff collected information on Jefferies and maybe even his associates. We need a head start in this," said Diane.

"Well, you know I always run a clean campaign. I

told Loraine that I didn't want any dirt dug up. Just pertinent information," said Sutton.

Loraine was nodding her head. "It was my job to do research. Maybe if I'd done it better . . ."

"It has been my experience that Jefferies was really good at hiding things," said Diane.

"Who knew he would pull things like this?" Her brother gestured at Diane's maps.

"You probably know," began Sutton, "that Spence Jefferies was from Atlanta. His mother was, at any rate. He was a military brat for a while. His mother and father divorced, and the mother moved him to Atlanta. You know he went to a good school, one of the ivy league schools."

"Pennsylvania?" said Diane.

This was just the initial dance. He was telling her ordinary background information to show her that was his focus. But Diane had no doubt he would get to the meatier information after the dance was over.

"That's it—Penn State."

Diane didn't correct him. And neither did his children, she noticed, though their faces said they noticed the error.

"Good business school. The others, Peeks and Bryce, went there too. They were just his campaign workers then. I had no idea he would reward them with such high positions. No matter how good the business school is, it didn't prepare them for work in law enforcement."

He shook his head. "Loraine headed up my research." He smiled at his daughter. The dance was over.

"I knew there was something about Jefferies . . . his eyes," Loraine said. "I didn't like him, and not because he was running against Dad."

"He did have that shark-eyed look," said Diane, hoping to encourage Loraine. She could see there was a reluctance to say anything bad about him right off the bat. Diane wanted to tell them to get on with it, that she didn't have all day. Instead she smiled and took a sip of coffee and a bite of the sugar cookie.

"That was it—like a shark. Cold and dark," she said, giving her body a small shake.

"Did you find out anything in your research?" asked Diane.

"I thought I had. I was really concerned that Dad not look like he was digging for dirt. We don't do that. I mainly tried to find out about a candidate's positions on issues. It's not easy if they've never held office, but we—the volunteers who were working with me—happened upon something that was suspicious. I told Dad I needed to follow up on this, and I did. But maybe I didn't go deep enough."

"What were you concerned about?" asked Diane.

"I was afraid he was abusing young people in some way," she said.

"Abusing how?" prompted Diane.

"It was Buckley who first noticed something. You remember Buckley Kramer, Dad."

Her father nodded. Her mother murmured that he was a nice boy.

"He was in Atlanta at a new restaurant. He saw Jefferies there with three young boys—I guess I should call them men—but they were high school and college age, Buckley said. They weren't as well dressed as Jefferies. But they were young people; it's hard to tell if they are poor dressers or just in style."

She stopped to take a drink of coffee. Diane imagined it was cold by now. It must have been, because she set the cup and saucer down on the coffee table.

"Jefferies was giving them gifts," she said. "Buckley couldn't see what kind of gifts, exactly, but they looked like watches." Diane raised her eyebrows a fraction.

"I know that's certainly not incriminating behavior," continued Loraine, "but Buckley said there was something about it that was creepy to him. Not all the kids looked happy."

Loraine called them kids, but it sounded like some of them were adults—young adults, but adults just the same. Still . . .

"What did you make of it?" said Diane.

"Nothing, at first. But we spoke with someone from his campaign who had quit. He said the mayor and his friends gave him the creeps. It looks like Jefferies gave everyone the creeps. I can't understand how he got elected. Sometimes I think people deserve the leaders they vote in." Her voice was vehement.

Diane could see that the election defeat had stung her too—and was still stinging.

"Now, Loraine," said her father. "He pulled the wool over everyone's eyes. Look at how the governor took to Jefferies. You know people don't deserve to suffer for making bad choices; let's just hope they learn from them."

He may have been gently chiding his daughter, but Diane could see he was feeling the same thing she had felt—vindication. She felt a bit ashamed of herself for it.

"Did the campaign worker tell you anything useful?" said Diane.

"Not at first. But then he told us he'd noticed Peeks was spending a lot of time talking to kids in chat rooms. He didn't know about what or which chat rooms. He only got a glance or two over his shoulder, but he read enough of the screen to see that Peeks was buttering up someone who was obviously much younger than he was."

"What did he do with the information?" asked Diane.

"There's the problem," said Loraine. "Nothing. He quit a few weeks later when he was verbally reprimanded rather harshly by Bryce for a mistake he made in a mailing. We thought the guy might be just a disgruntled volunteer. It happens in all campaigns. Some people think because they are volunteers they don't have to abide by a work ethic."

"Where is he now? Will he talk to me?" asked Diane.

"He's a manager at Wal-Mart. And, yes, Mother, I go to Wal-Mart sometimes. I like their craft section."

She smiled at her mother, who, Diane gathered, wouldn't be caught dead in a discount department store.

"Buckley and I got together to talk about what to do. The problem was, we really didn't have any information. Just vague suspicions about something that could be very innocent. Then Buckley remembered about Jefferies' business in Atlanta. We knew they made commercials—they would have film equipment. It occurred to us that he might be into, well, into porn with these kids. I know it was a stretch. But could we take a chance?"

"Oh, no," said Mrs. Sutton. "Tell me you didn't investigate that?"

"Well, yes, Mother, we did. That is, Buckley did. He said, being the candidate's daughter, I should stay out of it."

"Well, thank heaven for that," said her mother.

"Buckley knew someone who was having a commercial made by Jefferies' company. He went with them a couple of times and nosed around. Jefferies wasn't there. He has . . . had someone else run his business for him. Buckley couldn't find anything that suggested any kind of illegal activity at all. We thought it was a dead end. But Buckley wouldn't let it go."

Diane didn't quite see how they arrived at the notion that Jefferies was making porn from that scant evidence. It sounded to her like the beginnings of a smear campaign that Sutton's people had hoped to start. His supporters were known for planting malicious innuendos about political opponents, turning the most innocent things into something suspicious. Sutton himself had even helped spread rumors about Diane when she wouldn't agree to move the museum and sell the property. It was their bad luck that Jefferies was better at vicious campaigning than they were.

"What did Buckley do?" said Diane. Her body was starting to ache from sitting in one position for so long. She was more sore than she thought she would be.

Loraine looked at her father. "You know how loyal Buckley is," she said.

"Oh, Lord, what did he do?" said her father.

Loraine turned to Diane. "Dad's volunteers are very loyal to him. They know they are working for someone who has Rosewood's best interests at heart and they want to see him elected."

"I take it Buckley was at the forefront of loyalty," said Diane, smiling.

"He was. He followed one or the other of Jefferies or Peeks. He didn't stalk them or anything, but he'd follow them as they were leaving their headquarters, and if they didn't go home, he'd keep following. He wasn't really routine about it. Just when he had time. About the third time, he saw Peeks meeting with some kids. Two boys and a girl this time. He wrote down the license plate of their car. He found out who owned it and went to see him. The kid wouldn't talk with him at first except to say that he met Peeks at a job fair on campus. Buckley contacted the campus. You know you have to sign up to be at the job fair. We knew Peeks worked for a recruitment agency in Atlanta and we did find out that he placed several college students in jobs. They were legitimate jobs. We checked—phone company, banks, insurance offices, government agencies—all good jobs at legitimate places. We were at a dead end and decided to let it go. Then several days later the kid with the car called and told Buckley he wanted to meet with him."

"What did he want?" asked Diane, leaning forward.

"Don't know. The kid didn't show and he wouldn't answer Buckley's calls. Buckley went over to his house, but he wouldn't answer the door. That was it."

"What do you think that was about?" asked Diane.

Loraine shrugged. "Who knows? He was unreliable. He was one of those kids who, well, he dressed in ragged jeans, had a ring in his nose. Somehow you don't expect that from Asian kids, but there you are." Loraine stopped and looked at Diane. "Are you all right?"

Chapter 31

Diane must have gone pale, but there it was—Asian, nose ring, teenager. They all were staring at her. She put a hand to her cheek and gently rubbed it. "My face is hurting a little bit. It does that. I'm fine, really."

"Honestly, a man who would hit a woman," said Mrs. Sutton. "And he called himself a policeman. May I get you some ice?"

"I'll be all right. It's probably just healing twinges." Diane smiled at them and changed position in her chair. "Do you know the kid's name?" she asked.

"No, but I can find out. Just a minute. I'll call Buckley."

"An address and phone number for him would help a lot," said Diane.

Loraine stood up and went into an adjoining room. Diane heard her calling and asking for the name. There was a long silence. Diane imagined he was getting the information. They didn't talk long, but from what Diane heard, she guessed they probably had dated. May still be dating. There was a friendly playfulness to her voice usually reserved for someone close. Loraine didn't tell Buckley what it was about. Diane was grateful for that, but she had a feeling Loraine might call him back when she left.

"Count on Buckley for keeping good notes," Loraine said, coming back into the room.

She gave Diane an index card containing two names.

One had an address and phone number in Atlanta. The other had a local phone number.

"Malcolm Chen is the kid. Sid Larkin is the manager at Wal-Mart," said Loraine.

"Thank you," said Diane, taking the card and pocketing it. "This will be a big help. I appreciate all of you speaking with me. And thank you for the refreshments. I appreciate your hospitality."

"Glad to help," said Sutton. "I'm always glad to help."

They all rose as Diane stood. She was relieved to be leaving. She was starting to feel smothered by a room with so much fabric.

"Are you going to be all right to drive back?" asked Sutton.

"I'll be fine. I'm mostly just sore," she assured him.

"I'm glad Edward has taken the helm," he said. "He's a good man."

"He is," Diane agreed, edging toward the door.

Sutton cleared his throat. "Tell me, do you think he will run for mayor in the special election?"

Ah, thought Diane, *fishing for information about another potential rival.*

"He hasn't said anything to me, but I've always had the impression that if Edward were elected mayor, the first thing he would do is demand a recount."

Their laughter was far heartier than the joke warranted. Diane suspected it was mainly relief. There was no way that Walter Sutton could defeat Edward Van Ross in an election.

"Please come by again," said Mrs. Sutton.

"Thank you," said Diane.

Diane finally made it out the door and felt a distinct relief as it closed behind her. She climbed in her SUV and drove to Spence Jefferies' house.

At the entryway she pulled coveralls over her clothes and donned shoe and hair covers.

Whereas Mayor Sutton's house had been all fabric, tapestries, and deep colors, Mayor Jefferies' house was white marble and dark wood. Paintings of war and conquest were in abundance, all in classical Greek and Roman style, mounted in simple metal frames. There was the bust of Alexander the Great. And in the center of the dining room table was a sculpture of Bucephalus, Alexander's horse.

He was like a kid, thought Diane, pretending to be a great conqueror.

"Hey, boss. I thought I heard someone come in." Jin met her in the hallway.

She knew they would have processed the foyer first and would have made a safe walkway through the house—a trail that had been scrutinized for all the evidence they could discover.

"How are things going here?" she asked.

"Real good. David found something interesting. He'll tell you about it. Actually we could have found it in the lab, but we just now got to taking a closer look at the pictures."

"That sounds intriguing," said Diane. "Anything else?"

"Gee, boss, you expect a lot." Jin grinned. "I've mapped the blood pattern and taken lots of samples. I was just getting ready to go back to the lab. I checked the rest of the house for blood. I found some in the guest bathroom sink on this floor. There's a guest room back in the corner off the living room. Anyway, I think the shooter got a little spray on him and he washed up. The last team in here didn't think to check all the bathrooms for blood." Jin sounded cocky on the last comment.

"That's why we're here," said Diane. "I knew you would be thorough. Think maybe the shooter was hoping the guest bathroom would be skipped?"

Jin nodded. "That's what I think. There's a divider in front of the door, so it's kind of hidden—in a way."

"You have any luck with Sutton?" said Jin.

"Yes. Quite a bit. I'll tell all of you about it later," she said.

"Sure thing, boss. We've done the downstairs, so you can walk freely. The front stairs are done and they have half the second floor done. The others are up there now. They're teaching Rikki about search patterns. Izzy's in the study going through the books. He wanted to help, so David set him to work there."

"What is Izzy doing here?" asked Diane.

"He just showed up. I thought you told him to come," said Jin.

"No. I suppose the chief of police sent him," said Diane. "How is Rikki doing?" she asked as she walked back to the front door with Jin.

He took off his coveralls and removed the covering on his shoes and head and put them in a disposable bag from his crime scene kit.

"Complaining. But she's doing what David and Neva tell her." He lowered his voice. "Has anyone really looked at her educational background? I can't believe she had a minor in biology but has no concept of scientific method—and I can't believe she's ever had a course in criminology."

"You know, I haven't checked. We need to do that." Diane shook her head. "My brain's not working," she said.

"Probably from being hit on the head," said Jin.

"Thanks."

"Sure, boss. See you back at the lab."

He started for his car, then suddenly turned around.

"I'm glad to have you back in charge of the crime lab," he said. "We all are, especially David. This guy"—Jin gestured at the Jefferies' house—"he knocked the world off its axis for a lot of people. You're going to make it right again." Jin turned and went to his car.

Righting the world. Diane wished she could. She feared that her people expected more from her than she could deliver. She closed the front door and turned her attention back to the crime scene.

Jefferies' study and library was just to the left of the foyer. It had been labeled as a parlor on her floor plan. The door was half closed. She opened it and went in. Izzy, dressed in the coverings they wore to protect the crime scene from contamination, sat at a

library table looking through books. He looked quite
different in a shower cap.

Unlike the rest of the house, the study was mainly
wood. The bookcases, paneling, desk, and library table
were all rich brown colors of various kinds of woods
buffed to a high sheen. The glass doors to the banker's
bookshelves were raised and slid back into the case.
The shelves were empty. Most of the books were
stacked on the floor, table, and desk. She remembered
it being like this when she was here before with Colin
Prehoda—when they had discovered Edgar Peeks'
body with Garnett standing over it.

"Hi," Izzy said. "David put me to work down here
among the books."

"I'm surprised to see you," said Diane.

"Janice is working with another partner on this now.
This has priority in the department, so I'm helping."

Diane noticed that his answer was a tad carefully
worded for Izzy. He never really said who sent him.
Curious.

"We're looking for some kind of list that Bryce and
Rikki thought Jefferies had," he said.

Diane nodded. "It's what Pendleton said they were
looking for. I have no idea what kind of list or what
it looks like."

"Anybody asked Rikki?" he said.

"Not yet," said Diane. "We will later."

"She went through the books, too," said Izzy. He
pointed to scraps of paper littering the floor. "There's
bookmarks, envelopes, pieces of paper. I think what
Rikki did was shake everything to see what fell out."

"It seems that way, doesn't it?" said Diane, looking
at the papers. She picked up a torn envelope and examined it. There was only half of Jefferies' address on
it. The return address had been on the other half.
Apparently he tore it for a quick bookmark.

"I've been flipping through the books," said Izzy.
"I was thinking that if there is some list, he may have
written it inside a book on one of them blank pages."

"That's a good idea," agreed Diane. And a lot of

work, she thought. But she didn't know any other way to go through them except one by one.

"Lot of books here," said Izzy. "You think he read all these?"

Diane picked one up: Aristotle's *Poetics*. She looked at the spine and at the edges of the pages. "No one's read this one." She looked at the title page. *From Rebecca with love.* Diane wondered if that was a girl-friend. She examined a couple more: a biography of—who else?—Alexander the Great, and Sun Tzu's *The Art of War*, both signed by A. Houten *To my favorite student.* Both had bent spines and pages that had been turned. "Somebody read these."

"Lot of different kinds of books here," said Izzy. "I don't read much. Mainly the sports pages of the newspaper. Evie reads sometimes. Daniel was the reader in our house. Sometimes I pick up a book he's read and I read a page or two just to have something in my mind that was in his." He sighed and looked around at the books. "A lot of people's thoughts in here."

"Yes, there are." She noticed that Jefferies had leather-bound copies of the *Hundred Greatest Books*, history books, a lot of books on war, biographies—a fairly wide variety.

"I thumbed through something by Shakespeare," said Izzy. "*Hamlet*, I think. Saw several phrases I'd heard before."

"Shakespeare is one of the most quoted of writers," said Diane. She pulled a chair out and sat down.

" 'To be or not to be'—you hear that one a lot. What does it mean exactly?" said Izzy, opening a volume of *Hamlet* and pointing to a soliloquy.

"Hamlet's life isn't going well, and he's contemplating suicide," said Diane.

"I kind of thought that," he said.

She took the book and looked at the passage.

"He's wondering if it is better to struggle on and 'suffer the slings and arrows of outrageous fortune' or to end them and sleep. Sleep means death," she said.

"But he worries that if he kills himself, what happens after that might be worse—'for in the sleep of death what dreams may come.' "

Izzy was silent for a moment. "I can relate to that," he said.

"That's one of the reasons Shakespeare is so often quoted. He hit upon truths people can relate to today just as they did in his time," said Diane.

Izzy Wallace was the last person she thought she would ever be discussing Shakespeare with.

"You and me's suffered the slings and arrows of outrageous fortune, haven't we?" he said.

"There's no greater suffering to be had than losing a child," said Diane.

"No. There's not," he said. "That is for sure."

It was an unexpected confidence from Izzy, and Diane didn't know where to go with it.

"Did you ever think about it?" he said.

Diane knew what he meant. She wasn't sure how to answer.

"I never wanted to die. I just wanted to stop hurting," she said.

Izzy nodded his head. "I hear you there."

Diane looked up to see David in the doorway. He had several photographs in his hand.

"Hey, Diane. Did Izzy tell you what we found in the photographs?" he asked.

"No. We were discussing Shakespeare," she said.

David looked from one to the other. "Oh," he said, as if that didn't quite compute.

Diane smiled. "What did you find?"

"Something that's rather curious," he said. "It's a small thing. I'm not sure what to make of it."

Chapter 32

David came into the room and pulled out one of the chairs at the library table. Izzy moved a stack of books and put them on the floor. Diane noticed that Izzy had one of the notebooks they keep in the crime scene kits and was writing down all the names of the books. She wasn't sure that was necessary, but she wasn't going to tell him to stop at this point. He looked to be almost finished.

David sat down by Diane and put three photographs on the table in front of her. They showed different angles of Jefferies' body lying in the kitchen.

David tapped Jefferies' arm in one of the photographs with his finger.

"We hadn't noticed it before and it wasn't mentioned in his autopsy report, but his watch was on upside down. If he looked at it, the six would be at the top. He may have absentmindedly done it himself and just hadn't noticed, but I have a gut feeling it may have been put on his wrist after he was shot. For what reason I can't fathom. Jin is going to check it for blood spatters. If there aren't any, then there's a good possibility it wasn't on his wrist when he was shot."

"The ME didn't notice it when he undressed him?" asked Diane.

"If he did, he didn't see fit to mention it," said David.

"Watches keep coming up," said Diane almost to herself.

"We haven't found receipts for any of the watches, but Izzy's tracked down the serial number on the one we have," said David.

Izzy smiled and took a small notebook from his shirt pocket with a flourish of his arm. "It was purchased at Erinette Jewelers in Atlanta right before the elections," said Izzy. "He bought this watch." Izzy pointed to the photograph. "And he also bought three women's Carter . . . Cartier diamond watches—all Tank. I can't pronounce it. *F-R-A-N-C-A-I-S-E*," he spelled out. "And ten men's watches—three Chase-Durer Fighter Command watches, and seven TAG Heuer sports watches. I have the price here and all the serial numbers in case we run across a nest of expensive watches. And I mean expensive. Most of the cars I've owned didn't cost as much as one of these babies. I don't get it. They tell time. My fifty-dollar watch keeps perfect time. Of course it ain't got diamonds, but some of these don't either," he added. "What was he doing with them, you think?"

"Gifts," said Diane. "When you finish here, we'll debrief in my museum office," said Diane.

"You found out something, didn't you?" said David.

"Yes, I think so. I don't want to talk about it here," she said. "Have you noticed anything . . . unusual with Rikki?"

"After we searched the master bedroom, she showed a lot of interest in coming down and helping Izzy sort through all these books," he said. "Mainly, she's interested in how I'm going to decrypt the mayor's computer. By the way, Frank's working on it today. He said he has to be in Rosewood anyway. I told him to use your museum office. I hope that's okay," he said.

"That's fine. You think the two of you can get into the computer?" asked Diane.

"Depends." He shrugged. "We'll see."

"We've checked all the artwork, lamps, cereal boxes, everything we could think of for hidden compartments," said David. "Nothing." He grinned. "Neva found a Bic lighter in the back of a drawer.

You should have seen Rikki's eyes light up. She thought it was a flash drive. I think she's definitely waiting for us to find whatever it is they are looking for."

"Let's hope we don't disappoint her." Diane stood up. "I need to get back to the museum."

"Jin's found some good blood transfer," said David, rising from his chair. "Did you see him when you came in?"

"Yes. He told me about the guest bathroom," said Diane.

"Did he tell you about the stain under the chest in the foyer?" said David, pointing to the doorway.

"No, I guess he was saving it. What did he find?" she asked.

"We moved the chest to look under it because it was so close to Peeks' body. We found blood smears with a faint pattern in the middle of them, almost parallel lines. Don't know what it means. We're going to see if we can find an image when we get back to the lab," he said.

"Good work, guys," said Diane. "Seriously. You're doing very good work." Diane had to admit it felt good to be back in charge of the crime lab again.

"Hi, Andie," said Diane as she entered her office. "How was your gemology class?"

Andie was changing the ink cartridge in her printer. Today she was dressed in a black jumper, white sweater, and patent leather Mary Janes. She looked up from her task and grinned broadly. Diane noticed that she was working on the museum's newsletter.

"Great. Barb McConnel was back. Ethan didn't come. His father stayed home with him. She seemed to be having a good time. Did you know you can't let opals dry out or freeze? It's the water thing, which I still don't understand. I mean, water's wet. Anyway, Sheriff Canfield came by and left you a package. He said he didn't want to take it to the crime lab, even though you are back in charge. Which he was real glad about. He knew Rikki was still working there and didn't know if Bryce might pop back in. Is he really suing the city?"

Diane took the package from her. "Who, Bryce or Canfield?" asked Diane.

Andie grinned. "Bryce," she said.

"I've heard that he is," said Diane.

"Well, he won't win," said Andie.

"Probably not," she said. "You doing the newsletter this time?"

"Yeah. I've been getting a lot of calls on what the dress code is for 'white tie.' So I'm putting it in the newsletter," she said.

Diane smiled. "Excellent idea, Andie. Good thinking."

"I think there's going to be a lot of tiaras and prom dresses at the event. But I don't think tiaras are worn much anymore," said Andie, "except to proms." Diane agreed. "Though I've been looking at white-tie events on the Internet, and this woman is wearing a tiara that's more like a crown." Andie flipped views on her computer and pointed to a picture on the screen.

"Andie, that's the queen of England," said Diane.

"Oh." Andie squinted at the picture. "I think I need glasses. I thought it was the president's mother."

"I'll be in my office," said Diane. She walked past Andie's desk and opened the door that separated their offices. "I'll be here for a while if you need me."

"Frank's here," said Andie. "With a computer. He said you'd know what it is."

"I do," she said. "Thanks."

She took the package in and sat down behind her desk. *No one trusts the crime lab,* she thought, *not David or Frank. Not even me.* David told Frank to work in Diane's office. She told her crew to meet her here instead of at the lab. Establishing confidence again in the crime lab was going to be her top priority when this was over.

The box was wrapped in brown paper and tied with jute. It had her name on it and the address of the museum. The return address was the Rose County Sheriff's Office. She cut the jute and tore off the paper.

There was a note taped to the top of a cardboard box about half the size of a shoe box. It was from the sheriff saying they hadn't found anything more after a sweep of the area, except for a bullet, which was sent to the GBI ballistics lab. Canfield wasn't even trusting Rosewood ballistics. She couldn't blame him. Losing those bones was a major blunder. The note also had a PS: *I'm glad to see you back at the crime lab.*

She took the lid off and pulled away cotton batting. Four pieces of bone lay on another layer of cotton batting. She donned a pair of gloves. One of the bones was a front portion of a maxilla with a tooth still imbedded in it—an incisor. The other bone fragments consisted of a broken piece from the spinous process of a vertebrae, a piece of coracoid bone from the scapula, and the second cuneiform of the left foot. The most helpful was the incisor. The root of the tooth would be a good place to find usable DNA. She turned it over in her hand and saw that it was a shovel-tooth incisor—most common in Asian populations. The hunch she had at the Sutton house was looking stronger. There was nothing so far to rule it out. She repacked the bones, removed her gloves, and walked into her sitting room.

Frank had the computer on her table and was apparently taking it apart.

"David told me you'd be working here," she said. "Why are you dismantling the computer?"

"I'm not. I've just taken the case off the CPU," he said.

"Why?" she asked.

"Sometimes people write their encryption key inside the computer case, in the event they forget it. But I've been over every inch with a magnifying glass and I haven't found one."

"How about a black light?" said Diane.

"That was going to be my next step. You wouldn't happen to have a black light in your pocket, would you?" He winked at her and turned up one corner of his lips.

She grinned. "We have lots of black lights all over the building."

She called Andie and asked her to go up to the conservation lab and borrow a black light from Korey, her head conservator.

"Andie will be down with one in just a minute," said Diane.

Diane sat down at a small writing desk in the corner. She had the box of bones with her. She punched the sheriff's number into her cell and asked for him when the receptionist answered. It took a couple of minutes to get him on the line.

"Hey, Diane. I guess you got the package I sent you," he said.

"Yes, I did, and I have a name and address for you to check." She fished the paper from her pocket. "Malcolm Chen," she said, and gave the sheriff the Atlanta address. There was silence on the other end of the phone for several long moments.

"Hello? Are we still connected?" she asked.

"You know, I've been telling people you're good, but I had no idea. How in the world did you identify him from that paltry handful of bones?" he said.

Diane laughed. "I'd love to say my skills are—" She paused as she caught sight of Frank looking at her strangely. "Just a moment," she said and put a hand over the phone.

"What?" she asked.

"Malcolm Chen is a hacker," he said.

Chapter 33

"You know him?" said Diane. "You know Malcolm Chen?"

"I know the name," said Frank. "He's on a list of hackers I have. He's also known as Shogun."

"Interesting," said Diane.

Diane got back on the phone with the sheriff.

"Sheriff Canfield, Frank is here and he recognized the name. He says he may be a hacker called Shogun. Chen is Asian, he has a nose ring, and he is young. He fits the description of the kid in the field, and I have to tell you, this may not be him, but it's a lead. I've found nothing yet that would rule him out, but that's not the same as a positive ID, by any means. And you know what little I've had to work with. I'm hoping Jin will be able to extract DNA from the tooth. He's come up empty on the earlier samples."

"I'm going to call the Atlanta police right now and ask them to go to Chen's apartment. I tell you, Diane, I'm real impressed."

"Don't be too impressed. I was lucky to stumble onto something," she said. "I'll tell you about it later. Let me know what the Atlanta police say."

"I will," said the sheriff.

"Ask them to collect samples for DNA comparison," said Diane. "Toothbrush and hairbrush would be real good," said Diane.

"I'll do that," said the sheriff.

Diane hung up the phone and looked over at Frank. "A hacker?" she said.

"I've been looking at the usual suspects following this rash of identity thefts, and the names were on my mind," he said. "How did you come by his name?"

Diane went over to the couch and sat down. There was a stack of crime scene photos David had printed for her to examine, photographs that Rikki took before she dismantled the mayor's house in her search.

She didn't answer Frank. An idea was flitting through her mind and she wanted to follow through first. She picked up the stack of photographs. He watched her curiously, not pushing for an answer.

Andie came in with a black light.

"Okay, who gets it?" she said.

"Frank," said Diane without looking up from the photographs.

Andie handed the black light to Frank and left.

Diane flipped through the photographs, pulling out the ones from the library and laying them faceup, side by side on the table, looking closely at each one.

"Well, hell," said Frank.

"What?" said Diane, looking up.

"Look at this," he said.

Diane rose, went over to the table, and peered into the computer case. Under the black light, in neat block letters were the words *You won't find what you are looking for here*.

"What the—?" began Diane. "What does that mean?"

"It means this is going to be harder to decipher than I thought."

The door opened and Izzy walked in with his notebook under his arm.

"Hi, Diane, Frank. I can tell you right here and now that there is no list in that library. Not even a grocery list."

"It's probably in the machine, then," said Diane.

"Mind if I have a drink?" said Izzy.

"Sure," said Diane. "In the little fridge."

"Can I get anyone else one?" he asked. "The others will be here shortly. They're checking things into your evidence locker."

"You can bring me a green tea," said Diane.

Izzy got a Coke and gave Diane a bottle of green tea.

"Those any good?" he asked. He sat down on one of the couches, still clutching his notebook.

"I like them," said Diane.

She looked up at him. She had been wondering about Izzy. It had even crossed her mind briefly that he might be hanging around to find the list himself, in case it led to a lot of money. She wondered why he didn't go back to his job at the police station. It wasn't because he was guarding her, obviously.

"Izzy, don't get me wrong—you are doing a great job—but just why are you here? Did the chief of police send you?"

Izzy and Frank briefly exchanged glances as Frank sat down next to the computer.

"Well, it's like this. Evie's got her antidrug thing going and it's helping her through losing Daniel. She's making a difference, and that means something. Me, I work at a desk job. I'm just marking time. And my retirement ain't for many years yet. The stuff you do here catches people—like the people responsible for killing Daniel. I need to do something that makes a difference. And you guys laugh. I ain't laughed in a long time. I was thinking that since Jin is now mostly in the DNA lab, and I don't think you're going to keep li'l Gollum on after this is over, maybe you could ask the chief to assign me here. They have lots of guys approaching retirement who can work the desk."

Diane was shocked. She had no idea that was what was on Izzy's mind. When she didn't say anything, he continued.

"I'll never make detective in the department. I've known that for years. But I have a lot to offer as an investigator here. I have a lot of experience and I can learn the forensics."

"We don't do investigations; we collect crime scene evidence," said Diane.

Izzy smiled. "The hell you don't. The biggest complaint the detectives in the squad have with you is you tend sometimes to take over an investigation," he said.

Diane's jaw dropped. She hardly knew what to say. She looked over at Frank, but he was busy studying his shoes. She looked back at Izzy.

"Is that true?" she asked.

"Yeah. This time we asked you to, but we don't always do that," he said, laughing.

Diane stared at him a moment, thinking about the proposition. There would be an advantage to having one of the old boys on her crew. And Izzy was doing a good job. Of course he wasn't doing any collection of fingerprints or blood spatters, any trace evidence. But he had come up with good ideas.

She looked at Frank again. Apparently he'd found out all he could about his shoes because he looked at her and smiled.

"I'm not against the idea," she said. "Let me think about it. There would be a lot of benefits to both of us. I can see that."

"That's great," Izzy said, grinning. "Thanks."

"I didn't say yes," she said.

"But you didn't say no. Now, it's clear to me that no means no, but you didn't say that."

"I said maybe," she said. "I said I'll think about it."

"That's closer to a yes than to a no," he said. "So, Frankie, buddy. Did you find anything on the machine?"

Frank laughed and showed him the message under the black light.

"Well, I'll be damned. What do you make of that?" he asked.

"Looks like the work of another hacker on my list," said Frank. "I don't know his real name; we haven't found out his identity yet. But he goes by the nickname Black Light."

"Really?" said Diane looking up from the photographs she was examining. She went to the table and

picked up the magnifying glass that Frank was using
and inspected one of the pictures from the mayor's
library with it. "You don't think it was this Shogun
fellow who encrypted the computer, then?"

"Shogun? Now I've missed something," said Izzy.
"Jefferies had a book in his library called that. There
was a bunch of them by Clavell."

"Not that Shogun," said Diane.

"I missed something too," said Frank. "Why do you
think Malcolm Chen is connected to this case? By the
way, you never did tell me how you came by the name."

Diane used the magnifying glass and looked at a
photograph of the library bookcase.

"Jefferies had all the works of Dickens on one shelf
in alphabetical order by title. But one is missing."

"Izzy, would you hand me your list of books?"
she said.

He handed her the notebook containing the list in
Jefferies' library. He had abbreviated the titles, but
she thought she could decipher it easily enough.

"Are you going to withhold the information?"
said Frank.

"Do you want to discuss withholding information?"
she asked.

"No, I suppose not," he said.

"It's not on here," said Diane, tapping her finger
on the list.

"I got the names of all the books. I'm sure of it,"
said Izzy.

"I'm counting on it," said Diane.

"What's not there?" said Frank and Izzy together.

She handed them the photograph and magnifying
glass. "This picture was taken before Rikki took the
books out of the shelves. Look at the Dickens shelf.
There's a book missing between *Nicholas Nickleby*
and *Our Mutual Friend*," she said.

"And that would be . . . ," said Frank.

Diane saw him going over the titles and repeating
them to himself.

"*Oliver Twist*," said Frank. "It's not on the shelf."

"It's not in Izzy's notes either."

Izzy took the notebook from her and ran his finger down the list. "Not here," he said.

"The book was taken by someone—assuming the crew brought you all the books they found in the house," said Diane.

"They did," he said.

"If there really was a list, I think that's where Jefferies would have put it. He was into books—actually, he was into a fantasy life. He had sculptures and paintings of Alexander the Great all over the house."

"He had four biographies of him," said Izzy.

"Jefferies liked to see himself as bigger than life, like characters in his books. If he had a hard copy of a list with some connection to his real business, I think it makes sense that he would hide it in *Oliver Twist*."

"Why?" said Izzy. "I hate to admit it, but I've never read *Oliver Twist*. Or seen the movie—or the musical. Evie wanted to go, but I couldn't imagine sitting in the Fox Theater through a Broadway musical. Wish I had now."

Diane told the two of them what she had learned from Loraine Sutton about Jefferies and Peeks meeting with young people fresh out of high school and college, about getting them jobs in banking, insurance, and government agencies, and giving them expensive watches. About the boy who almost came forward—the boy who matched the description she had built out of the bones from the field Arlen Wilson plowed.

"Jefferies ran cybergangs," said Frank.

Chapter 34

"I think your case and mine just came crashing together," said Frank.

"You believe it's the same people?" said Diane.

"I'm having an upsurge in identity thefts and you have someone who might be running a cybergang," said Frank. "It may turn out that Malcolm Chen is alive and hacking his little heart out in his apartment and Jefferies was doing something completely different with his time, but with what we suspect right now, it's looking very much like they are related. It bears looking into."

"What's with *Oliver Twist*?" asked Izzy.

"Oliver Twist was an orphan who fell in with a gang of young thieves run by a bad guy," said Diane.

"Oh, well, that fits," said Izzy. "But what's cybergangs? Never heard of them before."

"That's more Frank's domain," said Diane.

Diane heard a commotion coming through Andie's office. It was her team. *Her* team. That sounded good. They were doing their usual bickering.

"We just had pizza," said Neva.

"You can never have too much pizza," said Jin. "It's essential food."

"You can have too much pizza," said David. "You might want to ask the rest of us before you just go pick up food for all of us."

Diane smelled the aroma of pizza coming through the door. Jin was carrying three large boxes.

"Hi," said Neva when she saw Diane. "We finished the house."

"You didn't happen to find a copy of *Oliver Twist* in any of the rooms?" said Diane.

"We gave all the books we found to Izzy," Neva said. "Why?"

Neva went to Diane's small refrigerator and began getting drinks out.

"Diane figured out that's where the list was," said Izzy.

The three of them stopped and looked at Diane.

"Really?" said David. "Well, you could have saved us a lot of time."

"The pizza smells really good," said Izzy.

Neva brought several drinks over and handed them out. She raised her eyebrows at Izzy and gave him a nod. Izzy nodded back and smiled. They were all in on it, thought Diane. Apparently Izzy had discussed his idea with all of them.

"So, why *Oliver Twist*?" asked David.

"It was missing on the shelf," said Izzy.

"Couldn't it have been loaned out?" said David.

"I don't think Jefferies loaned books," said Diane. "He liked them and he wanted to keep them—even the ones he didn't read."

"How could you know that?" said David.

"Just a feeling," said Diane.

"We need more," said David. He had a puzzled frown on his face, as if Diane was suddenly about to trade in her microscopes for a Ouija board.

"There's more," said Diane, smiling. "We'll have to eat on the coffee table. The computer's on the big table and it looks like it is going to stay there for a while."

"Any luck?" said David. He walked over to the computer and pulled up a chair.

"Depends on what you mean by luck," said Frank. He took the black light and showed David the message.

"Bit of a smart aleck," said David.

"What?" asked Jin. He and Neva came over and looked inside the computer case.

"What do you make of that?" said Neva.

"Let's eat the pizza before it gets cold," said Diane. "I'll tell you while you eat."

Diane got napkins from a cabinet and they all gathered around the coffee table, grabbing slices of pizza as Diane began her story.

"It started in the field that Arlen Wilson was plowing. He found some pieces of bones, told Sheriff Canfield, and brought them to me. I examined the bone fragments—which looked like they had gone through a wood chipper. They were possibly from a male in his late teens or early twenties who might have worn jewelry or a body piercing. When I told Canfield the bones were human, he had the field searched, and more pieces of bone were found along with black hair. This second set of bones and accompanying evidence were the ones that disappeared from the crime lab under Bryce's watch. After they disappeared, the sheriff went back to the field one more time and found a few more pieces and brought them to me. One was a maxilla with an incisor—a shovel-tooth incisor."

"I have shovel-tooth incisors. Want to see?" said Jin.

"Not with your mouth full of pizza," said Neva. "Jeez, Jin, it's bad enough that we have to eat pizza two days in a row without seeing it in your mouth."

"I'll swallow," said Jin.

"That's all right. We all know what they look like," said Neva.

"I don't," said Izzy.

"I'll show you one later," said Diane. "The point is, they're very common among Asians. Not nearly as common among other ethnic groups."

Diane took a bite of her pizza before it got completely cold and washed it down with a sip of Dr Pepper. They all watched her, waiting for the rest of her story.

"In the meantime," she continued, "David was having suspicions about the mayor and the people around him. He came up with credible evidence suggesting not only that Jefferies may have been responsible for the surge in burglaries that cost the former mayor the election, but that he may have been responsible for the murder of Judge McNevin and then framed some-one else for it. Then Edgar Peeks was killed at the mayor's house and we discovered that Bryce and Rikki may have been looking for some kind of list at the scene of the crime. It also came to our attention that the mayor was trying to bring the crime lab, the DNA lab, and the osteology lab under his control. We suspected that the mayor and his friends were in-volved in something criminal but didn't know what. Are you with me so far?" she said.

"Gotcha," said Jin, grabbing another slice.

The others nodded.

"I went to see former mayor Sutton today and we had a talk. This is what his daughter told me." Diane explained about Loraine's friend Buckley seeing the mayor having dinner with the young people and giving them watches. "One of the kids wanted to talk with Buckley. They set up a meeting, but the kid didn't show and couldn't be contacted. Buckley described him as young—late teens, early twenties—Asian, and with a body-piercing ring in his nose."

"Oh," said Neva. "Well, that's similar to the bones you described."

"Yes," said Diane. "And the last time Buckley saw the young man, whose name was Malcolm Chen, cor-responds roughly to the time I estimate the bones were deposited in the ground. However, keep in mind, all of this is a thin thread supported by mostly circum-stantial evidence. I'm only about eighty percent sure of the sex of the bones—and a set of characteristics is not by any means an identification."

"If you have a tooth," said Jin, "there's a good chance I can get DNA from the root."

"I'm hoping," said Diane.

"So what do you think is going on?" said Neva.

"When I was telling the sheriff to look into a person named Malcolm Chen, Frank recognized the name as one he has on a list of hackers."

"Okay, the plot thickens," said David. "So the late mayor had himself a cybergang."

"That's what Frank said. What is that exactly?" asked Izzy. "I know hardly nothing about computers."

Diane gestured to Frank. He finished his last bite of pizza, wiped his hands on a napkin, and took a drink.

"There are several types of cybergangs, from loosely organized groups of friends who hack because they can, to well-organized networks of people who commit crimes using computers. The money they make with identity theft, stealing financial and proprietary information, and laundering money is in the billions—it's now more lucrative than illegal drugs," said Frank.

Izzy whistled.

"Wow," said Neva. "Wow." She shook her head. "Wow."

"What's with the watches?" asked Izzy.

"It's like gang tattoos, or colors," said Frank. "A way to increase the tribal feeling of the members. It lets them know if they continue to work they are in for riches."

"I'd think the kids they're recruiting would prefer iPods," said Izzy.

"With electronics, you have to update them in a year. They're a commodity, temporary. The watches are a symbol of the long term and of wealth. At least I think that's what Jefferies had in mind," Frank said.

"It's like those identical signet rings worn by Jefferies and Peeks—and Bryce," said Diane. "Defines them as a group." Diane explained to Frank about the identical rings bearing the image of Alexander the Great.

Frank laughed. "Tribal leaders get to wear different markings," he said. "It fits the profile of a lot of gang culture."

"So," said David. "We've never really speculated on the content of this mysterious list. I was thinking offshore bank account numbers. But it could be the names of the cybergang members."

"Could be more than one list," said Frank.

"I'll bet Jefferies was the only person who knew what was on the list, or lists," said David. "Or maybe Jefferies and his top two lieutenants. And now all the people who knew are dead."

"The murderer could be anybody," said Neva. "Leaders of a rival organization, members of his own organization, Bryce, Rikki, Curtis Crabtree."

"I think it's time we tell Janice Warrick to sit Rikki and Bryce down and get serious," said Diane.

"You might want to give Janice the information and see how she wants to handle it," said Izzy, smiling.

"Yes," said Diane. "That's what I meant."

Chapter 35

Diane went to her office to call Janice Warrick while the others finished off the remainder of the pizza. Janice took a while to come to the phone. Diane played with a rock that had come loose from her desk fountain—pushing it back into place and taking it out again. She looked at her reflection in the blade of a letter opener, hoping that somehow the bruising on her face had vanished. It had not.

When Janice answered, Diane related the entire chain of events and linking suppositions again. It was helpful to keep going over it. It showed up any weakness in the logic and what needed to be dealt with. There were a lot of *ifs* connecting the links in the chain.

Diane wasn't sure how Janice felt about Frank knowing so much, but there wasn't much she could do about it. They'd asked Diane to look into things on the sly when she was just a private person. She couldn't undo the resources she had used before she became the director of the crime lab again.

"This is a lot to take in," Janice said.

"And most of it may or may not be true," said Diane.

"It sounds good, though. It all fits, doesn't it?" Janice said.

"It does," said Diane. *But sometimes that's a trap, getting seduced by the nice fit.* "Jin will try to get DNA

from the tooth. Sheriff Canfield asked the Atlanta PD
to go by Malcolm Chen's apartment. If Chen is missing, they will try to find some samples to test for
DNA—a toothbrush, hairbrush, that kind of thing.
Maybe we can find some firm connections for you to
deal with.''

Diane noticed that all the sharing was going one
way. Janice was not giving any information from her
end of the investigation—which was as it should be,
but it reminded her of what Izzy had said. The detectives had a problem with her butting into an investigation. As she thought back, most of the ones she had
been heavily involved in were ones where the perpetrator had involved her by coming after her, or the
FBI had asked her to get involved. She had never just
up and announced that she was going to take on a
case and they could all report to her. By far, most of
the crime scene data she and her team gathered was
sent to the detectives in charge of a case and that was
the end of her involvement. Diane felt a bit falsely
accused.

"I think it's about time I brought Bryce in for a
talk," said Janice. "I'd like you to keep Rikki Gillinick
on at the lab for a while. I think the longer they have
hope they'll find what they are looking for, the more
information we can get from them."

"All right," said Diane. "You might want to get the
GBI to do your crime scenes until we wrap this up. I
can't allow her to work on anything beyond what we
are doing now. We probably will have to rework cases
that came under Bryce's tenure the way it is."

"I see what you mean. Do you think she'll get suspicious, not working cases?" asked Janice.

"The first thing I did after I was reinstated was to
ask David to contact TechClean to do a top-to-bottom
cleaning of the lab," said Diane. "There was a layer
of dust on everything, and that can only mean the air
filters aren't working. We have to fix that problem. I
also told them we have to recalibrate all the equip-

ment. That will take as long as I let it. Rikki was present during all that discussion, so she knows we won't be doing much outside the lab for a while."

"Okay. That's what we will do. You let us know when you're ready to take new cases. Any luck with the computer?" asked Janice.

"David and Frank are working on it, and they're very good," Diane said. "Apparently it's slow going."

"Okay. Keep me informed and thanks for the information," she said.

"Sure," said Diane. "How is Garnett?"

"Lawyered up. Which is a good thing. This has been very hard for us to deal with. I told him that if the new chief tries to hang it on him, we'll all back him up," said Janice. "He probably thought I was playing him like a perp. Frankly, I think he's protecting someone. So does the chief."

"That makes more sense than him being a murderer," said Diane.

Diane put the phone back in the cradle and immediately her cell rang.

It was plugged in on her desk. She unplugged it and flipped it open. It was Sheriff Canfield.

"Interesting news," he said. "The Atlanta police can't locate the Chen kid. His landlord hasn't seen him in weeks and the rent is overdue. The landlord says Chen was real punctual with the rent despite the ring in his nose. They collected the things you asked for. I'll send them over tomorrow."

"That was fast. How in the world did you talk Atlanta PD into responding so quickly?" said Diane. "Rosewood has to fill out forms in triplicate to get anything from them. That's amazing."

"One of the detectives is my son-in-law. The boy knows to do what I tell him pronto," said Canfield.

Diane laughed.

"Have you heard from the GBI about the bullet?" asked Diane.

"That was my second bit of news. The GBI got a

hit, and I don't like it one bit. No, sirree, I don't like this one bit."

"What is it?" said Diane.

"The bullet we found in the field is from the same gun that killed Mayor Spence Jefferies. How's that for a bad day? Now I have to deal with Rosewood. Janice Warrick is the lead detective on this. She's not too bad," he commented. "I'm still shaking my head about Delamore trying to kill you. That's why I hate to deal with Rosewood. You never know when one of them isn't right in the head."

Talk of Delamore made Diane uneasy. The whole event was just starting to sink in. The shock of it had worn off, and what was left was the fear of what might have happened, and the guilt over what did happen.

"Hopefully, he was unique," she said. "I'm sure Janice will be glad to hear about the bullet. And I know she won't try to kill you."

The sheriff chuckled. "Don't count on it. My wife says I make people mad on purpose."

"Sounds like one shooter for the two murders," said Diane. "Chen and Jefferies. How odd."

Diane fiddled with the loose rock in the fountain and dropped it on the floor. It rolled under her desk. She bent and picked it up and put it back in its hole in the fountain.

"The bullet doesn't match the one that killed yourall's chief of detectives, Edgar Peeks," said Canfield. "I understand that was from Garnett's gun, and I have to tell you, I can't believe what I'm hearing. Garnett and I have never seen quite eye to eye, but I never figured him for a cold-blooded killer. I told my deputies, there has to be some mistake," he said. "You think this new ME of yours gave them the wrong bullet? Could he be a part of this?"

"Janice Warrick and Izzy Wallace witnessed the autopsy. They saw him take the bullet out of Peeks' brain and give it to them. Janice said it was from the gun they took off Garnett at the scene."

"I hate hearing that," said Canfield.

"So do I," said Diane. "He has been very support-
ive of me since we put the crime unit in, and very
protective of the museum."

"Before I talk to Janice, I'd like to speak with you
more about what's going on. You can explain to me
about this cybergang stuff you were talking about.
They don't like to share information in Rosewood.
They expect me to do all the sharing. That's why I
don't like dealing with them. They act like Rosewood's a big city and we're just rubes out here. I don't
live but a mile from the city limits, so I don't know
who they think they are fooling."

"I know what you mean about the sharing going
only one way," said Diane.

"Oh, one more thing," he said. "My wife wants to
know what you wear to a white-tie function. We've
never been to one."

Diane smiled. "Andie, my assistant, is putting together a newsletter that gives all the details. I'll make
sure you get a copy," she said.

"I would appreciate that. I told my wife I wouldn't
understand fashion advice even if I wrote it down. Just
tell me this, do I have to wear one of them top hats?
I told the wife that there are just some things where
I draw the line, and that's one of them."

"No. No top hat," said Diane.

"Good." He laughed. "Can't you just see me in one
of those?"

Diane seriously couldn't.

She hung up the phone and went back into her
sitting room. Neva was dusting the inside of the computer case for prints. David and Frank were at the
computer discussing the decryption procedures. Jin
was sitting on the sofa with Izzy, giving him a course
in DNA. Someone had cleaned up all the refuse from
the pizza dinner and disposed of it.

Diane pulled up a chair and sat down beside Frank.

"How are we doing?" she asked.

"We're just starting," said Frank. "If it's encrypted

using a very long key, then we may not be able to
break it before the end of this century."

"Well, how do hackers get in?" asked Diane. "How
do they break the encryption?"

"The best way is to not," said David.

"Is this Yoda talking?" said Diane.

David smiled. "No, it's me. One of the drawbacks
with encryption is that it doesn't work before the information is encrypted."

"No," agreed Diane. "I can see how it wouldn't."

"That's the power of recruiting computer-savvy
people to work in businesses the way Jefferies did,"
said Frank. "They have access to the information before it is encrypted. They can install their own software that steals and reroutes the information to a
place of their choosing."

David nodded. "According to Sutton's research,
Jefferies placed people in banking, insurance, and government agencies. It boggles the mind the amount of
information he had access to. At this point I don't
know which would be more useful, a list of bank account numbers or a list of people he had in place."

"One of the things the heads of these gangs do,"
said Frank, "is recruit someone from a technical field
that is not computer science, like, say, engineering.
Give him advanced computer training and get him a
job, for example, in the aerospace industry. Install him
as a sleeper in a company, doing work not directly
connected with sensitive information. Put him someplace where he would never be suspected. Give him
time to work his way up to a spot where he can use
those advanced computer skills you gave him to steal
company secrets, financial data, personal data—a whole
range of possibilities. A high-placed sleeper can rob
the company's databases and cover his tracks so no
one knows he's the thief. I use *him* as an example. It
could just as easily be a Mata Hari."

"It sounds very cold war," said Diane.

"It's like that exactly," said Frank. "They've adopted
old KGB tactics, and it works quite well."

Diane was letting everything David and Frank were telling her sink in. Suddenly, a red light on the wall began flashing and issuing a low but penetrating sound. They all looked at Diane.

"Someone's trying to break into the crime lab," she said.

Chapter 36

Diane looked at the computer. Neva was frozen over the case with a fingerprint card in her hand. Frank and David made eye contact with her, their faces creased in frowns. Izzy stood up behind her, ready to go.

"The computer. I'll bet someone's after the computer," said Diane. "They don't know it's here. In case they figure it out, all of you stay here."

She started for the door.

"Don't you need backup?" said Izzy.

"I have backup. My entire security department should be on their way. I need all of you to stay here and protect the computer."

Diane dashed out the doors, locking each one in turn behind her—her sitting room door, her office, Andie's office. When she got to the hallway she could see her security personnel hurrying out of the security office.

"What's going on?" she asked when she met up with Chanell, her chief of security.

"The guards on the museum side of the crime lab don't know anything. I haven't been able to get Mickey, the outside guard, to answer," she said.

There were two ways to get to the crime lab—from the museum side on the third floor, and from an elevator on the outside of the building. When she installed the crime lab, Diane had an elevator built on the outside of the museum that went directly to the third floor and opened into the crime lab. At ground level was a small room with an outside door that provided access to the elevator. That room always had a receptionist and a guard on duty in the daytime and a guard at night. It was that room that apparently was compromised.

Chanell sent two guards up to the third floor to reinforce the ones that were already there. Diane, Chanell, and two guards left the museum by the main front door and walked around the outside of the building toward the west wing.

It was already dark. The parking lot lights were on and the entire front lot was illuminated. Diane could see that some of the lights were out just ahead toward the west wing. Not good.

They had to thread through a stream of people entering and leaving through the door to the museum restaurant. Diane and the security personnel went at a fast walk, and Diane hoped they weren't attracting the attention of the diners.

It was cold. Diane hadn't thought to bring a coat. She walked faster.

Just ahead two security guards came out of the double doors of the main entrance to the west wing of the building.

The ropes were up that blocked people from parking on the west end after museum hours. They ducked under the ropes and proceeded to the end of the building.

This was taking too long. It was a flaw in the arrangement. They needed a quicker way to get to the outside entrance to the crime lab elevator. They stopped just as they got to the corner of the building.

"Send a couple of guards back through the dino room, out the back entrance. Have them come around the building from that way," said Diane.

"Good idea," said Chanell.

"Let's not have any shooting unless it's life or death. I don't want to alarm the restaurant visitors," said Diane.

Two security guards went back into the building. Another two went around the corner ahead of Diane and Chanell, who followed when they saw the guards gesture that it was clear.

There was no one outside the entrance to the small room at the base of the elevator. They couldn't see behind the room, but the two guards who went around the building should be there soon.

Diane listened for the sound of the elevator. She looked at the shaft on the side of the building that housed the elevator car—not that she could see anything. She supposed she looked because that's where the sound would come from if the elevator was in use. But there was no noise of any kind except the background noise of people entering and leaving the restaurant.

It was cold enough to produce puffs of fog with each breath. Diane's fingers were starting to ache. What was she thinking, not grabbing a coat and gloves? She blew into her hands.

She heard the noise first, for she was the first one to turn her head in the direction of the door. The door opened slowly, then stopped after a couple of inches. Her security staff trained their guns in that direction. Chanell motioned for Diane to get behind them.

Her heart thumped in her chest and made a lump in her throat. Suddenly and violently the door burst open. A figure dressed from head to foot in black came out of the door holding a young woman in front of him. He had one arm around her throat and was holding a gun to her head with the other hand. She was lightly dressed in jeans and a T-shirt.

Who is she? thought Diane.

There was silence for a moment: the figure holding a hostage confronting Diane's security guards. A face-off.

The male voice of the perp broke the silence.

"Leave us or I'll kill her."

So common. But Diane hadn't expected creativity.

"That's Mickey's wife," Chanell whispered to Diane.

Mickey was the security guard for this end of the building. That must be how the perp got Mickey to open the door—he used Mickey's wife. The problem for the perp, though, was that Mickey didn't know the key code to the crime lab door once the elevator got up there. Bad planning.

Mickey's wife coughed. The perp pushed the muzzle of the gun against her temple and told her to shut up.

"Let her go," said Diane in a calmer voice than she felt.

"I'll kill her," he said again.

He wasn't large. That was good. Not much body mass.

"You do that," said Diane, "and you lose your shield. These people are friends of Mickey. You kill his wife; they kill you." She hoped she sounded cold and menacing enough.

The woman's body trembled as she coughed again, and he squeezed her tighter and told her again to shut up.

"You're making her cough. You're holding her throat too tight. Ease up a little," said Diane.

He backed with his hostage in the direction of the woods bordering the museum. The access road that ran through the woods wasn't far away. Diane guessed that was where his getaway vehicle was parked.

"I have an offer," said Diane. "Exchange me for your hostage."

"No," whispered Chanell. "Not a good idea."

Diane ignored her. "In a show of good faith, I'll get the guards to back away," said Diane.

She told Chanell to back her people up. It was obvious Chanell didn't want to do it.

"Reduce the tension," said Diane. "Give him fifty feet of space so he will calm down."

"No tricks," he said. "No tricks, damn you."

"No tricks," said Diane.

Chanell and her guards backed off, leaving Diane facing the perp holding Mickey's wife.

"Listen to me," said Diane. "I think you are after the computer, aren't you?"

He said nothing.

"It's not in the crime lab. Even if you could get in there, you wouldn't find what you want. I have it somewhere else. The advantage to exchanging the young woman for me is that I know where the computer is. She doesn't."

He was quiet for several moments.

Where are the other two guards we sent through the building? Didn't they get the instructions right?

"Come over here slowly," he said. "Don't try anything, or I'll take out you and the woman before I go down."

"No one has to die," said Diane. "We all want to get out of this alive."

Diane stepped forward slowly. When she was directly in front of him, he told her to turn around, facing away from him. She did what he said. He shoved the girl to the ground and grabbed Diane from behind.

Okay, thought Diane, *so far the plan is working beautifully.*

She was suddenly knocked off her feet as the man yelled and fell down, kicking at something.

"What the—?" said Diane; then she saw that Mickey's wife had him by the leg and was biting him.

Diane was lying on his gun arm. She wrestled him for the weapon, and was joined in the effort by Mickey's wife, who held his hand down and bit his thumb. He screamed and released the gun, and Mickey's wife picked it up.

The man pushed himself unsteadily to his feet and backed up wildly, with Diane close after him. Mickey's wife stood aiming the gun at the man. Unfortunately, the way she was aiming, she could just as easily hit Diane, who stood between them, and it didn't appear that she was skilled with firearms.

Chanell and the guards were running toward them, and Chanell deflected the gun before Mickey's wife could shoot the wrong person. The man took advantage of the fact that Diane was standing in the line of fire and started running toward the woods. Diane ran after him, followed closely by Chanell.

His truck was parked on the access road, just as Diane had suspected. The driver's door was open. *Ready for a fast getaway*, thought Diane. She was just a few feet from him, but he jumped in the truck and slammed the door before she could tackle him. Diane ran up and grabbed at him through the open window, trying to rip his mask off. He held on to her and started the truck's engine.

Oh, hell, thought Diane.

Chapter 37

The man held her wrist tight with his left hand as he turned the key in the ignition. Diane grabbed his thumb in a panic and pulled. He yelled and tried to tighten his grip. Diane felt the nails of his fingers digging into her flesh. The truck didn't start immediately, but on the second turn of the key, the engine came to life and the truck started forward.

Diane pulled harder on his thumb. She ran alongside the truck, struggling to wrestle her arm from his grasp as the truck gained speed. He yelped as she broke his thumb back. She fell backward into the ditch on the side of the road, rolling, and scraping her face on the gravel.

She lay there for a second, too stunned to get up. She suddenly realized that the sound of the truck wasn't fading, but getting louder. She rose to her hands and knees and looked in the direction of the sound. The truck was backing up toward her. She leaped into the nearby bushes just before the truck's left rear tire hit the ditch where she had lain. The truck bounced and the rear slammed into the embankment; then, its tires spinning, it sped off, spraying gravel over Diane.

Diane stood and watched the truck fishtail down the access road and out of sight. She noted that it didn't have a tag. It was hard to see the color in the dark, but she thought it was either black, or navy blue, or perhaps dark green. She also noted that it was a Ford Ranger, around the year 2000, give or take.

Chanell came running up the road along with one of the security guards.

"Are you all right?" she said. "Dr. Fallon, you don't have enough excitement hanging off the side of a cliff; you have to go off trying to run down a maniac in a truck?"

"Apparently not," muttered Diane, dusting herself off. She shook out her hair, running her hands through it. She put a hand to her face and came away with blood on her fingers. Chanell gave her a tissue.

"How's Mickey?" said Diane. "Is he all right?"

"I don't know," said Chanell. "I hurried after you when we got the gun away from Shara—Mickey's wife."

"Did his wife say why she tried to shoot me?" said Diane.

Chanell gave a short, mirthless laugh. "She was scared and angry," said Chanell. "The woman has a temper. She was fighting us trying to get the gun out of her hand. I think she just panicked. You know how some people go all crazy when they're scared."

They hurried back to the museum. The other two security guards, the ones who were supposed to go through the building and out the back, were there looking sheepish.

"What in the hell did the two of you do?" said Chanell. "Stop for coffee?"

"One of the doors was blocked by that delivery truck," said one of the guards. "There was a storage container in front of the door on the loading dock. We had to go around to the restaurant's back entrance."

"That's the truck I told those guys not to leave unattended?" said Chanell.

"Well, they did leave it," said the other guard. "It was backed up against the door."

"I'll get on it right away, Dr. Fallon. I told those guys they had to unload and move the trucks, that they couldn't block the doors."

"Is that the material for the new exhibits?" said Diane.

"Yes, ma'am," said Chanell.

"They were supposed to go to the east wing loading dock with that anyway," said Diane.

"Don't I know it. These guys are stubborn and hard to deal with," said Chanell. "They've been giving our workers a fit."

"Then I'll cross them off our list of shippers," said Diane. "What was wrong with the outside door in the Arachnid Room?" said Diane.

"That room's being redone and it was locked off," the guard said. "We thought we could get out the restaurant door quicker. We're just really sorry."

"We can sort the access problems out tomorrow," said Diane. "What happened here?" Diane gestured toward Mickey and his wife. The two were huddled together.

Another of the security guards stepped forward and started to speak just as the police arrived, headed by Detective Janice Warrick. Out of the corner of her eye Diane saw Frank walking across the parking lot.

"What happened here?" said Warrick.

Diane allowed Chanell to explain to Janice what had happened. Chanell and the security guard who had released Mickey told Janice the story, from the sound of the alarm, to the almost apprehension of the perpetrator, to releasing Mickey.

Frank came and stood by Diane. He looked at her face for several moments and gave her a handkerchief to replace the Kleenex.

"Do you need to go to the emergency room?" said Janice.

"No," said Diane. "The last time I was there they offered me a season pass."

Everyone smiled or snickered except Frank.

"Where are the others?" Diane asked Frank in a low voice.

"With the computer in your office. Izzy wanted to come with me, but I told him if he wanted to work for you he had to start following your orders. I was under no such constraints. Are you all right?"

"Yes. I've had worse scrapes in a cave," she said.

"I know," said Frank.

Diane listened to the stories. Mickey and his wife walked over together and told Janice what happened. The wife had been grabbed at home as she was getting groceries out of her car. The man, whose face she never saw, told her he had a partner at her parents' home who would shoot them if she didn't come with him to the crime lab. At the lab she was forced to get her husband, Mickey, to open the door. When she did, the masked man pushed his way in, slapped Mickey on the side of the head with his gun, and made Mickey's wife cuff her husband with disposable restraints. The perp then restrained her and took the elevator to the third floor. He was there for several minutes before he came down and demanded the code to the crime lab door. Mickey, of course, didn't know it. The guy didn't believe him and was threatening Mickey's wife. Mickey told him help would be coming soon because the guy had set off the alarm by messing with the crime lab door, and that he, in fact, did not know the code for just such occasions. The perp cut the wife's ties and told her to open the door an inch and if she tried anything she was dead. That's when he burst out the door holding her.

Chanell explained the rest of the events, including Diane offering herself in exchange. Diane cringed. She knew Frank would be angry.

"Why did you do that?" said Janice.

"I could see Mickey's wife was frightened and I thought that if I could convince the guy I knew what he was looking for and could get it for him, he would let her go and we could get the upper hand. Then she grabbed his ankle, tripped him up, and bit him, and from there things got out of control."

"He threatened my family," said Shara. "He hit my husband and he touched me. Nobody touches me." She folded her arms under her breasts.

"Has anyone heard from your parents?" Janice asked Shara. "Are they okay?"

"Yes, the first thing I did was call them," said Shara. "They're fine. The jerk was lying. There wasn't anyone at their house."

"Let's focus on the perpetrator," said Janice. "Dr. Fallon, you think he was after the computer?"

Diane nodded. "He seemed to be. When you find him, he'll have a bite mark on his right leg, and his left thumb will be broken. And I imagine he'll have a few minor cuts and scrapes from the fall on the pavement."

"Do you have any idea who he might be?" said Janice. "Could he have been the shadowy figure in the video?"

There was that sword hanging over her again. Diane had almost forgotten about it.

"No," she said. "This guy was smaller."

Diane quickly gave a description of the man's build and his truck, hoping Janice wouldn't bring up the shadow man again.

"I know who I'd look at," said Diane. "Curtis Crabtree. He was the same size, and he figures in all this in some way. Plus, he seems to lack good judgment. I'd at least have a look at his ankle and thumb."

Frank insisted on taking Diane to the emergency room when they finished. She didn't argue, saving her words for when the real argument would come later. They waited an hour in the emergency room. It took another two hours for the tests that told her she was fine, just banged up.

She was standing outside waiting for Frank to drive around with the car when Shane Eastling, the ME, walked up to the door and started to enter. He stopped when he saw Diane. A shock of brown hair blew over his freckled face. He didn't shove it out of the way. She thought he was going to give her the kind of sympathetic comments she had gotten from everyone who saw her face—especially now that she looked even worse. He didn't.

"I don't appreciate you trying to tell me how to do my job," he said. "And I don't intend to do yours for you."

"What on earth are you talking about?" she asked.

"The watch that was on backward or upside down, or whatever. That Warrick woman was all over me about it and was questioning me about anything else I didn't put in my report. I autopsy bodies. If you can't do your little observations at the crime scene, don't ask me to do them for you. Who in the hell do you think you are?"

"For one thing, I'm the person who was *not* working the mayor's crime scene. That would be Bryce. Did you know him in school?" asked Diane. She looked at his finger for a signet ring. There was none.

"What?" Eastling looked annoyed and puzzled. "No. Why would you ask that?"

"You recommended Dr. Jeffcote-Smith to him," she said.

"No," he said slowly as if to a child. "It's she I went to school with once upon a time. Bryce mentioned he was looking for a good forensic anthropologist. I immediately thought of Jennifer."

"Look, Dr. Eastling, from here on out our paths are going to cross, and there will be times when we will have to work together. I would like to be able to do that as civilly as possible. If I have offended you, then I apologize. It was certainly not my intention."

He looked at her for a moment as if surprised. "As long as you understand what your job is, I don't see why we can't get along," he said.

"Good," said Diane. "Let me ask you, did you know any of the mayor's friends?" she asked. "They were all very well educated."

"Were they? I went to Cal State as an undergraduate and Chicago for med school. Where did they go?" He smirked as if expecting her to say Podunk U. Maybe he didn't know them.

"University of Pennsylvania, Wharton School of Business," she said.

His smirk faded. "Really? What the hell were they doing being policemen here? Did they flunk out?"

"No, they did quite well. I was hoping you knew them and could answer that question—what were they doing here? Puzzling isn't it?" she said.

"It is," he said. "Bryce go to school there too?"

"Bryce had the best grades of all of them," she said.

"I wouldn't have thought that," he said.

"Probably because he was working outside of his discipline," said Diane.

Eastling shook his head and thought for a minute as if processing the new information.

"Can't help you with any of them."

He brushed past her and went on in.

She watched him through the glass doors and saw him meet Jennifer Jeffcote-Smith, who must have been there ahead of him. They stood for a moment talking. It became clear to her now, he was smitten with Jennifer. From the body language, Diane wasn't sure if it was reciprocated. That's why he found her a job here. And possibly why he was so pissed with Diane. She had spoiled all his plans by being the rightful occupant of the osteology lab. They headed toward the cafeteria. An odd place for an assignation, but probably a safe one. Who would suspect a hospital cafeteria as the site for a romantic rendezvous?

Frank drove up and Diane got in the car. She was not looking forward to the ride home. Frank was very slow to anger, but she sensed she had crossed his threshold.

Chapter 38

They drove back home in silence. Diane dozed along the way and awoke with a start when the car stopped, realizing that her own vehicle was still parked at the museum.

Frank built a fire while Diane took a shower and put on a warm nightgown and robe. She sat on a sofa and watched the flames dancing in the fireplace. Occasionally the wood popped and tiny sparks flew onto the rock hearth. She smelled the hot chocolate Frank was making—one of his ultimate comfort foods for cold nights of fighting crime and maniacs. He'd made it for her more than once.

Frank came from the kitchen with two cups and gave her one. He sat down on the sofa opposite hers.

"How are you feeling?" he asked.

His voice always made him sound even tempered. It was one of the things Diane admired about him, but now she found it a bit annoying.

"Physically, I feel finc. I'm a little weary of waiting for the other shoe to drop. I know you're angry with me."

"Yes," he said, "I am. Why did you go running out after that guy? Why did you offer to exchange yourself for the hostage? You should never do that. Why didn't you just wait for the police to arrive? You have no training in that kind of physical police work." His voice wasn't as calm now. He set his cup down without taking a drink.

"I thought I could handle the situation," said Diane.

She jumped as a lightbulb blew out in the table lamp beside the sofa, plunging them into a darkness broken only by the firelight. Frank got up and turned on the overhead chandelier. Before he sat down again, he got a bulb from the closet in the hall. Diane watched him unscrew the old bulb and screw in the new one, an act that strangely tickled her brain and oddly reminded her of the loose rock in her desk fountain. Frank laid the old bulb on the table, turned off the chandelier, and sat back down.

As Diane watched him, she realized that was another idiosyncrasy she had always liked in Frank. He took care of problems in his house immediately. If a light blew, he replaced it. If a faucet dripped, he repaired it himself or had it fixed right away. If a door sagged, he had it straightened. If you wait, he said, it'll only get worse and you'll have a bigger repair. Consequently, his house was always in order—though not necessarily always neat. He did have a high tolerance for paper clutter, especially on the dining room table, that bothered Diane. But the house always worked. Nothing was ever broken for long.

That's what he was doing now. Fixing his home before the problem got worse. Frank's arguments were never accusations or recriminations, not like her ex-husband's arguments. Frank's were always about fixing things, sorting through things, getting to the bottom of things. He didn't like to go to bed angry. But sometimes Diane thought it was best to let matters alone. Sometimes they did just fix themselves.

"What was it about the situation you thought you could handle? Was it the gun in his hand, or the choke hold on the hostage?" said Frank.

Diane set her cup down. She hadn't taken a sip either. Hot chocolate just didn't fit her mood.

"Look, Frank, do you really expect an answer to

that? I did what I thought was right at the time. Was it the best thing? I don't know. We're all alive, no shots were fired, but we don't have the perp, so I guess it's just half and half."

"Diane, I know the directors of several state crime labs, and none of them ever have the . . . the incidents that you do. Why is that?"

"I don't know, Frank. I really don't. Do you think it's my fault Delamore attacked me?"

"Is that what you think this is about?" He wrinkled his brow. "Do you feel guilty over his death?"

"He died. Of course I feel guilty."

"Don't. The only difference between Delamore and a murderer is success. He was going to kill you." Frank hesitated a moment. "It's not Delamore you're feeling guilty about, is it? It's Ariel. It's this time of year in particular; you feel like you have to save everyone. Even if it means killing yourself. Isn't that it?"

Tears came to Diane's eyes at the mention of Ariel. "I have no desire to die," she said vehemently. "None."

"But you do feel like you always have to take action. To stop things before they get worse," said Frank.

Ariel was Diane's adopted daughter. Actually the adoption hadn't gone completely through. It was in progress, stuck in the slowness of bureaucracy. But the feelings Diane had for Ariel weren't stuck in the process. Ariel was her daughter. She was her heart.

Ariel had simply shown up at the mission where Diane and her human rights team were staying in South America. She had walked out of the jungle—a toddler, dirty, but unhurt, nameless. All efforts to find parents or relatives were fruitless. It was a surprise to Diane that she decided to adopt Ariel. She never thought of herself as particularly motherly, but Ariel had brought that out.

She didn't take her usual leaves of absence, but lived at the mission with Ariel, working out of there on her job with World Accord International. They had a good life until Diane became too successful at uncovering the evil deeds of a particularly vile dictator.

He retaliated by killing everyone at the mission while Diane and her team were away. She blamed herself for not just taking Ariel away, smuggling her out if the papers weren't ready. She had the contacts to do it. But she was so involved in doing things the legal way, she didn't even consider it. This month was the anniversary of the massacre, and it always made both her and David ache with the pain of their losses.

Frank was probably getting to the heart of why she did things the way she did. She didn't take action then, but she would now. Always take action before things get worse—a subconscious code she lived by. Not so subconscious. Diane wanted to make her corner of the world safe for people to live in.

Tears ran down her cheeks. She looked up at the picture on the mantel of herself and Ariel in their mother-daughter outfits she'd ordered from the States. Frank took her hand, then pulled her to him.

"Sometimes you have to let other people fix things," he said.

"Sometimes they don't," said Diane. "I waited for the government to issue Ariel's adoption papers; they never did. Sometimes you have to do things yourself."

"Let's go to bed," he said.

"Good idea. I'm very tired."

Frank got up, closed the fireplace screen, and turned out the lights.

Diane dreamed of changing lightbulbs. All over the house she was changing out the bulbs one after the other. Even if they didn't need it, she changed them anyway. She woke up with a start.

That was perhaps the stupidest dream I've ever had, she thought.

She looked at the clock. It was early. Frank was still asleep. He wasn't driving into Atlanta until the cybergang case was concluded. His bosses were excited by the discoveries about the mayor and the gang. They smelled a big case about to burst wide open. They, like everyone else, wanted what was hidden on the computer. Diane was lying there thinking that maybe it was a red herring. She had heard by way of Izzy—Janice was talking to him—that nothing was found on the computers of Edgar Peeks. Just business. It was the mayor's computer everyone had pinned their hopes on. It was the one that had the serious encryption.

Diane remembered she hadn't asked Frank about the latest on his Black Light hacker. Who was he? It was a fragile link—a message they could see only with a black light. But it was a good one, a good circumstantial clue to add to all the other circumstantial clues they had stacking up but couldn't verify.

Diane got out of bed and went to the kitchen to make pancakes. They were a favorite of Frank's. Maybe they would make up for almost getting herself killed—repeatedly.

She had to call Vanessa. Diane wasn't looking forward to that. She had just got the crime lab back and already the "danger" clause of the contract was violated. Would it always be a risky venture? Frank was right. None of the other crime labs attracted so much danger. Was it because it was in the museum and not at a police station that perps felt safe trying to break in? Maybe she should move it away from the museum and resign as crime lab director.

She started mixing the ingredients for the pancakes. As the griddle was heating up, she walked back to the bedroom to see if Frank was waking up. He was in the shower.

"I'm making pancakes," she said and heard him mumble something like, "Great . . . won't be long."

She poured batter on the griddle—always a messy operation for her. As the pancakes were cooking, she opened a drawer to dig for a spatula. Frank kept all his kitchen utensils in one big drawer. Diane kept meaning to straighten it out but had never gotten around to it. She searched for the particular spatula she liked to use. She pulled out a pair of ice tongs and put them down on the counter. She saw the spatula she wanted, pulled it out, and flipped the pancakes.

She looked down at the tongs. Great. She had laid them in pancake batter she had dribbled on the counter. She picked them up and stared at the pattern the batter made on the counter. She had seen a similar pattern before, and she knew why she had dreamed about lightbulbs all night.

Chapter 39

After breakfast, and after explaining her epiphany-bad-dream idea to Frank, and after she downloaded crime scene and autopsy photos, and after Frank drove her to the museum to get her SUV, Diane went to the police shooting range and asked to see the logbook.

The sergeant on duty was reluctant, even with Diane's freshly minted ID. He was torn, she could see. He liked Garnett and he knew that even though Diane was back at the crime lab and officially neutral, she was working in Garnett's favor. But he also had liked Harve Delamore.

Diane smiled in the friendliest manner she could muster and said if he needed it for his paperwork, she could call the chief of police for authorization. Grudgingly, he showed her the book. Diane wanted to ask him why he and others who felt the way he did thought it was all right for Delamore to try to kill her. Why was that okay with them? She didn't understand it, even accounting for the male-bonding thing. Surely morality should kick in and tell their conscience that Delamore was wrong to try to do what he did. Obviously it wasn't rational. It was just their feelings. They liked Delamore and now he was dead and Diane had something to do with it.

Diane examined the logbook and found something, though it was not exactly what she was looking for. It only added another link in the chain, but at least it didn't destroy it. She had to do a little rethinking of the sequence of events. Obviously, if she was right, there had been a change in plan along the way, a change in the intended target. Who could it have been?

Diane thanked the sergeant sincerely and drove to the city jail, where they were keeping Garnett. She didn't have any trouble seeing him. Odd, thought Diane, one would think he would be better guarded than a logbook at the gun range.

Garnett didn't look good. There were dark circles under his eyes and his whole body seemed to sag under the weight of his situation. Then again, he probably looked better than she did.

"There's something wrong." He began talking before Diane could say what she came for. His reticence with Janice apparently didn't roll over to Diane. His feelings poured out of him.

"Something's wrong. I didn't kill Edgar Peeks. I don't know who to trust. These are people I've known for a long time, and I can't believe they would be part of a conspiracy. But they have to be. I didn't shoot him. Not even my own lawyer believes me. Even my family is doubting me. This is a nightmare."

"I know," said Diane. "I believe you and I'm working on proving it. Let me tell you what I think happened."

There was more surprise on Garnett's face than relief. He stared at Diane, not speaking.

"I shouldn't be speaking to you, but just in case you may be able to remember something that will help, you need to know what's going on. You also need to have some hope. It must be like you've entered the Twilight Zone, or fell into a Kafka novel."

"You can explain this?" he said after a moment.

"I think so," said Diane. "The main problem you have is that a bullet from your gun was in Peeks' head. Janice and Izzy, both good, reliable witnesses, saw Shane Eastling remove it from Peeks' brain. And when they arrested you, you had your gun with you," said Diane.

"In a nutshell, yes, that's my problem. But they've made a mistake—"

Diane held up a hand. She wasn't sure where to start. She couldn't really tell him that she got the idea from fiddling with a loose rock in her fountain, or changing a lightbulb. But that was what triggered her idea: taking something out and putting something back in.

"I think someone got hold of one of your spent bullets when you were qualifying at the gun range. They killed Peeks with their gun, dug out their bullet with a pair of forceps, and replaced it with your bullet."

Garnett looked surprised and disbelieving, even though this would show him to be innocent. It was too far-fetched, he was probably thinking. And it was far-fetched. But he said nothing. He just waited for Diane to explain herself.

"I wondered why your bullet wasn't a through-and-through. Your gun has enough power to shoot a bullet all the way through the head at the close distance from which Peeks was shot. It didn't—but that can happen. Then I thought, what if he was really shot with a much smaller-caliber gun—something like a .22 would be powerful enough to pass through the skull bone and lodge in the brain, but would not be strong enough to break through the bone on the other side of the head. And there was the question of why there was so much damage to the brain tissue. There was no ricocheting of the bullet inside the skull cavity, just one straight path, with more damage to the brain tissue than you would expect. That can happen too.

"But all that got me to thinking. I began with the assumption that everyone around here is telling the truth. If that's the case, what happened?"

"Do you have any evidence?" said Garnett.

The wistfulness in his voice was pitiful, thought Diane.

"Jin and David found a bloodstain on the floor under the chest in the foyer where Peeks' body was found. It had a pattern in it. I think the pattern was made by a pair of bloody forceps."

She didn't mention that ice tongs and pancake batter make a similar pattern.

"Pendleton told me he saw Rikki Gillinick pocket something shiny at the crime scene. I think she found the forceps. Either she killed Peeks and was reclaiming evidence she left behind, or Bryce did it and she collected the forceps for him, or perhaps to keep and hold over him. If that's the case, the forceps are somewhere and we can find them. The forceps in our crime scene kits have a nice solid, shiny, flat place at the top that is great for fingerprints. And they would leave a pattern like the one Jin and David found in the blood."

Garnett looked a little less skeptical. In fact, he seemed to be warming up to the idea.

"How did they get one of my spent bullets?" he asked.

"At the shooting range," said Diane. "The logbook at the range shows that the last two times you were there, the only other person shooting was Edgar Peeks. Both of those times were before Jefferies and Peeks were killed. I think Peeks retrieved your bullets from a target after you left because he and his fellow conspirators were planning to kill someone and to frame you. Somewhere along the line the shit really hit the fan and the plans changed."

"I see where you're going with this," Garnett said. "Let's suppose they did need bullets fired from my gun. If it were me doing it, I'd find a way to get into the reference collection that's kept by Ballistics. They keep spent bullets from every officer's gun on file for comparison with bullets fired during a police action."

"Good idea," said Diane. "I should have thought of that."

"All this is plausible," he said. "But how can we prove it?"

"Bryce and Rikki are the keys," she said. "We have to find out from them somehow."

Garnett was silent a moment, quietly nodding his head. He rubbed his eyes with the heels of his hands.

"At least this gives me some hope," he said. "I know how paranoids feel now. I was thinking that Izzy and Janice were in on some plot against me, along with everyone else."

Diane smiled. "Just keep the faith. We'll figure this thing out."

Garnett looked better when she left than when she had arrived—a good sign. Diane went to find Janice Warrick.

Janice was at her desk going over some of the same crime photos that Diane had pored over earlier. Diane pulled up a chair and sat down.

"Do you know what this is?" Janice showed her a picture of the bloodstain under the hallway chest.

"I think so. That's why I wanted to talk with you."

Diane went over the scenario again. It was received better each time she presented it. Frank thought she was nuts at first. Garnett was cautiously optimistic. Janice was excited about it. Either she was getting really good at explaining her theory or Janice knew something Diane didn't.

"I hope this is helpful," said Diane, silently urging her to share.

"It is." Janice leaned closer. "One of the things we found in Peeks' apartment was a small jar of spent bullets. We gave them to Ballistics, but they weren't a priority. It just looked like he collected used bullets. But now . . . I'll check the Ballistics reference collection for anything missing."

Diane felt a remarkable sense of relief. Secretly, she herself had thought she was a little nuts.

"I spoke with Garnett," said Diane. "I thought he needed a boost, and I know you have to walk a pretty fine line. Actually, I do too, but they watch you more closely."

Janice's grin surprised Diane. She was all geared up to defend herself for meddling.

"I was also hoping Garnett would remember something. We'll see," added Diane. "Did you get a chance to speak with Curtis Crabtree?"

"Haven't been able to find him. We have an APB out." Janice grinned again. "I feel this coming to a good end."

Diane could see that a good end included commendations to Janice for solving Rosewood's case of the decade. Diane hoped it came to pass.

"I need to talk to Chief Monroe. Do you think he's in?" said Diane.

Janice looked a little suspicious. Diane was sure Janice didn't want her thunder stolen. Diane didn't blame her. Janice had to work hard in a sometimes hostile male-dominated police force to get to where she was. She needed credit when credit was due her.

"I think he is," said Janice. "He's been fielding calls from reporters. Having two leaders killed within a couple of days has brought us a lot of attention. It's very high profile. The chief is thinking about letting the FBI take a look at Jefferies' computer."

"Anyone who can crack it will be good," said Diane. She didn't say that it would piss David off, not to mention Frank.

Diane went upstairs to the office of the chief of police. Acting mayor Edward Van Ross was with him.

Chapter 40

"I'm glad you came by," said Mayor Van Ross. "I was going to call."

Even though it was Chief Monroe's office and the chief was sitting behind his desk, it was Edward Van Ross who motioned to a chair and indicated for Diane to sit down.

"I haven't spoken with Vanessa yet," said Diane, taking a seat. "Already, the 'Danger, Will Robinson' part of the contract has been violated."

Edward smiled. "That has something to do with science fiction, right? Mother said you are a fan. We got a lot of science fiction at the family reunion."

"So I understand," said Diane.

He seemed bemused by the whole idea.

"Didn't the report say you're having to rewire the security cameras back into the grid Bryce had disconnected?" said Edward. "I think we can call this a grace period—adjusting back to your rule."

My rule. An interesting phrase, thought Diane. "The cameras will be back in the security net tomorrow," she said.

"What I came to talk about is Izzy Wallace," said Diane. "I'd like him to be part of my team. I need someone to replace Jin in the crime lab, and Izzy has expressed a desire. He's also been very helpful and has shown a willingness to learn the process."

Chief Monroe nodded his head as though he liked the idea. Diane thought it was probably a done deal as far as the police were concerned. She suspected that perhaps Izzy had already set everything in motion.

"We have an officer who's injured and we want to put him on a desk job," said Chief Monroe, "so this will be a good move. Izzy's a good guy. It's a shame what happened to his family. What happened to a lot of families," he added.

"Yes," said Diane. "That was one of Rosewood's worst times." *Worse than now,* she thought, *because it was young people who died then.*

"I'll put through the paperwork," said the chief.

Diane went back downstairs. She spotted Izzy carrying a file to one of the detectives and waved to attract his attention.

"I've cleared it with Monroe," she said when he walked over to her. "If you want to back out, now's the time, before he gets the paperwork in."

Izzy grinned. "When do I start?"

"Chief Monroe will let you know. I imagine it will be right away," she said.

Izzy rubbed his hands together and looked around the room grinning. Diane realized this was his end run around the politics and bureaucracy that hadn't let him become a detective. He wouldn't be a detective now, exactly, but he would look like one and on occasion would get to do what detectives do. She really hoped this was the right course of action.

Janice motioned for Diane to come to her desk. She held a phone next to her ear and looked as if she was waiting.

"At first it looked like all Garnett's reference bullets were accounted for," Janice said. "But the clerk noticed that his file had been tampered with. I told him to verify all the bullets again. I also called the gun range and asked if Edgar Peeks liked to collect rounds. He did. Interesting, huh?" said Janice. She looked happy.

"This looks like a good lead, then," said Diane.

Janice nodded. "I'll let you know when I find out

anything." She got back on the phone and Diane left for the museum.

The desktop screen with all the little rows of software icons was still showing on Jefferies' computer when she walked into her office sitting room. It looked as if David and Frank had not made any progress. But they both looked upbeat. There were several flash drives lying beside the computer. She pulled up a chair. Frank reached over and squeezed her hand.

"The two of you look happy," she said.

"We're making progress. David and I pooled our decryption tools," said Frank. "David has written some impressive ones himself."

"Is that what's on all the flash drives?" she said.

Frank nodded. "We had an idea. Neva's gone over to the crime lab to get a gadget the mayor had."

"A gadget?" said Diane.

"You'll see," said David. "At first we thought it was a webcam. Actually it is a camera, but I noticed the other day it is also something else. In the meantime, Frank and I have been able to get into several programs. Unfortunately, none of which does us any good unless we want to play solitaire or work in Photoshop. We can't get into word processing, spreadsheets, calendars, or anything that might have useful information in it."

Neva came through the door carrying a box and handed it to David. He opened it and took out what indeed looked to be a webcam. The labeling on the box said it was an iris scanner.

"Iris scanner?" said Diane.

"The mayor liked gadgets. He had a lot of them. Most of them we left in the house, but we brought all his computer gadgets here. The picture on the box looks like a webcam and I didn't actually *read* the box. Or rather, it didn't register until now. Frank and I were talking about all the kinds of security measures that could be in effect, and it just hit me," said David. "Did you get the photographs too?"

"Of course," said Neva. She handed Frank a folder.

"Photographs?" said Diane.

"Of all the principals involved," said David.

Neva pulled up another chair, and they all sat around the computer.

"Where is Rikki?" asked Diane.

"She requested the day off to show a friend the museum," said Neva. "David, being in charge in your absence, gave it to her. She's probably lurking somewhere here in the museum. The crime lab is being cleaned. Jin agreed to babysit it while TechClean's in there doing their thing."

David connected the camera cable to the USB port and immediately the software came up on the screen.

"This is good," David said.

"Very good," said Frank.

"What are you going to do?" said Diane.

"We're going to see if the camera will recognize Jefferies' iris pattern," said Frank.

"It doesn't seem like it would be much use as a security device if you can use a picture instead of the real person," said Diane.

"It's not made for unsupervised applications," said Frank. "If the pictures are high-resolution enough, we should get some action." He smiled at her.

Frank apparently enjoyed this part of his job—decryption. In that respect, he and David were two of a kind.

David selected a full-face glossy publicity photo of Jefferies. He put one eye in the photo in front of the camera lens. A large image of the eye appeared in one window of the software. Another window printed a message and played accompanying music—the first line of the song "Bad Boys."

"That's interesting," said Frank.

"Are we making progress?" asked Neva.

"We are," said David, grinning. "We now have established a dialogue of sorts." He rubbed his hands together.

It reminded Diane of Izzy. She told them she had arranged for Izzy to join the team.

"Did I hear someone mention my name?" said Izzy, walking through the door.

"I suppose Andie will let just anybody in here," said Frank. "You're going to have to speak with her, Diane."

Frank shook his hand and congratulated him. Izzy pulled up a chair and sat down on the other side of David. All the team were there now except Jin. Diane didn't think another person would fit around the computer.

They tried a photograph of Peeks. Same message.

"What does this mean?" said Diane. "I don't think this is how the mayor would have it set up."

"Maybe you have to hold it longer," said Neva. "Don't you have to wait several seconds? And isn't there supposed to be some sort of laser scanning the eye?"

"That's what I was wondering," said Diane.

"You're thinking of retinal scans," said David. "Not the same thing. A retinal scan shines a low-energy infrared light into the eye and reads the pattern of blood vessels. We are just reading the pattern of the iris. It only takes a second."

"Still, this thing doesn't sound friendly to Jefferies or Peeks," said Diane.

"No," said Frank, "it doesn't."

David tried the photograph of Peeks again. Same message.

There was silence around the table.

"Well, watcha gon' do?" asked Neva, giggling.

"It's still progress," said David, unfazed. "We know it's reacting to them. I may be able to use this program to worm my way into some of the others."

Diane got up and looked over David's shoulder at the readout, as if maybe there was something in the lyrics of the song that would help. As she leaned in closer, the readout changed, as did the audio.

"Hello, Dr. Fallon. I've been waiting for you," it said in that quirky machine voice.

Chapter 41

"What the hell is that?" said Izzy, recovering his voice first.

They all turned to look at Diane. She stepped back and stared at the screen.

"This isn't normal, is it?" said Izzy. "I know I haven't been here long, and I don't know a thing about computers, but is this—normal?"

"Okay, this is weird," said David. "Really weird."

"It scanned my iris?" asked Diane. "It knows me? How?"

"Don't be alarmed," said the voice.

"Well, I am," said Diane, though she didn't know to whom. "What does this mean?" She looked from Frank to David as if they had done this as some kind of joke.

"We didn't do this," said David. "Honest. It knows you." He gestured to the machine.

"What does that mean exactly—it knows me?" said Diane.

She looked at the scanning camera. It now looked like a little creature with a big head and one big eye and a neck sitting on small shoulders. She almost expected it to tell her she was going to be assimilated.

"Let's ask," said Frank.

David touched a key and a screen popped up for him to type in. "How do you know me?" he asked.

"You are someone I trust with the information that

I have," said the voice. *"If you are hearing me, then my plan worked. It was a long shot."*

"Talky little fellow," muttered Izzy.

"Who are you?" typed in David.

"Who do you think I am?" said the voice.

"Is it alive?" asked Neva.

"That's what I want to know," said Izzy. "Is there someone somewhere listening to us?"

"Could it be bugged?" asked Diane.

"No," said David. "You know how I check things like that."

Izzy looked quizzically at David.

"Ask what it wants," said Diane.

Frank laughed. "Do you know how that sounds?"

"Yeah," said Diane, "I do."

David typed in the question. *What do you want?*

"I want to give Diane Fallon my information. I know you must have been looking for it if you got this far," said the voice.

"Jin is going to kick himself for not being here," said Neva.

Frank got up and went to his laptop, which was sitting on the coffee table. He started typing.

"What information?" asked Diane.

"Do you want to type?" said David getting up. "It wants to talk with you anyway."

Diane sat down in David's place at the keyboard.

What information do you have? she typed.

"Ah . . . that is the question, isn't it?" it said—which sounded really strange in the synthesized voice.

"I have two sets of information for you. The first is a list of names and businesses. I think you know what I'm talking about. Please be kind. Not everyone is a willing participant," it said.

Computer people? typed in Diane.

"Yes, I think," said the voice. *"But it would be easier if you would write a complete sentence."*

Is this a list of hackers? typed in Diane.

"Some of them are hackers," it said.

Now is the time for all good men to come to the aid of their country, Diane typed.

"I don't understand," said the voice. *"Please explain."*

"What was that about?" asked David.

"It seems awfully smart," said Diane. "I just wanted to type in a non sequitur and see what happened."

Give me the list, please, typed Diane.

"Look me in the eye," said the voice.

Diane looked at the camera.

A list of names scrolled by quickly. She started to say that it was too fast when she heard the sound of her printer on her desk in the adjoining room start to print.

"How are you doing that?" she typed and said aloud.

David laughed. "You notice she didn't ask us," he said to Frank.

Frank looked up from his keyboard and smiled. "I noticed."

"You have a local area network. I just tapped into it," it said. *"It's nothing to be alarmed about."*

Frank got up and went to the printer in the other room. He came back with several single-spaced pages of print.

He flipped through the pages. "I know some of these names," he said, shaking his head. "There are a lot of names here, and they're working in very data-sensitive places. No wonder identity thefts and cyber-crimes are up around here. They will be up all over the country. If the people are good—and I know many of them are—they can get at information all over the world through these businesses and institutions alone."

David looked over his shoulder at the printout.

"Wow, there's your case right there." He looked at the computer. "Way to go . . . cyberguy," he said.

Why are you doing this? typed Diane.

"To keep people from getting their life savings stolen," said the computer. *"People can lose their home and not even know what happened."*

"You notice how comfortable Diane is talking to a computer," said David. "She probably thinks it's an alien."

Diane ignored him.

"Well, I think it's fascinating," said Neva. "I want to know if there's a real person on the other end of this. You know, like instant mail."

"That's a good idea," said Diane.

Neva wants to know if you are a real person on another computer talking to us, she typed.

She made it a more complex sentence on purpose to see what kind of answer she would get.

"Hello, Neva," said the voice.

"Oh, my God," said Neva.

"I am not a person on another computer. I am in the computer," said the voice.

"This is unbelievable," said Neva.

Can we believe you? asked Diane.

"Yes. But that doesn't help you, does it? I could be lying," it said.

You sound real, typed Diane, who had decided it was a person after all and felt vaguely disappointed, like she would prefer to be talking to HAL.

"I know. That's the beauty of it," it said.

Do you know who killed Jefferies and Peeks? typed Diane.

"No. But you should have asked a better question," said the voice. *"Remember, I am a computer."*

I don't know what you mean, typed Diane.

"Good," said the voice.

Are you lying? typed Diane.

"I am exactly not lying," said the voice on the computer. *"Don't you want to ask what other information I have?"*

I'm sorry. I do want to know what other information you have, typed Diane.

"You are so polite. That's nice," said the voice.

I think you are real, typed Diane.

"That is the nicest compliment you could have given me," said the voice.

"I'm not getting anything going out or coming in,"

said Frank, looking at the screen on his laptop. "My guess is the guy is really good, or he's telling the truth and it's a program."

What is the other information you want to give me? typed Diane.

"I want to give you bank account numbers," it said. "I think you know whose."

Give me the numbers, typed Diane.

"*Look me in the eye,*" said the voice.

Diane looked into the camera. On the screen a set of numbers scrolled by with the names of banks beside them. Just at a glance, they looked like offshore accounts.

"I'll take those."

They all looked up sharply toward the new voice. Rikki Gillinick was standing in the doorway between Diane's office and her sitting room. She was holding a gun.

Chapter 42

"Rikki," said Diane, "I thought you were off today."

"I knew you guys were up to something and if I followed, I'd find my treasure. Give me the list of bank account numbers now."

Rikki carried a book bag on her arm; it looked empty. Diane wondered how long a list she was expecting. Rikki moved inside the room and kicked the door shut behind her.

Everyone stayed where they were around the computer, eyeing the gun.

"How did you get a gun into the museum?" said Diane. She might need to have a few words with her security personnel.

"Easy. A little chink in your security a while back. When Bryce was still running the crime lab and had his own guard, all he had to do was bring the gun into the museum from the crime lab side and find a place to hide it," she said.

"Why would he do that?" said Diane.

"You need to think about that real hard," said Rikki. "Now, quit stalling. I want the numbers."

"Is this the money Jefferies made in his little cyber-crime venture?" asked Diane.

"Yes. And it's not so little. I'm serious about getting those account numbers—about three hundred million dollars' worth of serious. They're the only reason Bryce and I stuck around."

"That's a lot of money," said Diane. "Did Jefferies make all of it with his cybergangs?"

"Mostly. His Atlanta business does well, but not that well," said Rikki.

"How do you expect to get out of the building?" said Diane. "Do you plan to take one of us hostage?"

Rikki laughed. "I have the best hostage of all," she said looking around the room. "Bryce saw people as mice he could poke a stick at and they would go scurrying. I told him he was making one mistake after another dealing with you, but he wouldn't listen. Typical male. But I'm not that way. I get to know people. And I know that more than anything, you will protect the museum. You don't want me even firing a gun into the air on museum property, and certainly not firing inside the building. You want no danger and no bad publicity; that's why you're going to let me just walk out of here with my bank numbers and my gun. You'll be willing to take the chance that I'll be apprehended when I'm well away from the museum. I know this about you, just like I know my mother will always choose the wrong men to shack up with and my father will always be a drunk."

"You're smarter than we gave you credit for," said Diane.

Rikki smiled. "It's the blond hair. Fools 'em every time."

"I suppose I don't need to tell you that you won't get far off museum property," said Diane.

"I have an escape plan," said Rikki. "Now, give me the numbers."

"They're in the printer tray in my office," said Diane, nodding toward the locked door. "That's where this"—she gestured to the computer—"this thing printed the list."

"How convenient. I knew you would crack the security. Bryce in his stupidity wanted to get the computer himself. Like he could have broken the encryption. I knew David could—given time. And for the record, I know you guys were on to me. I knew you weren't going to keep me on."

"For the record," said Diane. "We knew that you knew. We figured there must be a really big payoff."

"You see now that there was," said Rikki.

She opened the door behind her. "I'm going out to your office. If the list is not there, I'm going to be pissed, and you don't want that."

"Before you go," said Diane, "since you're clearing things up, did you kill Jefferies and Peeks?"

"No, I didn't. I liked Jefferies. He was an odd duck. He was a hard-ass for sure, but he was good to women. He gave me the watch," she said.

"He gave a lot of people watches," said Diane.

"I know. But mine was the most expensive," said Rikki. She backed out into Diane's office, still holding the gun. She glanced at the printer and back at the group in the sitting room. She reached for the paper in the printer tray, looked at it, and smiled.

"Three hundred million dollars. All mine. Now, David, I want you to take the hard disk out of the machine and put it in this bag." She threw the book bag over to them. "And please hurry. You don't have to be careful."

Diane nodded to David, and he began to dismantle the computer.

"It wasn't Bryce who tried to break in, I would have recognized him," said Diane. "Was it Curtis?"

"The two of them cooked it up. I told them they were being stupid, but they wouldn't listen. Curtis was sure he could just waltz in and take it, after I told them the lab was closing down for repairs. Bryce explained to him about the guard. I told him who it was. And I'm sorry about that. Curtis is a loose cannon. He almost messed everything up."

"Where is Curtis now?" said Diane.

"Don't know. He said he had his own plan. I haven't seen him since. Personally, I don't care where he is."

"You may think you have a good getaway plan," said Frank, who sat leaning forward with his forearms on his knees and his hands clasped in front of him like this kind of thing happened to him all the time and was no big deal. "But it's not easy to get away clean. Your best bet would be to simply give yourself up. I don't think you were directly involved in the murders."

"You're a policeman, aren't you? Let me worry about my plan," she said. "Have you got that thing out yet?" she said to David.

"Just a minute," said David.

When the screen to Jefferies' computer went blank, the first thing Diane thought of was who she had been talking to. He was gone now. Oddly, it made her a little sad.

"Pick up the book bag and put the hard disk in it," said Rikki.

David put the disk in the bag and held it out to her.

"It's heavy," he said.

"Set it down," she told him.

David complied. Rikki picked it up.

"It's not that heavy," she said. "I appreciate your cooperation. Diane, remember, I will fire the gun in the museum. I know you have security guards and they have guns, but they will be very reluctant to use them around visitors. Just let me leave and then you can try to find me," she said. "If I see any of you coming after me, I will fire the gun. Now, I really hate to run, but I gotta go."

Diane nodded. "You're free to go."

"I'm glad we have an agreement."

Rikki closed the door as she backed out. Diane heard her say good-bye to Andie as she left.

When Rikki was gone, Diane started for her computer in her office.

"You want us to go after her?" said Izzy.

"No," said Diane. "She had me pegged right. I won't take a chance on her firing a gun in the museum."

When Diane was at her computer, she called up a program that allowed her to see the security camera feeds on her monitor. Four screens came up, each in its own window. Diane caught sight of Rikki as she was going out the door. Diane switched to the parking lot cameras and watched her get in an orange Geo and drive down the hill, leaving the museum parking lot.

Diane picked up the phone and called the police.

"And you just let her go with the numbers?" said Janice.

"She had a gun," said Diane. "There are too many innocent people who could have been hurt. I'm sure you understand."

"Yes, I suppose so. You say she's in an orange Geo. Did you get the plates?"

"No, that will take a little finesse with the computers. I thought you would want to know right away. She can't have gotten far."

"Of course," said Janice. "We're on it right now."

"Tell them to block all the exits to the museum," said Frank.

"Hold the phone a minute," she said to Janice. "She'll be gone by then."

"Maybe not," said Frank. He took the phone from Diane. "Quicker this way," he said, smiling.

"Warrick," he said. "This is Frank Duncan. She may be changing cars before she gets off museum property. There are several access roads around the museum. Have your people get to those roads— quickly. Diane will have her security on the way too."

Diane called her security and told them basically what Frank had relayed to Janice. She put down the phone and looked at Frank.

"What makes you think that's what she's going to do?" said Diane.

"She said she had a plan," said Frank. "What's that movie that always cracks you up—*Tremors*? And what is it about a plan that guy says that you just love?"

" 'Running's not a plan; running's what you do when a plan fails,' " said Diane.

"Well, getting out on the highway in a car she knows you will have seen is not a plan. That's running."

Izzy laughed out loud.

Chapter 43

Diane, Frank, and Izzy were in Frank's car trailing the museum security SUV. Frank and Diane were in the front seat, Izzy in the back. Frank followed at a distance. They didn't want to capture Rikki themselves, but they did want to be extra eyes looking for her.

"I think she'll use that old roadway down by the river," said Frank.

He was speaking of the Dekanogee River—which was the river referred to in the RiverTrail Museum. He turned off onto the old dirt road, leaving the security vehicle to cover the more heavily used access roads.

"Why do you think she would come this way?" asked Diane.

"She wants to dispose of the hard disk so no one else can get the numbers," said Frank. "And she needs to get rid of it as soon as possible. I suspect she intends to throw the disk into the river. This is a good place to do that and a secluded place to change vehicles."

The woods were dense in this section of the property, and the roadbed was old and rough. The bottom of Frank's Camaro scraped the ground in the deep ruts, and the car bounced around badly enough that Diane tightened her seat belt and pressed the flat of her hand on the roof above her to hold herself in place.

"I have to tell you guys, my first day on the job has been a real kicker," said Izzy.

"It's not over yet," said Diane. "What's that?" she said, pointing toward some bushes just ahead.

Through the tangle of undergrowth Diane thought she saw a glint from a mirror and a flash of orange. Frank slowed the car as they approached. Diane rolled down her window so she could see better and listen for sounds.

Frank drove slowly past the place where Diane thought she saw the car. It was there in the bushes, only half concealed. He stopped the Camaro and called in their location. Izzy jumped out, pulled his gun, and ran in a crouch to the rear of the Geo. Cautiously, gun at the ready, he took a quick look through the windows of the vehicle and scanned the area. He turned toward them and shook his head.

"Up ahead," said Diane. "I hear a car."

Izzy heard it too. He ran back and jumped in the backseat.

"I think she's abandoned it all right," he said. He reached out his window and patted the roof of Frank's car. "Let's go," he said.

Frank looked over at Diane and smiled. He drove the narrow road at a speed greater than Diane felt comfortable with, but she said nothing and held on. Ahead of them they saw the rear of a dark blue Saturn just going out of sight around a curve in the road. Frank drove faster and the ride got bumpier.

As they rounded the curve, the Saturn was just ahead. The road was smoother here, mainly dirt, and the blue sedan was accelerating and kicking up dust. The Saturn drove out of sight again.

Frank sped up.

They popped over a low rise and suddenly they saw it again. It was backing fast toward them, running from police and museum security cars coming fast, head-on. Frank slid to a stop. Diane braced for impact. The Saturn's brake lights were glaring red; the car skidded to a stop just inches before it hit the front end of Frank's Camaro.

Izzy jumped out of the car, leaving the door open,

and drew his gun—as did Frank. Diane opened her door and stayed behind it. She had no gun.

She heard Janice's voice calling for the occupant of the car to come out, hands on head.

Diane watched the person sitting behind the steering wheel in the car. She saw black hair, she thought, but it was hard to see much with the glare of the sun on the window.

Janice repeated the command.

The door opened and Rikki stepped out, hands in the air. She was wearing a black wig. That was a relief. The thought had crossed Diane's mind that perhaps they had disturbed some innocent nature lovers who thought they were being chased by maniacs in a white Camaro. Janice spread Rikki against the car, patted her down, and put handcuffs on her. Only then did Diane stand up and Frank and Izzy let their guards down.

Rikki cast a wicked glance back at Diane.

Diane, Frank, and Izzy went to the interrogation room at the police station where Rikki was taken. They stood and looked through the two-way mirror at her sitting with her hands on top of the desk, beating out a tune with her palms.

"She doesn't look too worried," said Izzy. "Why is that, I wonder?"

"She has a Plan B," said Diane. "What I wonder is, did she have time to shift the money in the offshore accounts to some other bank account? How hard is that to do? Can you do it with a cell? A BlackBerry? An iPod?" she asked, smiling.

Frank laughed. "You can do it with a cell or a BlackBerry. It would be hard with an iPod."

"Is it difficult to track?" asked Diane.

"Depends," said Frank. "Could be very difficult. Even if you find it, you have to prove the money doesn't belong to the person who opened the account. Not easy with some of the offshore banking laws."

"What's her Plan B?" asked Izzy.

Janice Warrick entered the interview room and sat down opposite Rikki.

The observation room door opened and Chief of Police Buford Monroe entered. He stood beside Diane and the others, nodding to them.

"Finally getting somewhere," he said. "You say your guy cracked the encryption?"

"Yes, David and Frank," said Diane. "It had some very unusual aspects to it."

"I'll be anxious to hear about it," he said.

"We need to track down who encrypted it," said Diane.

Janice started speaking. Diane watched Rikki. She didn't look particularly defiant, and so far she hadn't asked for a lawyer.

"So tell me," said Janice. "When did you decide to kill Jefferies and Peeks?"

Rikki smiled. "I didn't kill anyone. I swear." She crossed her heart with her right index finger.

"You didn't, yet you knew about the money?" said Janice.

"Well, yeah, we all knew about the money."

"We all?" said Janice.

"People close to Jefferies."

"If you didn't kill them, who did?" asked Janice.

"For that, I need a deal and a lawyer," Rikki said.

"A deal?" said Janice.

But Monroe knocked on the glass. Rikki looked up, smiled, and waved as if she could see them on the other side.

"She's asked for a lawyer," said Monroe. "I might ought to have had one of the more senior detectives question her."

"Wouldn't have made any difference," said Diane. "Rikki's working on Plan B."

Diane and the others waited for Rikki's lawyer to show up. Diane tried to get a moment to speak to Janice, but she was busy running back and forth. Looking for ducks to get in a row, Diane supposed.

District Attorney Riddmann showed up first. He

was another bureaucrat whom Diane had managed to offend with her unpolished diplomatic skills. But he was friendly enough. He commented sympathetically on Diane's face. She looked forward to the day when the bruises would be gone.

Diane introduced the DA to Frank, but they knew each other already. Frank apparently could also have some unpolished diplomatic skills on occasion when it came to Riddmann.

"You're out of uniform, aren't you, Izzy?" Riddmann said, patting him on the arm.

"Nope. I'm working with the crime lab now. Quite exciting it is too. I had no idea what those folks were into over there," he said. "Why, decryption alone was worth the price of the ticket." He grinned broadly.

Riddmann nodded as if he understood what Izzy was talking about. It was awkward all the way around. Riddmann was not an easy man to make small talk with, even had Diane been good at small talk herself. Janice joined them.

"Sorry, I've been so busy. You'd think someone who has just stolen so much money could afford her own lawyer. The judge appointed LaCroix. She'll be here shortly."

"You think this will crack open the case?" asked Riddmann.

Janice shrugged. She looked at Diane. "Do you know what she has up her sleeve?"

"She wants to trade Bryce in exchange for a deal for herself," said Diane.

Janice raised her eyebrows.

"Does she have anything to deal with?" said Riddmann. "I understand she's been caught red-handed, as it were."

"She has the forceps Bryce used to take the bullet out of Edgar Peeks' skull, as well as the bullet," said Diane. "And quite a story, I would imagine."

Chapter 44

Rikki's lawyer came bustling in. She was a middle-aged woman, heavyset, with chunky turquoise jewelry and black frizzy hair. Riddmann didn't like her, mainly because he often lost to her, Diane knew.

Patsy LaCroix took one look at Diane and put her hand over her mouth. "Did the police do that to you?" she said.

"Your client is in here," said Janice. She ushered her into the interrogation room.

Diane thought she probably ought to go back to the museum, but she was curious to see how this turned out. She sat down with Frank on a bench out in the hallway. Izzy went to visit friends in the department, no doubt to tell them of his adventures so far. Riddmann and Janice stood talking with the chief of police, probably planning strategies, thought Diane.

"What did you make of the . . . I don't know what to call him," said Diane.

"AI, instant messenger?" said Frank. "I'm not sure if he was real or not either. I didn't detect any outside communications. What did I think of him? Interesting. Very intriguing."

"Someone must have gotten a photograph of me and programmed it into the computer for the camera to recognize. Is that how it was done?" said Diane. "There are publicity photographs of me available from the museum. It would be easy enough to get one."

Frank nodded. "It had to be a high-resolution pic-

ture. Publicity photographs are good for that. They
are usually high res."

"When?" said Diane. "When would they have
done that?"

Frank looked at her as if just recognizing the problem. "I don't know," he said.

"The computer was at the mayor's house until he
was killed. After that they would not have access to
it. At the time of his death I wasn't the director of
the crime lab. So, why me? Why would they think
I would have access to the crime scene evidence?"
she said.

"That's a good question," he said. "A very good
question."

Frank sat thinking for several moments. "Where was
the computer taken after it left the mayor's house?"

"The police station. They tried to get into it but
couldn't get past the encryption. Then it was brought
to the crime lab, where it sat on a shelf. It went from
there to my museum office," said Diane.

"Someone had remote access to it every time it was
turned on," said Frank.

"How?" asked Diane.

"Its wireless network adapter. It could connect itself
to whatever computer network it detected. The police
station and your museum both have local area networks with wireless connections," said Frank.

"But doesn't each computer have to be . . . I don't
know . . . don't they have to have a special card to
work with each network?" said Diane.

"Not with wireless connections," said Frank. "All
the fellow had to do was defeat the security regulating
wireless access to the network. For an experienced
hacker, that's a piece of cake, even for your museum
network . . . No offense. Whenever Jefferies' computer
was turned on, it could automatically connect itself to
the nearest wireless access point and send out a ping
to the hacker's computer."

"A ping?" said Diane.

"Computers talk to each other in the background

constantly. A ping is kind of like one computer ringing
the other's doorbell and saying, *Hi, it's me. I'm here,
you there?*"

"Its doorbell?" asked Diane.

"A metaphor," said Frank.

"An analogy," said Diane.

"A good one. I know how you hate bad ones. The
point is, for as long as Jefferies' computer was turned
on, our clever fellow could put anything on or take
anything off of it that he wanted—programs, data files,
photos of your iris, incriminating lists . . . anything."
Frank grinned. He seemed almost gleeful over his
analysis.

"Is nothing safe?" said Diane. The potential for in-
vasion of privacy was staggering to her.

"Not a lot. You need good protections. If I were you,
I'd let David take a look at your museum systems. He
is really good."

"Frank, please don't put him on your list," said
Diane suddenly. David would hate the very idea.

He reached over and squeezed her arm. "I won't.
Don't worry."

She looked at Frank. He wouldn't, she thought. Another thing she liked about Frank. He was decent.

Diane thought a moment. "So it was someone who
wanted to make things right. It's probably someone
on the list of hackers," she said.

"He or she probably took their name off the list,"
said Frank.

"So we can't find out who it is," said Diane.

Frank studied the wall opposite their bench, lost in
thought. "I can look at the list and see if there are
any businesses left off that should have been a prime
target—have a look at their employees. I can see if
there are any hackers that I know about who aren't
on the list," he said. "We know Edgar Peeks was recruiting at university job fairs. That's not uncommon;
many agencies recruit employees that way—easier to
find the kind of employee you want. The university
placement offices should have records on their fairs."

Diane sat up. "Could that guy, Malcolm Chen, have done it before . . ." Diane shook her head. "He died several months ago." She looked up again. "If those are his bones from the field. They might not be. Jin hasn't finished the DNA analysis yet."

"It's worth checking out," said Frank. "He may have just gone to ground—in another way," he added.

LaCroix came out and motioned for the DA and Janice. Frank, Diane, and the chief of police went back to the observation room.

"My client can offer you the murderer of Edgar Peeks all wrapped up with a bow. What can you offer her?" said LaCroix.

"What about the murderer of Jefferies?" said Janice Warrick.

"She doesn't know who killed him," said LaCroix.

"They weren't killed by the same person?" said Janice. She looked surprised.

"They may have been," said LaCroix. "But my client can only prove who killed Peeks. What can you offer her?"

"She held a gun on four people employed by the Rosewood Police Department and one Atlanta detective," said Riddmann. "Threatening to kill them. What kind of deal does she think she can get?"

"The gun wasn't loaded," said LaCroix. She looked over at Janice.

Janice shook her head. "It wasn't," she said.

"My client isn't a murderer. She is a victim caught up in some terrible conspiracies by these men."

"What about the money?" said Janice.

"What about it?" said LaCroix. "You have the account numbers. She didn't have time to do anything with them."

"We can give her six months," said Riddmann, "in the women's facility."

Diane thought that was awfully light, considering they didn't know what else she had done. *Ask her.* Diane wanted to knock on the window. She started to say something to the chief of police, but Janice spoke up.

"There were her activities in the employ of the mayor and his friends, and we don't know what her role was in the Peeks murder. She may have helped cover it up," said Janice. "Or plan it."

"I just worked for the crime lab," said Rikki. "You can look at the logs to see the crime scenes I was on. And as for Peeks, I didn't find out about his murder until after it was done. Sure the killer told me about it, but he threatened me. These are mean guys."

"You weren't too afraid to steal their money," said Janice.

"It was over a quarter of a billion dollars. I was overwhelmed by the thought of that much money. But I didn't hurt anyone and I wasn't one of the hackers who helped them get rich. They hired me to work in the crime lab because of my degree," said Rikki.

Riddmann nodded. "Do you take the deal?"

"Six months and immunity," said LaCroix.

Riddmann hesitated.

"It's a good story," said Rikki. "They were really bad guys."

He nodded. "Tell us your good story, Miss Gillinick."

Chapter 45

Rikki straightened herself up in her chair. She looked confident and not at all unhappy for someone who just lost over a quarter of a billion dollars, as she put it.

Janice said they had found the papers with the account numbers, passwords, and banks that Rikki got from Diane's office, but there were no electronic devices from which she could have transferred the money. *Not even a cell?* Diane had meant to ask, but things had been too hectic and the police were not inclined to stop and listen to her. They were wrapped up in solving the crime of the decade, and Diane could see they didn't really want to share the glory, especially not with Frank, an Atlanta detective, despite the help he had provided.

But they were letting Diane and Frank watch.

Patsy LaCroix sat beside Rikki, patting her hand. A court reporter was in the room transcribing the interview. They also had a tape recorder. They weren't taking any chances of missing anything.

"I really didn't get to know them all until after Jefferies was elected mayor. They hired me at a job fair at the university but told me the job wouldn't be ready for a couple of months and I could just take the time off. Jefferies gave me a watch—it was a real expensive diamond watch. He told me I would be well paid, but he wanted loyalty, that I would be part of a team. I had the watch appraised by a jeweler. It cost over ten thousand dollars!"

Her eyes grew wide just thinking about it.

"I'd never seen that much money, and there I was wearing it on my wrist," Rikki continued, caressing her bare wrist. "And he wasn't asking me for anything but loyalty. Sounded like a good deal to me, and working in a crime lab was something I wanted to do. I like all those TV shows. Can I have something to drink? Water, maybe? Mineral?"

Janice stepped out and asked someone to bring a bottle of water from the drink machine. Diane doubted it would be mineral.

"Go on, Miss Gillinick," said Riddmann. "They'll bring you the water."

"I knew there were other people on the team, but I didn't know who they were. I found out they were making a lot of money for Jefferies and his friends. I wasn't sure exactly how. I knew it involved computers. But my job was only to work in the crime lab and do what they told me to. That was important—that I do what I was told. Jefferies told me that when he got elected I would go to work. I asked him what if he didn't get elected, and he just laughed."

The water came and Rikki took a long drink.

"Well, he did get elected, and I went to work, and things were fine for a while. I liked the people I worked with. Neva and David were really nice to me, and Jin, when I saw him, was funny. We joked around a lot.

"Then I started learning more about Jefferies and the others, and it was scary. I heard them talking about having killed a judge. Whatever that was about happened before I came to work, and I don't know anything about it. It was just a stray comment I overheard Bryce tell Curtis. Curtis was Peeks' cousin. He's kind of creepy in a fun sort of way, and not very smart, if you know what I mean. I never let on that I overheard that."

"Where were you when you heard these conversations?" said Janice.

"Sometimes at the mayor's house. I was, uh, sort of

dating Curtis and we occasionally had dinner at the mayor's house. They didn't seem to care what I heard, I suppose, since they figured they had bought my loyalty."

She took another drink of water, this time a small sip, and she actually looked as if the memory scared her. Diane imagined it did, but not enough to overcome the glamour of the situation and the money that came with it. Along with her salary she was probably paid bonuses under the table.

"Continue, Miss Gillinick," said Riddmann. "We are anxious to hear about the murders."

Riddmann was inclined to be impatient. Diane thought they ought to just let the story unfold, not encourage her to skip over parts of it.

Rikki seemed to ignore him. She continued with her story the way she was telling it. She had the stage and was enjoying her part.

"They were real happy to get the crime lab. Bryce didn't want to be head of it, but they must have told him he had to. You know in movies how the good-looking guys will have a dweeb for a sidekick, and maybe he'll be smarter than them, but he's still a dweeb? Well, that was Bryce. He was the dweeb. But they told him the crime lab was the most important job of all. And I think they meant that. They weren't aware that the bone lab didn't come with it. At first they didn't pay much attention to it anyway. Then Bryce found out that it had all kinds of fancy equipment and he realized he could hire their own forensic anthropologist, so he started looking for one.

"But what Jefferies really wanted was the DNA lab. He knew it was owned by the museum, but he and the others had an idea of how to get it. They were first going to get Curtis on the inside to do all their DNA analysis. But Diane Fallon got in the way of that and they decided they had to get rid of her. They hired Harve Delamore to do it. He hated her anyway. Harve was always bragging about how he could have gone semipro. Well, that's what he was—semipro and not pro. He bungled it. When that didn't work out, they were going to frame her for his murder." She laughed. "Then it turned out that the GBI had jurisdiction. It was starting to get funny. Diane was like the Road Runner and they were Wile E. Coyote."

Diane was shocked that Rikki could talk about murdering someone with such ease, even laugh about it. She shivered. Life meant nothing to this woman. Nothing to Jefferies and his cronies either.

"Jefferies and Bryce drew up plans for what they would do with the whole third floor of the museum building," said Rikki. "But they had to get Dr. Fallon out of the way."

Diane was startled to hear that. How did they expect to get the whole third floor? she wondered.

Rikki leaned forward as if Riddmann and Janice could hear her better if she did.

"When Harve failed to kill her, Bryce smuggled a gun into the museum and hid it. It was easy because Bryce had his own guard at the door from the crime lab into the museum. They were planning to kill Dr. Fallon in the museum. They thought that might make it easier to close it down."

Diane sucked in her breath. Frank grabbed her hand and squeezed. The chief of police looked over at her, frowning himself, startled.

Rikki looked up at the two-way mirror as if she knew Diane was watching, and delighted in the shock of the revelation.

"You were just going to let that happen?" said Janice.

"What could I do? By this time I was thoroughly scared by these guys. If they were going to kill her, they wouldn't give a second thought about doing me."

"How did they think that would get them the DNA lab?" said Janice. "The museum would still own it."

"But Dr. Fallon was the force behind the crime aspect to it. They figured the next director wouldn't be

a forensic anthropologist and wouldn't be interested
in the labs. They knew some of the museum's board
of directors didn't like the forensic stuff being there."

"How were they planning to take over the whole
third floor?" asked Janice. "Killing Diane wouldn't
get them that either."

Diane could see that Janice was skeptical. Riddmann looked like he was getting impatient with Janice's questions. Diane wanted Janice to continue. She
wanted the answers to those questions.

"That wasn't all they had planned. I heard them say
that little old ladies could get mugged and what a tragedy that would be. They had planned to take out
Vanessa Van Ross too." She sat back in her chair. "See,
Mr. Riddmann, I told you this was a good story and
worth a little time off for good behavior," said Rikki.

Diane stepped back and leaned against the back
wall. She felt a strange retroactive fear of what might
have happened. Frank put an arm around her shoulder
and she leaned into him.

"How did we let this happen?" said Chief Monroe.
"How did we miss all of this?"

He didn't really expect an answer and Diane didn't
give him one. She didn't have one. She hadn't voted
for Jefferies. With her it was just a vague mistrust,
something she couldn't put into words, a gut feeling
that she acted on at the voting booth. But he had
appealed to a lot of people.

Diane could see that the three sitting in the room
with Rikki were just as stunned. She couldn't see Riddmann's and Janice's faces, but she saw them straighten
up and exchange glances. She saw the shock on Patsy
LaCroix's face. She had been periodically patting
Rikki on the hand, encouraging her. She took her
hands away and put them on the table in front of her.
Patsy LaCroix and Vanessa were friends.

Rikki saw their reaction, delighted in it for a moment, then straightened her own face to reflect the
seriousness of the situation.

"That's one of the reasons they were so furious with

Bryce when he gave Dr. Fallon the ammunition to get the crime lab out of the museum building. They could see all their carefully laid plans just collapsing. That's when they started fighting with each other. They tried to get Garnett to help them but he wouldn't. And that really pissed them off.

"They were trying to get rid of him anyway, and had planned to frame him for Dr. Fallon's murder. Bryce came up with the idea of substituting one bullet for another. He said it would be tricky. Bullets sometimes ricochet around in the body and you don't know where they might end up, but if it's done right, Bryce thought he could make it work by short loading the bullets, or something like that. He said he could reduce the energy of the bullet when it entered the body. He was just full of fun ideas." She laughed again.

"You think all this is funny?" said Janice.

"I do," said Rikki. "Do you want my story or not?"

"Please go on," said Riddmann.

Rikki nodded. "Just in case that didn't work—or they couldn't get the bullet out—they got a gun that couldn't be traced back to them. They also took Garnett's bullets from the Ballistics Department and were going to use them, but those were all in perfect shape and Bryce thought it would look suspicious. So they collected Garnett's bullets from the gun range."

"So all their plans collapsed," said Janice.

Rikki nodded. "First, Dr. Fallon shut down the crime lab and locked them out, so they couldn't get through the connecting door to get into the museum where the gun was and where they wanted to kill her. They didn't want to risk going through one of the main entrances. That meant passing under the video cameras and past people who might remember them. They thought about doing the Van Ross woman first, but she was out of town. They were trying to work all that out when Jefferies was murdered. That threw Peeks and Bryce for a loop. Let me tell you, it shook them bad. That's why I don't think they did it.

"After they got over being scared that they might be next, Peeks decided to take over where Jefferies left off. He was going to make Bryce the dweeb sidekick again, but Bryce wasn't going to have it. Him and Peeks were at Jefferies' house waiting for Garnett's lawyer to come with Dr. Fallon to look at the house when they had a real kickup. I wasn't there. Bryce told me about it later and said if I didn't help him, he would say I was in on it and would go to jail too—if I lived that long. I got with the program, but I protected myself.

"He shot Peeks in the back of the head and, just like he planned to do with Dr. Fallon, he took those long tweezers from the crime kit and dug the bullet out. I can't even bare to tweeze a splinter out of my finger; anyone can tell you that. Anyway, he found the bullet and pulled it out. He was carrying Garnett's bullet in his crime kit to use on Dr. Fallon, so he took the tweezers and pushed that bullet back through the bullet hole in Peeks' head. Pretty disgusting stuff, huh?

"Anyway, time was running out. He knew Dr. Fallon and the lawyer were coming soon. He was in a hurry and got careless. The bullet and the tweezers were knocked under the chest as he was getting the kit out of the way. He couldn't reach under the chest and he didn't have time to move it and clean everything up, so he left them, knowing he could get them later. He texted Garnett, pretending to be Prehoda's secretary, and told him to come and meet Prehoda and Dr. Fallon at the house. Then he hotfooted it out of there and got back to the crime lab just about the time we received the call from the police. That's when Bryce told me what happened and threatened me into helping him."

She took another long drink of water as if in the telling of it she was reliving it. She actually looked out of breath.

"It was busy when we got to the crime scene. He tried to hurry Dr. Fallon and the lawyer out of the way, but there was you and your partner to deal with too," she said to Janice. "I found the bullet and the tweezers under the chest and put them in a paper evidence bag and sealed it. I gave Bryce another bag just like it and told him it was the evidence. I took mine to the bank and put it in a safe deposit box. Then I stayed with a friend and didn't come to work until I found out Bryce had been fired and Dr. Fallon was back in charge. I wouldn't even take any calls from Curtis. I didn't really trust him either. I called Bryce and told him what I had and he'd better lay off me. He tried to make all nice and started talking about the money. Him and Curtis were making all these plans to get the computer, but they were so lame. They wanted me to stay working in the crime lab, and that's what you-all wanted too, so I did. I got to thinking that I'd get the money. I knew I would have to let you guys decode it first."

"Who encrypted it?" said Diane to the chief. "Get them to ask that. Find out if it was Malcolm Chen, and ask her what happened to the bones in the field."

Peabody Public Library
Columbia City, IN

Chapter 46

The chief of police, Buford Monroe, went into the room with Rikki and the others. He picked up a chair from the corner of the room, brought it over to the interview table, and sat down. Even in profile his face looked stern.

"Young lady," he asked, "do you know who encrypted the mayor's computer?"

Rikki looked at him a moment as if processing the question.

"I assume it was one of the hackers Jefferies hired. He had them over to his house sometimes. But I was never there when they were, and I didn't know any of them. I think Curtis knew who did it. He was always hinting at stuff. And of course Bryce knows many of the hackers. He's the only one left, in case you haven't noticed."

"Have you ever heard of a man named Malcolm Chen?" asked the chief.

"Not until recently when his bones were discovered. That was something else that really freaked them out. I heard Bryce on the phone with Jefferies. I sometimes listened in," she said without any embarrassment.

"Jefferies thought that was going to be the thing that would collapse their world. I didn't understand what it was about, but I got the idea that the last thing they wanted was for this guy to be identified and his death investigated.

"Bryce reminded them they had their own forensic

anthropologist. Up to then they thought he had jumped
the gun in hiring one and were giving him a hard time.
Everything was cool until Bryce realized the sheriff was
sending the bones to Dr. Fallon. Bryce hijacked them
and thought he was home free until he found out that
Dr. Fallon already had the few first ones that were
found. Jennifer told him there wasn't much Dr. Fallon
could do with a handful of bone fragments, that they
were too damaged and the DNA was probably de-
cayed."

"Was Jennifer in with them?" asked the chief.

"No, I didn't get that impression. Bryce told her he
wanted her to be the one to identify the bones and
not Dr. Fallon. That's how he explained his interest.
But I do think Bryce and the others thought they
could turn her. Jennifer was just out of the university,
and Bryce knew she wanted the job badly. She'd put
her career on hold while her husband went to school
and she raised the rug rats. Now she was old and
desperate. Bryce thought that would make her easier
to handle. He also thought she was having an affair
with the new medical examiner and he was going to
hold that over her. I told you, these were mean guys—
Bryce, Jefferies, and Peeks." Rikki smiled.

No loyalty there for Jennifer, thought Diane.

"It might interest you to know that Dr. Fallon did
discover the identity of the person who the handful of
broken bones came from," said the chief. He said it
as if he wanted her to know that the home team were
better all-around players than Jefferies' team.

Rikki grinned. "You'll have to tell that to Jennifer.
She'll have a cow. She got really jealous the way things
turned out."

"What happened to the bones that disappeared?"
asked Chief Monroe.

"Curtis took them and threw them in the river,"
she said.

"Where is the hard disk you took? Is that in the
river too?" asked the police chief.

"Yes," she said.

Diane wondered if they were regretting the great deal they gave her. Immunity is a great thing when you're up to your neck in crime.

"When Jefferies was killed, who did Peeks and Bryce think did it?" the police chief asked.

"They didn't know. We all talked about it. For about a minute I thought Bryce had. Jefferies was always on his butt for something, but he was really rattled by their deaths. I think Bryce did depend on them—even though they depended on him for their homework in that ivy league school they went to," said Rikki. "I guess you noticed their pinky rings. So seventh grade."

"Did Bryce or Peeks name anyone at all who they thought might have committed the murders?" asked the chief again.

"When it came down to it, they really thought Garnett may have done it. The only other people they mentioned were some of the hackers they hired, but they had no idea who. Peeks planned on going through the files to see if he could come up with anything. But as I said, their best guess was Garnett. Jefferies was really after him, and they thought he found out about them," said Rikki.

So they were back where they started, thought Diane. Back to Garnett. The chief would probably order him released, but Garnett would still have a cloud over him unless they could find out who killed Jefferies.

Diane thought of one person who would know.

"Let's go back to the museum," she said to Frank.

When the police chief came out of the interview room, Diane thanked him for letting her listen to the confession. He nodded. The chief was calm in the room with Rikki, but his face was red with anger when he came out.

"What do you make of all that?" he said.

"Right now, I'm shocked," said Diane.

"I can imagine you are. I am. I'm going to talk with Edward. He'll be outraged when he finds out his mother was on a hit list. Tell me, what were the voters thinking about when they went to the polls?" he said. "I wonder if you can sue voters; they're always so anxious to hold people accountable."

Diane didn't answer. She didn't think he really expected one. He was angry, and practically everyone to be angry with was dead.

"I've sent a car out to pick up Lloyd Bryce and Curtis Crabtree. Janice is going to the bank to get the evidence from the safety deposit box. She'll send it to the GBI for analysis, if that's all right with you. Edward said you have some repairs to make in the crime lab before it's ready for use again. I tell you, they're like an infestation of rats. And from the sound of things, there are a lot more of them out there lurking in peoples' businesses. Thank God we have a list."

"You can have Janice bring the evidence to us if you want. Jin can do the DNA faster and he can lift the prints in his lab. When he's finished he can send the bullet to Ballistics," said Diane.

The police chief nodded. "I like that better. Yes, I do. Let the people know we're on top of things despite all the rats' nests we have to clear out." He went to find Janice before she left for the bank.

"How do you feel?" asked Frank when they were ensconced in his car on the way back to the museum.

"Like I just escaped a bullet," she said. "I'm more astonished than angry at the moment. I can't believe what I just heard. Do you think she was telling the truth?"

"Most of it. I think she lightened her involvement considerably and she's been enjoying the life of a gun moll all this time."

"Could she have killed Jefferies and Peeks?" said Diane.

"It's a possibility they will look into," said Frank. "My gut feeling right now is, no. She is very driven by gathering things to herself. I can't see her murdering them unless she expected to get something big from it, and I can't see what that would be."

"How about all that money?" said Diane.

"I think she was after that anyway. That's why she listened in on conversations. Whether they were alive or dead, she was planning on stealing the money. When she held a gun on us, it was unloaded. She specifically did not want to do anything that would land her hard jail time. I may be wrong," he added.

"She wasn't afraid Jefferies would come after her if she stole his money?" asked Diane.

"She thought she could get away. She knew Jefferies' influence was local. He was in the process of building a gang. He didn't have members all over the country. He may have had sleepers in businesses in several places, but his organization was still new enough that he couldn't reach her every place she might go. I hope," he added.

"Doesn't she have immunity now?" said Diane.

Frank shook his head. "If she lies, all bets are off. At least that's the way we do it in Atlanta."

The crime lab was clean and almost ready to resume operation. The delicate machines were scheduled to be calibrated tomorrow. It looked and smelled cleaner when they walked in the door. David, Jin, and Neva were there. Diane had called and told them she was on her way.

Jin was having a fit. Apparently he had been in a tirade, as much of a tirade as Jin got in, ever since they told him about the computer person, or whatever it was. They were all at a loss as to what to call it.

"Why didn't anybody call me?" he said. "Something that cool is going on and nobody thinks to call me and let me see? How could you do that to me?"

"Jin, get over it already," said Neva. "It was probably just a guy on the other end of his instant messenger anyway."

"I'm glad you're back," said David. "Maybe you can do something with him."

Diane started to say something but was interrupted by a knock at the door. They all turned and looked accusingly at the door, as if it had done it. Visits from the museum side were unusual.

Diane opened the door. Jonas Briggs, the archaeologist, was standing on the other side, grinning. He had his laptop under his arm.

"It's the darnedest thing, but I thought I'd better tell you. So, this is the dark side," he said, coming in and looking around. It was what every museum staffer said when they came over.

"This is it," said Diane. "You said something is the darnedest thing?"

"Yes. This little guy who sounds for all the world like the physicist Stephen Hawking came up on my computer and asked me to play chess."

Chapter 47

They all stared at Jonas for several moments as he stood with his laptop under his arm, stretching his neck, looking around at the lab.

"He's in the system," said Diane to no one in particular. "What did you say in reply?" she asked Jonas.

"Nothing," Jonas said. "I started to. He knew my name. He called me Jonas, but I thought it might be a virus so I just turned off my computer. I hope that was right."

"That was fine, Jonas," said Diane. "We'll take it from here. Thanks for bringing it to my attention." She smiled, feeling like she was hurrying him out too fast. "Can we have your computer?"

"You said he's in the system," said Jonas. "He who?" Jonas apparently didn't feel hurried.

"We don't know yet. I would appreciate it if you wouldn't mention this to anyone," said Diane.

"I won't. I'll just mark it down as one of the many strange things that go on here." He handed her the computer.

"You'll get it back soon," said Diane.

"Okay. I'll be interested to hear the story when you can tell it," he said. "If the little fellow turns out to be okay, I'll be glad to play a game of chess with him."

He left and Diane watched him walk across the overlook, shaking his head. She handed the computer to David.

"Is this a virus?" she said, frowning. A virus in the museum network didn't bear thinking about.

"I don't know," said David. "I'll have a look."

"Can it get into the crime lab system?" asked Diane.

"No," said David. "I think I have that well protected. It would surprise me if it could get through my firewall."

"I don't want you to be surprised," said Diane.

"Would you feel better if we went to your office to turn this on?" said David.

"I don't want to hurt your feelings, but yes," said Diane. "I don't want to take the chance it'll jump into this system—if that's what it does." She was surprised at how ignorant she was of computers. She had thought she was a computer-savvy person until now.

Diane turned to Jin. "What's that you have in your hand?"

"Evidence from the Peeks murder. Detective Warrick brought it just before you got here," said Jin.

"What do we do with evidence around here?" said Diane.

"We process it," said Jin, "but—"

"Process it, then. This is very important evidence," she said. "It could clear Garnett and identify Peeks' killer. Take fingerprints first. You'll have to process everything down in your lab."

"Am I going to miss the cyberghost again?" he said.

"I'm sorry," said Diane.

Jin sighed. "That's what happens when you make yourself indispensable."

"Yes, it is," said Diane. "I am sorry, but right now your lab has to carry the load."

Jin nodded. "By the way. I did get DNA from the tooth and compared it with the samples from Malcolm Chen's house. It's a match. I told Detective Warrick. She seemed pleased."

"Thanks, Jin. You do great work and are appreciated," said Diane.

"I know. I have my own lab." He grinned.

It was almost time for the museum to shut down
for the evening. People were streaming out the door.
In about forty minutes the night lighting would come
on in the exhibit rooms and it would be quiet except
for the people still working in their labs and the few
classes going on in some of the departments.

On the way to her office Diane was stopped by
several members of the staff about various bits of museum business. She waved David, Frank, and Neva on
and told them to start without her.

No one who wanted to talk with her had anything
urgent, only the everyday things she needed to take
care of. Sometimes her staff just needed to see and
speak with her, or tell her of some particular unfortunate or even delightful thing that happened. It was
very calming compared to the last several days of
her life.

Andie was going out her door when Diane made it
to her office. She stopped to tell Diane she had put all
her messages on her desk—an unnecessary statement,
because Andie always put the messages on her desk
when she wasn't there.

"Thanks, Andie. Anything urgent?" asked Diane.

"Nope. Kendel is coming in sometime tomorrow.
We're all very excited to see the Neanderthal bones."

"That's great, Andie. Have a good evening. I'll see
you tomorrow," said Diane.

Frank, Neva, and David were ordering food from
the museum restaurant when Diane got to her sitting room.

"Not pizza," said Diane.

"No," said Neva and David together.

David was about to open the laptop when they
heard another knock on Diane's private back door.

"Someone else find the ghost?" said Neva.

Diane started to open it, but she stopped. "Who is
it?" she asked.

"Jin," the voice said.

She opened the door. "I thought you were working
on the evidence," said Diane, frowning at him.

"I lifted the prints. I found Bryce's. A thumb and partial index. I called Warrick with the information. I also matched the bullet. It's in the database as belonging to Bryce. I know we're not ballistics, but it was just a matter of photographing the striations and matching them to the database. I gave that info to Warrick too. She was giddy with excitement. The DNA analysis I can't get done tonight if I plan to eat dinner and go to bed at some point. So unless you want me to go down to my lab and work myself literally to the bone, I'd like to come and eat with you guys. You ordered dinner, didn't you? I'll bet it wasn't pizza."

"Come in, Jin. No, I don't want you to starve. Call the restaurant and add what you want to the Fallon order," said Diane.

While they waited for their food, Diane and Frank told them what Rikki had said in her statement. Jin, Neva, and David sat openmouthed at the revelation that Jefferies and company had begun implementation of a plan to kill Diane and Vanessa.

David stood up, his face flushed. "Are you telling me that if you hadn't kicked the crime lab out of the museum, you would be dead? Who in the hell do they think they are that they have the right to do that? Because they wanted something you have, they were going to kill you? This is what we left in South America. This is why Margaret died, and Damian, and Caridad, and Abigail, and Joe, and Martin, and, and Ariel." He stopped. "And all the others who were massacred by that monster," he whispered. Tears had settled in his eyes, not spilling down his cheeks, but damming up until his eyes were shiny black. "Are you sure we should be looking for their killer?" he said quietly.

Neva, Jin, and Frank sat in silence, looking sympathetically at David. Diane could see by the set of their mouths, the creases of their foreheads, they too were upset. On the way over in the car Frank hadn't let go of her hand but held on tight.

Diane looked up to see Izzy standing in the doorway. He looked as forlorn as David.

"I thought I would come see what you guys were doing," said Izzy. "Evie's at one of her meetings. I heard about Rikki's confession."

"Come in and sit down," said Diane. "We just ordered from the restaurant. It should be here in a minute. Why don't you call down for something?"

"I had a milk shake on the way over. I might order me a hamburger." Instead of going to the phone, he sat down on the sofa.

Diane went over and hugged David. "I'm here, and I really think they would have had a hard time killing me. Many have tried and failed,"

"Is that supposed to be funny?" he said.

"Yes. You mean it wasn't?" she said.

"Not in the least."

The moment was interrupted by the arrival of their dinner. Izzy placed an order for a hamburger and Diane gave the waiter a tip while the others were setting the food out on the table.

"I really understand you, David," said Izzy as they were putting chairs around Diane's table.

David smiled grimly. "It was just my turn to tirade. Jin's been doing it all day because he missed the cyberghost."

They told Izzy about the reappearance of the ghost to Jonas Briggs, the archaeologist.

"So he stayed on, did he?" said Izzy. "Can't say as I blame him."

Izzy was trying to be lighthearted, but Diane could see he too was feeling stinging anger at Jefferies and his buddies. All of them, all their eyes looked troubled. She understood. To think that there was someone out there plotting against her, plotting to kill her, and she didn't know it, wouldn't have known it until it was perhaps too late. How do you guard against things you don't know? How do you know to fight them? It was frightening and infuriating. Diane agreed with David. It was like the man who massacred their friends. Just like him.

"So, are we going to find Jefferies' and Peeks' killers or are we going to call them misdemeanor homicides and go after some really bad guys?" said Jin.

"Of course we are going to find the killers," said Diane. "The city needs some closure on this. We need to demonstrate that we are not to be messed with. And we need to put an end to this dirty business. Not for Jefferies and Peeks, but for all of us. Killing is not how we solve our problems. That's the whole point."

"You're not going to give a speech, are you?" said David. "Like *The Grapes of Wrath*, or *The Fountainhead*, because you really aren't as good as Henry Fonda or Gary Cooper."

"That was it. That was my speech," said Diane, smiling at him.

"So," said Neva. "How are we going to proceed? Do we know that Bryce didn't kill Spence Jefferies? He killed Edgar Peeks."

"No, we don't know," said Diane. "But I think there is someone who does. He as much as told me."

"Who?" said Neva.

"The cyberghost," said Diane.

Chapter 48

"The cyberghost told us?" said Neva, squeezing a slice of lemon over her salmon. "I must have missed that."

Diane was glad they had a name to call him. She was about to settle on Fred.

"Yes," said Diane, "he told us."

Diane took a bite of her salmon and they all settled into eating their meals of steaks, lasagna, and salmon. Diane supplied drinks from her refrigerator. It didn't take long for the restaurant staff to bring Izzy's hamburger, and he ate with the rest of them.

"Remember I asked it, 'Do you know who killed Jefferies and Peeks?' " said Diane after a moment. "It said, *'No. But you should have asked a better question. Remember I am a computer.'* I told it I didn't know what it meant and it said, *'Good.'* I asked it if it was lying and it said, *'I am exactly not lying.'* "

"You remember all that?" said Neva.

"It was an odd conversation," said Diane.

"I know, but still . . ." Neva let the sentence trail off.

"So," said David, "if you had said, 'Do you know who killed Jefferies *or* Peeks,' you would have gotten a different answer."

"Yes," said Diane, "exactly."

"You got me on that one," said Izzy.

"The words *and* and *or* are very important when you are talking to a computer," said David, "or a guy, or gal, pretending to be a computer."

He left his steak and went to Jonas' computer and started plugging it in. Diane took one more bite of her salmon and joined him. Gradually the others came over too, all looking over his shoulder. He plugged in a flash drive before he booted up.

The computer came to life with a low whirring sound and the glow of the screen. Other than that, nothing happened. No offers to play chess, no simulated voice, no ghost.

"Well, damn," said Jin. "You think it's me?"

"Yeah, Jin, it's you. He doesn't like you. If you left, he'd come back," said Neva, rolling her eyes.

David started typing, and several windows came up on the screen; one of them showed what looked to Diane like machine language. Presumably David was searching for an errant program. After a few minutes she went back to her food, as did everyone else except Frank. He and David sat, heads together, over the computer, muttering to each other. Diane couldn't understand anything they were saying. She was taking the last bite of her baked sweet potato when she heard the voice.

"Hello, Jonas. How about a nice game of chess?"

"How very *WarGames*!" cried Jin. He was the first to the computer. "Yes; say yes."

"Jin, will you please contain yourself in some way?" said David.

David and Frank watched the split windows as the voice spoke.

"You want to talk to it?" said David to Diane.

Diane sat down at the keyboard. *This is not Jonas. It is Diane,* she typed.

"Hello, Diane. This is a surprise. You are on Jonas' computer."

Yes. You startled Jonas, Diane typed.

"I am sorry. I did not mean to. I just wanted to play chess."

Why? Diane typed.

"I know how to play chess and so does he. It is something we have in common," it said.

How do you know Jonas knows how to play chess? Diane typed.

"He has Chessmaster on his computer. I found it," it said. *"Jonas beat Chessmaster twelve times. Do you play chess, Diane?"*

Yes. Jonas and I play often, Diane typed.

"Chess is good," it said.

"This is just so cool," said Jin.

"This is a computer program," said David, looking at Diane. "It's not a guy on instant messages."

"You are looking at me, Diane," it said. *"I see it."*

That is David and Frank looking at you, Diane typed.

"Dave and Frank. That is so funny. Do you know how that is funny, Diane?" it said.

"Okay, that was just plain weird," said Neva.

Yes. Those are the names of the astronauts in 2001: A Space Odyssey, Diane typed. *They talked to HAL, a computer. You are not like HAL, are you?*

"No, I am not like HAL," it said. *"HAL is not real."*

I need to ask you a question. Do you know who killed Jefferies or Peeks? she typed.

"You asked the right question. I will answer you. Yes, I know. Do you?" it asked.

No, typed Diane. *Will you tell me?*

"No. That is not a good thing to talk about," it said. *"I have to go now. I have enjoyed talking with you, Diane, but this conversation can serve no purpose anymore,"* it said, quoting a line from the movie. *"I made a joke. Did you get it? Good-bye."*

Diane tried several more questions, but she got no response.

"It deleted itself," said David.

"Can you undelete it?" asked Diane.

"I'll try, but I think that last message was designed to tell the program the game was over, so to speak," said David.

"I can see I'm going to have to spend more time at the movies," said Izzy. "Or reading books," he added.

"That was just the coolest thing," said Jin. "Where did it come from? Did it jump into the system?"

"Yes," said Frank. "That it did. What do you make of it, Diane?"

"It was a confession," she said.

"I think you're reading too much into it," said David. "AI programs can be very convincing, but they aren't sentient by a long shot."

"I agree," said Frank. "This was aimed at you, Diane. Whoever it was knew you and probably knew you are a science fiction fan."

"Perhaps," said Diane, "but to what purpose?"

"I don't know," said David.

"The main purpose of the program was to pass on information," said Frank.

"And then what?" said Diane. "Play chess? I'm not saying the thing is sentient, for heaven's sake, but I think whoever programmed it is the killer. I think it is one of the hackers and I think they want to confess, but can't manage to do it in person."

No one said anything. Diane took that to mean they disagreed with her.

Diane looked at Frank. "What do you know of this Black Light?" she said. "Isn't that who you thought wrote the message inside the computer case?"

"All I know is a name. He came up in our investigation only in passing. Shogun—Malcolm Chen—mentioned him in e-mails in terms that suggested that he thought Black Light was the best hacker. But I have no information on places he might have hacked. If he's active, then he is good, because he isn't on anyone's radar."

"We can contact some of the people on the list and see if they know him," said Diane.

Frank nodded. "We can do that tomorrow. I faxed

the list to my partner. I'll call him to see what he's found out."

"I think it's all but wrapped up," said Jin. "We have a lot of details to uncover, but I think Diane's right. The cyberghost did it. It may not be sentient, but the person behind it is."

"I agree," said Diane. "Now," she said to David, "do I have a virus in my system?"

David shook his head. "I'll examine the program, but I don't think so. I think it's dead now."

"You mean we can't start the whole thing up again if we scan my eye?" said Diane.

"No," said David. "I think it was programmed to know when it was done."

"Why did it escape from Jefferies' computer into the museum system?" asked Diane.

"I don't know," said David.

"It wasn't finished delivering the message," said Neva. "It's kind of like an angel."

"Angel?" said Izzy. "How's that?"

"They're messengers," said Neva. "Not all messages are good. This was a messenger from it's creator— Black Light, or whoever."

Frank built a fire, and he and Diane sat in front of it and watched the flames. Earlier, Frank had called his partner and the two of them discussed everything they knew about Black Light, which took about five minutes. They didn't really know if he existed or was a fantasy made up by a few hackers. Frank decided they should contact all the hackers who had mentioned Black Light in their correspondence. That would be the best bet. He was thinking the cyberghost would be one of them.

"I'll contact the university too," said Frank. "ACM may know something. They deal with a lot of gifted computer programmers."

Diane nodded. Then her eyes got wide and she sat up and looked at Frank.

"What?" he said.

"HAL. Did you know, if you advance one letter in the alphabet, HAL turns into IBM? Arthur C. Clarke said it was unintentional, but it's kind of cool."

"I agree," said Frank. "It's cool. So . . . why did that make you suddenly sit up and take notice?"

"If you do the same to Black Light, *BL*, you get *CM*," she said. "I know who Black Light is."

Chapter 49

"Who is CM?" asked Frank. "I don't remember a mention of a CM."

"Because, like your Black Light, he is completely under the radar. He's a student in Advanced Computational Methods, he quit his job at a bank right after the murders of Jefferies and Peeks, and he took a photograph of me just a few days ago with his digital camera. His name is Caleb Miller and he is a great kid who loves his brother, does well in school, and— I hope I'm wrong."

"I haven't heard the name," said Frank, as if that was in Caleb's favor. "Malcolm Chen's initials are CM backwards, as in Chen, Malcolm. I don't know if that mean's anything, but there it is."

Diane nodded. "And he was a hacker. But was he a programmer? Aren't there different levels of skill among hackers?" she asked. "And he has been dead for a couple of months."

"There are levels, and programmers are the top of the hacker pyramid in many cases, but the levels are very blurred. To tell you the truth, I don't know if Chen was a programmer. And yes, he's been dead for months, but his program—if it is his program—could remain active years after his death."

"We still have the same problem: Why contact me? At the time of his death, Chen wouldn't have any idea that I would be back in charge of the crime lab. Caleb would *know* that I am," said Diane.

She looked at her watch. It was a little after ten p.m. "We have to go see him," she said.

"Do you know where he lives?" said Frank. "We'll have to ask Janice to go with us."

"He's not in her jurisdiction," she said.

Diane called Sheriff Bruce Canfield and gave him a brief summary of why she needed to talk with Caleb.

"I know Caleb is involved in computers, but I find it hard to believe he would be mixed up in this," said the sheriff. "He's a nice young man. He's never given his grandparents a minute's trouble. Neither of the boys have."

"From the brief times I met with him, I found him to be a great kid too," said Diane, "but I would like to speak with him just the same."

"Can't this wait until tomorrow? It's mighty late. The Wilsons are farmers," he said. "They go to bed early and get up early."

"It would be good if we could get this done soon," said Diane.

"Wait a minute," said the sheriff. "I just remembered. My cousin does some of Arlen's chores when he has to be out of town, and he mentioned something about Arlen going into Atlanta with the family to visit the boys' Miller kin. He said they would be back late. We may catch them up. Meet me at my office and I'll drive you out there. But I have to tell you, I think this is thin."

"I agree that it is not conclusive," said Diane. "But Caleb may know some of the people we're interested in because of the classes he takes at the university. He may be able to help us with the program that was on Jefferies' computer if we describe it to him."

"All this computer stuff is just so much Greek to me. I'll see you at my office. I'm driving my pickup. It's a big silver Super Duty. I'll be out front. Are you bringing Rosewood detectives?"

"No. Frank will be with me," said Diane.

"That's okay then. I don't want Rosewood thinking they can cross the city limits anytime they want."

Frank drove out to the Rose County Sheriff's Office. Bruce Canfield was waiting for them when they drove up, standing by his silver truck dressed not in his uniform, but in jeans, a flannel shirt, and an open fleece-lined denim jacket.

He and Frank shook hands and they climbed into the cab of the truck. Diane sat between them.

"Buckle up. I didn't call to tell them we're coming, just in case you're right and he is involved in this somehow. But I'll be real surprised if he is."

"Me too," said Diane, fastening her seat belt. "By the way, we found out Bryce had a man named Curtis Crabtree throw your bones in the river."

"That son of a bitch threw them in the river? I ought to make him wade out until he finds them."

As the sheriff drove out to Arlen Wilson's farm, Diane and Frank gave him a rundown on current events. The sheriff whistled.

"If that's not just the worst bunch of . . ." Words seemed to fail him. "You're telling me they were planning on killing you and Mrs. Van Ross? What is Rosewood coming to? When that Jefferies was running for mayor, I didn't like him one bit. Too slick. But of course it didn't matter, since I wasn't voting in that election. The wife said he couldn't be trusted. She saw his picture in the paper with the governor a lot. Said she didn't like his face. 'Course, the wife doesn't like any politicians. I wasn't fond of Mayor Sutton, but he's a damn sight better than Jefferies was. You people sure know how to pick 'em. Now, I've heard people say some real nice things about Edward Van Ross. That family's been around here a long time. I know a lot of people would like to see him run in the special election. You think he will?"

Diane liked Canfield, but he surely was a talker. "I don't know," she said. "Sutton wanted to know the same thing when I spoke with him."

The sheriff laughed out loud. "I'll bet he did. So let me get this straight. Jefferies was running some kind of cybergang that stole peoples' identities—like running up their credit cards and stuff like that?''

"Or borrowing money from a mortgage company using a victim's house as collateral, then pocketing the money and defaulting on the loan," said Frank. "They also apply for new credit cards with a stolen identity and register a change of address for the victim. That way, the bills never reach the victim and he never even knows what has happened until thousands of dollars in charges have been rung up. They have a thousand different ways to steal money from you if they have the right information," said Frank.

"That just boggles the mind. I guess you get a lot of that kind of thing in Atlanta." Canfield said *Atlanta* the same way he would have said *Sodom* or *Gomorrah*.

"We do. But it's everywhere. I imagine you get a lot here in the county, but most of the time people don't report it. They just try to settle it with the card companies. It takes a couple of years on the average for a person to get their credit straightened out."

Canfield turned off the highway onto a dirt road. It was in good condition but still a little rough for Diane. There weren't many houses in the area—mostly farms. It was beautiful in the daylight, but all that was visible in the dark was the road ahead, running between farm fences, patches of woods, and an occasional pair of animal eyes shining back from the darkness. The sheriff turned down another dirt road, and Diane thought she saw a mailbox at the intersection with the name *Wilson* on it, but she wasn't sure. He drove another half mile or so until he came to a white one-story farmhouse. In the truck's headlights she could see a red barn about a hundred feet from the house.

There were lights on inside the house and a car and two pickup trucks were parked in the drive. They got out of the sheriff's truck and walked up to the house. The sheriff knocked, and Diane heard footsteps coming to the door. It was opened by a woman whom Diane assumed to be Mrs. Wilson.

An electric shock ran through Diane. Not even thinking, her heart pounding, she sucked in her breath, readying herself to jump out of danger. It was the kind of autonomic fear response that comes from stepping on a snake.

But it was not a snake. There was no place to jump. It was a man standing in the shadow behind the open door. He was pointing a gun straight at Diane.

In the same instant she saw him, Diane realized that one of the pickup trucks in the driveway was a dark Ford Ranger—just like the perp had used at the museum. The one that had tried to run her down.

Chapter 50

It was the gun that Diane's eyes froze on. A big, high-caliber silver and black thing, one that would make a big entry hole and an even bigger exit hole. Her gaze shifted to the face of the man holding the gun. It was Curtis Crabtree. She glanced at his left hand, the one not holding the gun. It was wrapped in a bandage meant to immobilize the thumb. He probably had a bite mark on his ankle.

Frank was just behind Diane. He had a hand on her upper arm, holding her tight in his grip. The three of them were stuck on the porch in the open doorway. No way to flee, not wanting to enter the house.

"Well, I'll be damned," said Curtis. "Aren't we in luck? Just the person we needed to see. Gage, when the boy gets here we'll have everything we need."

Gage? There was someone else in the room. Gage Shipman, the third-floor overlook troll. Great. Two hotheads with guns.

Diane looked at Mrs. Wilson. She was dressed in a blue flowered robe and had rollers in her hair and a grave look on her face. Diane could see she was trembling. She didn't blame her. She was about to start shaking herself.

"Now, hold on here," said the sheriff. "What do you think you're up to?"

"Getting us a truckload of money. Now, get in here." Curtis backed up, pulling Mrs. Wilson with him. "Do it," he barked at them, "or I'll start shooting.

Gage and me only need one hostage apiece, so a lot of you are just extra. Now, get in here and sit your asses down. You, put your gun on the table," said Curtis, aiming his gun at the sheriff.

The sheriff complied and the three of them went in and sat down together on a sofa. Mrs. Wilson sat in a straight-backed chair.

Diane was sure the three of them—she, the sheriff, and Frank—were thinking the same thing, and hoped it didn't show on their faces. Curtis and Gage didn't know Frank was a detective and they hadn't searched him for a gun. A bit of good luck. But it also meant they were probably high on something and weren't thinking clearly. A bad situation.

The problem was, Frank's gun was inside his zipped-up suede jacket. Not easily accessible at the moment, but it was there. A small kernel of luck on their side.

Gage Shipman grinned at Diane. He had Henry sitting on the floor next to his chair, a gun near Henry's head but not pointing at him. Arlen Wilson was sitting in an easy chair that was probably where he sat to watch television. He had blood running down the side of his face. Probably hit with a gun when the two men came in the house. He was dressed in his pajamas, as was Henry.

"What exactly are you doing here?" said the sheriff.

Frank sat quietly with his arms folded. Diane guessed that he wouldn't say much lest he be outed as a detective. She tried to think of some way to distract the two thugs so Frank could get at his gun. But one thing she remembered Frank telling her—it's not the gun you have that's important; it's the gun the other guy has.

Curtis and Gage ignored the sheriff.

"Who's this guy?" Curtis pointed his gun at Frank.

"Boyfriend," said Frank.

"You mean you've actually got a boyfriend?" Curtis said to Diane. "Well, no accounting for taste. What do you do?" he asked Frank.

"Accounting," Frank said.

"Accounting?" He laughed as if that were a joke. "Hey, Gage, we have an accountant." He emphasized each syllable. "Maybe he can help us count our money."

"I told you, we don't have any money," said Arlen Wilson. "We're just farmers. Just leave us alone. We ain't rich folks."

"I know, you dumb ass," said Curtis. "Caleb is the one who knows how to get the money. I told you." He slurred his words just enough that Diane was sure Curtis was high on something.

"Caleb's just a student," said Mrs. Wilson. "He don't have any money."

Curtis stood in the middle of the room, looked at the ceiling, and gestured, palms up. Diane was afraid the gun would go off accidently.

"Is everybody in here stupid?" he said.

He went over to Mrs. Wilson and stared at her, nose to nose. She cringed back in her seat.

"Look, you dumb old woman, I didn't say he *has* money. I said he can get it. Get it? He can get it."

"Stop calling my grandparents names," said Henry. "They're smarter than you are."

"Yeah? Well if they're so smart, how come I'm the one here holding the gun? Tell me that."

"What money are you talking about?" said the sheriff. "What money could a college student get his hands on that's got you boys so riled up and raring to go?"

Curtis looked at him for a long moment. "It's in a bank. The kid knows how to get the account numbers and passwords off a computer," he said. "It's a lot of money, and Gage and me's going to get it, with the help of Caleb and the Fallon woman. Now, are we all on the same page here?"

"Caleb won't help the likes of you," said Mrs. Wilson. Apparently the presence of the sheriff and other people was making her more courageous.

Curtis walked over to Henry and patted him on the cheek. Henry shrunk back away from his hand.

"We know Caleb will do anything to keep his little brother safe. Anything."

His voice was suddenly very calm, and it frightened Diane more than when he was yelling.

"Where is Caleb?" asked the sheriff.

"He's out on a date," said Mrs. Wilson. "A girl in one of his classes."

"When will he be getting back?" said the sheriff.

"He doesn't have a curfew," said Arlen Wilson. "He's a grown man now. I don't know when he'll be in."

"Why are you guys here?" said Gage, apparently just now thinking to ask.

"The same reason you are," said Diane. "We've been trying to get into the mayor's computer. We know Caleb is good with computers so we thought we would ask him if he could break the code."

"Oh, he can break it all right," said Curtis. "He probably wrote it."

"Caleb doesn't do things like that," said Mrs. Wilson.

"Why don't you allow Mrs. Wilson and me to make some coffee?" said Diane. "It looks like we might be here a while."

Curtis thought a moment. He looked at Gage, who shrugged.

"All right. But I'm going to stand in the doorway and watch. Don't try to get a knife or anything," he said.

"We'll just put on some coffee," said Diane. "Trying to make things a little easier, that's all."

"Tell you what, Curtis," said Gage. "You watch young Henry, and I'll watch them in the kitchen."

"Whatever," said Curtis. He went over and sat down in the chair vacated by Gage Shipman.

Diane helped Mrs. Wilson into the kitchen. Shipman followed and stood close to Diane. He grinned at her, and Diane could see he was just dying to get even with her for the incident on the third-floor overlook.

But they needed her. When Caleb came, it would be her, Henry, and Caleb that they needed—Henry to be a hostage to make Caleb do the work, and Diane to get the computer.

Frank and the others would be just excess baggage then. Diane had no doubt they would shoot Frank, the sheriff, and the Wilsons when Caleb got there. The thought terrified her.

She or Frank or the sheriff would have to do something before then. Unfortunately, she couldn't think of a thing to do. The best she could come up with so far was to split them up and give Curtis fewer targets if Frank tried something. Perhaps Frank and the sheriff would come up with a plan. The problem was Henry. He was too close to Curtis.

Shipman put a hand on the back of Diane's hair and flipped it. She brushed him away as she rinsed out the coffeepot. It was clean, but she was trying to waste time. Mrs. Wilson seemed to understand. She slowly laid out coffee filters, a measuring spoon, and several cups.

Shipman put his fingertips on Diane's neck, then her cheek. She brushed his hands away. She filled the pot with water and turned off the faucet. He reached up to tickle her ear and she turned to him.

"Did you never get out of third grade?" she said.

"I'm just being nice," he said, grinning. "Doesn't your accountant boyfriend ever touch you like this?" He reached for her ear again, sticking out his tongue.

"What kind of coffee?" Mrs. Wilson said. "We have some chocolate raspberry that's good and some vanilla. We have the regular kind too."

"Chocolate raspberry sounds just fine," said Shipman. "I bet you like chocolate raspberry," he said to Diane. She slapped his hand away again and he laughed. "We might have a long night ahead of us. We'll have to find something to entertain ourselves with."

Diane had the coffeepot filled with water in her right hand. It had weight to it. One good hit and she could knock the gun from his hand just as she had with the rock and Harve Delamore's gun.

"Don't go thinking about trying anything with that pot," said Shipman. "You'd just make me mad." He laughed and for a moment Diane wondered how she telegraphed her intentions.

"I wouldn't dream of it," she said. "If we all stay calm, we can all get what we want."

"What we want. You know what I'm wanting right now?" Shipman caressed her cheek with the knuckle of his index finger.

Diane handed the pot to Mrs. Wilson, who slipped a knife in her hand at the same time. It startled Diane, and she almost jumped. It was small and it was for peeling potatoes—not one that would cut. She wasn't sure what help it would be, but it was obviously the only one that Mrs. Wilson could get her hands on. Diane held the knife to her side, trying to come up with a plan.

"Mrs. Wilson," said Shipman, "would you like to watch as I bend Diane here over your kitchen table?"

Mrs. Wilson sucked in her breath. "Don't do that. Why would you do that?"

"To fucking get even!" he shouted and slapped Diane at the same time.

Diane hadn't seen it coming. She fell to the floor, hitting her elbow. Electric pain coursed through her arm where the hard surface of the floor hit a nerve bundle. She bit her lip to keep from yelling out and causing Frank to take some action before he was ready. She heard Mrs. Wilson suck in her breath and let out a whimper. Diane held on to the knife as Shipman reached down and jerked her up by her other arm.

"Mrs. Wilson," said Shipman, "while the coffee's making you can go sit by your husband. Diane and I want to be alone."

"Don't do this, young man," said Mrs. Wilson.

"You want to be next? Fucking do what I tell you," he said through his clenched teeth.

"It's all right, Mrs. Wilson," said Diane. "Why don't you go back in with the others?"

"See, she wants it too," said Shipman grinning.

Diane watched Mrs. Wilson slowly walk out of the kitchen. She was softly crying.

"Now, bitch . . ." Shipman laid the barrel of his gun beside her head. "Bend over."

Chapter 51

"No," said Diane. She stood up straight and looked him in the eyes. "That isn't going to happen."

"It isn't, huh?" He put the barrel of the gun to her temple. "You rather I blow your brains out instead?" He put his face close to her ear, still gripping her arm tight with his right hand. "That might just be more fun—watching your brains splatter all over the old lady's refrigerator."

He laughed and Diane smelled the odor of alcohol.

"Except it would be over too fast," he said. "One squeeze . . ." He pushed the gun until the end of the barrel hurt against her skin. "Bang, it's all over."

"Instead of bang, bang, and it's all over?" said Diane.

She wanted to make him mad, make him let go of her even if it was to hit her. She needed an opening. She needed him to be distracted—just for a second.

It took him a moment to understand he had been insulted. He just looked at her, processing her words in his alcohol-fogged brain.

Suddenly he got it. His face twisted in anger.

"Is that what you think? You damn fucking bitch."

He glared at her and lay the gun down on the counter, and in one angry move pulled his arm back, his hand balled into a powerful fist.

It was now or never.

Diane rammed the knife with all her strength into

the hollow of Shipman's throat just above the sternum.
He would have yelled, but she had pierced his trachea
and cut off the air flow to his larynx.

In sudden panic he grabbed at his throat and pulled
at the knife. The dull serrated edges made it stick fast.
Diane grabbed the gun as he struggled to breathe and
hit him across the temple. He went down like a
fallen tree.

She was almost to the living room when she saw
headlights reflect against the wall. Caleb was home.

"Gage, here he comes. Get in here," yelled Crabtree.

Diane quickly and quietly retraced her steps and
headed for the kitchen door. Her hand was on the
knob when the loud report of two shots filled the
house.

"No, please," she whispered.

She ran to the living room, gun in hand pointing
straight ahead. Frank was bending over Crabtree.
Henry was almost to the front door, the sheriff going
after him, when a voice came from the porch.

"Whoever's in there, if you've hurt my family, I'll
kill you. You won't get out of the house."

"Caleb," yelled Henry. "It's okay. We're all right."
He ran to the door and opened it and hugged his
brother.

Caleb walked in, wide-eyed, surveying the room. He
saw his grandparents huddled together and went over
to them. Henry followed.

Diane still had the gun aiming toward where
Crabtree had been sitting. She slowly dropped her
arm.

Crabtree was on the floor, bleeding from his chest.

Diane knelt beside Frank and leaned against him.
"I was afraid it was you," she said.

"I'm fine. Are you all right?" he said. "I was . . .
afraid for you. Crabtree had his gun on Henry the
whole time . . ."

"I'm fine," she said. "Thanks to Mrs. Wilson. She

managed to slip me a potato peeler. Fine weapons, potato peelers." Diane was shaking and she hugged Frank closer, trying to stop shivering.

Fortunately, like Delamore, Shipman was a taunter. Taunters waste a lot of time—time enough for Diane to have formulated a plan. Things could have turned out so different. Diane fought back a wave of nausea.

She looked down at Curtis Crabtree. He was shot twice in the chest, but he wasn't dead. His breathing was fast and shallow. Frank took a throw from the chair and applied pressure to his chest.

Sheriff Canfield walked toward the kitchen to check on Shipman, his own gun in his hand. After a while she heard his voice speaking to someone. He came back several moments later.

"I called for an ambulance," said the sheriff. "He's not dead, but his breathing is real bad. I didn't know if I should take the knife out or not."

Another chill ran through Diane. She leaned against Frank again as he tended to Curtis.

"What happened in here?" she asked.

"I'd been mentally rehearsing how I was going to get at my gun, when Caleb drove up. Henry made a dash for the door. He was so quick, it caught Curtis off guard. He started after him, but Henry was too far away to reach quickly. Crabtree realized his mistake in going after Henry, so he turned around, but by that time I had my gun and shot him. It was all very fast."

Crabtree turned his head and looked up at Caleb. There was a lot of hate in his eyes, but nothing compared to the black hatred in Caleb's eyes.

"Who are these people?" asked Mrs. Wilson. "Caleb, what have you to do with these people?"

Mrs. Wilson's question remained unanswered while the sheriff tended to the aftermath. The ambulance came and took both Shipman and Crabtree to the hospital. Several Rose County deputies arrived and stood on the porch, guarding it, Diane guessed. She wasn't sure from whom. It could have been from another of

Jefferies' thugs, or it could have been from the Rosewood police in case they decided to show up.

The sheriff called his wife and briefly told her what
had happened and that Henry would be staying the
night with them. Henry didn't want to go, but Caleb
talked him into it. Caleb wanted to tell his story, but
he didn't want his little brother to hear it. A deputy
left with Henry.

"Okay, Caleb," said the sheriff, "we're listening.
You know you can have a lawyer, don't you?"

"Yes, I know. But right now I just want to get this
off my chest."

They were sitting in the living room. Mrs. Wilson
had put a rug over Crabtree's bloodstains. Mr. Wilson
had declined to go to the hospital for examination. He
was holding ice in a ziplock bag to the side of his head
where he had been struck. He and Mrs. Wilson were
still in their pajamas and robes, but Mrs. Wilson had
taken the rollers out of her hair. She sat on the couch
with her husband and motioned for Caleb to sit between them. But he shook his head.

"I'll sit right here," he said and took a seat across
from the sheriff.

Diane and Frank pulled up dining room chairs. All
eyes were on Caleb. He looked so thin and small.

He glanced over at Diane. "You got my message?"
he asked.

"If you are the ghost in the machine," said Diane.
"That's why we're here. We figured out it was you."

He smiled. "I'm a little surprised. I thought, if you
figure it out, that's fine, but if you don't, then maybe
it was meant for me to be home free."

"Free from what, Caleb?" asked Mr. Wilson.

"The things I've done," he said.

"Did Spence Jefferies recruit you?" asked Diane.

"Not the way he did other people. He recruited
Malcolm Chen. Malcolm was my friend. He's the one
who came up with the Black Light thing. I thought it
was kind of silly, but he thought it was cool. He knew

I like the movies *WarGames* and *2001: A Space Odyssey*."

"You wrote the AI program?" said Frank.

Caleb nodded. "I wanted to write a program that could be used maybe to help the disabled use computers more easily, or maybe in business. Like it could just flow around in the network keeping track of what people are doing. And if someone on the fifth floor could use the information that someone on the first floor had, the program could tell them. That kind of thing."

"It seemed real," said Diane. "For a long time we thought it was someone using some kind of instant-messaging program."

Caleb smiled. "I started by writing a chess-playing algorithm. Playing chess is one of the best things to start programming with. It has pure rules, but it also has strategies and thinking ahead, and personality. There's lots of chess programs out there, but I wanted to write my own for the practice. It looks for people to play with; you may have found that out."

"Yes, it found its way to Jonas Briggs' computer and asked him to play. He was rather surprised," said Diane.

Caleb smiled. "It's almost become a bug in the program," he said. "I started by teaching it to look for people who play. I tried to change it, but it won't stop."

"But it's more than a chess program now," said Frank.

Caleb nodded. "I gave it a database of information. A fairly large one. I was trying to get it to learn, so when it gets new information, it compares it to what it knows. If there is no conflict, it keeps it and stores it according to a hierarchy of probable accuracy— another algorithm I worked out."

"How did you make it sound human?" said Diane.

"It parses sentences and conversations, so when you ask it a question, it not only analyzes what you asked, but analyzes everything that was said previously. There is a little problem in changing topics sometimes."

Caleb's eyes grew bright when he talked about his program. Diane was seeing just how very gifted he was. She was starting to feel heartsick.

"I made algorithms from interrogation techniques and from the way some psychiatrists do therapy—you know, kind of Rogerian—by making a statement and then asking what the person understands or what they think it means. That kind of thing. Or answering a question with a question. I also put in a small-talk algorithm. If certain concepts or phrases come up in the conversation, it searches for references in pop culture or movies."

"We noticed that," said Frank. "We were all impressed. My name is Frank, and the other guy working on it was Dave."

Caleb grinned for the first time. "Did it recognize that? Did it say something?"

"Yes," said Frank. "It said it was funny and asked us if we knew why it was funny."

Caleb laughed and slapped his thighs. Diane could hear the joy in his voice—like a parent enjoying what his child had learned to do.

If the sheriff or the Wilsons were getting impatient, they didn't show it. The sheriff appeared to be content to let Caleb's story unfold the way he wanted it to. Diane felt that it was important to understand his programming abilities, for that seemed to be the basis for the crimes.

Caleb hesitated a moment, as if he knew he needed to get to the topic at hand. His face grew solemn and he looked as if he was about to tear up.

"Malcolm Chen, as I said, was a friend," he said, "and I killed him."

Chapter 52

Arlen and Mary Wilson sat up straight. She put a hand over her mouth.

"No," she whispered.

"You are entitled to have a lawyer," Diane repeated.

"You need to do that, son," said the sheriff.

"Listen to them," said Arlen. He started to rise from his chair.

Caleb shook his head violently.

"Look . . . Let's just say that everything I say is hypothetical and leave it at that. Will that be all right? Everything I'm going to tell you is hypothetical. But I need to tell you."

"Okay, son," said the sheriff. "Tell us your hypothetical story."

Arlen sat back down.

"You asked me if Spence Jefferies recruited me. He recruited Mal—Malcolm—to work as a hacker. Mal was so easily impressed and thought he was on the inside. But Jefferies didn't just want hackers, he wanted programmers. Mal was a good hacker, but he couldn't see the ones and zeros, I mean really see them," he said, looking at each of them.

"I know what you mean," said Frank.

"Were you the one who hacked Jefferies' computer?" Caleb asked.

Frank shook his head. "It was another guy. I just offered suggestions."

"But you understand about seeing the math?" he said.

"Yes," said Frank.

"Mal told Jefferies about me. I wasn't interested in the job fairs, or even getting that kind of job. I was interested in working with AI. I was still in school and wanted to go to graduate school. But Mal told him about me and told him I was the best."

Caleb frowned, looking angry.

"Jefferies came after me. He tried to bribe me. First with watches. What the hell kind of bribe is that? I don't need a watch that costs ten thousand dollars. Who does? Then he offered me money. A lot of it. I didn't like what they were doing. I knew it was a cybergang. I told Mal it wasn't a game. It was serious business, and these guys were criminals. He just laughed."

"He couldn't bribe you?" prompted Frank.

Caleb shook his head.

"Then he started threatening my family. The farm. He was rich and he said he could take Grampa's farm away from him. He owed a lot of money and Jefferies said he would buy out his mortgage like they were doing to other people. So I gave in. I told him I would write his programs. What he wanted was trojans carrying viruses to gather information. Do you know about that?" he asked.

"I'm a detective in the Metro-Atlanta Fraud and Computer Forensics Unit," said Frank. "I've been working on the rise in identity thefts caused by Jefferies' cybergang."

Caleb nodded. "So you know the damage those viruses can do. Jefferies wanted me to write one that was harder to detect. One that didn't hog the CPU use, so it would be harder to discover. He also wanted me to work in the Rosewood Bank and install one of my viruses to steal information about the patrons and about other banks in the Federal Reserve System. Jefferies was fascinated with programmers. He thought we were a cross between magicians and pets."

"What happened with Malcolm Chen?" asked Frank. "Hypothetically."

"Stupid." Caleb shook his head. "He got stupid. I couldn't convince him these guys weren't to be messed with. He bought into their hype that he was some kind of special expert that no one could touch. He figured out how much money Jefferies was raking in and decided to steal some of it. He hacked into Jefferies' computer and stole some of his offshore account numbers and transferred the money to an account he set up."

Caleb shook his head again. "He didn't tell me. If he had told me, I could have helped him cover it up. I discovered that Mayor Jefferies' computer had been hacked when he asked me to work on it. I told Jefferies he had been hacked, and he was furious. I didn't know it was Mal because Mal hadn't told me, don't you see?"

Caleb stopped for a moment as if to catch his breath. He looked at each of them and his gaze lingered on his grandparents, who smiled at him.

"Jefferies asked me if I knew where there was some land away from everything where he could hide something. He didn't tell me what. I told him about McCarthy's land. You know, Grampa, the guy from Detroit who can't decide what he wants to do with his little piece of property."

His grandfather nodded. "I told them about him," he said.

"Jefferies made me take him out there to show him. Curtis Crabtree and Edgar Peeks were with him. When we got there they opened the trunk of the car, and there was Mal in the trunk, tied up and gagged. They dragged him out and called that other guy, Gage Shipman, on Jefferies' cell. The phone was on speaker and Shipman described my brother Henry doing his chores. Shipman was here at our farm. Over in the woods. He was right here, watching Henry."

Diane had a sick feeling in her stomach. She saw Arlen and his wife reach for each other.

Tears began to flow from Caleb's eyes, spilling onto his cheeks as he started crying. His eyes grew red and puffy. He got the hiccups, and it was hard for him to catch his breath. Frank handed him a box of Kleenex from an end table and went to the kitchen and brought back a glass of water. Caleb wiped his eyes and blew his nose. He took a long drink, almost to the bottom of the glass.

"Jefferies put a gun in my hand and told me if I didn't shoot Malcolm, they would tell Gage Shipman to kill my little brother."

Caleb stopped and cried again, his shoulders heaving with the flow of tears that dripped onto his hands. His grandmother gasped and held a hand to her mouth. Both she and her husband were tearing up.

"How do you make a decision like that? How do you do that? You've seen Henry, how special he is. He's my brother. How could they ask me to make that kind of decision?"

He sniffed and blew his nose again.

"Mal begged me. He was crying and begging me not to shoot him. But I did. They called Shipman off and they took the gun from me. Jefferies told me I was a murderer now and that he owned me. He said it wouldn't be too bad because I would make a lot of money. He took Mal's watch off him and gave it to me and told me that as long as I did what he wanted, Henry would be safe."

"So you killed Jefferies," said Diane.

Caleb was silent for a long while. No one said anything.

"It's funny," Caleb said. "I wrote the virus Jefferies wanted, and it never occurred to him that I would put it on his computer." Caleb looked at Diane. "I owned his network. I knew everything he did, including where he kept all his money, who he had hired, and where they worked. I had their programs. I had everything. I had it all sent to my computer here."

Frank raised his eyebrows. Diane could imagine what he was thinking.

He drank the last of his water. He'd stopped crying, and his face was like stone. His eyes were mere slits, and his mouth was set in a grim frown.

"Jefferies so admired Alexander the Great. Well, I knew about Alexander the Great too. And I knew what he would do to defeat an enemy. He'd cut off its head. To kill a snake, you take off the head. In this case it was more like a hydra and two more would grow back. I had to kill the others too. I shot Jefferies. I was going to kill Peeks, but someone beat me to it. I was going to get everyone who wore that stupid pinky ring. It was the only way I could make sure Henry would be safe. After I shot Jefferies, I put Mal's watch on him. He could have the damn thing back."

"Why didn't you come to us, Caleb?" said Arlen. "We would have helped."

Caleb looked at his grandparents. "You would have done the right thing, and you would have been killed for it. I had no place to go for help."

"You should have come straight to me, son," said the sheriff. "I would have handled it. You didn't have to kill them."

"I couldn't take the chance with Henry's life, Sheriff, I'm sorry. You're a good man, but there's one of you and a whole gang of them. All of them vicious and cold-blooded. Jefferies was the mayor; Peeks was the chief of police. They'd hired a bunch of their own cops. His friend Bryce controlled the crime lab. Jefferies had a judge killed and was friends with the governor. He bragged that he was going to get someone inside the GBI. Where could I go? Who was I supposed to go to? Who could I trust? As far as I was concerned, he had broken the social contract." Caleb looked at Diane. "Are you familiar with John Locke?" he asked.

Diane nodded. "You no longer had to give up your right to aggressively protect yourself and your family, because the government had not fulfilled its part of the bargain. From your point of view, the government could not maintain social order. Does that sum up your position?" said Diane.

Caleb nodded. "What else could I have done?"

David was faced with the same dilemma exactly, thought Diane. He dropped out and started his own investigation. He skirted the law a little, but he wouldn't have killed. But then, David was a lot older than Caleb; he had a world more experience, resources to use, and maturity. It makes a difference. Caleb was essentially a kid. He was a kid for how long—almost twenty years? And a young adult for one.

What would any of us have done if our families had been threatened in that way? What would I have done had I known what Ivan Santos had in mind for Ariel and our friends at the mission? thought Diane. *Would I have gone after him?*

Epilogue

The aftermath to the whole Jefferies episode was unsettling to everyone in Rosewood. The meth lab explosion the previous year had brought people together. But this series of events and disclosures was divisive. The fallout reached everyone from the governor, whose PR people tried to spin the damage by explaining that photo ops with Jefferies didn't mean they were bosom buddies, to individual families like the McConnels, whose son, Ethan, wandered onto the museum overlook and was threatened by security guard Gage Shipman.

Andie told Diane she heard from Mrs. McConnel that she and her husband might divorce. The policeman friend of Mr. McConnel's buddy, Barrel, turned out to be one of Jefferies' hires. Mr. McConnel, who had voted for Jefferies based on his law-and-order stance, now felt betrayed and humiliated, and his wife was not kind. Like a lot of people, she couldn't resist the I-told-you-so's.

Frank and his department came out well. Caleb's computer was a gold mine—literally. It had every single thing in it Frank needed to untangle Jefferies' empire. Caleb gave Frank a flash drive containing a total copy of the information. He seemed to understand that Rosewood might not be eager to share with Atlanta. Caleb gave David all his algorithms to ponder. David, a lover of algorithms, was bubbly with excitement.

Janice Warrick never discovered who the shadow man was on the security tape.

Rikki was the most disappointed. She thought she sent a chunk of Jefferies' money to her own account in the Caribbean via her cell phone, which she threw in the river along with the hard disk. She had no way of knowing that Caleb had already emptied all but a thousand dollars from each account. He put the money in a holding account for the authorities to figure out what to do with. The prison guards said Rikki stomped around her cell for days ranting at her bad luck.

Jennifer Jeffcote-Smith received an undisclosed sum from the city, but she wasn't happy either. Her reputation was tarnished by her proximity to the Jefferies gang, and her husband's relatives were as relentless with her as Mrs. McConnel was with her husband. Diane had seen her one last time in passing at the post office as Jennifer was leaving town. Her in-laws were laughing, telling all their friends to move to Georgia, where they pay you a lot of money for being stupid. Jennifer was probably heading for a divorce too, thought Diane.

Many on the city council wanted Douglas Garnett to run for mayor. But he really liked being chief of detectives, and Edward Van Ross reinstated him. Garnett and his wife sent Diane a bouquet of red roses.

Former mayor Walter Sutton was as disappointed as Rikki Gillinick. The citizens of Rosewood did not want him as mayor again. They somehow blamed him too for the corruption in city hall, though Diane wasn't sure why. Edward Van Ross was pressed into service for a term as mayor. He told everyone it was just until Rosewood got back to normal. Diane wasn't sure that would ever happen. A group of people actually approached her to run in the special election. Diane couldn't think of anything she had rather not do than run for mayor. She politely declined.

Curtis Crabtree died on the way to the hospital. Shipman clung to life and slowly recovered in the

prison hospital. Caleb told Diane and Frank that
Crabtree and Shipman tormented him over how they
cut up his friend Malcolm and fed him into the wood
chipper. The one nice thing that Jefferies had done
for Caleb was to tell Curtis and Shipman to lay off—
but, Caleb added, that was just so his work wouldn't
be affected.

Diane had asked Colin Prehoda to take Caleb's
case. He loved it. Diane had invited him to lunch in
her office and told him about Caleb and what happened.

"I can get the kid a medal," he said. "My wife can
get him a movie."

Diane frowned. "For himself, he needs to know that
killing wasn't the answer," said Diane. "He doesn't
need to go the rest of his life thinking there was no
alternative. Everyone needs to know you can't get off
scot-free for murder, no matter what the circumstances."

"Was there an alternative?" said Prehoda. "Where
could he go in his situation? It's a valid question, one
I can make the jury understand. Have you talked with
Vanessa lately? If Jefferies wasn't already dead, she
said she would have killed him. She said she might
just dig him up and shoot him anyway. People can't
just go around doing what he did and not expect
someone to bite back really hard."

"I'm talking about—" began Diane.

"I know, you're talking about the kid's soul. But
my job is to give him a good defense, and I cannot
do otherwise. You'll have to let his grandparents look
after his soul," said Prehoda.

"I suppose. He's a kid with a conscience, and I want
him to be able to be happy sometime in his life," said
Diane. "He has a real talent. I don't think he can ever
be happy without some kind of accounting."

"Redemption requires atonement?" Prehoda
shrugged. "That's not my jurisdiction. Right now, settle for his freedom. I can get him out of hard jail
time, even though it looks like he premeditated the

murders. Jefferies and his gang didn't give him any options, and they were relentless in their threats to his family. It doesn't help the prosecution that Jefferies had Karen McNevin killed. A lot of us liked her. A lot of us like you and Vanessa. The discovery that he planned to kill the two of you isn't sitting well with anyone. The kid's not going to jail over this."

"Probably not," she said.

"Besides, you have no evidence physically linking him to any of the murders. You only have his hypothetical story about what happened," said Prehoda.

Prehoda had been right. He made a deal with the DA that Caleb would get intensive counseling and five years' probation. But Diane worried, as did Frank, especially when they found out the college classmate Caleb was on a date with that fateful night was Star, Frank's daughter. Frank sort of freaked out when he learned that.

Jefferies had a file that detailed how Curtis had killed Judge McNevin. Prehoda was right about that too. People were very angry about a well-respected judge being murdered. Suddenly everyone in town knew who John Locke, Jean-Jacques Rousseau, and Thomas Hobbes were and what the concept of *social contract* meant. It was a strange time for Rosewood.

"Here's a dilemma for you," Diane told Prehoda. "Bryce killed Edgar Peeks. He confessed, and we have the evidence. But he also keeps saying he was framed. We thought he had just gone nuts until I realized that we have the bloodstains on the forceps—along with his bloody thumbprints on them—but we don't have a trail left by the incriminating bloody bullet that was supposed to have rolled under the chest. I think Bryce did take his bullet away from the scene, but Rikki, in her sneaky little fashion, had a spent bullet from Bryce's gun that she swabbed in the blood and brain tissue before she dropped it in the evidence bag. That would make not all the evidence against him true, but he did do it."

" 'For 'tis the sport to have the enginer / Hoist with

his own petar,' " was Prehoda's only comment, and they enjoyed the rest of the meal talking about the upcoming Neanderthal exhibit.

Diane managed to get her world back to what passed for normal, even if it would take a long time for Rosewood to get back on track. She didn't think about Jefferies or any of them when she went down to check on how the Pleistocene Room was coming along.

Kendel Williams, the assistant director, had brought back an almost complete Neanderthal skeleton. The brown bones lay in a glass case like Snow White waiting to be awakened. Neva was working on a facial reconstruction to be shown at the event.

The museum would be having the white-tie party in the Pleistocene Room. Diane was putting the Neanderthal diorama and bones temporarily in the huge room so the Friends of the Museum could get a preview of the new acquisition at the party.

Henry, who was now a museum intern after school, worked with Jonas Briggs on the exhibit. Diane knew the Wilsons worried about their grandsons Caleb and Henry. The Wilsons were religious people and were having a hard time of it. Diane was sure atonement was on their minds as well.

She didn't know if justice had been served. She didn't know anymore if complete justice was possible. She touched the glass case that held the bones of the young female Neanderthal and wondered what she would make of the world now.

Professor Emeritus Alexander de Houten sat in his leather chair twirling the pinky ring on his finger. He pulled it from his finger and angrily threw it in the trash. The anger was directed at himself for miscalculating. It was a mistake to trust sociopaths. He thought people free of emotions would carry out his ideas in perfect order. But he hadn't realized that sociopaths aren't free of emotions, just empathy. They have plenty of emotions for themselves. They are selfish to

their core. He wouldn't make that mistake again. And
Rosewood had been such a perfect place for his
plan—small town, easily manipulated, with its own
crime lab. Just perfect. He sighed. He should just
count himself lucky they didn't connect him with their
unfortunate events.

He turned on his computer and watched as it
booted up. He touched his mouse. A screen with text
popped up—and a voice.

*"Hello, Professor de Houten. Would you like to play
a nice game of chess?"*

"What the hell is this?" he said loud enough for his
secretary to hear and knock on his door.

Peabody Public Library
Columbia City, IN

Peabody Public Library
Columbia City, IN

ABOUT THE AUTHOR

Beverly Connor is the author of the Diane Fallon Forensic Investigation series and the Lindsay Chamberlain archaeology mystery series. She holds undergraduate and graduate degrees in archaeology, anthropology, sociology, and geology. Before she began her writing career, Beverly worked as an archaeologist in the southeastern United States, specializing in bone identification and analysis of stone tool debitage. Originally from Oak Ridge, Tennessee, she weaves her professional experiences from archaeology and her knowledge of the South into interlinked stories of the past and present. Beverly's books have been translated into German, Dutch, and Czech, and are available in standard and large print in the UK.

Also Available from

BEVERLY CONNOR

Dead Guilty

A Diane Fallon
Forensic Investigation

In the shadow of Diane Fallon's new forensic lab in Georgia, a land survey crew has discovered three bodies hanging in an isolated patch of woods. The sensational case has aroused the interest of the media, unnerved the locals—and inspired a gruesome game between the killer and Diane. It begins with taunting emails and chilling phone calls. Where it leads is a dangerously personal investigation as each bizarre clue brings Diane closer to a heartless betrayal and a desperate man's obsession for justice—and revenge.

Available wherever books are sold or at penguin.com

Also Available from

BEVERLY CONNOR

One Grave Too Many

A Diane Fallon Forensic Investigation

Leaving a troubled past behind her, Diane Fallon is starting over as director of the RiverTrail Museum of Natural History in Georgia—until former love Detective Frank Duncan tracks her down. He needs her unique experience as a forensic anthropologist to examine a bone found in the woods. Diane can't resist Frank's request—on both a professional and personal level. Because the secrets of bones are in her blood—and theirs.

Available wherever books are sold or at penguin.com

Also Available from

BEVERLY CONNOR

Dead Secret

A Diane Fallon
Forensic Investigation

When forensic anthropologist Diane Fallon
discovers a trio of decades-old skeletons, she
also unearths the key to a mystery that reaches
back seventy years in a legacy of love, greed,
and murder—and an unearthed family secret
that still holds the power to kill.

**Available wherever books are sold or
at penguin.com**

Also Available from

BEVERLY CONNOR

Dead Past

A Diane Fallon
Forensic Investigation

As a child, Juliet Price witnessed the bloody
slaying of an entire family. Then the killer
chased her down, brutalized her, and left her
for dead. The police were never able to find
the man responsible. For years, Juliet's
traumatized mind hid the events from her.
Then she sees a television show featuring the
unsolved cold case, and the horrors come to
her in her nightmares. She shares her fears
with Diane Fallon, who realizes that Juliet's
shattered visions recall not one, but two
intertwined crimes—crimes that Diane intends
to uncover.

**Available wherever books are sold or
at penguin.com**

Also Available from

BEVERLY CONNOR

Dead Hunt

A Diane Fallon
Forensic Investigation

Clymene O'Riley is in prison for killing her
husband—though Diane Fallon is sure she killed
another, and suspects she may have left a veritable
graveyard of dead men in her wake. So when
Clymene informs her that one of the prison guards
may be in danger from a serial killer, Diane
is suspicious.

And when Clymene escapes from jail, Diane
becomes the prime suspect in a bloody murder that
puts her in the path of an angry killer who wants
her dead...

**Available wherever books are sold or
at penguin.com**

Peabody Public Library

DISCARD